THE '

By Honore De Balzac

Translated by Katharine Prescott Wormeley

DEDICATION
To Monsieur Charles Nodier, member of the French Academy, etc.

Here, my dear Nodier, is a book filled with deeds that are screened from the action of the laws by the closed doors of domestic life; but as to which the finger of God, often called chance, supplies the place of human justice, and in which the moral is none the less striking and instructive because it is pointed by a scoffer.

To my mind, such deeds contain great lessons for the Family and for Maternity. We shall some day realize, perhaps too late, the effects produced by the diminution of paternal authority. That authority, which formerly ceased only at the death of the father, was the sole human tribunal before which domestic crimes could be arraigned; kings themselves, on special occasions, took part in executing its judgments. However good and tender a mother may be, she cannot fulfil the function of the patriarchal royalty any more than a woman can take the place of a king upon the throne. Perhaps I have never drawn a picture that shows more plainly how essential to European society is the indissoluble marriage bond, how fatal the results of feminine weakness, how great the dangers arising from selfish interests when indulged without restraint. May a society which is based solely on the power of wealth shudder as it sees the impotence of the law in dealing with the workings of a system which deifies success, and pardons every means of attaining it. May it return to the Catholic religion, for the purification of its masses through the inspiration of religious feeling, and by means of an education other than that of a lay university.

In the "Scenes from Military Life" so many fine natures, so many high and noble self-devotions will be set forth, that I may here be allowed to point out the depraving effect of the necessities of war upon certain minds who venture to act in domestic life as if upon the field of battle.

You have cast a sagacious glance over the events of our own time; its philosophy shines, in more than one bitter reflection, through your elegant pages; you have appreciated, more clearly than other men, the havoc wrought in the mind of our country by the existence of four distinct political systems. I cannot, therefore, place this history under the protection of a more competent authority. Your name may, perhaps, defend my work against the criticisms that are certain to follow it,—for where is the patient who keeps silence when the surgeon lifts the dressing from his wound?

To the pleasure of dedicating this Scene to you, is joined the pride I feel in thus making known your friendship for one who here subscribes himself

Your sincere admirer,   *De Balzac*

Paris, November, 1842.

THE TWO BROTHERS

CHAPTER I

In 1792 the townspeople of Issoudun enjoyed the services of a physician named Rouget, whom they held to be a man of consummate malignity. Were we to believe certain bold tongues, he made his wife extremely unhappy, although she was the most beautiful woman of the neighborhood. Perhaps, indeed, she was rather silly. But the prying of friends, the slander of enemies, and the gossip of acquaintances, had never succeeded in laying bare the interior of that household. Doctor Rouget was a man of whom we say in common parlance, "He is not pleasant to deal with." Consequently, during his lifetime, his townsmen kept silence about him and treated him civilly. His wife, a demoiselle Descoings, feeble in health during her girlhood (which was said to be a reason why the doctor married her), gave birth to a son, and also to a daughter who arrived, unexpectedly, ten years after her brother, and whose birth took the husband, doctor though he were, by surprise. This late-comer was named Agathe.

These little facts are so simple, so commonplace, that a writer seems scarcely justified in placing them in the fore-front of his history; yet if they are not known, a man of Doctor Rouget's stamp would be thought a monster, an unnatural father, when, in point of fact, he was only following out the evil tendencies which many people shelter under the terrible axiom that "men should have strength of character,"—a masculine phrase that has caused many a woman's misery.

The Descoings, father-in-law and mother-in-law of the doctor, were commission merchants in the wool-trade, and did a double business by selling for the producers and buying for the manufacturers of the golden fleeces of Berry; thus pocketing a commission on both sides. In this way they grew rich and miserly—the outcome of many such lives. Descoings the son, younger brother of Madame Rouget, did not like Issoudun. He went to seek his fortune in Paris, where he set up as a grocer in the rue Saint-Honore. That step led to his ruin. But nothing could have hindered it: a grocer is drawn to his business by an attracting force quite equal to the repelling force which drives artists away from it. We do not sufficiently study the social potentialities which make up the various vocations of life. It would be interesting to know what determines one man to be a stationer rather than a baker; since, in our day, sons are not compelled to follow the calling of their fathers, as they were among the Egyptians. In this instance, love decided the vocation of Descoings. He said to himself, "I, too, will be a grocer!" and in the same breath he said (also to himself) some other things regarding his employer,—a beautiful creature, with whom he had fallen desperately in love. Without other help than patience and the trifling sum of money his father and mother sent him, he married the widow of his predecessor, Monsieur Bixiou.

In 1792 Descoings was thought to be doing an excellent business. At that time, the old Descoings were still living. They had retired from the wool-trade, and were employing their capital in buying up the forfeited estates,—another golden fleece! Their son-in-law Doctor Rouget, who, about this time, felt pretty sure that he should soon have to mourn for the death of his wife, sent his daughter to Paris to the care of his brother-in-law, partly to let her see the capital, but still more to carry out an artful scheme of his own. Descoings had no children. Madame Descoings, twelve years older than her husband, was in good health, but as fat as a thrush after harvest; and the canny Rouget knew enough professionally to be certain that Monsieur and Madame Descoings, contrary to the moral of fairy tales, would live happy ever after without having any children. The pair might therefore become attached to Agathe.

That young girl, the handsomest maiden in Issoudun, did not resemble either father or mother. Her birth had caused a lasting breach between Doctor Rouget and his intimate friend Monsieur Lousteau, a former sub-delegate who had lately removed from the town. When a family expatriates itself, the natives of a place as attractive as Issoudun have a right to inquire into the reasons of so surprising a step. It was said by certain sharp tongues that Doctor Rouget, a vindictive man, had been heard to exclaim that Monsieur Lousteau should die by his hand. Uttered by a physician, this declaration had the force of a cannon-ball. When the National Assembly suppressed the sub-delegates, Lousteau and his family left Issoudun, and never returned there. After their departure Madame Rouget spent most of her time with the sister of the late sub-delegate, Madame Hochon, who was the godmother of her daughter, and the only person to whom she confided her griefs. The little that the good town of Issoudun ever really knew of the beautiful Madame Rouget was told by Madame Hochon,—though not until after the doctor's death.

The first words of Madame Rouget, when informed by her husband that he meant to send Agathe to Paris, were: "I shall never see my daughter again."

"And she was right," said the worthy Madame Hochon.

After this, the poor mother grew as yellow as a quince, and her appearance did not contradict the tongues of those who declared that Doctor Rouget was killing her by inches. The behavior of her booby of a son must have added to the misery of the poor woman so unjustly accused. Not restrained, possibly encouraged by his father, the young fellow, who was in every way stupid, paid her neither the attentions nor the respect which a son owes to a mother. Jean-Jacques Rouget was like his father, especially on the latter's worst side; and the doctor at his best was far from satisfactory, either morally or physically.

The arrival of the charming Agathe Rouget did not bring happiness to her uncle Descoings; for in the same week (or rather, we should say decade, for the Republic had then been proclaimed) he was imprisoned on a hint from Robespierre given to Fouquier-Tinville. Descoings, who was imprudent enough to think the famine fictitious, had the additional folly, under the impression that opinions were free, to express that opinion to several of his male and female customers as he served them in the grocery. The citoyenne Duplay, wife of a cabinet-maker with whom Robespierre lodged, and who looked after the affairs of that eminent citizen, patronized, unfortunately, the Descoings establishment. She considered the opinions of the grocer insulting to Maximilian the First. Already displeased with the manners of Descoings, this illustrious "tricoteuse" of the Jacobin club regarded the beauty of his wife as a kind of aristocracy. She infused a venom of her own into the grocer's remarks when she repeated them to her good and gentle master, and the poor man was speedily arrested on the well-worn charge of "accaparation."

No sooner was he put in prison, than his wife set to work to obtain his release. But the steps she took were so ill-judged that any one hearing her talk to the arbiters of his fate might have thought that she was in reality seeking to get rid of him. Madame Descoings knew Bridau, one of the secretaries of Roland, then minister of the interior,—the right-hand man of all the ministers who succeeded each other in that office. She put Bridau on the war-path to save her grocer. That incorruptible official—one of the virtuous dupes who are always admirably disinterested—was careful not to corrupt the men on whom the fate of the poor grocer depended; on the contrary, he endeavored to enlighten them. Enlighten people in those days! As well might he have begged them to bring back the Bourbons. The Girondist minister, who was then contending against Robespierre, said to his secretary, "Why do you meddle in the matter?" and all others to whom the worthy Bridau appealed made the same atrocious reply: "Why do you meddle?" Bridau then sagely advised Madame Descoings to keep quiet and await events. But instead of conciliating Robespierre's housekeeper, she fretted and fumed against that informer, and even complained to a member of the Convention, who, trembling for himself, replied hastily, "I will speak of it to Robespierre." The handsome petitioner put faith in this promise, which the other carefully forgot. A few loaves of sugar, or a bottle or two of good liqueur, given to the citoyenne Duplay would have saved Descoings.

This little mishap proves that in revolutionary times it is quite as dangerous to employ honest men as scoundrels; we should rely on ourselves alone. Descoings perished; but he had the glory of going to the scaffold with Andre Chenier. There, no doubt, grocery and poetry embraced for the first time in the flesh; although they have, and ever have had, intimate secret relations. The death of Descoings produced far more sensation than that of Andre Chenier. It has taken thirty years to prove to France that she lost more by the death of Chenier than by that of Descoings.

This act of Robespierre led to one good result: the terrified grocers let politics alone until 1830. Descoings's shop was not a hundred yards from Robespierre's lodging. His successor was scarcely more fortunate than himself. Cesar Birotteau, the celebrated perfumer of the "Queen of Roses," bought the premises; but, as if the scaffold had left some inexplicable contagion behind it, the inventor of the "Paste of Sultans" and the "Carminative Balm" came to his ruin in that very shop. The solution of the problem here suggested belongs to the realm of occult science.

During the visits which Roland's secretary paid to the unfortunate Madame Descoings, he was struck with the cold, calm, innocent beauty of Agathe Rouget. While consoling the widow, who, however, was too inconsolable to carry on the business of her second deceased husband, he married the charming girl, with the consent of her father, who hastened to give his approval to the match. Doctor Rouget, delighted to hear that matters were going beyond his expectations,—for his wife, on the death of her brother, had become sole heiress of the Descoings,—rushed to Paris, not so much to be present at the wedding as to see that the marriage contract was drawn to suit him. The ardent and disinterested love of citizen Bridau gave carte blanche to the perfidious doctor, who made the most of his son-in-law's blindness, as the following history will show.

Madame Rouget, or, to speak more correctly, the doctor, inherited all the property, landed and personal, of Monsieur and Madame Descoings the elder, who died within two years of each other; and soon after that, Rouget got the better, as we may say, of his wife, for she died at the beginning of the year 1799. So he had vineyards and he bought farms, he owned iron-works and he sold fleeces. His well-beloved son was stupidly incapable of doing anything; but the father destined him for the state in life of a land proprietor and allowed him to grow up in wealth and silliness, certain that the lad would know as much as the wisest if he simply let himself live and die. After 1799, the cipherers of Issoudun put, at the very least, thirty thousand francs' income to the doctor's credit. From the time of his wife's death he led a debauched life, though he regulated it, so to speak, and kept it within the closed doors of his own house. This man, endowed with "strength of character," died in 1805, and God only knows what the townspeople of Issoudun said about him then, and how many anecdotes they related of his horrible private life. Jean-Jacques Rouget, whom his father, recognizing his stupidity, had latterly treated with severity, remained a bachelor for certain reasons, the explanation of which will form an important part of this history. His celibacy was partly his father's fault, as we shall see later.

Meantime, it is well to inquire into the results of the secret vengeance the doctor took on a daughter whom he did not recognize as his own, but who, you must understand at once, was legitimately his. Not a person in Issoudun had noticed one of those capricious facts that make the whole subject of generation a vast abyss in which science flounders. Agathe bore a strong likeness to the mother of Doctor Rouget. Just as gout is said to skip a generation and pass from grandfather to grandson, resemblances not uncommonly follow the same course.

In like manner, the eldest of Agathe's children, who physically resembled his mother, had the moral qualities of his grandfather, Doctor Rouget. We will leave the solution of this problem to the twentieth century, with a fine collection of microscopic animalculae; our descendants may perhaps write as much nonsense as the scientific schools of the nineteenth century have uttered on this mysterious and perplexing question.

Agathe Rouget attracted the admiration of everyone by a face destined, like that of Mary, the mother of our Lord, to continue ever virgin, even after marriage. Her portrait, still to be seen in the atelier of Bridau, shows a perfect oval and a clear whiteness of complexion, without the faintest tinge of color, in spite of her golden hair. More than one artist, looking at the pure brow, the discreet, composed mouth, the delicate nose, the small ears, the long lashes, and the dark-blue eyes filled with tenderness,—in short, at the whole countenance expressive of placidity,—has asked the great artist, "Is that a copy of a Raphael?" No man ever acted under a truer inspiration than the minister's secretary when he married this young girl. Agathe was an embodiment of the ideal housekeeper brought up in the provinces and never parted from her mother. Pious, though far from sanctimonious, she had no other education than that given to women by the Church. Judged, by ordinary standards, she was an accomplished wife, yet her ignorance of life paved the way for great misfortunes. The epitaph on the Roman matron, "She did needlework and kept the house," gives a faithful picture of her simple, pure, and tranquil existence.

Under the Consulate, Bridau attached himself fanatically to Napoleon, who placed him at the head of a department in the ministry of the interior in 1804, a year before the death of Doctor Rouget. With a salary of twelve thousand francs and very handsome emoluments, Bridau was quite indifferent to the scandalous settlement of the property at Issoudun, by which Agathe was deprived of her rightful inheritance. Six months before Doctor Rouget's death he had sold one-half of his property to his son, to whom the other half was bequeathed as a gift, and also in accordance with his rights as heir. An advance of fifty thousand francs on her inheritance, made to Agathe at the time of her marriage, represented her share of the property of her father and mother.

Bridau idolized the Emperor, and served him with the devotion of a Mohammedan for his prophet; striving to carry out the vast conceptions of the modern demi-god, who, finding the whole fabric of France destroyed, went to work to reconstruct everything. The new official never showed fatigue, never cried "Enough." Projects, reports, notes, studies, he accepted all, even the hardest labors, happy in the consciousness of aiding his Emperor. He loved him as a man, he adored him as a sovereign, and he would never allow the least criticism of his acts or his purposes.

From 1804 to 1808, the Bridaus lived in a handsome suite of rooms on the Quai Voltaire, a few steps from the ministry of the interior and close to the Tuileries. A cook and footman were the only servants of the household during this period of Madame Bridau's grandeur. Agathe, early afoot, went to market with her cook. While the latter did the rooms, she prepared the breakfast. Bridau never went to the ministry before eleven o'clock. As long as their union lasted, his wife took the same unwearying pleasure in preparing for him an exquisite breakfast, the only meal he really enjoyed. At all seasons and in all weathers, Agathe watched her husband from the window as he walked toward his office, and never drew in her head until she had seen him turn the corner of the rue du Bac. Then she cleared the breakfast-table herself, gave an eye to the arrangement of the rooms, dressed for the day, played with her children and took them to walk, or received the visits of friends; all the while waiting in spirit for Bridau's return. If her husband brought him important business that had to be attended to, she would station herself close to the writing-table in his study, silent as a statue, knitting while he wrote, sitting up as late as he did, and going to bed only a few moments before him. Occasionally, the pair went to some theatre, occupying one of the ministerial boxes. On those days, they dined at a restaurant, and the gay scenes of that establishment never ceased to give Madame Bridau the same lively pleasure they afford to provincials who are new to Paris. Agathe, who was obliged to accept the formal dinners sometimes given to the head of a department in a ministry, paid due attention to the luxurious requirements of the then mode of dress, but she took off the rich apparel with delight when she returned home, and resumed the simple garb of a provincial. One day in the week, Thursday, Bridau received his friends, and he also gave a grand ball, annually, on Shrove Tuesday.

These few words contain the whole history of their conjugal life, which had but three events; the births of two children, born three years apart, and the death of Bridau, who died in 1808, killed by overwork at the very moment when the Emperor was about to appoint him director-general, count, and councillor of state. At this period of his reign, Napoleon was particularly absorbed in the affairs of the interior; he overwhelmed Bridau with work, and finally wrecked the health of that dauntless bureaucrat. The Emperor, of whom Bridau had never asked a favor, made inquiries into his habits and fortune. Finding that this devoted servant literally had nothing but his situation, Napoleon recognized him as one of the incorruptible natures which raised the character of his government and gave moral weight to it, and he wished to surprise him by the gift of some distinguished reward. But the effort to complete a certain work, involving immense labor, before the departure of the Emperor for Spain caused the death of the devoted servant, who was seized with an inflammatory fever. When the Emperor, who remained in Paris for a few days after his return to prepare for the campaign of 1809, was told of Bridau's death he said: "There are men who can never be replaced." Struck by the spectacle of a devotion which could receive none of the brilliant recognitions that reward a soldier, the Emperor resolved to create an order to requite civil services, just as he had already created the Legion of honor to reward the military. The impression he received from the death of Bridau led him to plan the order of the Reunion. He had not time, however, to mature this aristocratic scheme, the recollection of which is now so completely effaced that many of my readers may ask what were its insignia: the order was worn with a blue ribbon. The Emperor called it the Reunion, under the idea of uniting the order of the Golden Fleece of Spain with the order of the Golden Fleece of Austria. "Providence," said a Prussian diplomatist, "took care to frustrate the profanation."

After Bridau's death the Emperor inquired into the circumstances of his widow. Her two sons each received a scholarship in the Imperial Lyceum, and the Emperor paid the whole costs of their education from his privy purse. He gave Madame Bridau a pension of four thousand francs, intending, no doubt, to advance the fortune of her sons in future years.

From the time of her marriage to the death of her husband, Agathe had held no communication with Issoudun. She lost her mother just as she was on the point of giving birth to her youngest son, and when her father, who, as she well knew, loved her little, died, the coronation of the Emperor was at hand, and that event gave Bridau so much additional work that she was unwilling to leave him. Her brother, Jean-Jacques Rouget, had not written to her since she left Issoudun. Though grieved by the tacit repudiation of her family, Agathe had come to think seldom of those who never thought of her. Once a year she received a letter from her godmother, Madame Hochon, to whom she replied with commonplaces, paying no heed to the advice which that pious and excellent woman gave to her, disguised in cautious words.

Some time before the death of Doctor Rouget, Madame Hochon had written to her goddaughter warning her that she would get nothing from her father's estate unless she gave a power of attorney to Monsieur Hochon. Agathe was very reluctant to harass her brother. Whether it were that Bridau thought the spoliation of his wife in accordance with the laws and customs of Berry, or that, high-minded as he was, he shared the magnanimity of his wife, certain it is that he would not listen to Roguin, his notary, who advised him to take advantage of his ministerial position to contest the deeds by which the father had deprived the daughter of her legitimate inheritance. Husband and wife thus tacitly sanctioned what was done at Issoudun. Nevertheless, Roguin had forced Bridau to reflect upon the future interests of his wife which were thus compromised. He saw that if he died before her, Agathe would be left without property, and this led him to look into his own affairs. He found that between 1793 and 1805 his wife and he had been obliged to use nearly thirty thousand of the fifty thousand francs in cash which old Rouget had given to his daughter at the time of her marriage. He at once invested the remaining twenty thousand in the public funds, then quoted at forty, and from this source Agathe received about two thousand francs a year. As a widow, Madame Bridau could live suitably on an income of six thousand francs. With provincial good sense, she thought of changing her residence, dismissing the footman, and keeping no servant except a cook; but her intimate friend, Madame Descoings, who insisted on being considered her aunt, sold her own establishment and came to live with Agathe, turning the study of the late Bridau into her bedroom.

The two widows clubbed their revenues, and so were in possession of a joint income of twelve thousand francs a year. This seems a very simple and natural proceeding. But nothing in life is more deserving of attention than the things that are called natural; we are on our guard against the unnatural and extraordinary. For this reason, you will find men of experience— lawyers, judges, doctors, and priests—attaching immense importance to simple matters; and they are often thought over-scrupulous. But the serpent amid flowers is one of the finest myths that antiquity has bequeathed for the guidance of our lives. How often we hear fools, trying to excuse themselves in their own eyes or in the eyes of others, exclaiming, "It was all so natural that any one would have been taken in."

In 1809, Madame Descoings, who never told her age, was sixty-five. In her heyday she had been popularly called a beauty, and was now one of those rare women whom time respects. She owed to her excellent constitution the privilege of preserving her good looks, which, however, would not bear close examination. She was of medium height, plump, and fresh, with fine shoulders and a rather rosy complexion. Her blond hair, bordering on chestnut, showed, in spite of her husband's catastrophe, not a tinge of gray. She loved good cheer, and liked to concoct nice little made dishes; yet, fond as she was of eating, she also adored the theatre and cherished a vice which she wrapped in impenetrable mystery—she bought into lotteries. Can that be the abyss of which mythology warns us under the fable of the Danaides and their cask? Madame Descoings, like other women who are lucky enough to keep young for many years, spend rather too much upon her dress; but aside from these trifling defects she was the pleasantest of women to live with. Of every one's opinion, never opposing anybody, her kindly and communicative gayety gave pleasure to all. She had, moreover, a Parisian quality which charmed the retired clerks and elderly merchants of her circle,—she could take and give a jest. If she did not marry a third time it was no doubt the fault of the times. During the wars of the Empire, marrying men found rich and handsome girls too easily to trouble themselves about women of sixty.

Madame Descoings, always anxious to cheer Madame Bridau, often took the latter to the theatre, or to drive; prepared excellent little dinners for her delectation, and even tried to marry her to her own son by her first husband, Bixiou. Alas! to do this, she was forced to reveal a terrible secret, carefully kept by her, by her late husband, and by her notary. The young and beautiful Madame Descoings, who passed for thirty-six years old, had a son who was thirty-five, named Bixiou, already a widower, a major in the Twenty-Fourth Infantry, who subsequently perished at Lutzen, leaving behind him an only son. Madame Descoings, who only saw her grandson secretly, gave out that he was the son of the first wife of her first husband. The revelation was partly a prudential act; for this grandson was being educated with Madame Bridau's sons at the Imperial Lyceum, where he had a half-scholarship. The lad, who was clever and shrewd at school, soon after made himself a great reputation as draughtsman and designer, and also as a wit.

Agathe, who lived only for her children, declined to re-marry, as much from good sense as from fidelity to her husband. But it is easier for a woman to be a good wife than to be a good mother. A widow has two tasks before her, whose duties clash: she is a mother, and yet she must exercise parental authority. Few women are firm enough to understand and practise this double duty. Thus it happened that Agathe, notwithstanding her many virtues, was the innocent cause of great unhappiness. In the first place, through her lack of intelligence and the blind confidence to which such noble natures are prone, Agathe fell a victim to Madame Descoings, who brought a terrible misfortune on the family. That worthy soul was nursing up a combination of three numbers called a "trey" in a lottery, and lotteries give no credit to their customers. As manager of the joint household, she was able to pay up her stakes with the money intended for their current expenses, and she went deeper and deeper into debt, with the hope of ultimately enriching her grandson Bixiou, her dear Agathe, and the little Bridaus. When the debts amounted to ten thousand francs, she increased her stakes, trusting that her favorite trey, which had not turned up in nine years, would come at last, and fill to overflowing the abysmal deficit.

From that moment the debt rolled up rapidly. When it reached twenty thousand francs, Madame Descoings lost her head, still failing to win the trey. She tried to mortgage her own property to pay her niece, but Roguin, who was her notary, showed her the impossibility of carrying out that honorable intention. The late Doctor Rouget had laid hold of the property of the brother-in-law after the grocer's execution, and had, as it were, disinherited Madame Descoings by securing to her a life-interest on the property of his own son, Jean-Jacques Rouget. No money-lender would think of advancing twenty thousand francs to a woman sixty-six years of age, on an annuity of about four thousand, at a period when ten per cent could easily be got for an investment. So one morning Madame Descoings fell at the feet of her niece, and with sobs confessed the state of things. Madame Bridau did not reproach her; she sent away the footman and cook, sold all but the bare necessities of her furniture, sold also three-fourths of her government funds, paid off the debts, and bade farewell to her *appartement*.

CHAPTER II

One of the worst corners in all Paris is undoubtedly that part of the rue Mazarin which lies between the rue Guenegard and its junction with the rue de Seine, behind the palace of the Institute. The high gray walls of the college and of the library which Cardinal Mazarin presented to the city of Paris, and which the French Academy was in after days to inhabit, cast chill shadows over this angle of the street, where the sun seldom shines, and the north wind blows. The poor ruined widow came to live on the third floor of a house standing at this damp, dark, cold corner. Opposite, rose the Institute buildings, in which were the dens of ferocious animals known to the bourgeoisie under the name of artists,—under that of tyro, or rapin, in the studios. Into these dens' they enter rapins, but they may come forth prix de Rome. The transformation does not take place without extraordinary uproar and disturbance at the time of year when the examinations are going on, and the competitors are shut up in their cells. To win a prize, they were obliged, within a given time, to make, if a sculptor, a clay model; if a painter, a picture such as may be seen at the Ecole des Beaux-Arts; if a musician, a cantata; if an architect, the plans for a public building. At the time when we are penning the words, this menagerie has already been removed from these cold and cheerless buildings, and taken to the elegant Palais des Beaux-Arts, which stands near by.

6

From the windows of Madame Bridau's new abode, a glance could penetrate the depths of those melancholy barred cages. To the north, the view was shut in by the dome of the Institute; looking up the street, the only distraction to the eye was a file of hackney-coaches, which stood at the upper end of the rue Mazarin. After a while, the widow put boxes of earth in front of her windows, and cultivated those aerial gardens that police regulations forbid, though their vegetable products purify the atmosphere. The house, which backed up against another fronting on the rue de Seine, was necessarily shallow, and the staircase wound round upon itself. The third floor was the last. Three windows to three rooms, namely, a dining-room, a small salon, and a chamber on one side of the landing; on the other, a little kitchen, and two single rooms; above, an immense garret without partitions. Madame Bridau chose this lodging for three reasons: economy, for it cost only four hundred francs a year, so that she took a lease of it for nine years; proximity to her sons' school, the Imperial Lyceum being at a short distance; thirdly, because it was in the quarter to which she was used.

The inside of the *appartement* was in keeping with the general look of the house. The dining-room, hung with a yellow paper covered with little green flowers, and floored with tiles that were not glazed, contained nothing that was not strictly necessary,—namely, a table, two sideboards, and six chairs, brought from the other *appartement*. The salon was adorned with an Aubusson carpet given to Bridau when the ministry of the interior was refurnished. To the furniture of this room the widow added one of those commonplace mahogany sofas with the Egyptian heads that Jacob Desmalter manufactured by the gross in 1806, covering them with a silken green stuff bearing a design of white geometric circles. Above this piece of furniture hung a portrait of Bridau, done in pastel by the hand of an amateur, which at once attracted the eye. Though art might have something to say against it, no one could fail to recognize the firmness of the noble and obscure citizen upon that brow. The serenity of the eyes, gentle, yet proud, was well given; the sagacious mind, to which the prudent lips bore testimony, the frank smile, the atmosphere of the man of whom the Emperor had said, "Justum et tenacem," had all been caught, if not with talent, at least with fidelity. Studying that face, an observer could see that the man had done his duty. His countenance bore signs of the incorruptibility which we attribute to several men who served the Republic. On the opposite wall, over a card-table, flashed a picture of the Emperor in brilliant colors, done by Vernet; Napoleon was riding rapidly, attended by his escort.

Agathe had bestowed upon herself two large birdcages; one filled with canaries, the other with Java sparrows. She had given herself up to this juvenile fancy since the loss of her husband, irreparable to her, as, in fact, it was to many others. By the end of three months, her widowed chamber had become what it was destined to remain until the appointed day when she left it forever,—a litter of confusion which words are powerless to describe. Cats were domiciled on the sofa. The canaries, occasionally let loose, left their commas on the furniture. The poor dear woman scattered little heaps of millet and bits of chickweed about the room, and put tidbits for the cats in broken saucers. Garments lay everywhere. The room breathed of the provinces and of constancy. Everything that once belonged to Bridau was scrupulously preserved. Even the implements in his desk received the care which the widow of a paladin might have bestowed upon her husband's armor. One slight detail here will serve to bring the tender devotion of this woman before the reader's mind. She had wrapped up a pen and sealed the package, on which she wrote these words, "Last pen used by my dear husband." The cup from which he drank his last draught was on the fireplace; caps and false hair were tossed, at a later period, over the glass globes which covered these precious relics. After Bridau's death not a trace of coquetry, not even a woman's ordinary care of her person, was left in the young widow of thirty-five. Parted from the only man she had ever known, esteemed, and loved, from one who had never caused her the slightest unhappiness, she was no longer conscious of her womanhood; all things were as nothing to her; she no longer even thought of her dress. Nothing was ever more simply done or more complete than this laying down of conjugal happiness and personal charm. Some human beings obtain through love the power of transferring their self—their I—to the being of another; and when death takes that other, no life of their own is possible for them.

Agathe, who now lived only for her children, was infinitely sad at the thought of the privations this financial ruin would bring upon them. From the time of her removal to the rue Mazarin a shade of melancholy came upon her face, which made it very touching. She hoped a little in the Emperor; but the Emperor at that time could do no more than he was already doing; he was giving three hundred francs a year to each child from his privy purse, besides the scholarships.

As for the brilliant Descoings, she occupied an *appartement* on the second floor similar to that of her niece above her. She had made Madame Bridau an assignment of three thousand francs out of her annuity. Roguin, the notary, attended to this in Madame Bridau's interest; but it would take seven years of such slow repayment to make good the loss. The Descoings, thus reduced to an income of twelve hundred francs, lived with her niece in a small way. These excellent but timid creatures employed a woman-of-all-work for the morning hours only. Madame Descoings, who liked to cook, prepared the dinner. In the evenings a few old friends, persons employed at the ministry who owed their places to Bridau, came for a game of cards with the two widows. Madame Descoings still cherished her trey, which she declared was obstinate about turning up. She expected, by one grand stroke, to repay the enforced loan she had made upon her niece. She was fonder of the little Bridaus than she was of her grandson Bixiou,—partly from a sense of the wrong she had done them, partly because she felt the kindness of her niece, who, under her worst deprivations, never uttered a word of reproach. So Philippe and Joseph were cossetted, and the old gambler in the Imperial Lottery of France (like others who have a vice or a weakness to atone for) cooked them nice little dinners with plenty of sweets. Later on, Philippe and Joseph could extract from her pocket, with the utmost facility, small sums of money, which the younger used for pencils, paper, charcoal and prints, the elder to buy tennis-shoes, marbles, twine, and pocket-knives. Madame Descoings's passion forced her to be content with fifty francs a month for her domestic expenses, so as to gamble with the rest.

On the other hand, Madame Bridau, motherly love, kept her expenses down to the same sum. By way of penance for her former over-confidence, she heroically cut off her own little enjoyments. As with other timid souls of limited intelligence, one shock to her feelings rousing her distrust led her to exaggerate a defect in her character until it assumed the consistency of a virtue. The Emperor, she said to herself, might forget them; he might die in battle; her pension, at any rate, ceased with her life. She shuddered at the risk her children ran of being left alone in the world without means. Quite incapable of understanding Roguin when he explained to her that in seven years Madame Descoings's assignment would replace the money she had sold out of the Funds, she persisted in trusting neither the notary nor her aunt, nor even the government; she believed in nothing but herself and the privations she was practising. By laying aside three thousand francs every year from her pension, she would have thirty thousand francs at the end of ten years; which would give fifteen hundred a year to her children. At thirty-six, she might expect to live twenty years longer; and if she kept to the same system of economy she might leave to each child enough for the bare necessaries of life.

Thus the two widows passed from hollow opulence to voluntary poverty,—one under the pressure of a vice, the other through the promptings of the purest virtue. None of these petty details are useless in teaching the lesson which ought to be learned from this present history, drawn as it is from the most commonplace interests of life, but whose bearings are, it may be, only the more widespread. The view from the windows into the student dens; the tumult of the rapins below; the necessity of looking up at the sky to escape the miserable sights of the damp angle of the street; the presence of that portrait, full of soul and grandeur despite the workmanship of an amateur painter; the sight of the rich colors, now old and harmonious, in that calm and placid home; the preference of the mother for her eldest child; her opposition to the tastes of the younger; in short, the whole body of facts and circumstances which make the preamble of this history are perhaps the generating causes to which we owe Joseph Bridau, one of the greatest painters of the modern French school of art.

Philippe, the elder of the two sons, was strikingly like his mother. Though a blond lad, with blue eyes, he had the daring look which is readily taken for intrepidity and courage. Old Claparon, who entered the ministry of the interior at the same time as Bridau, and was one of the faithful friends who played whist every night with the two widows, used to say of Philippe two or three times a month, giving him a tap on the cheek, "Here's a young rascal who'll stand to his guns!" The boy, thus stimulated, naturally and out of bravado, assumed a resolute manner. That turn once given to his character, he became very adroit at all bodily exercises; his fights at the Lyceum taught him the endurance and contempt for pain which lays the foundation of military valor. He also acquired, very naturally, a distaste for study; public education being unable to solve the difficult problem of developing "pari passu" the body and the mind.

Agathe believed that the purely physical resemblance which Philippe bore to her carried with it a moral likeness; and she confidently expected him to show at a future day her own delicacy of feeling, heightened by the vigor of manhood. Philippe was fifteen years old when his mother moved into the melancholy *appartement* in the rue Mazarin; and the winning ways of a lad of that age went far to confirm the maternal beliefs. Joseph, three years younger, was like his father, but only on the defective side. In the first place, his thick black hair was always in disorder, no matter what pains were taken with it; while Philippe's, notwithstanding his vivacity, was invariably neat. Then, by some mysterious fatality, Joseph could not keep his clothes clean; dress him in new clothes, and he immediately made them look like old ones. The elder, on the other hand, took care of his things out of mere vanity. Unconsciously, the mother acquired a habit of scolding Joseph and holding up his brother as an example to him. Agathe did not treat the two children alike; when she went to fetch them from school, the thought in her mind as to Joseph always was, "What sort of state shall I find him in?" These trifles drove her heart into the gulf of maternal preference.

No one among the very ordinary persons who made the society of the two widows—neither old Du Bruel nor old Claparon, nor Desroches the father, nor even the Abbe Loraux, Agathe's confessor—noticed Joseph's faculty for observation. Absorbed in the line of his own tastes, the future colorist paid no attention to anything that concerned himself. During his childhood this disposition was so like torpor that his father grew uneasy about him. The remarkable size of the head and the width of the brow roused a fear that the child might be liable to water on the brain. His distressful face, whose originality was thought ugliness by those who had no eye for the moral value of a countenance, wore rather a sullen expression during his childhood. The features, which developed later in life, were pinched, and the close attention the child paid to what went on about him still further contracted them. Philippe flattered his mother's vanity, but Joseph won no compliments. Philippe sparkled with the clever sayings and lively answers that lead parents to believe their boys will turn out remarkable men; Joseph was taciturn, and a dreamer. The mother hoped great things of Philippe, and expected nothing of Joseph.

Joseph's predilection for art was developed by a very commonplace incident. During the Easter holidays of 1812, as he was coming home from a walk in the Tuileries with his brother and Madame Descoings, he saw a pupil drawing a caricature of some professor on the wall of the Institute, and stopped short with admiration at the charcoal sketch, which was full of satire. The next day the child stood at the window watching the pupils as they entered the building by the door on the rue Mazarin; then he ran downstairs and slipped furtively into the long courtyard of the Institute, full of statues, busts, half-finished marbles, plasters, and baked clays; at all of which he gazed feverishly, for his instinct was awakened, and his vocation stirred within him. He entered a room on the ground-floor, the door of which was half open; and there he saw a dozen young men drawing from a statue, who at once began to make fun of him.

"Hi! little one," cried the first to see him, taking the crumbs of his bread and scattering them at the child.

"Whose child is he?"

"Goodness, how ugly!"

For a quarter of an hour Joseph stood still and bore the brunt of much teasing in the atelier of the great sculptor, Chaudet. But after laughing at him for a time, the pupils were struck with his persistency and with the expression of his face. They asked him what he wanted. Joseph answered that he wished to know how to draw; thereupon they all encouraged him. Won by such friendliness, the child told them he was Madame Bridau's son.

"Oh! if you are Madame Bridau's son," they cried, from all parts of the room, "you will certainly be a great man. Long live the son of Madame Bridau! Is your mother pretty? If you are a sample of her, she must be stylish!"

"Ha! you want to be an artist?" said the eldest pupil, coming up to Joseph, "but don't you know that that requires pluck; you'll have to bear all sorts of trials,—yes, trials,—enough to break your legs and arms and soul and body. All the fellows you see here have gone through regular ordeals. That one, for instance, he went seven days without eating! Let me see, now, if you can be an artist."

He took one of the child's arms and stretched it straight up in the air; then he placed the other arm as if Joseph were in the act of delivering a blow with his fist.

"Now that's what we call the telegraph trial," said the pupil. "If you can stand like that, without lowering or changing the position of your arms for a quarter of an hour, then you'll have proved yourself a plucky one."

"Courage, little one, courage!" cried all the rest. "You must suffer if you want to be an artist."

Joseph, with the good faith of his thirteen years, stood motionless for five minutes, all the pupils gazing solemnly at him.

"There! you are moving," cried one.

"Steady, steady, confound you!" cried another.

"The Emperor Napoleon stood a whole month as you see him there," said a third, pointing to the fine statue by Chaudet, which was in the room.

That statue, which represents the Emperor standing with the Imperial sceptre in his hand, was torn down in 1814 from the column it surmounted so well.

At the end of ten minutes the sweat stood in drops on Joseph's forehead. At that moment a bald-headed little man, pale and sickly in appearance, entered the atelier, where respectful silence reigned at once.

"What you are about, you urchins?" he exclaimed, as he looked at the youthful martyr.

"That is a good little fellow, who is posing," said the tall pupil who had placed Joseph.

"Are you not ashamed to torture a poor child in that way?" said Chaudet, lowering Joseph's arms. "How long have you been standing there?" he asked the boy, giving him a friendly little pat on the cheek.

"A quarter of an hour."

"What brought you here?"

"I want to be an artist."

"Where do you belong? where do you come from?"

"From mamma's house."

"Oh! mamma!" cried the pupils.

"Silence at the easels!" cried Chaudet. "Who is your mamma?"

"She is Madame Bridau. My papa, who is dead, was a friend of the Emperor; and if you will teach me to draw, the Emperor will pay all you ask for it."

"His father was head of a department at the ministry of the Interior," exclaimed Chaudet, struck by a recollection. "So you want to be an artist, at your age?"

"Yes, monsieur."

"Well, come here just as much as you like; we'll amuse you. Give him a board, and paper, and chalks, and let him alone. You are to know, you young scamps, that his father did me a service. Here, Corde-a-puits, go and get some cakes and sugar-plums," he said to the pupil who had tortured Joseph, giving him some small change. "We'll see if you are to be artist by the way you gobble up the dainties," added the sculptor, chucking Joseph under the chin.

Then he went round examining the pupils' works, followed by the child, who looked and listened, and tried to understand him. The sweets were brought, Chaudet, himself, the child, and the whole studio all had their teeth in them; and Joseph was petted quite as much as he had been teased. The whole scene, in which the rough play and real heart of artists were revealed, and which the boy instinctively understood, made a great impression on his mind. The apparition of the sculptor,—for whom the Emperor's protection opened a way to future glory, closed soon after by his premature death,—was like a vision to little Joseph. The child said nothing to his mother about this adventure, but he spent two hours every Sunday and every Thursday in Chaudet's atelier. From that time forth, Madame Descoings, who humored the fancies of the two cherubim, kept Joseph supplied with pencils and red chalks, prints and drawing-paper. At school, the future colorist sketched his masters, drew his comrades, charcoaled the dormitories, and showed surprising assiduity in the drawing-class. Lemire, the drawing-master, struck not only with the lad's inclination but also with his actual progress, came to tell Madame Bridau of her son's faculty. Agathe, like a true provincial, who knows as little of art as she knows much of housekeeping, was terrified. When Lemire left her, she burst into tears.

"Ah!" she cried, when Madame Descoings went to ask what was the matter. "What is to become of me! Joseph, whom I meant to make a government clerk, whose career was all marked out for him at the ministry of the interior, where, protected by his father's memory, he might have risen to be chief of a division before he was twenty-five, he, my boy, he wants to be a painter,—a vagabond! I always knew that child would give me nothing but trouble."

Madame Descoings confessed that for several months past she had encouraged Joseph's passion, aiding and abetting his Sunday and Thursday visits to the Institute. At the Salon, to which she had taken him, the little fellow had shown an interest in the pictures, which was, she declared, nothing short of miraculous.

"If he understands painting at thirteen, my dear," she said, "your Joseph will be a man of genius."

"Yes; and see what genius did for his father,—killed him with overwork at forty!"

At the close of autumn, just as Joseph was entering his fourteenth year, Agathe, contrary to Madame Descoings's entreaties, went to see Chaudet, and requested that he would cease to debauch her son. She found the sculptor in a blue smock, modelling his last statue; he received the widow of the man who formerly had served him at a critical moment, rather roughly; but, already at death's door, he was struggling with passionate ardor to do in a few hours work he could hardly have accomplished in several months. As Madame Bridau entered, he had just found an effect long sought for, and was handling his tools and clay with spasmodic jerks and movements that seemed to the ignorant Agathe like those of a maniac. At any other time Chaudet would have laughed; but now, as he heard the mother bewailing the destiny he had opened to her child, abusing art, and insisting that Joseph should no longer be allowed to enter the atelier, he burst into a holy wrath.

"I was under obligations to your deceased husband, I wished to help his son, to watch his first steps in the noblest of all careers," he cried. "Yes, madame, learn, if you do not know it, that a great artist is a king, and more than a king; he is happier, he is independent, he lives as he likes, he reigns in the world of fancy. Your son has a glorious future before him. Faculties like his are rare; they are only disclosed at his age in such beings as the Giottos, Raphaels, Titians, Rubens, Murillos,—for, in my opinion, he will make a better painter than sculptor. God of heaven! if I had such a son, I should be as happy as the Emperor is to have given himself the King of Rome. Well, you are mistress of your child's fate. Go your own way, madame; make him a fool, a miserable quill-driver, tie him to a desk, and you've murdered him! But I hope, in spite if all your efforts, that he will stay an artist. A true vocation is stronger than all the obstacles that can be opposed to it. Vocation! why the very word means a call; ay, the election of God himself! You will make your child unhappy, that's all." He flung the clay he no longer needed violently into a tub, and said to his model, "That will do for to-day."

Agathe raised her eyes and saw, in a corner of the atelier where her glance had not before penetrated, a nude woman sitting on a stool, the sight of whom drove her away horrified.

"You are not to have the little Bridau here any more," said Chaudet to his pupils, "it annoys his mother."

"Eugh!" they all cried, as Agathe closed the door.

No sooner did the students of sculpture and painting find out that Madame Bridau did not wish her son to be an artist, than their whole happiness centred on getting Joseph among them. In spite of a promise not to go to the Institute which his mother exacted from him, the child often slipped into Regnauld the painter's studio, where he was encouraged to daub canvas. When the widow complained that the bargain was not kept, Chaudet's pupils assured her that Regnauld was not Chaudet, and they hadn't the bringing up of her son, with other impertinences; and the atrocious young scamps composed a song with a hundred and thirty-seven couplets on Madame Bridau.

On the evening of that sad day Agathe refused to play at cards, and sat on her sofa plunged in such grief that the tears stood in her handsome eyes.

"What is the matter, Madame Bridau?" asked old Claparon.

"She thinks her boy will have to beg his bread because he has got the bump of painting," said Madame Descoings; "but, for my part, I am not the least uneasy about the future of my step-son, little Bixiou, who has a passion for drawing. Men are born to get on."

"You are right," said the hard and severe Desroches, who, in spite of his talents, had never himself got on in the position of assistant-head of a department. "Happily I have only one son; otherwise, with my eighteen hundred francs a year, and a wife who makes barely twelve hundred out of her stamped-paper office, I don't know what would become of me. I have just placed my boy as under-clerk to a lawyer; he gets twenty-five francs a month and his breakfast. I give him as much more, and he dines and sleeps at home. That's all he gets; he must manage for himself, but he'll make his way. I keep the fellow harder at work than if he were at school, and some day he will be a barrister. When I give him money to go to the theatre, he is as happy as a king and kisses me. Oh, I keep a tight hand on him, and he renders me an account of all he spends. You are too good to your children, Madame Bridau; if your son wants to go through hardships and privations, let him; they'll make a man of him."

"As for my boy," said Du Bruel, a former chief of a division, who had just retired on a pension, "he is only sixteen; his mother dotes on him; but I shouldn't listen to his choosing a profession at his age,—a mere fancy, a notion that may pass off. In my opinion, boys should be guided and controlled."

"Ah, monsieur! you are rich, you are a man, and you have but one son," said Agathe.

"Faith!" said Claparon, "children do tyrannize over us—over our hearts, I mean. Mine makes me furious; he has nearly ruined me, and now I won't have anything to do with him—it's a sort of independence. Well, he is the happier for it, and so am I. That fellow was partly the cause of his mother's death. He chose to be a commercial traveller; and the trade just suited him, for he was no sooner in the house than he wanted to be out of it; he couldn't keep in one place, and he wouldn't learn anything. All I ask of God is that I may die before he dishonors my name. Those who have no children lose many pleasures, but they escape great sufferings."

"And these men are fathers!" thought Agathe, weeping anew.

"What I am trying to show you, my dear Madame Bridau, is that you had better let your boy be a painter; if not, you will only waste your time."

"If you were able to coerce him," said the sour Desroches, "I should advise you to oppose his tastes; but weak as I see you are, you had better let him daub if he likes."

"Console yourself, Agathe," said Madame Descoings, "Joseph will turn out a great man."

After this discussion, which was like all discussions, the widow's friends united in giving her one and the same advice; which advice did not in the least relieve her anxieties. They advised her to let Joseph follow his bent.

"If he doesn't turn out a genius," said Du Bruel, who always tried to please Agathe, "you can then get him into some government office."

When Madame Descoings accompanied the old clerks to the door she assured them, at the head of the stairs, that they were "Grecian sages."

"Madame Bridau ought to be glad her son is willing to do anything," said Claparon.

"Besides," said Desroches, "if God preserves the Emperor, Joseph will always be looked after. Why should she worry?"

"She is timid about everything that concerns her children," answered Madame Descoings. "Well, my good girl," she said, returning to Agathe, "you see they are unanimous; why are you still crying?"

"If it was Philippe, I should have no anxiety. But you don't know what goes on in that atelier; they have naked women!"

"I hope they keep good fires," said Madame Descoings.

A few days after this, the disasters of the retreat from Moscow became known. Napoleon returned to Paris to organize fresh troops, and to ask further sacrifices from the country. The poor mother was then plunged into very different anxieties. Philippe, who was tired of school, wanted to serve under the Emperor; he saw a review at the Tuileries,—the last Napoleon ever held,—and he became infatuated with the idea of a soldier's life. In those days military splendor, the show of uniforms, the authority of epaulets, offered irresistible seductions to a certain style of youth. Philippe thought he had the same vocation for the army that his brother Joseph showed for art. Without his mother's knowledge, he wrote a petition to the Emperor, which read as follows:—

Sire,—I am the son of your Bridau; eighteen years of age, five feet six inches; I have good legs, a good constitution, and wish to be one of your soldiers. I ask you to let me enter the army, etc.

Within twenty-four hours, the Emperor had sent Philippe to the Imperial Lyceum at Saint-Cyr, and six months later, in November, 1813, he appointed him sub-lieutenant in a regiment of cavalry. Philippe spent the greater part of that winter in cantonments, but as soon as he knew how to ride a horse he was dispatched to the front, and went eagerly. During the campaign in France he was made a lieutenant, after an affair at the outposts where his bravery had saved his colonel's life. The Emperor named him captain at the battle of La Fere-Champenoise, and took him on his staff. Inspired by such promotion, Philippe won the cross at Montereau. He witnessed Napoleon's farewell at Fontainebleau, raved at the sight, and refused to serve the Bourbons. When he returned to his mother, in July, 1814, he found her ruined.

Joseph's scholarship was withdrawn after the holidays, and Madame Bridau, whose pension came from the Emperor's privy purse, vainly entreated that it might be inscribed on the rolls of the ministry of the interior. Joseph, more of a painter than ever, was delighted with the turn of events, and entreated his mother to let him go to Monsieur Regnauld, promising to earn his own living. He declared he was quite sufficiently advanced in the second class to get on without rhetoric. Philippe, a captain at nineteen and decorated, who had, moreover, served the Emperor as an aide-de-camp in two battles, flattered the mother's vanity immensely. Coarse, blustering, and without real merit beyond the vulgar bravery of a cavalry officer, he was to her mind a man of genius; whereas Joseph, puny and sickly, with unkempt hair and absent mind, seeking peace, loving quiet, and dreaming of an artist's glory, would only bring her, she thought, worries and anxieties.

The winter of 1814-1815 was a lucky one for Joseph. Secretly encouraged by Madame Descoings and Bixiou, a pupil of Gros, he went to work in the celebrated atelier of that painter, whence a vast variety of talent issued in its day, and there he formed the closest intimacy with Schinner. The return from Elba came; Captain Bridau joined the Emperor at Lyons, accompanied him to the Tuileries, and was appointed to the command of a squadron in the dragoons of the Guard. After the battle of Waterloo—in which he was slightly wounded, and where he won the cross of an officer of the Legion of honor—he happened to be near Marshal Davoust at Saint-Denis, and was not with the army of the Loire. In consequence of this, and through Davoust's intercession, his cross and his rank were secured to him, but he was placed on half-pay.

Joseph, anxious about his future, studied all through this period with an ardor which several times made him ill in the midst of these tumultuous events.

"It is the smell of the paints," Agathe said to Madame Descoings. "He ought to give up a business so injurious to his health."

However, all Agathe's anxieties were at this time for her son the lieutenant-colonel. When she saw him again in 1816, reduced from the salary of nine thousand francs (paid to a commander in the dragoons of the Imperial Guard) to a half-pay of three hundred francs a month, she fitted up her attic rooms for him, and spent her savings in doing so. Philippe was one of the faithful Bonapartes of the cafe Lemblin, that constitutional Boeotia; he acquired the habits, manners, style, and life of a half-pay officer; indeed, like any other young man of twenty-one, he exaggerated them, vowed in good earnest a mortal enmity to the Bourbons, never reported himself at the War department, and even refused opportunities which were offered to him for employment in the infantry with his rank of lieutenant-colonel. In his mother's eyes, Philippe seemed in all this to be displaying a noble character.

"The father himself could have done no more," she said.

Philippe's half-pay sufficed him; he cost nothing at home, whereas all Joseph's expenses were paid by the two widows. From that moment, Agathe's preference for Philippe was openly shown. Up to that time it had been secret; but the persecution of this faithful servant of the Emperor, the recollection of the wound received by her cherished son, his courage in adversity, which, voluntary though it were, seemed to her a glorious adversity, drew forth all Agathe's tenderness. The one sentence, "He is unfortunate," explained and justified everything. Joseph himself,—with the innate simplicity which superabounds in the artist-soul in its opening years, and who was, moreover, brought up to admire his big brother,—so far from being hurt by the preference of their mother, encouraged it by sharing her worship of the hero who had carried Napoleon's orders on two battlefields, and was wounded at Waterloo. How could he doubt the superiority of the grand brother, whom he had beheld in the green and gold uniform of the dragoons of the Guard, commanding his squadron on the Champ de Mars?

Agathe, notwithstanding this preference, was an excellent mother. She loved Joseph, though not blindly; she simply was unable to understand him. Joseph adored his mother; Philippe let his mother adore him. Towards her, the dragoon softened his military brutality; but he never concealed the contempt he felt for Joseph,—expressing it, however, in a friendly way. When he looked at his brother, weak and sickly as he was at seventeen years of age, shrunken with determined toil, and over-weighted with his powerful head, he nicknamed him "Cub." Philippe's patronizing manners would have wounded any one less carelessly indifferent than the artist, who had, moreover, a firm belief in the goodness of heart which soldiers hid, he thought, beneath a brutal exterior. Joseph did not yet know, poor boy, that soldiers of genius are as gentle and courteous in manner as other superior men in any walk of life. All genius is alike, wherever found.

"Poor boy!" said Philippe to his mother, "we mustn't plague him; let him do as he likes."

To his mother's eyes the colonel's contempt was a mark of fraternal affection.

"Philippe will always love and protect his brother," she thought to herself.

CHAPTER III

In 1816, Joseph obtained his mother's permission to convert the garret which adjoined his attic room into an atelier, and Madame Descoings gave him a little money for the indispensable requirements of the painter's trade;—in the minds of the two widows, the art of painting was nothing but a trade. With the feeling and ardor of his vocation, the lad himself arranged his humble atelier. Madame Descoings persuaded the owner of the house to put a skylight in the roof. The garret was turned into a vast hall painted in chocolate-color by Joseph himself. On the walls he hung a few sketches. Agathe contributed, not without reluctance, an iron stove; so that her son might be able to work at home, without, however, abandoning the studio of Gros, nor that of Schinner.

The constitutional party, supported chiefly by officers on half-pay and the Bonapartists, were at this time inciting "emeutes" around the Chamber of Deputies, on behalf of the Charter, though no one actually wanted it. Several conspiracies were brewing. Philippe, who dabbled in them, was arrested, and then released for want of proof; but the minister of war cut short his half-pay by putting him on the active list,—a step which might be called a form of discipline. France was no longer safe; Philippe was liable to fall into some trap laid for him by spies,— provocative agents, as they were called, being much talked of in those days.

While Philippe played billiards in disaffected cafes, losing his time and acquiring the habit of wetting his whistle with "little glasses" of all sorts of liquors. Agathe lived in mortal terror for the safety of the great man of the family. The Grecian sages were too much accustomed to wend their nightly way up Madame Bridau's staircase, finding the two widows ready and waiting, and hearing from them all the news of their day, ever to break up the habit of coming to the green salon for their game of cards. The ministry of the interior, though purged of its former *employes* in 1816, had retained Claparon, one of those cautious men, who whisper the news of the "Moniteur," adding invariably, "Don't quote me." Desroches, who had retired from active service some time after old Du Bruel, was still battling for his pension. The three friends, who were witnesses of Agathe's distress, advised her to send the colonel to travel in foreign countries.

"They talk about conspiracies, and your son, with his disposition, will be certain to fall a victim in some of them; there is plenty of treachery in these days."

"Philippe is cut from the wood the Emperor made into marshals," said Du Bruel, in a low voice, looking cautiously about him; "and he mustn't give up his profession. Let him serve in the East, in India—"

"Think of his health," said Agathe.

"Why doesn't he get some place, or business?" said old Desroches; "there are plenty of private offices to be had. I am going as head of a bureau in an insurance company, as soon as I have got my pension."

"Philippe is a soldier; he would not like to be any thing else," said the warlike Agathe.

"Then he ought to have the sense to ask for employment—"

"And serve *these others!*" cried the widow. "Oh! I will never give him that advice."

"You are wrong," said Du Bruel. "My son has just got an appointment through the Duc de Navarreins. The Bourbons are very good to those who are sincere in rallying to them. Your son could be appointed lieutenant-colonel to a regiment."

"They only appoint nobles in the cavalry. Philippe would never rise to be a colonel," said Madame Descoings.

Agathe, much alarmed, entreated Philippe to travel abroad, and put himself at the service of some foreign power who, she thought, would gladly welcome a staff officer of the Emperor.

"Serve a foreign nation!" cried Philippe, with horror.

Agathe kissed her son with enthusiasm.

"His father all over!" she exclaimed.

"He is right," said Joseph. "France is too proud of her heroes to let them be heroic elsewhere. Napoleon may return once more."

However, to satisfy his mother, Philippe took up the dazzling idea of joining General Lallemand in the United States, and helping him to found what was called the Champ d'Asile, one of the most disastrous swindles that ever appeared under the name of national subscription. Agathe gave ten thousand francs to start her son, and she went to Havre to see him off. By the end of 1817, she had accustomed herself to live on the six hundred francs a year which remained to her from her property in the Funds; then, by a lucky chance, she made a good investment of the ten thousand francs she still kept of her savings, from which she obtained an interest of seven per cent. Joseph wished to emulate his mother's devotion. He dressed like a bailiff; wore the commonest shoes and blue stockings; denied himself gloves, and burned charcoal; he lived on bread and milk and Brie cheese. The poor lad got no sympathy, except from Madame Descoings, and from Bixiou, his student-friend and comrade, who was then making those admirable caricatures of his, and filling a small office in the ministry.

"With what joy I welcomed the summer of 1818!" said Joseph Bridau in after-years, relating his troubles; "the sun saved me the cost of charcoal."

As good a colorist by this time as Gros himself, Joseph now went to his master for consultation only. He was already meditating a tilt against classical traditions, and Grecian conventionalities, in short, against the leading-strings which held down an art to which Nature *as she is* belongs, in the omnipotence of her creations and her imagery. Joseph made ready for a struggle which, from the day when he first exhibited in the Salon, has never ceased. It was a terrible year. Roguin, the notary of Madame Descoings and Madame Bridau, absconded with the moneys held back for seven years from Madame Descoings's annuity, which by that time were producing two thousand francs a year. Three days after this disaster, a bill of exchange for a thousand francs, drawn by Philippe upon his mother, arrived from New York. The poor fellow, misled like so many others, had lost his all in the Champ d'Asile. A letter, which accompanied the bill, drove Agathe, Joseph, and the Descoings to tears, and told of debts contracted in New York, where his comrades in misfortunes had indorsed for him.

"It was I who made him go!" cried the poor mother, eager to divert the blame from Philippe.

"I advise you not to send him on many such journeys," said the old Descoings to her niece.

Madame Descoings was heroic. She continued to give the three thousand francs a year to Madame Bridau, but she still paid the dues on her trey which had never turned up since the year 1799. About this time, she began to doubt the honesty of the government, and declared it was capable of keeping the three numbers in the urn, so as to excite the shareholders to put in enormous stakes. After a rapid survey of all their resources, it seemed to the two women impossible to raise the thousand francs without selling out the little that remained in the Funds. They talked of pawning their silver and part of the linen, and even the needless pieces of furniture. Joseph, alarmed at these suggestions, went to see Gerard and told him their circumstances. The great painter obtained an order from the household of the king for two copies of a portrait of Louis XVIII., at five hundred francs each. Though not naturally generous, Gros took his pupil to an artist-furnishing house and fitted him out with the necessary materials. But the thousand francs could not be had till the copies were delivered, so Joseph painted four panels in ten days, sold them to the dealers and brought his mother the thousand francs with which to meet the bill of exchange when it fell due. Eight days later, came a letter from the colonel, informing his mother that he was about to return to France on board a packet from New York, whose captain had trusted him for the passage-money. Philippe announced that he should need at least a thousand francs on his arrival at Havre.

"Good," said Joseph to his mother, "I shall have finished my copies by that time, and you can carry him the money."

"Dear Joseph!" cried Agathe in tears, kissing her son, "God will bless you. You do love him, then, poor persecuted fellow? He is indeed our glory and our hope for the future. So young, so brave, so unfortunate! everything is against him; we three must always stand by him."

"You see now that painting is good for something," cried Joseph, overjoyed to have won his mother's permission to be a great artist.

Madame Bridau rushed to meet her beloved son, Colonel Philippe, at Havre. Once there, she walked every day beyond the round tower built by Francois I., to look out for the American packet, enduring the keenest anxieties. Mothers alone know how such sufferings quicken maternal love. The vessel arrived on a fine morning in October, 1819, without delay, and having met with no mishap. The sight of a mother and the air of one's native land produces a certain affect on the coarsest nature, especially after the miseries of a sea-voyage. Philippe gave way to a rush of feeling, which made Agathe think to herself, "Ah! how he loves me!" Alas, the hero loved but one person in the world, and that person was Colonel Philippe. His misfortunes in Texas, his stay in New York,—a place where speculation and individualism are carried to the highest pitch, where the brutality of self-interest attains to cynicism, where man, essentially isolated, is compelled to push his way for himself and by himself, where politeness does not exist,—in fact, even the minor events of Philippe's journey had developed in him the worst traits of an old campaigner: he had grown brutal, selfish, rude; he drank and smoked to excess; physical hardships and poverty had depraved him. Moreover, he considered himself persecuted; and the effect of that idea is to make persons who are unintelligent persecutors and bigots themselves. To Philippe's conception of life, the universe began at his head and ended at his feet, and the sun shone for him alone. The things he had seen in New York, interpreted by his practical nature, carried away his last scruples on the score of morality. For such beings, there are but two ways of existence. Either they believe, or they do not believe; they have the virtues of honest men, or they give themselves up to the demands of necessity; in which case they proceed to turn their slightest interests and each passing impulse of their passions into necessities.

Such a system of life carries a man a long way. It was only in appearance that Colonel Philippe retained the frankness, plain-dealing, and easy-going freedom of a soldier. This made him, in reality, very dangerous; he seemed as guileless as a child, but, thinking only of himself, he never did anything without reflecting what he had better do,—like a wily lawyer planning some trick "a la Maitre Gonin"; words cost him nothing, and he said as many as he could to get people to believe. If, unfortunately, some one refused to accept the explanations with which he justified the contradictions between his conduct and his professions, the colonel, who was a good shot and could defy the most adroit fencing-master, and possessed the coolness of one to whom life is indifferent, was quite ready to demand satisfaction for the first sharp word; and when a man shows himself prepared for violence there is little more to be said. His imposing stature had taken on a certain rotundity, his face was bronzed from exposure in Texas, he was still succinct in speech, and had acquired the decisive tone of a man obliged to make himself feared among the populations of a new world. Thus developed, plainly dressed, his body trained to endurance by his recent hardships, Philippe in the eyes of his mother was a hero; in point of fact, he had simply become what people (not to mince matters) call a blackguard.

Shocked at the destitution of her cherished son, Madame Bridau bought him a complete outfit of clothes at Havre. After listening to the tale of his woes, she had not the heart to stop his drinking and eating and amusing himself as a man just returned from the Champ d'Asile was likely to eat and drink and divert himself. It was certainly a fine conception,—that of conquering Texas with the remains of the imperial army. The failure was less in the idea than in the men who conceived it; for Texas is to-day a republic, with a future full of promise. This scheme of Liberalism under the Restoration distinctly proves that the interests of the party were purely selfish and not national, seeking power and nothing else. Neither men, nor occasion, nor cause, nor devotion were lacking; only the money and the support of the hypocritical party at home who dispensed enormous sums, but gave nothing when it came to recovering empire. Household managers like Agathe have a plain common-sense which enables them to perceive such political chicane: the poor woman saw the truth through the lines of her son's tale; for she had read, in the exile's interests, all the pompous editorials of the constitutional journals, and watched the management of the famous subscription, which produced barely one hundred and fifty thousand francs when it ought to have yielded five or six millions. The Liberal leaders soon found out that they were playing into the hands of Louis XVIII. by exporting the glorious remnants of our grand army, and they promptly abandoned to their fate the most devoted, the most ardent, the most enthusiastic of its heroes,—those, in short, who had gone in the advance. Agathe was never able, however, to make her son see that he was more duped than persecuted. With blind belief in her idol, she supposed herself ignorant, and deplored, as Philippe did, the evil times which had done him such wrong. Up to this time he was, to her mind, throughout his misfortunes, less faulty than victimized by his noble nature, his energy, the fall of the Emperor, the duplicity of the Liberals, and the rancor of the Bourbons against the Bonapartists. During the week at Havre, a week which was horribly costly, she dared not ask him to make terms with the royal government and apply to the minister of war. She had hard work to get him away from Havre, where living is very expensive, and to bring him back to Paris before her money gave out. Madame Descoings and Joseph, who were awaiting their arrival in the courtyard of the coach-office of the Messageries Royales, were struck with the change in Agathe's face.

"Your mother has aged ten years in two months," whispered the Descoings to Joseph, as they all embraced, and the two trunks were being handed down.

"How do you do, mere Descoings?" was the cool greeting the colonel bestowed on the old woman whom Joseph was in the habit of calling "maman Descoings."

"I have no money to pay for a hackney-coach," said Agathe, in a sad voice.

"I have," replied the young painter. "What a splendid color Philippe has turned!" he cried, looking at his brother.

"Yes, I've browned like a pipe," said Philippe. "But as for you, you're not a bit changed, little man."

Joseph, who was now twenty-one, and much thought of by the friends who had stood by him in his days of trial, felt his own strength and was aware of his talent; he represented the art of painting in a circle of young men whose lives were devoted to science, letters, politics, and philosophy. Consequently, he was wounded by his brother's contempt, which Philippe still further emphasized with a gesture, pulling his ears as if he were still a child. Agathe noticed the coolness which succeeded the first glow of tenderness on the part of Joseph and Madame Descoings; but she hastened to tell them of Philippe's sufferings in exile, and so lessened it. Madame Descoings, wishing to make a festival of the return of the prodigal, as she called him under her breath, had prepared one of her good dinners, to which old Claparon and the elder Desroches were invited. All the family friends were to come, and did come, in the evening. Joseph had invited Leon Giraud, d'Arthez, Michel Chrestien, Fulgence Ridal, and Horace Bianchon, his friends of the fraternity. Madame Descoings had promised Bixiou, her so-called step-son, that the young people should play at ecarte. Desroches the younger, who had now taken, under his father's stern rule, his degree at law, was also of the party. Du Bruel, Claparon, Desroches, and the Abbe Loraux carefully observed the returned exile, whose manners and coarse features, and voice roughened by the abuse of liquors, together with his vulgar glance and phraseology, alarmed them not a little. While Joseph was placing the card-tables, the more intimate of the family friends surrounded Agathe and asked,—

"What do you intend to make of Philippe?"

"I don't know," she answered, "but he is determined not to serve the Bourbons."

"Then it will be very difficult for you to find him a place in France. If he won't re-enter the army, he can't be readily got into government employ," said old Du Bruel. "And you have only to listen to him to see he could never, like my son, make his fortune by writing plays."

The motion of Agathe's eyes, with which alone she replied to this speech, showed how anxious Philippe's future made her; they all kept silence. The exile himself, Bixiou, and the younger Desroches were playing at ecarte, a game which was then the rage.

"Maman Descoings, my brother has no money to play with," whispered Joseph in the good woman's ear.

The devotee of the Royal Lottery fetched twenty francs and gave them to the artist, who slipped them secretly into his brother's hand. All the company were now assembled. There were two tables of boston; and the party grew lively. Philippe proved a bad player: after winning for awhile, he began to lose; and by eleven o'clock he owed fifty francs to young Desroches and to Bixiou. The racket and the disputes at the ecarte table resounded more than once in the ears of the more peaceful boston players, who were watching Philippe surreptitiously. The exile showed such signs of bad temper that in his final dispute with the younger Desroches, who was none too amiable himself, the elder Desroches joined in, and though his son was decidedly in the right, he declared he was in the wrong, and forbade him to play any more. Madame Descoings did the same with her grandson, who was beginning to let fly certain witticisms; and although Philippe, so far, had not understood him, there was always a chance that one of the barbed arrows might piece the colonel's thick skull and put the sharp jester in peril.

"You must be tired," whispered Agathe in Philippe's ear; "come to bed."

"Travel educates youth," said Bixiou, grinning, when Madame Bridau and the colonel had disappeared.

Joseph, who got up at dawn and went to bed early, did not see the end of the party. The next morning Agathe and Madame Descoings, while preparing breakfast, could not help remarking that soires would be terribly expensive if Philippe were to go on playing that sort of game, as the Descoings phrased it. The worthy old woman, then seventy-six years of age, proposed to sell her furniture, give up her *appartement* on the second floor (which the owner was only too glad to occupy), and take Agathe's parlor for her chamber, making the other room a sitting-room and dining-room for the family. In this way they could save seven hundred francs a year; which would enable them to give Philippe fifty francs a month until he could find something to do. Agathe accepted the sacrifice. When the colonel came down and his mother had asked how he liked his little bedroom, the two widows explained to him the situation of the family. Madame Descoings and Agathe possessed, by putting all their resources together, an income of five thousand three hundred francs, four thousand of which belonged to Madame Descoings and were merely a life annuity. The Descoings made an allowance of six hundred a year to Bixiou, whom she had acknowledged as her grandson during the last few months, also six hundred to Joseph; the rest of her income, together with that of Agathe, was spent for the household wants. All their savings were by this time eaten up.

"Make yourselves easy," said the lieutenant-colonel. "I'll find a situation and put you to no expense; all I need for the present is board and lodging."

Agathe kissed her son, and Madame Descoings slipped a hundred francs into his hand to pay for his losses of the night before. In ten days the furniture was sold, the *appartement* given up, and the change in Agathe's domestic arrangements accomplished with a celerity seldom seen outside of Paris. During those ten days, Philippe regularly decamped after breakfast, came back for dinner, was off again for the evening, and only got home about midnight to go to bed. He contracted certain habits half mechanically, and they soon became rooted in him; he got his boots blacked on the Pont Neuf for the two sous it would have cost him to go by the Pont des Arts to the Palais-Royal, where he consumed regularly two glasses of brandy while reading the newspapers,—an occupation which employed him till midday; after that he sauntered along the rue Vivienne to the cafe Minerve, where the Liberals congregated, and where he played at billiards with a number of old comrades. While winning and losing, Philippe swallowed four or five more glasses of divers liquors, and smoked ten or a dozen cigars in going and coming, and idling along the streets. In the evening, after consuming a few pipes at the Hollandais smoking-rooms, he would go to some gambling-place towards ten o'clock at night. The waiter handed him a card and a pin; he always inquired of certain well-seasoned players about the chances of the red or the black, and staked ten francs when the lucky moment seemed to come; never playing more than three times, win or lose. If he won, which usually happened, he drank a tumbler of punch and went home to his garret; but by that time he talked of smashing the ultras and the Bourbon body-guard, and trolled out, as he mounted the staircase, "We watch to save the Empire!" His poor mother, hearing him, used to think "How gay Philippe is to-night!" and then she would creep up and kiss him, without complaining of the fetid odors of the punch, and the brandy, and the pipes.

"You ought to be satisfied with me, my dear mother," he said, towards the end of January; "I lead the most regular of lives."

The colonel had dined five times at a restaurant with some of his army comrades. These old soldiers were quite frank with each other on the state of their own affairs, all the while talking of certain hopes which they based on the building of a submarine vessel, expected to bring about the deliverance of the Emperor. Among these former comrades, Philippe particularly liked an old captain of the dragoons of the Guard, named Giroudeau, in whose company he had seen his first service. This friendship with the late dragoon led Philippe into completing what Rabelais called "the devil's equipage"; and he added to his drams, and his tobacco, and his play, a "fourth wheel."

One evening at the beginning of February, Giroudeau took Philippe after dinner to the Gaite, occupying a free box sent to a theatrical journal belonging to his nephew Finot, in whose office Giroudeau was cashier and secretary. Both were dressed after the fashion of the Bonapartist officers who now belonged to the Constitutional Opposition; they wore ample overcoats with square collars, buttoned to the chin and coming down to their heels, and decorated with the rosette of the Legion of honor; and they carried malacca canes with loaded knobs, which they held by strings of braided leather. The late troopers had just (to use one of their own expressions) "made a bout of it," and were mutually unbosoming their hearts as they entered the box. Through the fumes of a certain number of bottles and various glasses of various liquors, Giroudeau pointed out to Philippe a plump and agile little ballet-girl whom he called Florentine, whose good graces and affection, together with the box, belonged to him as the representative of an all-powerful journal.

"But," said Philippe, "I should like to know how far her good graces go for such an iron-gray old trooper as you."

"Thank God," replied Giroudeau, "I've stuck to the traditions of our glorious uniform. I have never wasted a farthing upon a woman in my life."

"What's that?" said Philippe, putting a finger on his left eye.

"That is so," answered Giroudeau. "But, between ourselves, the newspaper counts for a good deal. To-morrow, in a couple of lines, we shall advise the managers to let Mademoiselle Florentine dance a particular step, and so forth. Faith, my dear boy, I'm uncommonly lucky!"

"Well!" thought Philippe; "if this worthy Giroudeau, with a skull as polished as my knee, forty-eight years, a big stomach, a face like a ploughman, and a nose like a potato, can get a ballet-girl, I ought to be the lover of the first actress in Paris. Where does one find such luck?" he said aloud.

"I'll show you Florentine's place to-night. My Dulcinea only earns fifty francs a month at the theatre," added Giroudeau, "but she is very prettily set up, thanks to an old silk dealer named Cardot, who gives her five hundred francs a month."

"Well, but—?" exclaimed the jealous Philippe.

"Bah!" said Giroudeau; "true love is blind."

When the play was over Giroudeau took Philippe to Mademoiselle Florentine's *appartement*, which was close to the theatre, in the rue de Crussol.

"We must behave ourselves," said Giroudeau. "Florentine's mother is here. You see, I haven't the means to pay for one, so the worthy woman is really her own mother. She used to be a concierge, but she's not without intelligence. Call her Madame; she makes a point of it."

Florentine happened that night to have a friend with her,—a certain Marie Godeschal, beautiful as an angel, cold as a danseuse, and a pupil of Vestris, who foretold for her a great choregraphic destiny. Mademoiselle Godeschal, anxious to make her first appearance at the Panorama-Dramatique under the name of Mariette, based her hopes on the protection and influence of a first gentleman of the bedchamber, to whom Vestris had promised to introduce her. Vestris, still green himself at this period, did not think his pupil sufficiently trained to risk the introduction. The ambitious girl did, in the end, make her pseudonym of Mariette famous; and the motive of her ambition, it must be said, was praiseworthy. She had a brother, a clerk in Derville's law office. Left orphans and very poor, and devoted to each other, the brother and sister had seen life such as it is in Paris. The one wished to be a lawyer that he might support his sister, and he lived on ten sous a day; the other had coldly resolved to be a dancer, and to profit by her beauty as much as by her legs that she might buy a practice for her brother. Outside of their feeling for each other, and of their mutual life and interests, everything was to them, as it once was to the Romans and the Hebrews, barbaric, outlandish, and hostile. This generous affection, which nothing ever lessened, explained Mariette to those who knew her intimately.

The brother and sister were living at this time on the eighth floor of a house in the Vieille rue du Temple. Mariette had begun her studies when she was ten years old; she was now just sixteen. Alas! for want of becoming clothes, her beauty, hidden under a coarse shawl, dressed in calico, and ill-kept, could only be guessed by those Parisians who devote themselves to hunting grisettes and the quest of beauty in misfortune, as she trotted past them with mincing step, mounted on iron pattens. Philippe fell in love with Mariette. To Mariette, Philippe was commander of the dragoons of the Guard, a staff-officer of the Emperor, a young man of twenty-seven, and above all, the means of proving herself superior to Florentine by the evident superiority of Philippe over Giroudeau. Florentine and Giroudeau, the one to promote his comrade's happiness, the other to get a protector for her friend, pushed Philippe and Mariette into a "mariage en detrempe,"—a Parisian term which is equivalent to "morganatic marriage," as applied to royal personages. Philippe when they left the house revealed his poverty to Giroudeau, but the old roue reassured him.

18

"I'll speak to my nephew Finot," he said. "You see, Philippe, the reign of phrases and quill-drivers is upon us; we may as well submit. To-day, scribblers are paramount. Ink has ousted gunpowder, and talk takes the place of shot. After all, these little toads of editors are pretty good fellows, and very clever. Come and see me to-morrow at the newspaper office; by that time I shall have said a word for you to my nephew. Before long you'll have a place on some journal or other. Mariette, who is taking you at this moment (don't deceive yourself) because she literally has nothing, no engagement, no chance of appearing on the stage, and I have told her that you are going on a newspaper like myself,—Mariette will try to make you believe she is loving you for yourself; and you will believe her! Do as I do,—keep her as long as you can. I was so much in love with Florentine that I begged Finot to write her up and help her to a debut; but my nephew replied, 'You say she has talent; well, the day after her first appearance she will turn her back on you.' Oh, that's Finot all over! You'll find him a knowing one."

The next day, about four o'clock, Philippe went to the rue de Sentier, where he found Giroudeau in the entresol,—caged like a wild beast in a sort of hen-coop with a sliding panel; in which was a little stove, a little table, two little chairs, and some little logs of wood. This establishment bore the magic words, SUBSCRIPTION OFFICE, painted on the door in black letters, and the word "Cashier," written by hand and fastened to the grating of the cage. Along the wall that lay opposite to the cage, was a bench, where, at this moment, a one-armed man was breakfasting, who was called Coloquinte by Giroudeau, doubtless from the Egyptian colors of his skin.

"A pretty hole!" exclaimed Philippe, looking round the room. "In the name of thunder! what are you doing here, you who charged with poor Colonel Chabert at Eylau? You—a gallant officer!"

"Well, yes! broum! broum!—a gallant officer keeping the accounts of a little newspaper," said Giroudeau, settling his black silk skull-cap. "Moreover, I'm the working editor of all that rubbish," he added, pointing to the newspaper itself.

"And I, who went to Egypt, I'm obliged to stamp it," said the one-armed man.

"Hold your tongue, Coloquinte," said Giroudeau. "You are in presence of a hero who carried the Emperor's orders at the battle of Montereau."

Coloquinte saluted. "That's were I lost my missing arm!" he said.

"Coloquinte, look after the den. I'm going up to see my nephew."

The two soldiers mounted to the fourth floor, where, in an attic room at the end of a passage, they found a young man with a cold light eye, lying on a dirty sofa. The representative of the press did not stir, though he offered cigars to his uncle and his uncle's friend.

"My good fellow," said Giroudeau in a soothing and humble tone, "this is the gallant cavalry officer of the Imperial Guard of whom I spoke to you."

"Eh! well?" said Finot, eyeing Philippe, who, like Giroudeau, lost all his assurance before the diplomatist of the press.

"My dear boy," said Giroudeau, trying to pose as an uncle, "the colonel has just returned from Texas."

"Ah! you were taken in by that affair of the Champ d'Asile, were you? Seems to me you were rather young to turn into a Soldier-laborer."

The bitterness of this jest will only be understood by those who remember the deluge of engravings, screens, clocks, bronzes, and plaster-casts produced by the idea of the Soldier-laborer, a splendid image of Napoleon and his heroes, which afterwards made its appearance on the stage in vaudevilles. That idea, however, obtained a national subscription; and we still find, in the depths of the provinces, old wall-papers which bear the effigy of the Soldier-laborer. If this young man had not been Giroudeau's nephew, Philippe would have boxed his ears.

"Yes, I was taken in by it; I lost my time, and twelve thousand francs to boot," answered Philippe, trying to force a grin.

"You are still fond of the Emperor?" asked Finot.

"He is my god," answered Philippe Bridau.

"You are a Liberal?"

"I shall always belong to the Constitutional Opposition. Oh Foy! oh Manuel! oh Laffitte! what men they are! They'll rid us of these others,—these wretches, who came back to France at the heels of the enemy."

"Well," said Finot coldly, "you ought to make something out of your misfortunes; for you are the victim of the Liberals, my good fellow. Stay a Liberal, if you really value your opinions, but threaten the party with the follies in Texas which you are ready to show up. You never got a farthing of the national subscription, did you? Well, then you hold a fine position: demand an account of that subscription. I'll tell you how you can do it. A new Opposition journal is just starting, under the auspices of the deputies of the Left; you shall be the cashier, with a salary of three thousand francs. A permanent place. All you want is some one to go security for you in twenty thousand francs; find that, and you shall be installed within a week. I'll advise the Liberals to silence you by giving you the place. Meantime, talk, threaten,—threaten loudly."

Giroudeau let Philippe, who was profuse in his thanks, go down a few steps before him, and then he turned back to say to his nephew, "Well, you are a queer fellow! you keep me here on twelve hundred francs—"

"That journal won't live a year," said Finot. "I've got something better for you."

"Thunder!" cried Philippe to Giroudeau. "He's no fool, that nephew of yours. I never once thought of making something, as he calls it, out of my position."

That night at the cafe Lemblin and the cafe Minerve Colonel Philippe fulminated against the Liberal party, which had raised subscriptions, sent heroes to Texas, talked hypocritically of Soldier-laborers, and left them to starve, after taking the money they had put into it, and keeping them in exile for two years.

"I am going to demand an account of the moneys collected by the subscription for the Champ d'Asile," he said to one of the frequenters of the cafe, who repeated it to the journalists of the Left.

Philippe did not go back to the rue Mazarin; he went to Mariette and told her of his forthcoming appointment on a newspaper with ten thousand subscribers, in which her choregraphic claims should be warmly advanced.

Agathe and Madame Descoings waited up for Philippe in fear and trembling, for the Duc de Berry had just been assassinated. The colonel came home a few minutes after breakfast; and when his mother showed her uneasiness at his absence, he grew angry and asked if he were not of age.

"In the name of thunder, what's all this! here have I brought you some good news, and you both look like tombstones. The Duc de Berry is dead, is he?—well, so much the better! that's one the less, at any rate. As for me, I am to be cashier of a newspaper, with a salary of three thousand francs, and there you are, out of all your anxieties on my account."

"Is it possible?" cried Agathe.

"Yes; provided you can go security for me in twenty thousand francs; you need only deposit your shares in the Funds, you will draw the interest all the same."

The two widows, who for nearly two months had been desperately anxious to find out what Philippe was about, and how he could be provided for, were so overjoyed at this prospect that they gave no thought to their other catastrophes. That evening, the Grecian sages, old Du Bruel, Claparon, whose health was failing, and the inflexible Desroches were unanimous; they all advised Madame Bridau to go security for her son. The new journal, which fortunately was started before the assassination of the Duc de Berry, just escaped the blow which Monsieur Decazes then launched at the press. Madame Bridau's shares in the Funds, representing thirteen hundred francs' interest, were transferred as security for Philippe, who was then appointed cashier. That good son at once promised to pay one hundred francs every month to the two widows, for his board and lodging, and was declared by both to be the best of sons. Those who had thought ill of him now congratulated Agathe.

"We were unjust to him," they said.

Poor Joseph, not to be behind his brother in generosity, resolved to pay for his own support, and succeeded.

CHAPTER IV

Three months later, the colonel, who ate and drank enough for four men, finding fault with the food and compelling the poor widows, on the score of his payments, to spend much money on their table, had not yet paid down a single penny. His mother and Madame Descoings were unwilling, out of delicacy, to remind him of his promise. The year went by without one of those coins which Leon Gozlan so vigorously called "tigers with five claws" finding its way from Philippe's pocket to the household purse. It is true that the colonel quieted his conscience on this score by seldom dining at home.

"Well, he is happy," said his mother; "he is easy in mind; he has a place."

Through the influence of a feuilleton, edited by Vernou, a friend of Bixiou, Finot, and Giroudeau, Mariette made her appearance, not at the Panorama-Dramatique but at the Porte-Saint-Martin, where she triumphed beside the famous Begrand. Among the directors of the theatre was a rich and luxurious general officer, in love with an actress, for whose sake he had made himself an impresario. In Paris, we frequently meet with men so fascinated with actresses, singers, or ballet-dancers, that they are willing to become directors of a theatre out of love. This officer knew Philippe and Giroudeau. Mariette's first appearance, heralded already by Finot's journal and also by Philippe's, was promptly arranged by the three officers; for there seems to be solidarity among the passions in a matter of folly.

The mischievous Bixiou was not long in revealing to his grandmother and the devoted Agathe that Philippe, the cashier, the hero of heroes, was in love with Mariette, the celebrated ballet-dancer at the Porte-Saint-Martin. The news was a thunder-clap to the two widows; Agathe's religious principles taught her to think that all women on the stage were brands in the burning; moreover, she thought, and so did Madame Descoings, that women of that kind dined off gold, drank pearls, and wasted fortunes.

"Now do you suppose," said Joseph to his mother, "that my brother is such a fool as to spend his money on Mariette? Such women only ruin rich men."

"They talk of engaging Mariette at the Opera," said Bixiou. "Don't be worried, Madame Bridau; the diplomatic body often comes to the Porte-Saint-Martin, and that handsome girl won't stay long with your son. I did hear that an ambassador was madly in love with her. By the bye, another piece of news! Old Claparon is dead, and his son, who has become a banker, has ordered the cheapest kind of funeral for him. That fellow has no education; they wouldn't behave like that in China."

Philippe, prompted by mercenary motives, proposed to Mariette that she should marry him; but she, knowing herself on the eve of an engagement at the Grand Opera, refused the offer, either because she guessed the colonel's motive, or because she saw how important her independence would be to her future fortune. For the remainder of this year, Philippe never came more than twice a month to see his mother. Where was he? Either at his office, or the theatre, or with Mariette. No light whatever as to his conduct reached the household of the rue Mazarin. Giroudeau, Finot, Bixiou, Vernou, Lousteau, saw him leading a life of pleasure. Philippe shared the gay amusements of Tullia, a leading singer at the Opera, of Florentine, who took Mariette's place at the Porte-Saint-Martin, of Florine and Matifat, Coralie and Camusot. After four o'clock, when he left his office, until midnight, he amused himself; some party of pleasure had usually been arranged the night before,—a good dinner, a card-party, a supper by some one or other of the set. Philippe was in his element.

This carnival, which lasted eighteen months, was not altogether without its troubles. The beautiful Mariette no sooner appeared at the Opera, in January, 1821, than she captured one of the most distinguished dukes of the court of Louis XVIII. Philippe tried to make head against the peer, and by the month of April he was compelled by his passion, notwithstanding some luck at cards, to dip into the funds of which he was cashier. By May he had taken eleven hundred francs. In that fatal month Mariette started for London, to see what could be done with the lords while the temporary opera house in the Hotel Choiseul, rue Lepelletier, was being prepared. The luckless Philippe had ended, as often happens, in loving Mariette notwithstanding her flagrant infidelities; she herself had never thought him anything but a dull-minded, brutal soldier, the first rung of a ladder on which she had never intended to remain long. So, foreseeing the time when Philippe would have spent all his money, she captured other journalistic support which released her from the necessity of depending on him; nevertheless, she did feel the peculiar gratitude that class of women acknowledge towards the first man who smooths their way, as it were, among the difficulties and horrors of a theatrical career.

Forced to let his terrible mistress go to London without him, Philippe went into winter quarters, as he called it,—that is, he returned to his attic room in his mother's *appartement*. He made some gloomy reflections as he went to bed that night, and when he got up again. He was conscious within himself of the inability to live otherwise than as he had been living the last year. The luxury that surrounded Mariette, the dinners, the suppers, the evenings in the side-scenes, the animation of wits and journalists, the sort of racket that went on around him, the delights that tickled both his senses and his vanity,—such a life, found only in Paris, and offering daily the charm of some new thing, was now more than habit,—it had become to Philippe as much a necessity as his tobacco or his brandy. He saw plainly that he could not live without these continual enjoyments. The idea of suicide came into his head; not on account of the deficit which must soon be discovered in his accounts, but because he could no longer live with Mariette in the atmosphere of pleasure in which he had disported himself for over a year. Full of these gloomy thoughts, he entered for the first time his brother's painting-room, where he found the painter in a blue blouse, copying a picture for a dealer.

"So that's how pictures are made," said Philippe, by way of opening the conversation.

"No," said Joseph, "that is how they are copied."

"How much do they pay you for that?"

"Eh! never enough; two hundred and fifty francs. But I study the manner of the masters and learn a great deal; I found out the secrets of their method. There's one of my own pictures," he added, pointing with the end of his brush to a sketch with the colors still moist.

"How much do you pocket in a year?"

"Unfortunately, I am known only to painters. Schinner backs me; and he has got me some work at the Chateau de Presles, where I am going in October to do some arabesques, panels, and other decorations, for which the Comte de Serizy, no doubt, will pay well. With such trifles and with orders from the dealers, I may manage to earn eighteen hundred to two thousand francs a year over and above the working expenses. I shall send that picture to the next exhibition; if it hits the public taste, my fortune is made. My friends think well of it."

"I don't know anything about such things," said Philippe, in a subdued voice which caused Joseph to turn and look at him.

"What is the matter?" said the artist, seeing that his brother was very pale.

"I should like to know how long it would take you to paint my portrait?"

"If I worked steadily, and the weather were clear, I could finish it in three or four days."

"That's too long; I have only one day to give you. My poor mother loves me so much that I wished to leave her my likeness. We will say no more about it."

"Why! are you going away again?"

"I am going never to return," replied Philippe with an air of forced gayety.

"Look here, Philippe, what is the matter? If it is anything serious, I am a man and not a ninny. I am accustomed to hard struggles, and if discretion is needed, I have it."

"Are you sure?"

"On my honor."

"You will tell no one, no matter who?"

"No one."

"Well, I am going to blow my brains out."

"You!—are you going to fight a duel?"

"I am going to kill myself."

"Why?"

"I have taken eleven hundred francs from the funds in my hands; I have got to send in my accounts to-morrow morning. Half my security is lost; our poor mother will be reduced to six hundred francs a year. That would be nothing! I could make a fortune for her later; but I am dishonored! I cannot live under dishonor—"

"You will not be dishonored if it is paid back. To be sure, you will lose your place, and you will only have the five hundred francs a year from your cross; but you can live on five hundred francs."

"Farewell!" said Philippe, running rapidly downstairs, and not waiting to hear another word.

Joseph left his studio and went down to breakfast with his mother; but Philippe's confession had taken away his appetite. He took Madame Descoings aside and told her the terrible news. The old woman made a frightened exclamation, let fall the saucepan of milk she had in her hand, and flung herself into a chair. Agathe rushed in; from one exclamation to another the mother gathered the fatal truth.

"He! to fail in honor! the son of Bridau to take the money that was trusted to him!"

The widow trembled in every limb; her eyes dilated and then grew fixed; she sat down and burst into tears.

"Where is he?" she cried amid the sobs. "Perhaps he has flung himself into the Seine."

"You must not give up all hope," said Madame Descoings, "because a poor lad has met with a bad woman who has led him to do wrong. Dear me! we see that every day. Philippe has had such misfortunes! he has had so little chance to be happy and loved that we ought not to be surprised at his passion for that creature. All passions lead to excess. My own life is not without reproach of that kind, and yet I call myself an honest woman. A single fault is not vice; and after all, it is only those who do nothing that are never deceived."

Agathe's despair overcame her so much that Joseph and the Descoings were obliged to lessen Philippe's wrong-doings by assuring her that such things happened in all families.

"But he is twenty-eight years old," cried Agathe, "he is no longer a child."

Terrible revelation of the inward thought of the poor woman on the conduct of her son.

"Mother, I assure you he thought only of your sufferings and of the wrong he had done you," said Joseph.

"Oh, my God! let him come back to me, let him live, and I will forgive all," cried the poor mother, to whose mind a horrible vision of Philippe dragged dead out of the river presented itself.

Gloomy silence reigned for a short time. The day went by with cruel alternations of hope and fear; all three ran to the window at the least sound, and gave way to every sort of conjecture. While the family were thus grieving, Philippe was quietly getting matters in order at his office. He had the audacity to give in his accounts with a statement that, fearing some accident, he had retained eleven hundred francs at his own house for safe keeping. The scoundrel left the office at five o'clock, taking five hundred francs more from the desk, and coolly went to a gambling-house, which he had not entered since his connection with the paper, for he knew very well that a cashier must not be seen to frequent such a place. The fellow was not wanting in acumen. His past conduct proved that he derived more from his grandfather Rouget than from his virtuous sire, Bridau. Perhaps he might have made a good general; but in private life, he was one of those utter scoundrels who shelter their schemes and their evil actions behind a screen of strict legality, and the privacy of the family roof.

At this conjuncture Philippe maintained his coolness. He won at first, and gained as much as six thousand francs; but he let himself be dazzled by the idea of getting out of his difficulties at one stroke. He left the trente-et-quarante, hearing that the black had come up sixteen times at the roulette table, and was about to put five thousand francs on the red, when the black came up for the seventeenth time. The colonel then put a thousand francs on the black and won. In spite of this remarkable piece of luck, his head grew weary; he felt it, though he continued to play. But that divining sense which leads a gambler, and which comes in flashes, was already failing him. Intermittent perceptions, so fatal to all gamblers, set in. Lucidity of mind, like the rays of the sun, can have no effect except by the continuity of a direct line; it can divine only on condition of not breaking that line; the curvettings of chance bemuddle it. Philippe lost all. After such a strain, the careless mind as well as the bravest weakens. When Philippe went home that night he was not thinking of suicide, for he had never really meant to kill himself; he no longer thought of his lost place, nor of the sacrificed security, nor of his mother, nor of Mariette, the cause of his ruin; he walked along mechanically. When he got home, his mother in tears, Madame Descoings, and Joseph, all fell on his neck and kissed him and brought him joyfully to a seat by the fire.

"Bless me!" thought he, "the threat has worked."

The brute at once assumed an air suitable to the occasion; all the more easily, because his ill-luck at cards had deeply depressed him. Seeing her atrocious Benjamin so pale and woe-begone, the poor mother knelt beside him, kissed his hands, pressed them to her heart, and gazed at him for a long time with eyes swimming in tears.

"Philippe," she said, in a choking voice, "promise not to kill yourself, and all shall be forgotten."

Philippe looked at his sorrowing brother and at Madame Descoings, whose eyes were full of tears, and thought to himself, "They are good creatures." Then he took his mother in his arms, raised her and put her on his knee, pressed her to his heart and whispered as he kissed her, "For the second time, you give me life."

The Descoings managed to serve an excellent dinner, and to add two bottles of old wine with a little "liqueur des iles," a treasure left over from her former business.

"Agathe," she said at dessert, "we must let him smoke his cigars," and she offered some to Philippe.

These two poor creatures fancied that if they let the fellow take his ease, he would like his home and stay in it; both, therefore, tried to endure his tobacco-smoke, though each loathed it. That sacrifice was not so much as noticed by Philippe.

On the morrow, Agathe looked ten years older. Her terrors calmed, reflection came back to her, and the poor woman had not closed an eye throughout that horrible night. She was now reduced to six hundred francs a year. Madame Descoings, like all fat women fond of good eating, was growing heavy; her step on the staircase sounded like the chopping of logs; she might die at any moment; with her life, four thousand francs would disappear. What folly to rely on that resource! What should she do? What would become of them? With her mind made up to become a sick-nurse rather than be supported by her children, Agathe did not think of herself. But Philippe? what would he do if reduced to live on the five hundred francs of an officer of the Legion of honor? During the past eleven years, Madame Descoings, by giving up three thousand francs a year, had paid her debt twice over, but she still continued to sacrifice her grandson's interests to those of the Bridau family. Though all Agathe's honorable and upright feelings were shocked by this terrible disaster, she said to herself: "Poor boy! is it his fault? He is faithful to his oath. I have done wrong not to marry him. If I had found him a wife, he would not have got entangled with this danseuse. He has such a vigorous constitution—"

Madame Descoings had likewise reflected during the night as to the best way of saving the honor of the family. At daybreak, she got out of bed and went to her friend's room.

"Neither you nor Philippe should manage this delicate matter," she urged. "Our two old friends Du Bruel and Claparon are dead, but we still have Desroches, who is very sagacious. I'll go and see him this morning. He can tell the newspaper people that Philippe trusted a friend and has been made a victim; that his weakness in such respects makes him unfit to be a cashier; what has now happened may happen again, and that Philippe prefers to resign. That will prevent his being turned off."

Agathe, seeing that this business lie would save the honor of her son, at any rate in the eyes of strangers, kissed Madame Descoings, who went out early to make an end of the dreadful affair.

Philippe, meanwhile, had slept the sleep of the just. "She is sly, that old woman," he remarked, when his mother explained to him why breakfast was late.

Old Desroches, the last remaining friend of these two poor women, who, in spite of his harsh nature, never forgot that Bridau had obtained for him his place, fulfilled like an accomplished diplomat the delicate mission Madame Descoings had confided to him. He came to dine that evening with the family, and notified Agathe that she must go the next day to the Treasury, rue Vivienne, sign the transfer of the funds involved, and obtain a coupon for the six hundred francs a year which still remained to her. The old clerk did not leave the afflicted household that night without obliging Philippe to sign a petition to the minister of war, asking for his reinstatement in the active army. Desroches promised the two women to follow up the petition at the war office, and to profit by the triumph of a certain duke over Philippe in the matter of the danseuse, and so obtain that nobleman's influence.

"Philippe will be lieutenant-colonel in the Duc de Maufrigneuse's regiment within three months," he declared, "and you will be rid of him."

Desroches went away, smothered with blessings from the two poor widows and Joseph. As to the newspaper, it ceased to exist at the end of two months, just as Finot had predicted. Philippe's crime had, therefore, so far as the world knew, no consequences. But Agathe's motherhood had received a deadly wound. Her belief in her son once shaken, she lived in perpetual fear, mingled with some satisfactions, as she saw her worst apprehensions unrealized.

When men like Philippe, who are endowed with physical courage, and yet are cowardly and ignoble in their moral being, see matters and things resuming their accustomed course about them after some catastrophe in which their honor and decency is well-nigh lost, such family kindness, or any show of friendliness towards them is a premium of encouragement. They count on impunity; their minds distorted, their passions gratified, only prompt them to study how it happened that they succeeded in getting round all social laws; the result is they become alarmingly adroit.

A fortnight later, Philippe, once more a man of leisure, lazy and bored, renewed his fatal cafe life,—his drams, his long games of billiards embellished with punch, his nightly resort to the gambling-table, where he risked some trifling stake and won enough to pay for his dissipations. Apparently very economical, the better to deceive his mother and Madame Descoings, he wore a hat that was greasy, with the nap rubbed off at the edges, patched boots, a shabby overcoat, on which the red ribbon scarcely showed so discolored and dirty was it by long service at the buttonhole and by the spatterings of coffee and liquors. His buckskin gloves, of a greenish tinge, lasted him a long while; and he only gave up his satin neckcloth when it was ragged enough to look like wadding. Mariette was the sole object of the fellow's love, and her treachery had greatly hardened his heart. When he happened to win more than usual, or if he supped with his old comrade, Giroudeau, he followed some Venus of the slums, with brutal contempt for the whole sex. Otherwise regular in his habits, he breakfasted and dined at home and came in every night about one o'clock. Three months of this horrible life restored Agathe to some degree of confidence.

As for Joseph, who was working at the splendid picture to which he afterwards owed his reputation, he lived in his atelier. On the prediction of her grandson Bixiou, Madame Descoings believed in Joseph's future glory, and she showed him every sort of motherly kindness; she took his breakfast to him, she did his errands, she blacked his boots. The painter was never seen till dinner-time, and his evenings were spent at the Cenacle among his friends. He read a great deal, and gave himself that deep and serious education which only comes through the mind itself, and which all men of talent strive after between the ages of twenty and thirty. Agathe, seeing very little of Joseph, and feeling no uneasiness about him, lived only for Philippe, who gave her the alternations of fears excited and terrors allayed, which seem the life, as it were, of sentiment, and to be as necessary to maternity as to love. Desroches, who came once a week to see the widow of his patron and friend, gave her hopes. The Duc de Maufrigneuse had asked to have Philippe in his regiment; the minister of war had ordered an inquiry; and as the name of Bridau did not appear on any police list, nor an any record at the Palais de Justice, Philippe would be reinstated in the army early in the coming year.

To arrive at this result, Desroches set all the powers that he could influence in motion. At the prefecture of police he learned that Philippe spent his evenings in the gambling-house; and he thought it best to tell this fact privately to Madame Descoings, exhorting her keep an eye on the lieutenant-colonel, for one outbreak would imperil all; as it was, the minister of war was not likely to inquire whether Philippe gambled. Once restored to his rank under the flag of his country, he would perhaps abandon a vice only taken up from idleness. Agathe, who no longer received her friends in the evening, sat in the chimney-corner reading her prayers, while Madame Descoings consulted the cards, interpreted her dreams, and applied the rules of the "cabala" to her lottery ventures. This jovial fanatic never missed a single drawing; she still pursued her trey,—which never turned up. It was nearly twenty-one years old, just approaching its majority; on this ridiculous idea the old woman now pinned her faith. One of its three numbers had stayed at the bottom of all the wheels ever since the institution of the lottery. Accordingly, Madame Descoings laid heavy stakes on that particular number, as well as on all the combinations of the three numbers. The last mattress remaining to her bed was the place where she stored her savings; she unsewed the ticking, put in from time to time the bit of gold saved from her needs, wrapped carefully in wool, and then sewed the mattress up again. She intended, at the last drawing, to risk all her savings on the different combinations of her treasured trey.

This passion, so universally condemned, has never been fairly studied. No one has understood this opium of poverty. The lottery, all-powerful fairy of the poor, bestowed the gift of magic hopes. The turn of the wheel which opens to the gambler a vista of gold and happiness, lasts no longer than a flash of lightning, but the lottery gave five days' existence to that magnificent flash. What social power can to-day, for the sum of five sous, give us five days' happiness and launch us ideally into all the joys of civilization? Tobacco, a craving far more immoral than play, destroys the body, attacks the mind, and stupefies a nation; while the lottery did nothing of the kind. This passion, moreover, was forced to keep within limits by the long periods that occurred between the drawings, and by the choice of wheels which each investor individually clung to. Madame Descoings never staked on any but the "wheel of Paris." Full of confidence that the trey cherished for twenty-one years was about to triumph, she now imposed upon herself enormous privations, that she might stake a large amount of savings upon the last drawing of the year. When she dreamed her cabalistic visions (for all dreams did not correspond with the numbers of the lottery), she went and told them to Joseph, who was the sole being who would listen, and not only not scold her, but give her the kindly words with which an artist knows how to soothe the follies of the mind. All great talents respect and understand a real passion; they explain it to themselves by finding the roots of it in their own hearts or minds. Joseph's ideas was, that his brother loved tobacco and liquors, Maman Descoings loved her trey, his mother loved God, Desroches the younger loved lawsuits, Desroches the elder loved angling,—in short, all the world, he said, loved something. He himself loved the "beau idéal" in all things; he loved the poetry of Lord Byron, the painting of Gericault, the music of Rossini, the novels of Walter Scott. "Every one to his taste, maman," he would say; "but your trey does hang fire terribly."

"It will turn up, and you will be rich, and my little Bixiou as well."

"Give it all to your grandson," cried Joseph; "at any rate, do what you like best with it."

"Hey! when it turns up I shall have enough for everybody. In the first place, you shall have a fine atelier; you sha'n't deprive yourself of going to the opera so as to pay for your models and your colors. Do you know, my dear boy, you make me play a pretty shabby part in that picture of yours?"

By way of economy, Joseph had made the Descoings pose for his magnificent painting of a young courtesan taken by an old woman to a Doge of Venice. This picture, one of the masterpieces of modern painting, was mistaken by Gros himself for a Titian, and it paved the way for the recognition which the younger artists gave to Joseph's talent in the Salon of 1823.

"Those who know you know very well what you are," he answered gayly. "Why need you trouble yourself about those who don't know you?"

For the last ten years Madame Descoings had taken on the ripe tints of a russet apple at Easter. Wrinkles had formed in her superabundant flesh, now grown pallid and flabby. Her eyes, full of life, were bright with thoughts that were still young and vivacious, and might be considered grasping; for there is always something of that spirit in a gambler. Her fat face bore traces of dissimulation and of the mental reservations hidden in the depths of her heart. Her vice necessitated secrecy. There were also indications of gluttony in the motion of her lips. And thus, although she was, as we have seen, an excellent and upright woman, the eye might be misled by her appearance. She was an admirable model for the old woman Joseph wished to paint. Coralie, a young actress of exquisite beauty who died in the flower of her youth, the mistress of Lucien de Rubempre, one of Joseph's friends, had given him the idea of the picture. This noble painting has been called a plagiarism of other pictures, while in fact it was a splendid arrangement of three portraits. Michel Chrestien, one of his companions at the Cenacle, lent his republican head for the senator, to which Joseph added a few mature tints, just as he exaggerated the expression of Madame Descoings's features. This fine picture, which was destined to make a great noise and bring the artist much hatred, jealousy, and admiration, was just sketched out; but, compelled as he was to work for a living, he laid it aside to make copies of the old masters for the dealers; thus he penetrated the secrets of their processes, and his brush is therefore one of the best trained of the modern school. The shrewd sense of an artist led him to conceal the profits he was beginning to lay by from his mother and Madame Descoings, aware that each had her road to ruin,—the one in Philippe, the other in the lottery. This astuteness is seldom wanting among painters; busy for days together in the solitude of their studios, engaged in work which, up to a certain point, leaves the mind free, they are in some respects like women,—their thoughts turn about the little events of life, and they contrive to get at their hidden meaning.

Joseph had bought one of those magnificent chests or coffers of a past age, then ignored by fashion, with which he decorated a corner of his studio, where the light danced upon the bas-reliefs and gave full lustre to a masterpiece of the sixteenth century artisans. He saw the necessity for a hiding-place, and in this coffer he had begun to accumulate a little store of money. With an artist's carelessness, he was in the habit of putting the sum he allowed for his monthly expenses in a skull, which stood on one of the compartments of the coffer. Since his brother had returned to live at home, he found a constant discrepancy between the amount he spent and the sum in this receptacle. The hundred francs a month disappeared with incredible celerity. Finding nothing one day, when he had only spent forty or fifty francs, he remarked for the first time: "My money must have got wings." The next month he paid more attention to his accounts; but add as he might, like Robert Macaire, sixteen and five are twenty-three, he could make nothing of them. When, for the third time, he found a still more important discrepancy, he communicated the painful fact to Madame Descoings, who loved him, he knew, with that maternal, tender, confiding, credulous, enthusiastic love that he had never had from his own mother, good as she was,—a love as necessary to the early life of an artist as the care of the hen is to her unfledged chickens. To her alone could he confide his horrible suspicions. He was as sure of his friends as he was of himself; and the Descoings, he knew, would take nothing to put in her lottery. At the idea which then suggested itself the poor woman wrung her hands. Philippe alone could have committed this domestic theft.

"Why didn't he ask me, if he wanted it?" cried Joseph, taking a dab of color on his palette and stirring it into the other colors without seeing what he did. "Is it likely I should refuse him?"

"It is robbing a child!" cried the Descoings, her face expressing the deepest disgust.

"No," replied Joseph, "he is my brother; my purse is his: but he ought to have asked me."

"Put in a special sum, in silver, this morning, and don't take anything out," said Madame Descoings. "I shall know who goes into the studio; and if he is the only one, you will be certain it is he."

The next day Joseph had proof of his brother's forced loans upon him. Philippe came to the studio when his brother was out and took the little sum he wanted. The artist trembled for his savings.

"I'll catch him at it, the scamp!" he said, laughing, to Madame Descoings.

"And you'll do right: we ought to break him of it. I, too, I have missed little sums out of my purse. Poor boy! he wants tobacco; he's accustomed to it."

"Poor boy! poor boy!" cried the artist. "I'm rather of Fulgence and Bixiou's opinion: Philippe is a dead-weight on us. He runs his head into riots and has to be shipped to America, and that costs the mother twelve thousand francs; he can't find anything to do in the forests of the New World, and so he comes back again, and that costs twelve thousand more. Under pretence of having carried two words of Napoleon to a general, he thinks himself a great soldier and makes faces at the Bourbons; meantime, what does he do? amuse himself, travel about, see foreign countries! As for me, I'm not duped by his misfortunes; he doesn't look like a man who fails to get the best of things! Somebody finds him a good place, and there he is, leading the life of a Sardanapalus with a ballet-girl, and guzzling the funds of his journal; that costs the mother another twelve thousand francs! I don't care two straws for myself, but Philippe will bring that poor woman to beggary. He thinks I'm of no account because I was never in the dragoons of the Guard; but perhaps I shall be the one to support that poor dear mother in her old age, while he, if he goes on as he does, will end I don't know how. Bixiou often says to me, 'He is a downright rogue, that brother of yours.' Your grandson is right. Philippe will be up to some mischief that will compromise the honor of the family, and then we shall have to scrape up another ten or twelve thousand francs! He gambles every night; when he comes home, drunk as a templar, he drops on the staircase the pricked cards on which he marks the turns of the red and black. Old Desroches is trying to get him back into the army, and, on my word on honor, I believe he would hate to serve again. Would you ever have believed that a boy with such heavenly blue eyes and the look of Bayard could turn out such a scoundrel?"

CHAPTER V

In spite of the coolness and discretion with which Philippe played his trifling game every night, it happened every now and then that he was what gamblers call "cleaned out." Driven by the irresistible necessity of having his evening stake of ten francs, he plundered the household, and laid hands on his brother's money and on all that Madame Descoings or Agathe left about. Already the poor mother had had a dreadful vision in her first sleep: Philippe entered the room and took from the pockets of her gown all the money he could find. Agathe pretended to sleep, but she passed the rest of the night in tears. She saw the truth only too clearly. "One wrong act is not a vice," Madame Descoings had declared; but after so many repetitions, vice was unmistakable. Agathe could doubt no longer; her best-beloved son had neither delicacy nor honor.

On the morrow of that frightful vision, before Philippe left the house after breakfast, she drew him into her chamber and begged him, in a tone of entreaty, to ask her for what money he needed. After that, the applications were so numerous that in two weeks Agathe was drained of all her savings. She was literally without a penny, and began to think of finding work. The means of earning money had been discussed in the evenings between herself and Madame Descoings, and she had already taken patterns of worsted work to fill in, from a shop called the "Pere de Famille,"—an employment which pays about twenty sous a day. Notwithstanding Agathe's silence on the subject, Madame Descoings had guessed the motive of this desire to earn money by women's-work. The change in her appearance was eloquent: her fresh face had withered, the skin clung to the temples and the cheek-bones, and the forehead showed deep lines; her eyes lost their clearness; an inward fire was evidently consuming her; she wept the greater part of the night. A chief cause of these outward ravages was the necessity of hiding her anguish, her sufferings, her apprehensions. She never went to sleep until Philippe came in; she listened for his step, she had learned the inflections of his voice, the variations of his walk, the very language of his cane as it touched the pavement. Nothing escaped her. She knew the degree of drunkenness he had reached, she trembled as she heard him stumble on the stairs; one night she picked up some pieces of gold at the spot where he had fallen. When he had drunk and won, his voice was gruff and his cane dragged; but when he had lost, his step had something sharp, short and angry about it; he hummed in a clear voice, and carried his cane in the air as if presenting arms. At breakfast, if he had won, his behavior was gay and even affectionate; he joked roughly, but still he joked, with Madame Descoings, with Joseph, and with his mother; gloomy, on the contrary, when he had lost, his brusque, rough speech, his hard glance, and his depression, frightened them. A life of debauch and the abuse of liquors debased, day by day, a countenance that was once so handsome. The veins of the face were swollen with blood, the features became coarse, the eyes lost their lashes and grew hard and dry. No longer careful of his person, Philippe exhaled the miasmas of a tavern and the smell of muddy boots, which, to an observer, stamped him with debauchery.

"You ought," said Madame Descoings to Philippe during the last days of December, "you ought to get yourself new-clothed from head to foot."

"And who is to pay for it?" he answered sharply. "My poor mother hasn't a sou; and I have five hundred francs a year. It would take my whole year's pension to pay for the clothes; besides I have mortgaged it for three years—"

"What for?" asked Joseph.

"A debt of honor. Giroudeau borrowed a thousand francs from Florentine to lend me. I am not gorgeous, that's a fact; but when one thinks that Napoleon is at Saint Helena, and has sold his plate for the means of living, his faithful soldiers can manage to walk on their bare feet," he said, showing his boots without heels, as he marched away.

"He is not bad," said Agathe, "he has good feelings."

"You can love the Emperor and yet dress yourself properly," said Joseph. "If he would take any care of himself and his clothes, he wouldn't look so like a vagabond."

"Joseph! you ought to have some indulgence for your brother," cried Agathe. "You do the things you like, while he is certainly not in his right place."

"What did he leave it for?" demanded Joseph. "What can it matter to him whether Louis the Eighteenth's bugs or Napoleon's cuckoos are on the flag, if it is the flag of his country? France is France! For my part, I'd paint for the devil. A soldier ought to fight, if he is a soldier, for the love of his art. If he had stayed quietly in the army, he would have been a general by this time."

"You are unjust to him," said Agathe, "your father, who adored the Emperor, would have approved of his conduct. However, he has consented to re-enter the army. God knows the grief it has caused your brother to do a thing he considers treachery."

Joseph rose to return to his studio, but his mother took his hand and said:—

"Be good to your brother; he is so unfortunate."

When the artist got back to his painting-room, followed by Madame Descoings, who begged him to humor his mother's feelings, and pointed out to him how changed she was, and what inward suffering the change revealed, they found Philippe there, to their great amazement.

"Joseph, my boy," he said, in an off-hand way, "I want some money. Confound it! I owe thirty francs for cigars at my tobacconist's, and I dare not pass the cursed shop till I've paid it. I've promised to pay it a dozen times."

"Well, I like your present way best," said Joseph; "take what you want out of the skull."

"I took all there was last night, after dinner."

"There was forty-five francs."

"Yes, that's what I made it," replied Philippe. "I took them; is there any objection?"

"No, my friend, no," said Joseph. "If you were rich, I should do the same by you; only, before taking what I wanted, I should ask you if it were convenient."

"It is very humiliating to ask," remarked Philippe; "I would rather see you taking as I do, without a word; it shows more confidence. In the army, if a comrade dies, and has a good pair of boots, and you have a bad pair, you change, that's all."

"Yes, but you don't take them while he is living."

"Oh, what meanness!" said Philippe, shrugging his shoulders. "Well, so you haven't got any money?"

"No," said Joseph, who was determined not to show his hiding-place.

"In a few days we shall be rich," said Madame Descoings.

"Yes, you; you think your trey is going to turn up on the 25th at the Paris drawing. You must have put in a fine stake if you think you can make us all rich."

"A paid-up trey of two hundred francs will give three millions, without counting the couplets and the singles."

"At fifteen thousand times the stake—yes, you are right; it is just two hundred you must pay up!" cried Philippe.

Madame Descoings bit her lips; she knew she had spoken imprudently. In fact, Philippe was asking himself as he went downstairs:—

"That old witch! where does she keep her money? It is as good as lost; I can make a better use of it. With four pools at fifty francs each, I could win two hundred thousand francs, and that's much surer than the turning up of a trey."

He tried to think where the old woman was likely to have hid the money. On the days preceding festivals, Agathe went to church and stayed there a long time; no doubt she confessed and prepared for the communion. It was now the day before Christmas; Madame Descoings would certainly go out to buy some dainties for the "reveillon," the midnight meal; and she might also take occasion to pay up her stake. The lottery was drawn every five days in different localities, at Bordeaux, Lyons, Lille, Strasburg, and Paris. The Paris lottery was drawn on the twenty-fifth of each month, and the lists closed on the twenty-fourth, at midnight. Philippe studied all these points and set himself to watch. He came home at midday; the Descoings had gone out, and had taken the key of the *appartement*. But that was no difficulty. Philippe pretended to have forgotten something, and asked the concierge to go herself and get a locksmith, who lived close by, and who came at once and opened the door. The villain's first thought was the bed; he uncovered it, passed his hands over the mattress before he examined the bedstead, and at the lower end felt the pieces wrapped up in paper. He at once ripped the ticking, picked out twenty napoleons, and then, without taking time to sew up the mattress, re-made the bed neatly enough, so that Madame Descoings could suspect nothing.

The gambler stole off with a light foot, resolving to play at three different times, three hours apart, and each time for only ten minutes. Thorough-going players, ever since 1786, the time at which public gaming-houses were established,—the true players whom the government dreaded, and who ate up, to use a gambling term, the money of the bank,—never played in any other way. But before attaining this measure of experience they lost fortunes. The whole science of gambling-houses and their gains rests upon three things: the impassibility of the bank; the even results called "drawn games," when half the money goes to the bank; and the notorious bad faith authorized by the government, in refusing to hold or pay the player's stakes except optionally. In a word, the gambling-house, which refuses the game of a rich and cool player, devours the fortune of the foolish and obstinate one, who is carried away by the rapid movement of the machinery of the game. The croupiers at "trente et quarante" move nearly as fast as the ball.

Philippe had ended by acquiring the sang-froid of a commanding general, which enables him to keep his eye clear and his mind prompt in the midst of tumult. He had reached that statesmanship of gambling which in Paris, let us say in passing, is the livelihood of thousands who are strong enough to look every night into an abyss without getting a vertigo. With his four hundred francs, Philippe resolved to make his fortune that day. He put aside, in his boots, two hundred francs, and kept the other two hundred in his pocket. At three o'clock he went to the gambling-house (which is now turned into the theatre of the Palais-Royal), where the bank accepted the largest sums. He came out half an hour later with seven thousand francs in his pocket. Then he went to see Florentine, paid the five hundred francs which he owed to her, and proposed a supper at the Rocher de Cancale after the theatre. Returning to his game, along the rue de Sentier, he stopped at Giroudeau's newspaper-office to notify him of the gala. By six o'clock Philippe had won twenty-five thousand francs, and stopped playing at the end of ten minutes as he had promised himself to do. That night, by ten o'clock, he had won seventy-five thousand francs. After the supper, which was magnificent, Philippe, by that time drunk and confident, went back to his play at midnight. In defiance of the rule he had imposed upon himself, he played for an hour and doubled his fortune. The bankers, from whom, by his system of playing, he had extracted one hundred and fifty thousand francs, looked at him with curiosity.

"Will he go away now, or will he stay?" they said to each other by a glance. "If he stays he is lost."

Philippe thought he had struck a vein of luck, and stayed. Towards three in the morning, the hundred and fifty thousand francs had gone back to the bank. The colonel, who had imbibed a considerable quantity of grog while playing, left the place in a drunken state, which the cold of the outer air only increased. A waiter from the gambling-house followed him, picked him up, and took him to one of those horrible houses at the door of which, on a hanging lamp, are the words: "Lodgings for the night." The waiter paid for the ruined gambler, who was put to bed, where he remained till Christmas night. The managers of gambling-houses have some consideration for their customers, especially for high players. Philippe awoke about seven o'clock in the evening, his mouth parched, his face swollen, and he himself in the grip of a nervous fever. The strength of his constitution enabled him to get home on foot, where meanwhile he had, without willing it, brought mourning, desolation, poverty, and death.

The evening before, when dinner was ready, Madame Descoings and Agathe expected Philippe. They waited dinner till seven o'clock. Agathe always went to bed at ten; but as, on this occasion, she wished to be present at the midnight mass, she went to lie down as soon as dinner was over. Madame Descoings and Joseph remained alone by the fire in the little salon, which served for all, and the old woman asked the painter to add up the amount of her great stake, her monstrous stake, on the famous trey, which she was to pay that evening at the Lottery office. She wished to put in for the doubles and singles as well, so as to seize all chances. After feasting on the poetry of her hopes, and pouring the two horns of plenty at the feet of her adopted son, and relating to him her dreams which demonstrated the certainty of success, she felt no other uneasiness than the difficulty of bearing such joy, and waiting from mid-night until ten o'clock of the morrow, when the winning numbers were declared. Joseph, who saw nothing of the four hundred francs necessary to pay up the stakes, asked about them. The old woman smiled, and led him into the former salon, which was now her bed-chamber.

"You shall see," she said.

Madame Descoings hastily unmade the bed, and searched for her scissors to rip the mattress; she put on her spectacles, looked at the ticking, saw the hole, and let fall the mattress. Hearing a sigh from the depths of the old woman's breast, as though she were strangled by a rush of blood to the heart, Joseph instinctively held out his arms to catch the poor creature, and placed her fainting in a chair, calling to his mother to come to them. Agathe rose, slipped on her dressing-gown, and ran in. By the light of a candle, she applied the ordinary remedies,—eau-de-cologne to the temples, cold water to the forehead, a burnt feather under the nose,—and presently her aunt revived.

"They were there is morning; HE has taken them, the monster!" she said.

"Taken what?" asked Joseph.

"I had twenty louis in my mattress; my savings for two years; no one but Philippe could have taken them."

"But when?" cried the poor mother, overwhelmed, "he has not been in since breakfast."

29

"I wish I might be mistaken," said the old woman. "But this morning in Joseph's studio, when I spoke before Philippe of my stakes, I had a presentiment. I did wrong not to go down and take my little all and pay for my stakes at once. I meant to, and I don't know what prevented me. Oh, yes!—my God! I went out to buy him some cigars."

"But," said Joseph, "you left the door locked. Besides, it is so infamous. I can't believe it. Philippe couldn't have watched you, cut open the mattress, done it deliberately,—no, no!"

"I felt them this morning, when I made my bed after breakfast," repeated Madame Descoings.

Agathe, horrified, went down stairs and asked if Philippe had come in during the day. The concierge related the tale of his return and the locksmith. The mother, heart-stricken, went back a changed woman. White as the linen of her chemise, she walked as we might fancy a spectre walks, slowly, noiselessly, moved by some superhuman power, and yet mechanically. She held a candle in her hand, whose light fell full upon her face and showed her eyes, fixed with horror. Unconsciously, her hands by a desperate movement had dishevelled the hair about her brow; and this made her so beautiful with anguish that Joseph stood rooted in awe at the apparition of that remorse, the vision of that statue of terror and despair.

"My aunt," she said, "take my silver forks and spoons. I have enough to make up the sum; I took your money for Philippe's sake; I thought I could put it back before you missed it. Oh! I have suffered much."

She sat down. Her dry, fixed eyes wandered a little.

"It was he who did it," whispered the old woman to Joseph.

"No, no," cried Agathe; "take my silver plate, sell it; it is useless to me; we can eat with yours."

She went to her room, took the box which contained the plate, felt its light weight, opened it, and saw a pawnbroker's ticket. The poor mother uttered a dreadful cry. Joseph and the Descoings ran to her, saw the empty box, and her noble falsehood was of no avail. All three were silent, and avoided looking at each other; but the next moment, by an almost frantic gesture, Agathe laid her finger on her lips as if to entreat a secrecy no one desired to break. They returned to the salon, and sat beside the fire.

"Ah! my children," cried Madame Descoings, "I am stabbed to the heart: my trey will turn up, I am certain of it. I am not thinking of myself, but of you two. Philippe is a monster," she continued, addressing her niece; "he does not love you after all that you have done for him. If you do not protect yourself against him he will bring you to beggary. Promise me to sell out your Funds and buy a life-annuity. Joseph has a good profession and he can live. If you will do this, dear Agathe, you will never be an expense to Joseph. Monsieur Desroches has just started his son as a notary; he would take your twelve thousand francs and pay you an annuity."

Joseph seized his mother's candlestick, rushed up to his studio, and came down with three hundred francs.

"Here, Madame Descoings!" he cried, giving her his little store, "it is no business of ours what you do with your money; we owe you what you have lost, and here it is, almost in full."

"Take your poor little all?—the fruit of those privations that have made me so unhappy! are you mad, Joseph?" cried the old woman, visibly torn between her dogged faith in the coming trey, and the sacrilege of accepting such a sacrifice.

"Oh! take it if you like," said Agathe, who was moved to tears by this action of her true son.

Madame Descoings took Joseph by the head, and kissed him on the forehead:—

"My child," she said, "don't tempt me. I might only lose it. The lottery, you see, is all folly."

No more heroic words were ever uttered in the hidden dramas of domestic life. It was, indeed, affection triumphant over inveterate vice. At this instant, the clocks struck midnight.

"It is too late now," said Madame Descoings.

"Oh!" cried Joseph, "here are your cabalistic numbers."

The artist sprang at the paper, and rushed headlong down the staircase to pay the stakes. When he was no longer present, Agathe and Madame Descoings burst into tears.

"He has gone, the dear love," cried the old gambler; "but it shall all be his; he pays his own money."

Unhappily, Joseph did not know the way to any of the lottery-offices, which in those days were as well known to most people as the cigarshops to a smoker in ours. The painter ran along, reading the street names upon the lamps. When he asked the passers-by to show him a lottery-office, he was told they were all closed, except the one under the portico of the Palais-Royal which was sometimes kept open a little later. He flew to the Palais-Royal: the office was shut.

"Two minutes earlier, and you might have paid your stake," said one of the vendors of tickets, whose beat was under the portico, where he vociferated this singular cry: "Twelve hundred francs for forty sous," and offered tickets all paid up.

By the glimmer of the street lamp and the lights of the cafe de la Rotonde, Joseph examined these tickets to see if, by chance, any of them bore the Descoings's numbers. He found none, and returned home grieved at having done his best in vain for the old woman, to whom he related his ill-luck. Agathe and her aunt went together to the midnight mass at Saint-Germain-des-Pres. Joseph went to bed. The collation did not take place. Madame Descoings had lost her head; and in Agathe's heart was eternal mourning.

The two rose late on Christmas morning. Ten o'clock had struck before Madame Descoings began to bestir herself about the breakfast, which was only ready at half-past eleven. At that hour, the oblong frames containing the winning numbers are hung over the doors of the lottery-offices. If Madame Descoings had paid her stake and held her ticket, she would have gone by half-past nine o'clock to learn her fate at a building close to the ministry of Finance, in the rue Neuve-des-Petits Champs, a situation now occupied by the Theatre Ventadour in the place of the same name. On the days when the drawings took place, an observer might watch with curiosity the crowd of old women, cooks, and old men assembled about the door of this building; a sight as remarkable as the cue of people about the Treasury on the days when the dividends are paid.

"Well, here you are, rolling in wealth!" said old Desroches, coming into the room just as the Descoings was swallowing her last drop of coffee.

"What do you mean?" cried poor Agathe.

"Her trey has turned up," he said, producing the list of numbers written on a bit of paper, such as the officials of the lottery put by hundreds into little wooden bowls on their counters.

Joseph read the list. Agathe read the list. The Descoings read nothing; she was struck down as by a thunderbolt. At the change in her face, at the cry she gave, old Desroches and Joseph carried her to her bed. Agathe went for a doctor. The poor woman was seized with apoplexy, and she only recovered consciousness at four in the afternoon; old Haudry, her doctor, then said that, in spite of this improvement, she ought to settle her worldly affairs and think of her salvation. She herself only uttered two words:—

"Three millions!"

Old Desroches, informed by Joseph, with due reservations, of the state of things, related many instances where lottery-players had seen a fortune escape them on the very day when, by some fatality, they had forgotten to pay their stakes; but he thoroughly understood that such a blow might be fatal when it came after twenty years' perseverance. About five o'clock, as a deep silence reigned in the little *appartement*, and the sick woman, watched by Joseph and his mother, the one sitting at the foot, the other at the head of her bed, was expecting her grandson Bixiou, whom Desroches had gone to fetch, the sound of Philippe's step and cane resounded on the staircase.

"There he is! there he is!" cried the Descoings, sitting up in bed and suddenly able to use her paralyzed tongue.

Agathe and Joseph were deeply impressed by this powerful effect of the horror which violently agitated the old woman. Their painful suspense was soon ended by the sight of Philippe's convulsed and purple face, his staggering walk, and the horrible state of his eyes, which were deeply sunken, dull, and yet haggard; he had a strong chill upon him, and his teeth chattered.

"Starvation in Prussia!" he cried, looking about him. "Nothing to eat or drink?—and my throat on fire! Well, what's the matter? The devil is always meddling in our affairs. There's my old Descoings in bed, looking at me with her eyes as big as saucers."

"Be silent, monsieur!" said Agathe, rising. "At least, respect the sorrows you have caused."

"*Monsieur*, indeed!" he cried, looking at his mother. "My dear little mother, that won't do. Have you ceased to love your son?"

"Are you worthy of love? Have you forgotten what you did yesterday? Go and find yourself another home; you cannot live with us any longer,—that is, after to-morrow," she added; "for in the state you are in now it is difficult—"

"To turn me out,—is that it?" he interrupted. "Ha! are you going to play the melodrama of 'The Banished Son'? Well done! is that how you take things? You are all a pretty set! What harm have I done? I've cleaned out the old woman's mattress. What the devil is the good of money kept in wool? Do you call that a crime? Didn't she take twenty thousand francs from you? We are her creditors, and I've paid myself as much as I could get,—that's all."

"My God! my God!" cried the dying woman, clasping her hands and praying.

"Be silent!" exclaimed Joseph, springing at his brother and putting his hand before his mouth.

31

"To the right about, march! brat of a painter!" retorted Philippe, laying his strong hand on Joseph's head, and twirling him round, as he flung him on a sofa. "Don't dare to touch the moustache of a commander of a squadron of the dragoons of the Guard!"

"She has paid me back all that she owed me," cried Agathe, rising and turning an angry face to her son; "and besides, that is my affair. You have killed her. Go away, my son," she added, with a gesture that took all her remaining strength, "and never let me see you again. You are a monster."

"I kill her?"

"Her trey has turned up," cried Joseph, "and you stole the money for her stake."

"Well, if she is dying of a lost trey, it isn't I who have killed her," said the drunkard.

"Go, go!" said Agathe. "You fill me with horror; you have every vice. My God! is this my son?"

A hollow rattle sounded in Madame Descoings's throat, increasing Agathe's anger.

"I love you still, my mother,—you who are the cause of all my misfortunes," said Philippe. "You turn me out of doors on Christmas-day. What did you do to grandpa Rouget, to your father, that he should drive you away and disinherit you? If you had not displeased him, we should all be rich now, and I should not be reduced to misery. What did you do to your father,— you who are a good woman? You see by your own self, I may be a good fellow and yet be turned out of house and home,—I, the glory of the family—"

"The disgrace of it!" cried the Descoings.

"You shall leave this room, or you shall kill me!" cried Joseph, springing on his brother with the fury of a lion.

"My God! my God!" cried Agathe, trying to separate the brothers.

At this moment Bixiou and Haudry the doctor entered. Joseph had just knocked his brother over and stretched him on the ground.

"He is a regular wild beast," he cried. "Don't speak another word, or I'll—"

"I'll pay you for this!" roared Philippe.

"A family explanation," remarked Bixiou.

"Lift him up," said the doctor, looking at him. "He is as ill as Madame Descoings; undress him and put him to bed; get off his boots."

"That's easy to say," cried Bixiou, "but they must be cut off; his legs are swollen."

Agathe took a pair of scissors. When she had cut down the boots, which in those days were worn outside the clinging trousers, ten pieces of gold rolled on the floor.

"There it is,—her money," murmured Philippe. "Cursed fool that I was, I forgot it. I too have missed a fortune."

He was seized with a horrible delirium of fever, and began to rave. Joseph, assisted by old Desroches, who had come back, and by Bixiou, carried him to his room. Doctor Haudry was obliged to write a line to the Hopital de la Charite and borrow a strait-waistcoat; for the delirium ran so high as to make him fear that Philippe might kill himself,—he was raving. At nine o'clock calm was restored. The Abbe Loraux and Desroches endeavored to comfort Agathe, who never ceased to weep at her aunt's bedside. She listened to them in silence, and obstinately shook her head; Joseph and the Descoings alone knew the extent and depth of her inward wound.

"He will learn to do better, mother," said Joseph, when Desroches and Bixiou had left.

"Oh!" cried the widow, "Philippe is right,—my father cursed me: I have no right to— Here, here is your money," she said to Madame Descoings, adding Joseph's three hundred francs to the two hundred found on Philippe. "Go and see if your brother does not need something," she said to Joseph.

"Will you keep a promise made to a dying woman?" asked Madame Descoings, who felt that her mind was failing her.

"Yes, aunt."

"Then swear to me to give your property to young Desroches for a life annuity. My income ceases at my death; and from what you have just said, I know you will let that wretch wring the last farthing out of you."

"I swear it, aunt."

The old woman died on the 31st of December, five days after the terrible blow which old Desroches had so innocently given her. The five hundred francs—the only money in the household—were barely enough to pay for her funeral. She left a small amount of silver and some furniture, the value of which Madame Bixiou paid over to her grandson Bixiou. Reduced to eight hundred francs' annuity paid to her by young Desroches, who had bought a business without clients, and himself took the capital of twelve thousand francs, Agathe gave up her *appartement* on the third floor, and sold all her superfluous furniture. When, at the end of a month, Philippe seemed to be convalescent, his mother coldly explained to him that the costs of his illness had taken all her ready money, that she should be obliged in future to work for her living, and she urged him, with the utmost kindness, to re-enter the army and support himself.

"You might have spared me that sermon," said Philippe, looking at his mother with an eye that was cold from utter indifference. "I have seen all along that neither you nor my brother love me. I am alone in the world; I like it best!"

"Make yourself worthy of our affection," answered the poor mother, struck to the very heart, "and we will give it back to you—"

"Nonsense!" he cried, interrupting her.

He took his old hat, rubbed white at the edges, stuck it over one ear, and went downstairs, whistling.

"Philippe! where are you going without any money?" cried his mother, who could not repress her tears. "Here, take this—"

She held out to him a hundred francs in gold, wrapped up in paper. Philippe came up the stairs he had just descended, and took the money.

"Well; won't you kiss me?" she said, bursting into tears.

He pressed his mother in his arms, but without the warmth of feeling which was all that could give value to the embrace.

"Where shall you go?" asked Agathe.

"To Florentine, Girodeau's mistress. Ah! they are real friends!" he answered brutally.

He went away. Agathe turned back with trembling limbs, and failing eyes, and aching heart. She fell upon her knees, prayed God to take her unnatural child into His own keeping, and abdicated her woeful motherhood.

CHAPTER VI

By February, 1822, Madame Bridau had settled into the attic room recently occupied by Philippe, which was over the kitchen of her former *appartement*. The painter's studio and bedroom was opposite, on the other side of the staircase. When Joseph saw his mother thus reduced, he was determined to make her as comfortable as possible. After his brother's departure he assisted in the re-arrangement of the garret room, to which he gave an artist's touch. He added a rug; the bed, simple in character but exquisite in taste, had something monastic about it; the walls, hung with a cheap glazed cotton selected with taste, of a color which harmonized with the furniture and was newly covered, gave the room an air of elegance and nicety. In the hallway he added a double door, with a "portiere" to the inner one. The window was shaded by a blind which gave soft tones to the light. If the poor mother's life was reduced to the plainest circumstances that the life of any woman could have in Paris, Agathe was at least better off than all others in a like case, thanks to her son.

To save his mother from the cruel cares of such reduced housekeeping, Joseph took her every day to dine at a table-d'hote in the rue de Beaune, frequented by well-bred women, deputies, and titled people, where each person's dinner cost ninety francs a month. Having nothing but the breakfast to provide, Agathe took up for her son the old habits she had formerly had with the father. But in spite of Joseph's pious lies, she discovered the fact that her dinner was costing him nearly a hundred francs a month. Alarmed at such enormous expense, and not imaging that her son could earn much money by painting naked women, she obtained, thanks to her confessor, the Abbe Loraux, a place worth seven hundred francs a year in a lottery-office belonging to the Comtesse de Bauvan, the widow of a Chouan leader. The lottery-offices of the government, the lot, as one might say, of privileged widows, ordinarily sufficed for the support of the family of each person who managed them. But after the Restoration the difficulty of rewarding, within the limits of constitutional government, all the services rendered to the cause, led to the custom of giving to reduced women of title not only one but two lottery-offices, worth, usually, from six to ten thousand a year. In such cases, the widow of a general or nobleman thus "protected" did not keep the lottery-office herself; she employed a paid manager. When these managers were young men they were obliged to employ an assistant; for, according to law, the offices had to be kept open till midnight; moreover, the reports required by the minister of finance involved considerable writing. The Comtesse de Bauvan, to whom the Abbe Loraux explained the circumstances of the widow Bridau, promised, in case her manager should leave, to give the place to Agathe; meantime she stipulated that the widow should be taken as assistant, and receive a salary of six hundred francs. Poor Agathe, who was obliged to be at the office by ten in the morning, had scarcely time to get her dinner. She returned to her work at seven in the evening, remaining there till midnight. Joseph never, for two years, failed to fetch his mother at night, and bring her back to the rue Mazarin; and often he went to take her to dinner; his friends frequently saw him leave the opera or some brilliant salon to be punctually at midnight at the office in the rue Vivienne.

Agathe soon acquired the monotonous regularity of life which becomes a stay and a support to those who have endured the shock of violent sorrows. In the morning, after doing up her room, in which there were no longer cats and little birds, she prepared the breakfast at her own fire and carried it into the studio, where she ate it with her son. She then arranged Joseph's bedroom, put out the fire in her own chamber, and brought her sewing to the studio, where she sat by the little iron stove, leaving the room if a comrade or a model entered it. Though she understood nothing whatever of art, the silence of the studio suited her. In the matter of art she made not the slightest progress; she attempted no hypocrisy; she was utterly amazed at the importance they all attached to color, composition, drawing. When the Cenacle friends or some brother-painter, like Schinner, Pierre Grassou, Leon de Lora,—a very youthful "rapin" who was called at that time Mistigris,—discussed a picture, she would come back afterwards, examine it attentively, and discover nothing to justify their fine words and their hot disputes. She made her son's shirts, she mended his stockings, she even cleaned his palette, supplied him with rags to wipe his brushes, and kept things in order in the studio. Seeing how much thought his mother gave to these little details, Joseph heaped attentions upon her in return. If mother and son had no sympathies in the matter of art, they were at least bound together by signs of tenderness. The mother had a purpose. One morning as she was petting Joseph while he was sketching a large picture (finished in after years and never understood), she said, as it were, casually and aloud,—

"My God! what is he doing?"

"Doing? who?"

"Philippe."

"Oh, ah! he's sowing his wild oats; that fellow will make something of himself by and by."

"But he has gone through the lesson of poverty; perhaps it was poverty which changed him to what he is. If he were prosperous he would be good—"

"You think, my dear mother, that he suffered during that journey of his. You are mistaken; he kept carnival in New York just as he does here—"

"But if he is suffering at this moment, near to us, would it not be horrible?"

"Yes," replied Joseph. "For my part, I will gladly give him some money; but I don't want to see him; he killed our poor Descoings."

"So," resumed Agathe, "you would not be willing to paint his portrait?"

"For you, dear mother, I'd suffer martyrdom. I can make myself remember nothing except that he is my brother."

"His portrait as a captain of dragoons on horseback?"

"Yes, I've a copy of a fine horse by Gros and I haven't any use for it."

"Well, then, go and see that friend of his and find out what has become of him."

"I'll go!"

Agathe rose; her scissors and work fell at her feet; she went and kissed Joseph's head, and dropped two tears on his hair.

"He is your passion, that fellow," said the painter. "We all have our hopeless passions."

That afternoon, about four o'clock, Joseph went to the rue du Sentier and found his brother, who had taken Giroudeau's place. The old dragoon had been promoted to be cashier of a weekly journal established by his nephew. Although Finot was still proprietor of the other newspaper, which he had divided into shares, holding all the shares himself, the proprietor and editor "de visu" was one of his friends, named Lousteau, the son of that very sub-delegate of Issoudun on whom the Bridaus' grandfather, Doctor Rouget, had vowed vengeance; consequently he was the nephew of Madame Hochon. To make himself agreeable to his uncle, Finot gave Philippe the place Giroudeau was quitting; cutting off, however, half the salary. Moreover, daily, at five o'clock, Giroudeau audited the accounts and carried away the receipts. Coloquinte, the old veteran, who was the office boy and did errands, also kept an eye on the slippery Philippe; who was, however, behaving properly. A salary of six hundred francs, and the five hundred of his cross sufficed him to live, all the more because, living in a warm office all day and at the theatre on a free pass every evening, he had only to provide himself with food and a place to sleep in. Coloquinte was departing with the stamped papers on his head, and Philippe was brushing his false sleeves of green linen, when Joseph entered.

"Bless me, here's the cub!" cried Philippe. "Well, we'll go and dine together. You shall go to the opera; Florine and Florentine have got a box. I'm going with Giroudeau; you shall be of the party, and I'll introduce you to Nathan."

He took his leaded cane, and moistened a cigar.

"I can't accept your invitation; I am to take our mother to dine at a table d'hote."

"Ah! how is she, the poor, dear woman?"

34

nothing more. You needn't be uneasy; no one knows this secret but myself. Go to Issoudun with your mother. You have good sense; try to save the property."

"Come, my poor mother, Desroches is right," said Joseph, rejoining Agathe on the staircase. "I have sold my two pictures, let us start for Berry; you have two weeks' leave of absence."

After writing to her godmother to announce their arrival, Agathe and Joseph started the next evening for their trip to Issoudun, leaving Philippe to his fate. The diligence rolled through the rue d'Enfer toward the Orleans highroad. When Agathe saw the Luxembourg, to which Philippe had been transferred, she could not refrain from saying,—

"If it were not for the Allies he would never be there!"

Many sons would have made an impatient gesture and smiled with pity; but the artist, who was alone with his mother in the coupe, caught her in his arms and pressed her to his heart, exclaiming:—

"Oh, mother! you are a mother just as Raphael was a painter. And you will always be a fool of a mother!"

Madame Bridau's mind, diverted before long from her griefs by the distractions of the journey, began to dwell on the purpose of it. She re-read the letter of Madame Hochon, which had so stirred up the lawyer Desroches. Struck with the words "concubine" and "slut," which the pen of a septuagenarian as pious as she was respectable had used to designate the woman now in process of getting hold of Jean-Jacques Rouget's property, struck also with the word "imbecile" applied to Rouget himself, she began to ask herself how, by her presence at Issoudun, she was to save the inheritance. Joseph, poor disinterested artist that he was, knew little enough about the Code, and his mother's last remark absorbed his mind.

"Before our friend Desroches sent us off to protect our rights, he ought to have explained to us the means of doing so," he exclaimed.

"So far as my poor head, which whirls at the thought of Philippe in prison,—without tobacco, perhaps, and about to appear before the Court of Peers!—leaves me any distinct memory," returned Agathe, "I think young Desroches said we were to get evidence of undue influence, in case my brother has made a will in favor of that—that—woman."

"He is good at that, Desroches is," cried the painter. "Bah! if we can make nothing of it I'll get him to come himself."

"Well, don't let us trouble our heads uselessly," said Agathe. "When we get to Issoudun my godmother will tell us what to do."

This conversation, which took place just after Madame Bridau and Joseph changed coaches at Orleans and entered the Sologne, is sufficient proof of the incapacity of the painter and his mother to play the part the inexorable Desroches had assigned to them.

In returning to Issoudun after thirty years' absence, Agathe was about to find such changes in its manners and customs that it is necessary to sketch, in a few words, a picture of that town. Without it, the reader would scarcely understand the heroism displayed by Madame Hochon in assisting her goddaughter, or the strange situation of Jean-Jacques Rouget. Though Doctor Rouget had taught his son to regard Agathe in the light of a stranger, it was certainly a somewhat extraordinary thing that for thirty years a brother should have given no signs of life to a sister. Such a silence was evidently caused by peculiar circumstances, and any other sister and nephew than Agathe and Joseph would long ago have inquired into them. There is, moreover, a certain connection between the condition of the city of Issoudun and the interests of the Bridau family, which can only be seen as the story goes on.

CHAPTER VII

Issoudun, be it said without offence to Paris, is one of the oldest cities in France. In spite of the historical assumption which makes the emperor Probus the Noah of the Gauls, Caesar speaks of the excellent wine of Champ-Fort ("de Campo Forti") still one of the best vintages of Issoudun. Rigord writes of this city in language which leaves no doubt as to its great population and its immense commerce. But these testimonies both assign a much lesser age to the city than its ancient antiquity demands. In fact, the excavations lately undertaken by a learned archaeologist of the place, Monsieur Armand Peremet, have brought to light, under the celebrated tower of Issoudun, a basilica of the fifth century, probably the only one in France. This church preserves, in its very materials, the sign-manual of an anterior civilization; for its stones came from a Roman temple which stood on the same site.

Issoudun, therefore, according to the researches of this antiquary, like other cities of France whose ancient or modern autonym ends in "Dun" ("dunum") bears in its very name the certificate of an autochthonous existence. The word "Dun," the appanage of all dignity consecrated by Druidical worship, proves a religious and military settlement of the Celts. Beneath the Dun of the Gauls must have lain the Roman temple to Isis. From that comes, according to Chaumon, the name of the city, Issous-Dun,—"Is" being the abbreviation of "Isis." Richard Coeur-de-lion undoubtedly built the famous tower (in which he coined money) above the basilica of the fifth century,—the third monument of the third religion of this ancient town. He used the church as a necessary foundation, or stay, for the raising of the rampart; and he preserved it by covering it with feudal fortifications as with a mantle. Issoudun was at that time the seat of the ephemeral power of the Routiers and the Cottereaux, adventurers and free-lancers, whom Henry II. sent against his son Richard, at the time of his rebellion as Comte de Poitou.

The history of Aquitaine, which was not written by the Benedictines, will probably never be written, because there are no longer Benedictines: thus we are not able to light up these archaeological tenebrae in the history of our manners and customs on every occasion of their appearance. There is another testimony to the ancient importance of Issoudun in the conversion into a canal of the Tournemine, a little stream raised several feet above the level of the Theols which surrounds the town. This is undoubtedly the work of Roman genius. Moreover, the suburb which extends from the castle in a northerly direction is intersected by a street which for more than two thousand years has borne the name of the rue de Rome; and the inhabitants of this suburb, whose racial characteristics, blood, and physiognomy have a special stamp of their own, call themselves descendants of the Romans. They are nearly all vine-growers, and display a remarkable inflexibility of manners and customs, due, undoubtedly, to their origin,—perhaps also to their victory over the Cottereaux and the Routiers, whom they exterminated on the plain of Charost in the twelfth century.

After the insurrection of 1830, France was too agitated to pay much attention to the rising of the vine-growers of Issoudun; a terrible affair, the facts of which have never been made public,—for good reasons. In the first place, the bourgeois of Issoudun refused to allow the military to enter the town. They followed the use and wont of the bourgeoisie of the Middle Ages and declared themselves responsible for their own city. The government was obliged to yield to a sturdy people backed up by seven or eight thousand vine-growers, who had burned all the archives, also the offices of "indirect taxation," and had dragged through the streets a customs officer, crying out at every street lantern, "Let us hang him here!" The poor man's life was saved by the national guard, who took him to prison on pretext of drawing up his indictment. The general in command only entered the town by virtue of a compromise made with the vine-growers; and it needed some courage to go among them. At the moment when he showed himself at the hotel-de-ville, a man from the faubourg de Rome slung a "volant" round his neck (the "volant" is a huge pruning-hook fastened to a pole, with which they trim trees) crying out, "No more clerks, or there's an end to compromise!" The fellow would have taken off that honored head, left untouched by sixteen years of war, had it not been for the hasty intervention of one of the leaders of the revolt, to whom a promise had been made that *the chambers should be asked to suppress the excisemen.*

In the fourteenth century, Issoudun still had sixteen or seventeen thousand inhabitants, remains of a population double that number in the time of Rigord. Charles VII. possessed a mansion which still exists, and was known, as late as the eighteenth century, as the Maison du Roi. This town, then a centre of the woollen trade, supplied that commodity to the greater part of Europe, and manufactured on a large scale blankets, hats, and the excellent Chevreautin gloves. Under Louis XIV., Issoudun, the birthplace of Baron and Bourdaloue, was always cited as a city of elegance and good society, where the language was correctly spoken. The curate Poupard, in his History of Sancerre, mentions the inhabitants of Issoudun as remarkable among the other Berrichons for subtlety and natural wit. To-day, the wit and the splendor have alike disappeared. Issoudun, whose great extent of ground bears witness to its ancient importance, has now barely twelve thousand inhabitants, including the vine-dressers of four enormous suburbs,—those of Saint-Paterne, Vilatte, Rome, and Alouette, which are really small towns. The bourgeoisie, like that of Versailles, are spread over the length and breadth of the streets. Issoudun still holds the market for the fleeces of Berry; a commerce now threatened by improvements in the stock which are being introduced everywhere except in Berry.

The vineyards of Issoudun produce a wine which is drunk throughout the two departments, and which, if manufactured as Burgundy and Gascony manufacture theirs, would be one of the best wines in France. Alas, "to do as our fathers did," with no innovations, is the law of the land. Accordingly, the vine-growers continue to leave the refuse of the grape in the juice during its fermentation, which makes the wine detestable, when it might be a source of ever-springing wealth, and an industry for the community. Thanks to the bitterness which the refuse infuses into the wine, and which, they say, lessens with age, a vintage will keep a century. This reason, given by the vine-grower in excuse for his obstinacy, is of sufficient importance to oenology to be made public here; Guillaume le Breton has also proclaimed it in some lines of his "Phillippide."

The decline of Issoudun is explained by this spirit of sluggishness, sunken to actual torpor, which a single fact will illustrate. When the authorities were talking of a highroad between Paris and Toulouse, it was natural to think of taking it from Vierzon to Chateauroux by way of Issoudun. The distance was shorter than to make it, as the road now is, through Vatan, but the leading people of the neighborhood and the city council of Issoudun (whose discussion of the matter is said to be recorded), demanded that it should go by Vatan, on the ground that if the highroad went through their town, provisions would rise in price and they might be forced to pay thirty sous for a chicken. The only analogy to be found for this proceeding is in the wilder parts of Sardinia, a land once so rich and populous, now so deserted. When Charles Albert, with a praiseworthy intention of civilization, wished to unite Sassari, the second capital of the island, with Cagliari by a magnificent highway (the only one ever made in that wild waste by name Sardinia), the direct line lay through Bornova, a district inhabited by lawless people, all the more like our Arab tribes because they are descended from the Moors. Seeing that they were about to fall into the clutches of civilization, the savages of Bornova, without taking the trouble to discuss the matter, declared their opposition to the road. The government took no notice of it. The first engineer who came to survey it, got a ball through his head, and died on his level. No action was taken on this murder, but the road made a circuit which lengthened it by eight miles!

The continual lowering of the price of wines drunk in the neighborhood, though it may satisfy the desire of the bourgeoisie of Issoudun for cheap provisions, is leading the way to the ruin of the vine-growers, who are more and more burdened with the costs of cultivation and the taxes; just as the ruin of the woollen trade is the result of the non-improvement in the breeding of sheep. Country-folk have the deepest horror of change; even that which is most conducive to their interests. In the country, a Parisian meets a laborer who eats an enormous quantity of bread, cheese, and vegetables; he proves to him that if he would substitute for that diet a certain portion of meat, he would be better fed, at less cost; that he could work more, and would not use up his capital of health and strength so quickly. The Berrichon sees the correctness of the calculation, but he answers, "Think of the gossip, monsieur." "Gossip, what do you mean?" "Well, yes, what would people say of me?" "He would be the talk of the neighborhood," said the owner of the property on which this scene took place; "they would think him as rich as a tradesman. He is afraid of public opinion, afraid of being pointed at, afraid of seeming ill or feeble. That's how we all are in this region." Many of the bourgeoisie utter this phrase with feelings of inward pride.

While ignorance and custom are invincible in the country regions, where the peasants are left very much to themselves, the town of Issoudun itself has reached a state of complete social stagnation. Obliged to meet the decadence of fortunes by the practice of sordid economy, each family lives to itself. Moreover, society is permanently deprived of that distinction of classes which gives character to manners and customs. There is no opposition of social forces, such as that to which the cities of the Italian States in the Middle Ages owed their vitality. There are no longer any nobles in Issoudun. The Cottereaux, the Routiers, the Jacquerie, the religious wars and the Revolution did away with the nobility. The town is proud of that triumph. Issoudun has repeatedly refused to receive a garrison, always on the plea of cheap provisions. She has thus lost a means of intercourse with the age, and she has also lost the profits arising from the presence of troops. Before 1756, Issoudun was one of the most delightful of all the garrison towns. A judicial drama, which occupied for a time the attention of France, the feud of a lieutenant-general of the department with the Marquis de Chapt, whose son, an officer of dragoons, was put to death,—justly perhaps, yet traitorously, for some affair of gallantry,—deprived the town from that time forth of a garrison. The sojourn of the forty-fourth demi-brigade, imposed upon it during the civil war, was not of a nature to reconcile the inhabitants to the race of warriors.

Bourges, whose population is yearly decreasing, is a victim of the same social malady. Vitality is leaving these communities. Undoubtedly, the government is to blame. The duty of an administration is to discover the wounds upon the body-politic, and remedy them by sending men of energy to the diseased regions, with power to change the state of things. Alas, so far from that, it approves and encourages this ominous and fatal tranquillity. Besides, it may be asked, how could the government send new administrators and able magistrates? Who, of such men, is willing to bury himself in the arrondissements, where the good to be done is without glory? If, by chance, some ambitious stranger settles there, he soon falls into the inertia of the region, and tunes himself to the dreadful key of provincial life. Issoudun would have benumbed Napoleon.

As a result of this particular characteristic, the arrondissement of Issoudun was governed, in 1822, by men who all belonged to Berry. The administration of power became either a nullity or a farce,—except in certain cases, naturally very rare, which by their manifest importance compelled the authorities to act. The procureur du roi, Monsieur Mouilleron, was cousin to the entire community, and his substitute belonged to one of the families of the town. The judge of the court, before attaining that dignity, was made famous by one of those provincial sayings which put a cap and bells on a man's head for the rest of his life. As he ended his summing-up of all the facts of an indictment, he looked at the accused and said: "My poor Pierre! the thing is as plain as day; your head will be cut off. Let this be a lesson to you." The commissary of police, holding office since the Restoration, had relations throughout the arrondissement. Moreover, not only was the influence of religion null, but the curate himself was held in no esteem.

It was this bourgeoisie, radical, ignorant, and loving to annoy others, which now related tales, more or less comic, about the relations of Jean-Jacques Rouget with his servant-woman. The children of these people went none the less to Sunday-school, and were as scrupulously prepared for their communion: the schools were kept up all the same; mass was said; the taxes were paid (the sole thing that Paris extracts of the provinces), and the mayor passed resolutions. But all these acts of social existence were done as mere routine, and thus the laxity of the local government suited admirably with the moral and intellectual condition of the governed. The events of the following history will show the effects of this state of things, which is not as unusual in the provinces as might be supposed. Many towns in France, more particularly in the South, are like Issoudun. The condition to which the ascendency of the bourgeoisie has reduced that local capital is one which will spread over all France, and even to Paris, if the bourgeois continues to rule the exterior and interior policy of our country.

Now, one word of topography. Issoudun stretches north and south, along a hillside which rounds towards the highroad to Chateauroux. At the foot of the hill, a canal, now called the "Riviere forcee" whose waters are taken from the Theols, was constructed in former times, when the town was flourishing, for the use of manufactories or to flood the moats of the rampart. The "Riviere forcee" forms an artificial arm of a natural river, the Tournemine, which unites with several other streams beyond the suburb of Rome. These little threads of running water and the two rivers irrigate a tract of wide-spreading meadow-land, enclosed on all sides by little yellowish or white terraces dotted with black speckles; for such is the aspect of the vineyards of Issoudun during seven months of the year. The vine-growers cut the plants down yearly, leaving only an ugly stump, without support, sheltered by a barrel. The traveller arriving from Vierzon, Vatan, or Chateauroux, his eyes weary with monotonous plains, is agreeably surprised by the meadows of Issoudun,—the oasis of this part of Berry, which supplies the inhabitants with vegetables throughout a region of thirty miles in circumference. Below the suburb of Rome, lies a vast tract entirely covered with kitchen-gardens, and divided into two sections, which bear the name of upper and lower Baltan. A long avenue of poplars leads from the town across the meadows to an ancient convent named Frapesle, whose English gardens, quite unique in that arrondissement, have received the ambitious name of Tivoli. Loving couples whisper their vows in its alleys of a Sunday.

Traces of the ancient grandeur of Issoudun of course reveal themselves to the eyes of a careful observer; and the most suggestive are the divisions of the town. The chateau, formerly almost a town itself with its walls and moats, is a distinct quarter which can only be entered, even at the present day, through its ancient gateways,—by means of three bridges thrown across the arms of the two rivers,—and has all the appearance of an ancient city. The ramparts show, in places, the formidable strata of their foundations, on which houses have now sprung up. Above the chateau, is the famous tower of Issoudun, once the citadel. The conqueror of the city, which lay around these two fortified points, had still to gain possession of the tower and the castle; and possession of the castle did not insure that of the tower, or citadel.

The suburb of Saint-Paterne, which lies in the shape of a palette beyond the tower, encroaching on the meadow-lands, is so considerable that in the very earliest ages it must have been part of the city itself. This opinion derived, in 1822, a sort of certainty from the then existence of the charming church of Saint-Paterne, recently pulled down by the heir of the individual who bought it of the nation. This church, one of the finest specimens of the Romanesque that France possessed, actually perished without a single drawing being made of the portal, which was in perfect preservation. The only voice raised to save this monument of a past art found no echo, either in the town itself or in the department. Though the castle of Issoudun has the appearance of an old town, with its narrow streets and its ancient mansions, the city itself, properly so called, which was captured and burned at different epochs, notably during the Fronde, when it was laid in ashes, has a modern air. Streets that are spacious in comparison with those of other towns, and well-built houses form a striking contrast to the aspect of the citadel,— a contrast that has won for Issoudun, in certain geographies, the epithet of "pretty."

In a town thus constituted, without the least activity, even business activity, without a taste for art, or for learned occupations, and where everybody stayed in the little round of his or her own home, it was likely to happen, and did happen under the Restoration in 1816 when the war was over, that many of the young men of the place had no career before them, and knew not where to turn for occupation until they could marry or inherit the property of their fathers. Bored in their own homes, these young fellows found little or no distraction elsewhere in the city; and as, in the language of that region, "youth must shed its cuticle" they sowed their wild oats at the expense of the town itself. It was difficult to carry on such operations in open day, lest the perpetrators should be recognized; for the cup of their misdemeanors once filled, they were liable to be arraigned at their next peccadillo before the police courts; and they therefore judiciously selected the night time for the performance of their mischievous pranks. Thus it was that among the traces of divers lost civilizations, a vestige of the spirit of drollery that characterized the manners of antiquity burst into a final flame.

The young men amused themselves very much as Charles IX. amused himself with his courtiers, or Henry V. of England and his companions, or as in former times young men were wont to amuse themselves in the provinces. Having once banded together for purposes of mutual help, to defend each other and invent amusing tricks, there presently developed among them, through the clash of ideas, that spirit of malicious mischief which belongs to the period of youth and may even be observed among animals. The confederation, in itself, gave them the mimic delights of the mystery of an organized conspiracy. They called themselves the "Knights of Idleness." During the day these young scamps were youthful saints; they all pretended to extreme quietness; and, in fact, they habitually slept late after the nights on which they had been playing their malicious pranks. The "Knights" began with mere commonplace tricks, such as unhooking and changing signs, ringing bells, flinging casks left before one house into the cellar of the next with a crash, rousing the occupants of the house by a noise that seemed to their frightened ears like the explosion of a mine. In Issoudun, as in many country towns, the cellar is entered by an opening near the door of the house, covered with a wooden scuttle, secured by strong iron hinges and a padlock.

In 1816, these modern Bad Boys had not altogether given up such tricks as these, perpetrated in the provinces by all young lads and gamins. But in 1817 the Order of Idleness acquired a Grand Master, and distinguished itself by mischief which, up to 1823, spread something like terror in Issoudun, or at least kept the artisans and the bourgeoisie perpetually uneasy.

This leader was a certain Maxence Gilet, commonly called Max, whose antecedents, no less than his youth and his vigor, predestined him for such a part. Maxence Gilet was supposed by all Issoudun to be the natural son of the sub-delegate Lousteau, that brother of Madame Hochon whose gallantries had left memories behind them, and who, as we have seen, drew down upon himself the hatred of old Doctor Rouget about the time of Agathe's birth. But the friendship which bound the two men together before their quarrel was so close that, to use an expression of that region and that period, "they willingly walked the same road." Some people said that Maxence was as likely to be the son of the doctor as of the sub-delegate; but in fact he belonged to neither the one nor the other,—his father being a charming dragoon officer in garrison at Bourges. Nevertheless, as a result of their enmity, and very fortunately for the child, Rouget and Lousteau never ceased to claim his paternity.

Max's mother, the wife of a poor sabot-maker in the Rome suburb, was possessed, for the perdition of her soul, of a surprising beauty, a Trasteverine beauty, the only property which she transmitted to her son. Madame Gilet, pregnant with Maxence in 1788, had long desired that blessing, which the town attributed to the gallantries of the two friends,—probably in the hope of setting them against each other. Gilet, an old drunkard with a triple throat, treated his wife's misconduct with a collusion that is not uncommon among the lower classes. To make sure of protectors for her son, Madame Gilet was careful not to enlighten his reputed fathers as to his parentage. In Paris, she would have turned out a millionaire; at Issoudun she lived sometimes at her ease, more often miserably, and, in the long run, despised. Madame Hochon, Lousteau's sister, paid sixty francs a year for the lad's schooling. This liberality, which Madame Hochon was quite unable to practise on her own account because of her husband's stinginess, was naturally attributed to her brother, then living at Sancerre.

When Doctor Rouget, who certainly was not lucky in sons, observed Max's beauty, he paid the board of the "young rogue," as he called him, at the seminary, up to the year 1805. As Lousteau died in 1800, and the doctor apparently obeyed a feeling of vanity in paying the lad's board until 1805, the question of the paternity was left forever undecided. Maxence Gilet, the butt of many jests, was soon forgotten,—and for this reason: In 1806, a year after Doctor Rouget's death, the lad, who seemed to have been created for a venturesome life, and was moreover gifted with remarkable vigor and agility, got into a series of scrapes which more or less threatened his safety. He plotted with the grandsons of Monsieur Hochon to worry the grocers of the city; he gathered fruit before the owners could pick it, and made nothing of scaling walls. He had no equal at bodily exercises, he played base to perfection, and could have outrun a hare. With a keen eye worthy of Leather-stocking, he loved hunting passionately. His time was passed in firing at a mark, instead of studying; and he spent the money extracted from the old doctor in buying powder and ball for a wretched pistol that old Gilet, the sabot-maker, had given him. During the autumn of 1806, Maxence, then seventeen, committed an involuntary murder, by frightening in the dusk a young woman who was pregnant, and who came upon him suddenly while stealing fruit in her garden. Threatened with the guillotine by Gilet, who doubtless wanted to get rid of him, Max fled to Bourges, met a regiment then on its way to Egypt, and enlisted. Nothing came of the death of the young woman.

A young fellow of Max's character was sure to distinguish himself, and in the course of three campaigns he did distinguish himself so highly that he rose to be a captain, his lack of education helping him strenuously. In Portugal, in 1809, he was left for dead in an English battery, into which his company had penetrated without being able to hold it. Max, taken prisoner by the English, was sent to the Spanish hulks at the island of Cabrera, the most horrible of all stations for prisoners of war. His friends begged that he might receive the cross of the Legion of honor and the rank of major; but the Emperor was then in Austria, and he reserved his favors for those who did brilliant deeds under his own eye: he did not like officers or men who allowed themselves to be taken prisoner, and he was, moreover, much dissatisfied with events in Portugal. Max was held at Cabrera from 1810 to 1814.(1) During those years he became utterly demoralized, for the hulks were like galleys, minus crime and infamy. At the outset, to maintain his personal free will, and protect himself against the corruption which made that horrible prison unworthy of a civilized people, the handsome young captain killed in a duel (for duels were fought on those hulks in a space scarcely six feet square) seven bullies among his fellow-prisoners, thus ridding the island of their tyranny to the great joy of the other victims. After this, Max reigned supreme in his hulk, thanks to the wonderful ease and address with which he handled weapons, to his bodily strength, and also to his extreme cleverness.

(1) *The cruelty of the Spaniards to the French prisoners at Cabrera was very great. In the spring of 1811, H.M. brig "Minorca," Captain Wormeley, was sent by Admiral Sir Charles Cotton, then commanding the Mediterranean fleet, to make a report of their condition. As she neared the island, the wretched prisoners swam out to meet her. They were reduced to skin and bone; many of them were naked; and their miserable condition so moved the seamen of the "Minorca" that they came aft to the quarter-deck, and asked permission to subscribe three days' rations for the relief of the sufferers. Captain Wormeley carried away some of the prisoners, and his report to Sir Charles Cotton, being sent to the Admiralty, was made the basis of a remonstrance on the part of the British government with Spain on the subject of its cruelties. Sir Charles Cotton despatched Captain Wormeley a second time to Cabrera with a good many head of live cattle and a large supply of other provisions.—Tr.*

But he, in turn, committed arbitrary acts; there were those who curried favor with him, and worked his will, and became his minions. In that school of misery, where bitter minds dreamed only of vengeance, where the sophistries hatched in such brains were laying up, inevitably, a store of evil thoughts, Max became utterly demoralized. He listened to the opinions of those who longed for fortune at any price, and did not shrink from the results of criminal actions, provided they were done without discovery. When peace was proclaimed, in April, 1814, he left the island, depraved though still innocent. On his return to Issoudun he found his father and mother dead. Like others who give way to their passions and make life, as they call it, short and sweet, the Gilets had died in the almshouse in the utmost poverty. Immediately after his return, the news of Napoleon's landing at Cannes spread through France; Max could do no better than go to Paris and ask for his rank as major and for his cross. The marshal who was at that time minister of war remembered the brave conduct of Captain Gilet in Portugal. He put him in the Guard as captain, which gave him the grade of major in the infantry; but he could not get him the cross. "The Emperor says that you will know how to win it at the first chance," said the marshal. In fact, the Emperor did put the brave captain on his list for decoration the evening after the fight at Fleurus, where Gilet distinguished himself.

After the battle of Waterloo Max retreated to the Loire. At the time of the disbandment, Marshal Feltre refused to recognize Max's grade as major, or his claim to the cross. The soldier of Napoleon returned to Issoudun in a state of exasperation that may well be conceived; he declared that he would not serve without either rank or cross. The war-office considered these conditions presumptuous in a young man of twenty-five without a name, who might, if they were granted, become a colonel at thirty. Max accordingly sent in his resignation. The major—for among themselves Bonapartists recognized the grades obtained in 1815—thus lost the pittance called half-pay which was allowed to the officers of the army of the Loire. But all Issoudun was roused at the sight of the brave young fellow left with only twenty napoleons in his possession; and the mayor gave him a place in his office with a salary of six hundred francs. Max kept it a few months, then gave it up of his own accord, and was replaced by a captain named Carpentier, who, like himself, had remained faithful to Napoleon.

By this time Gilet had become grand master of the Knights of Idleness, and was leading a life which lost him the good-will of the chief people of the town; who, however, did not openly make the fact known to him, for he was violent and much feared by all, even by the officers of the old army who, like himself, had refused to serve under the Bourbons, and had come home to plant their cabbages in Berry. The little affection felt for the Bourbons among the natives of Issoudun is not surprising when we recall the history which we have just given. In fact, considering its size and lack of importance, the little place contained more Bonapartists than any other town in France. These men became, as is well known, nearly all Liberals.

In Issoudun and its neighborhood there were a dozen officers in Max's position. These men admired him and made him their leader,—with the exception, however, of Carpentier, his successor, and a certain Monsieur Mignonnet, ex-captain in the artillery of the Guard. Carpentier, a cavalry officer risen from the ranks, had married into one of the best families in the town,—the Borniche-Herau. Mignonnet, brought up at the Ecole Polytechnique, had served in a corps which held itself superior to all others. In the Imperial armies there were two shades of distinction among the soldiers themselves. A majority of them felt a contempt for the bourgeois, the "civilian," fully equal to the contempt of nobles for their serfs, or conquerors for the conquered. Such men did not always observe the laws of honor in their dealings with civilians; nor did they much blame those who rode rough-shod over the bourgeoisie. The others, and particularly the artillery, perhaps because of its republicanism, never adopted the doctrine of a military France and a civil France, the tendency of which was nothing less than to make two nations. So, although Major Potel and Captain Renard, two officers living in the Rome suburb, were friends to Maxence Gilet "through thick and thin," Major Mignonnet and Captain Carpentier took sides with the bourgeoisie, and thought his conduct unworthy of a man of honor.

Major Mignonnet, a lean little man, full of dignity, busied himself with the problems which the steam-engine requires us to solve, and lived in a modest way, taking his social intercourse with Monsieur and Madame Carpentier. His gentle manners and ways, and his scientific occupations won him the respect of the whole town; and it was frequently said of him and of Captain Carpentier that they were "quite another thing" from Major Potel and Captain Renard, Maxence, and other frequenters of the cafe Militaire, who retained the soldierly manners and the defective morals of the Empire.

At the time when Madame Bridau returned to Issoudun, Max was excluded from the society of the place. He showed, moreover, proper self-respect in never presenting himself at the club, and in never complaining of the severe reprobation that was shown him; although he was the handsomest, the most elegant, and the best dressed man in the place, spent a great deal of money, and kept a horse,—a thing as amazing at Issoudun as the horse of Lord Byron at Venice. We are now to see how it was that Maxence, poor and without apparent means, was able to become the dandy of the town. The shameful conduct which earned him the contempt of all scrupulous or religious persons was connected with the interests which brought Agathe and Joseph to Issoudun.

Judging by the audacity of his bearing, and the expression of his face, Max cared little for public opinion; he expected, no doubt, to take his revenge some day, and to lord it over those who now condemned him. Moreover, if the bourgeoisie of Issoudun thought ill of him, the admiration he excited among the common people counterbalanced their opinion; his courage, his dashing appearance, his decision of character, could not fail to please the masses, to whom his degradations were, for the most part, unknown, and indeed the bourgeoisie themselves scarcely suspected its extent. Max played a role at Issoudun which was something like that of the blacksmith in the "Fair Maid of Perth"; he was the champion of Bonapartism and the Opposition; they counted upon him as the burghers of Perth counted upon Smith on great occasions. A single incident will put this hero and victim of the Hundred-Days into clear relief.

In 1819, a battalion commanded by royalist officers, young men just out of the Maison Rouge, passed through Issoudun on its way to go into garrison at Bourges. Not knowing what to do with themselves in so constitutional a place as Issoudun, these young gentlemen went to while away the time at the cafe Militaire. In every provincial town there is a military cafe. That of Issoudun, built on the place d'Armes at an angle of the rampart, and kept by the widow of an officer, was naturally the rendezvous of the Bonapartists, chiefly officers on half-pay, and others who shared Max's opinions, to whom the politics of the town allowed free expression of their idolatry for the Emperor. Every year, dating from 1816, a banquet was given in Issoudun to commemorate the anniversary of his coronation. The three royalists who first entered asked for the newspapers, among others, for the "Quotidienne" and the "Drapeau Blanc." The politics of

Issoudun, especially those of the cafe Militaire, did not allow of such royalist journals. The establishment had none but the "Commerce,"—a name which the "Constitutionel" was compelled to adopt for several years after it was suppressed by the government. But as, in its first issue under the new name, the leading article began with these words, "Commerce is essentially constitutional," people continued to call it the "Constitutionel," the subscribers all understanding the sly play of words which begged them to pay no attention to the label, as the wine would be the same.

The fat landlady replied from her seat at the desk that she did not take those papers. "What papers do you take then?" asked one of the officers, a captain. The waiter, a little fellow in a blue cloth jacket, with an apron of coarse linen tied over it, brought the "Commerce."

"Is that your paper? Have you no other?"

"No," said the waiter, "that's the only one."

The captain tore it up, flung the pieces on the floor, and spat upon them, calling out,—

"Bring dominos!"

In ten minutes the news of the insult offered to the Constitution Opposition and the Liberal party, in the supersacred person of its revered journal, which attacked priests with courage and the wit we all remember, spread throughout the town and into the houses like light itself; it was told and repeated from place to place. One phrase was on everybody's lips,—

"Let us tell Max!"

Max soon heard of it. The royalist officers were still at their game of dominos when that hero entered the cafe, accompanied by Major Potel and Captain Renard, and followed by at least thirty young men, curious to see the end of the affair, most of whom remained outside in the street. The room was soon full.

"Waiter, *my* newspaper," said Max, in a quiet voice.

Then a little comedy was played. The fat hostess, with a timid and conciliatory air, said, "Captain, I have lent it!"

"Send for it," cried one of Max's friends.

"Can't you do without it?" said the waiter; "we have not got it."

The young royalists were laughing and casting sidelong glances at the new-comers.

"They have torn it up!" cried a youth of the town, looking at the feet of the young royalist captain.

"Who has dared to destroy that paper?" demanded Max, in a thundering voice, his eyes flashing as he rose with his arms crossed.

"And we spat upon it," replied the three young officers, also rising, and looking at Max.

"You have insulted the whole town!" said Max, turning livid.

"Well, what of that?" asked the youngest officer.

With a dexterity, quickness, and audacity which the young men did not foresee, Max slapped the face of the officer nearest to him, saying,—

"Do you understand French?"

They fought near by, in the allee de Frapesle, three against three; for Potel and Renard would not allow Max to deal with the officers alone. Max killed his man. Major Potel wounded his so severely, that the unfortunate young man, the son of a good family, died in the hospital the next day. As for the third, he got off with a sword cut, after wounding his adversary, Captain Renard. The battalion left for Bourges that night. This affair, which was noised throughout Berry, set Max up definitely as a hero.

The Knights of Idleness, who were all young, the eldest not more than twenty-five years old, admired Maxence. Some among them, far from sharing the prudery and strict notions of their families concerning his conduct, envied his present position and thought him fortunate. Under such a leader, the Order did great things. After the month of May, 1817, never a week passed that the town was not thrown into an uproar by some new piece of mischief. Max, as a matter of honor, imposed certain conditions upon the Knights. Statutes were drawn up. These young demons grew as vigilant as the pupils of Amoros,—bold as hawks, agile at all exercises, clever and strong as criminals. They trained themselves in climbing roofs, scaling houses, jumping and walking noiselessly, mixing mortar, and walling up doors. They collected an arsenal of ropes, ladders, tools, and disguises. After a time the Knights of Idleness attained to the beau-ideal of malicious mischief, not only as to the accomplishment but, still more, in the invention of their pranks. They came at last to possess the genius for evil that Panurge so much delighted in; which provokes laughter, and covers its victims with such ridicule that they dare not complain. Naturally, these sons of good families of Issoudun possessed and obtained information in their households, which gave them the ways and means for the perpetration of their outrages.

Sometimes the young devils incarnate lay in ambush along the Grand'rue or the Basse rue, two streets which are, as it were, the arteries of the town, into which many little side streets open.

Crouching, with their heads to the wind, in the angles of the wall and at the corners of the streets, at the hour when all the households were hushed in their first sleep, they called to each other in tones of terror from ambush to ambush along the whole length of the town: "What's the matter?" "What is it?" till the repeated cries woke up the citizens, who appeared in their shirts and cotton night-caps, with lights in their hands, asking questions of one another, holding the strangest colloquies, and exhibiting the queerest faces.

A certain poor bookbinder, who was very old, believed in hobgoblins. Like most provincial artisans, he worked in a small basement shop. The Knights, disguised as devils, invaded the place in the middle of the night, put him into his own cutting-press, and left him shrieking to himself like the souls in hell. The poor man roused the neighbors, to whom he related the apparitions of Lucifer; and as they had no means of undeceiving him, he was driven nearly insane.

In the middle of a severe winter, the Knights took down the chimney of the collector of taxes, and built it up again in one night apparently as it was before, without making the slightest noise, or leaving the least trace of their work. But they so arranged the inside of the chimney as to send all the smoke into the house. The collector suffered for two months before he found out why his chimney, which had always drawn so well, and of which he had often boasted, played him such tricks; he was then obliged to build a new one.

At another time, they put three trusses of hay dusted with brimstone, and a quantity of oiled paper down the chimney of a pious old woman who was a friend of Madame Hochon. In the morning, when she came to light her fire, the poor creature, who was very gentle and kindly, imagined she had started a volcano. The fire-engines came, the whole population rushed to her assistance. Several Knights were among the firemen, and they deluged the old woman's house, till they had frightened her with a flood, as much as they had terrified her with the fire. She was made ill with fear.

When they wished to make some one spend the night under arms and in mortal terror, they wrote an anonymous letter telling him that he was about to be robbed; then they stole softly, one by one, round the walls of his house, or under his windows, whistling as if to call each other.

One of their famous performances, which long amused the town, where in fact it is still related, was to write a letter to all the heirs of a miserly old lady who was likely to leave a large property, announcing her death, and requesting them to be promptly on hand when the seals were affixed. Eighty persons arrived from Vatan, Saint-Florent, Vierzon and the neighboring country, all in deep mourning,—widows with sons, children with their fathers, some in carrioles, some in wicker gigs, others in dilapidated carts. Imagine the scene between the old woman's servants and the first arrivals! and the consultations among the notaries! It created a sort of riot in Issoudun.

At last, one day the sub-prefect woke up to a sense that this state of things was all the more intolerable because it seemed impossible to find out who was at the bottom of it. Suspicion fell on several young men; but as the National Guard was a mere name in Issoudun, and there was no garrison, and the lieutenant of police had only eight gendarmes under him, so that there were no patrols, it was impossible to get any proof against them. The sub-prefect was immediately posted in the "order of the night," and considered thenceforth fair game. This functionary made a practice of breakfasting on two fresh eggs. He kept chickens in his yard, and added to his mania for eating fresh eggs that of boiling them himself. Neither his wife nor his servant, in fact no one, according to him, knew how to boil an egg properly; he did it watch in hand, and boasted that he carried off the palm of egg-boiling from all the world. For two years he had boiled his eggs with a success which earned him many witticisms. But now, every night for a whole month, the eggs were taken from his hen-house, and hard-boiled eggs substituted. The sub-prefect was at his wits' end, and lost his reputation as the "sous-prefet a l'oeuf." Finally he was forced to breakfast on other things. Yet he never suspected the Knights of Idleness, whose trick had been cautiously played. After this, Max managed to grease the sub-prefect's stoves every night with an oil which sent forth so fetid a smell that it was impossible for any one to stay in the house. Even that was not enough; his wife, going to mass one morning, found her shawl glued together on the inside with some tenacious substance, so that she was obliged to go without it. The sub-prefect finally asked for another appointment. The cowardly submissiveness of this officer had much to do with firmly establishing the weird and comic authority of the Knights of Idleness.

Beyond the rue des Minimes and the place Misere, a section of a quarter was at that time enclosed between an arm of the "Riviere forcee" on the lower side and the ramparts on the other, beginning at the place d'Armes and going as far as the pottery market. This irregular square is filled with poor-looking houses crowded one against the other, and divided here and there by streets so narrow that two persons cannot walk abreast. This section of the town, a sort of cour des Miracles, was occupied by poor people or persons working at trades that were little remunerative,—a population living in hovels, and buildings called picturesquely by the familiar term of "blind houses." From the earliest ages this has no doubt been an accursed quarter, the haunt of evil-doers; in fact one thoroughfare is named "the street of the Executioner." For more than five centuries it has been customary for the executioner to have a red door at the entrance of his house. The assistant of the executioner of Chateauroux still lives there,—if we are to believe public rumor, for the townspeople never see him: the vine-dressers alone maintain an intercourse with this mysterious being, who inherits from his predecessors the gift of curing wounds and fractures. In the days when Issoudun assumed the airs of a capital city the women of the town made this section of it the scene of their wanderings. Here came the second-hand sellers of things that look as if they never could find a purchaser, old-clothes dealers whose wares infected the air; in short, it was the rendezvous of that apocryphal population which is to be found in nearly all such portions of a city, where two or three Jews have gained an ascendency.

At the corner of one of these gloomy streets in the livelier half of the quarter, there existed from 1815 to 1823, and perhaps later, a public-house kept by a woman commonly called Mere Cognette. The house itself was tolerably well built, in courses of white stone, with the intermediary spaces filled in with ashlar and cement, one storey high with an attic above. Over the door was an enormous branch of pine, looking as though it were cast in Florentine bronze. As if this symbol were not explanatory enough, the eye was arrested by the blue of a poster which was pasted over the doorway, and on which appeared, above the words "Good Beer of Mars," the picture of a soldier pouring out, in the direction of a very decolletee woman, a jet of foam which spurted in an arched line from the pitcher to the glass which she was holding towards him; the whole of a color to make Delacroix swoon.

The ground-floor was occupied by an immense hall serving both as kitchen and dining-room, from the beams of which hung, suspended by huge nails, the provisions needed for the custom of such a house. Behind this hall a winding staircase led to the upper storey; at the foot of the staircase a door led into a low, long room lighted from one of those little provincial courts, so narrow, dark, and sunken between tall houses, as to seem like the flue of a chimney. Hidden by a shed, and concealed from all eyes by walls, this low room was the place where the Bad Boys of Issoudun held their plenary court. Ostensibly, Pere Cognet boarded and lodged the country-people on market-days; secretly, he was landlord to the Knights of Idleness. This man, who was formerly a groom in a rich household, had ended by marrying La Cognette, a cook in a good family. The suburb of Rome still continues, like Italy and Poland, to follow the Latin custom of putting a feminine termination to the husband's name and giving it to the wife.

By uniting their savings Pere Cognet and his spouse had managed to buy their present house. La Cognette, a woman of forty, tall and plump, with the nose of a Roxelane, a swarthy skin, jet-black hair, brown eyes that were round and lively, and a general air of mirth and intelligence, was selected by Maxence Gilet, on account of her character and her talent for cookery, as the Leonarde of the Order. Pere Cognet might be about fifty-six years old; he was thick-set, very much under his wife's rule, and, according to a witticism which she was fond of repeating, he only saw things with a good eye—for he was blind of the other. In the course of seven years, that is, from 1816 to 1823, neither wife nor husband had betrayed what went on nightly at their house, or who they were that shared in the plot; they felt the liveliest regard for the Knights; their devotion was absolute. But this may seem less creditable if we remember that self-interest was the security of their affection and their silence. No matter at what hour of the night the Knights dropped in upon the tavern, the moment they knocked in a certain way Pere Cognet, recognizing the signal, got up, lit the fire and the candles, opened the door, and went to the cellar for a particular wine that was laid in expressly for the Order; while La Cognette cooked an excellent supper, eaten either before or after the expeditions, which were usually planned the previous evening or in the course of the preceding day.

CHAPTER VIII

While Joseph and Madame Bridau were journeying from Orleans to Issoudun, the Knights of Idleness perpetrated one of their best tricks. An old Spaniard, a former prisoner of war, who after the peace had remained in the neighborhood, where he did a small business in grain, came early one morning to market, leaving his empty cart at the foot of the tower of Issoudun. Maxence, who arrived at a rendezvous of the Knights, appointed on that occasion at the foot of the tower, was soon assailed with the whispered question, "What are we to do to-night?"

"Here's Pere Fario's cart," he answered. "I nearly cracked my shins over it. Let us get it up on the embankment of the tower in the first place, and we'll make up our minds afterwards."

When Richard Coeur-de-Lion built the tower of Issoudun he raised it, as we have said, on the ruins of the basilica, which itself stood above the Roman temple and the Celtic Dun. These ruins, each of which represents a period of several centuries, form a mound big with the monuments of three distinct ages. The tower is, therefore, the apex of a cone, from which the descent is equally steep on all sides, and which is only approached by a series of steps. To give in a few words an idea of the height of this tower, we may compare it to the obelisk of Luxor on its pedestal. The pedestal of the tower of Issoudun, which hid within its breast such archaeological treasures, was eighty feet high on the side towards the town. In an hour the cart was taken off its wheels and hoisted, piece by piece, to the top of the embankment at the foot of the tower itself,—a work that was somewhat like that of the soldiers who carried the artillery over the pass of the Grand Saint-Bernard. The cart was then remounted on its wheels, and the Knights, by this time hungry and thirsty, returned to Mere Cognette's, where they were soon seated round the table in the low room, laughing at the grimaces Fario would make when he came after his barrow in the morning.

The Knights, naturally, did not play such capers every night. The genius of Sganarelle, Mascarille, and Scapin combined would not have sufficed to invent three hundred and sixty-five pieces of mischief a year. In the first place, circumstances were not always propitious: sometimes the moon shone clear, or the last prank had greatly irritated their betters; then one or another of their number refused to share in some proposed outrage because a relation was involved. But if the scamps were not at Mere Cognette's every night, they always met during the day, enjoying together the legitimate pleasures of hunting, or the autumn vintages and the winter skating. Among this assemblage of twenty youths, all of them at war with the social somnolence of the place, there are some who were more closely allied than others to Max, and who made him their idol. A character like his often fascinates other youths. The two grandsons of Madame Hochon—Francois Hochon and Baruch Borniche—were his henchmen. These young fellows, accepting the general opinion of the left-handed parentage of Lousteau, looked upon Max as their cousin. Max, moreover, was liberal in lending them money for their pleasures, which their grandfather Hochon refused; he took them hunting, let them see life, and exercised a much greater influence over them than their own family. They were both orphans, and were kept, although each had attained his majority, under the guardianship of Monsieur Hochon, for reasons which will be explained when Monsieur Hochon himself comes upon the scene.

At this particular moment Francois and Baruch (we will call them by their Christian names for the sake of clearness) were sitting, one on each side of Max, at the middle of a table that was rather ill lighted by the fuliginous gleams of four tallow candles of eight to the pound. A dozen to fifteen bottles of various wines had just been drunk, for only eleven of the Knights were present. Baruch—whose name indicates pretty clearly that Calvinism still kept some hold on Issoudun— said to Max, as the wine was beginning to unloose all tongues,—

"You are threatened in your stronghold."

"What do you mean by that?" asked Max.

"Why, my grandmother has had a letter from Madame Bridau, who is her goddaughter, saying that she and her son are coming here. My grandmother has been getting two rooms ready for them."

"What's that to me?" said Max, taking up his glass and swallowing the contents at a gulp with a comic gesture.

Max was then thirty-four years old. A candle standing near him threw a gleam upon his soldierly face, lit up his brow, and brought out admirably his clear skin, his ardent eyes, his black and slightly curling hair, which had the brilliancy of jet. The hair grew vigorously upward from the forehead and temples, sharply defining those five black tongues which our ancestors used to call the "five points." Notwithstanding this abrupt contrast of black and white, Max's face was very sweet, owing its charm to an outline like that which Raphael gave to the faces of his Madonnas, and to a well-cut mouth whose lips smiled graciously, giving an expression of countenance which Max had made distinctively his own. The rich coloring which blooms on a Berrichon cheek added still further to his look of kindly good-humor. When he laughed heartily, he showed thirty-two teeth worthy of the mouth of a pretty woman. In height about five feet six inches, the young man was admirably well-proportioned,—neither too stout nor yet too thin. His hands, carefully kept, were white and rather handsome; but his feet recalled the suburb and the foot-soldier of the Empire. Max would certainly have made a good general of division; he had shoulders that were worth a fortune to a marshal of France, and a breast broad enough to wear all the orders of Europe. Every movement betrayed intelligence; born with grace and charm, like nearly all the children of love, the noble blood of his real father came out in him.

"Don't you know, Max," cried the son of a former surgeon-major named Goddet—now the best doctor in the town—from the other end of the table, "that Madame Hochon's goddaughter is the sister of Rouget? If she is coming here with her son, no doubt she means to make sure of getting the property when he dies, and then—good-by to your harvest!"

Max frowned. Then, with a look which ran from one face to another all round the table, he watched the effect of this announcement on the minds of those present, and again replied,—

"What's that to me?"

"But," said Francois, "I should think that if old Rouget revoked his will,—in case he has made one in favor of the Rabouilleuse—"

Here Max cut short his henchman's speech. "I've stopped the mouths of people who have dared to meddle with you, my dear Francois," he said; "and this is the way you pay your debts? You use a contemptuous nickname in speaking of a woman to whom I am known to be attached."

Max had never before said as much as this about his relations with the person to whom Francois had just applied a name under which she was known at Issoudun. The late prisoner at Cabrera—the major of the grenadiers of the Guard—knew enough of what honor was to judge rightly as to the causes of the disesteem in which society held him. He had therefore never allowed any one, no matter who, to speak to him on the subject of Mademoiselle Flore Brazier, the servant-mistress of Jean-Jacques Rouget, so energetically termed a "slut" by the respectable Madame Hochon. Everybody knew it was too ticklish a subject with Max, ever to speak of it unless he began it; and hitherto he had never begun it. To risk his anger or irritate him was altogether too dangerous; so that even his best friends had never joked him about the Rabouilleuse. When they talked of his liaison with the girl before Major Potel and Captain Renard, with whom he lived on intimate terms, Potel would reply,—

"If he is the natural brother of Jean-Jacques Rouget where else would you have him live?"

"Besides, after all," added Captain Renard, "the girl is a worthless piece, and if Max does live with her where's the harm?"

After this merited snub, Francois could not at once catch up the thread of his ideas; but he was still less able to do so when Max said to him, gently,—

"Go on."

"Faith, no!" cried Francois.

"You needn't get angry, Max," said young Goddet; "didn't we agree to talk freely to each other at Mere Cognette's? Shouldn't we all be mortal enemies if we remembered outside what is said, or thought, or done here? All the town calls Flore Brazier the Rabouilleuse; and if Francois did happen to let the nickname slip out, is that a crime against the Order of Idleness?"

"No," said Max, "but against our personal friendship. However, I thought better of it; I recollected we were in session, and that was why I said, 'Go on.'"

A deep silence followed. The pause became so embarrassing for the whole company that Max broke it by exclaiming:—

"I'll go on for him," (sensation) "—for all of you," (amazement) "—and tell you what you are thinking" (profound sensation). "You think that Flore, the Rabouilleuse, La Brazier, the housekeeper of Pere Rouget,—for they call him so, that old bachelor, who can never have any children!—you think, I say, that that woman supplies all my wants ever since I came back to Issoudun. If I am able to throw three hundred francs a month to the dogs, and treat you to suppers,—as I do to-night,—and lend money to all of you, you think I get the gold out of Mademoiselle Flore Brazier's purse? Well, yes" (profound sensation). "Yes, ten thousand times yes! Yes, Mademoiselle Brazier is aiming straight for the old man's property."

"She gets it from father to son," observed Goddet, in his corner.

"You think," continued Max, smiling at Goddet's speech, "that I intend to marry Flore when Pere Rouget dies, and so this sister and her son, of whom I hear to-night for the first time, will endanger my future?"

"That's just it," cried Francois.

"That is what every one thinks who is sitting round this table," said Baruch.

"Well, don't be uneasy, friends," answered Max. "Forewarned is forearmed! Now then, I address the Knights of Idleness. If, to get rid of these Parisians I need the help of the Order, will you lend me a hand? Oh! within the limits we have marked out for our fooleries," he added hastily, perceiving a general hesitation. "Do you suppose I want to kill them,—poison them? Thank God I'm not an idiot. Besides, if the Bridaus succeed, and Flore has nothing but what she stands in, I should be satisfied; do you understand that? I love her enough to prefer her to Mademoiselle Fichet,—if Mademoiselle Fichet would have me."

Mademoiselle Fichet was the richest heiress in Issoudun, and the hand of the daughter counted for much in the reported passion of the younger Goddet for the mother. Frankness of speech is a pearl of such price that all the Knights rose to their feet as one man.

"You are a fine fellow, Max!"

50

"Well said, Max; we'll stand by you!"

"A fig for the Bridaus!"

"We'll bridle them!"

"After all, it is only three swains to a shepherdess."

"The deuce! Pere Lousteau loved Madame Rouget; isn't it better to love a housekeeper who is not yoked?"

"If the defunct Rouget was Max's father, the affair is in the family."

"Liberty of opinion now-a-days!"

"Hurrah for Max!"

"Down with all hypocrites!"

"Here's a health to the beautiful Flore!"

Such were the eleven responses, acclamations, and toasts shouted forth by the Knights of Idleness, and characteristic, we may remark, of their excessively relaxed morality. It is now easy to see what interest Max had in becoming their grand master. By leading the young men of the best families in their follies and amusements, and by doing them services, he meant to create a support for himself when the day for recovering his position came. He rose gracefully and waved his glass of claret, while all the others waited eagerly for the coming allocution.

"As a mark of the ill-will I bear you, I wish you all a mistress who is equal to the beautiful Flore! As to this irruption of relations, I don't feel any present uneasiness; and as to the future, we'll see what comes—"

"Don't let us forget Fario's cart!"

"Hang it! that's safe enough!" said Goddet.

"Oh! I'll engage to settle that business," cried Max. "Be in the market-place early, all of you, and let me know when the old fellow goes for his cart."

It was striking half-past three in the morning as the Knights slipped out in silence to go to their homes; gliding close to the walls of the houses without making the least noise, shod as they were in list shoes. Max slowly returned to the place Saint-Jean, situated in the upper part of the town, between the port Saint-Jean and the port Vilatte, the quarter of the rich bourgeoisie. Maxence Gilet had concealed his fears, but the news had struck home. His experience on the hulks at Cabrera had taught him a dissimulation as deep and thorough as his corruption. First, and above all else, the forty thousand francs a year from landed property which old Rouget owned was, let it be clearly understood, the constituent element of Max's passion for Flore Brazier. By his present bearing it is easy to see how much confidence the woman had given him in the financial future she expected to obtain through the infatuation of the old bachelor. Nevertheless, the news of the arrival of the legitimate heirs was of a nature to shake Max's faith in Flore's influence. Rouget's savings, accumulating during the last seventeen years, still stood in his own name; and even if the will, which Flore declared had long been made in her favor, were revoked, these savings at least might be secured by putting them in the name of Mademoiselle Brazier.

"That fool of a girl never told me, in all these seven years, a word about the sister and nephews!" cried Max, turning from the rue de la Marmouse into the rue l'Avenier. "Seven hundred and fifty thousand francs placed with different notaries at Bourges, and Vierzon, and Chateauroux, can't be turned into money and put into the Funds in a week, without everybody knowing it in this gossiping place! The most important thing is to get rid of these relations; as soon as they are driven away we ought to make haste to secure the property. I must think it over."

Max was tired. By the help of a pass-key, he let himself into Pere Rouget's house, and went to bed without making any noise, saying to himself,—

"To-morrow, my thoughts will be clear."

It is now necessary to relate where the sultana of the place Saint-Jean picked up the nickname of "Rabouilleuse," and how she came to be the quasi-mistress of Jean-Jacques Rouget's home.

As old Doctor Rouget, the father of Jean-Jacques and Madame Bridau, advanced in years, he began to perceive the nonentity of his son; he then treated him harshly, trying to break him into a routine that might serve in place of intelligence. He thus, though unconsciously, prepared him to submit to the yoke of the first tyranny that threw its halter over his head.

Coming home one day from his professional round, the malignant and vicious old man came across a bewitching little girl at the edge of some fields that lay along the avenue de Tivoli. Hearing the horse, the child sprang up from the bottom of one of the many brooks which are to be seen from the heights of Issoudun, threading the meadows like ribbons of silver on a green robe. Naiad-like, she rose suddenly on the doctor's vision, showing the loveliest virgin head that painters ever dreamed of. Old Rouget, who knew the whole country-side, did not know this miracle of beauty. The child, who was half naked, wore a forlorn little petticoat of coarse woollen stuff, woven in alternate strips of brown and white, full of holes and very ragged. A sheet of rough writing paper, tied on by a shred of osier, served her for a hat. Beneath this paper— covered with pot-hooks and round O's, from which it derived the name of "schoolpaper"—the loveliest mass of blonde hair that ever a daughter of Eve could have desired, was twisted up, and held in place by a species of comb made to comb out the tails of horses. Her pretty tanned bosom, and her neck, scarcely covered by a ragged fichu which was once a Madres handkerchief, showed edges of the white skin below the exposed and sun-burned parts. One end of her petticoat was drawn between the legs and fastened with a huge pin in front, giving that garment the look of a pair of bathing drawers. The feet and the legs, which could be seen through the clear water in which she stood, attracted the eye by a delicacy which was worthy of a sculptor of the middle ages. The charming limbs exposed to the sun had a ruddy tone that was not without beauty of its own. The neck and bosom were worthy of being wrapped in silks and cashmeres; and the nymph had blue eyes fringed with long lashes, whose glance might have made a painter or a poet fall upon his knees. The doctor, enough of an anatomist to trace the exquisite figure, recognized the loss it would be to art if the lines of such a model were destroyed by the hard toil of the fields.

"Where do you come from, little girl? I have never seen you before," said the old doctor, then sixty-two years of age. This scene took place in the month of September, 1799.

"I belong in Vatan," she answered.

Hearing Rouget's voice, an ill-looking man, standing at some distance in the deeper waters of the brook, raised his head. "What are you about, Flore?" he said, "While you are talking instead of catching, the creatures will get away."

"Why have you come here from Vatan?" continued the doctor, paying no heed to the interruption.

"I am catching crabs for my uncle Brazier here."

"Rabouiller" is a Berrichon word which admirably describes the thing it is intended to express; namely, the action of troubling the water of a brook, making it boil and bubble with a branch whose end-shoots spread out like a racket. The crabs, frightened by this operation, which they do not understand, come hastily to the surface, and in their flurry rush into the net the fisher has laid for them at a little distance. Flore Brazier held her "rabouilloir" in her hand with the natural grace of childlike innocence.

"Has your uncle got permission to hunt crabs?"

"Hey! are not we all under a Republic that is one and indivisible?" cried the uncle from his station.

"We are under a Directory," said the doctor, "and I know of no law which allows a man to come from Vatan and fish in the territory of Issoudun"; then he said to Flore, "Have you got a mother, little one!"

"No, monsieur; and my father is in the asylum at Bourges. He went mad from a sun-stroke he got in the fields."

"How much do you earn?"

"Five sous a day while the season lasts; I catch 'em as far as the Braisne. In harvest time, I glean; in winter, I spin."

"You are about twelve years old?"

"Yes, monsieur."

"Do you want to come with me? You shall be well fed and well dressed, and have some pretty shoes."

"No, my niece will stay with me; I am responsible to God and man for her," said Uncle Brazier who had come up to them. "I am her guardian, d'ye see?"

The doctor kept his countenance and checked a smile which might have escaped most people at the aspect of the man. The guardian wore a peasant's hat, rotted by sun and rain, eaten like the leaves of a cabbage that has harbored several caterpillars, and mended, here and there, with white thread. Beneath the hat was a dark and sunken face, in which the mouth, nose, and eyes, seemed four black spots. His forlorn jacket was a bit of patchwork, and his trousers were of crash towelling.

"I am Doctor Rouget," said that individual; "and as you are the guardian of the child, bring her to my house, in the place Saint-Jean. It will not be a bad day's work for you; nor for her, either."

Without waiting for an answer, and sure that Uncle Brazier would soon appear with his pretty "rabouilleuse," Doctor Rouget set spurs to his horse and returned to Issoudun. He had hardly sat down to dinner, before his cook announced the arrival of the citoyen and citoyenne Brazier.

"Sit down," said the doctor to the uncle and niece.

Flore and her guardian, still barefooted, looked round the doctor's dining-room with wondering eyes; never having seen its like before.

The house, which Rouget inherited from the Descoings estate, stands in the middle of the place Saint-Jean, a so-called square, very long and very narrow, planted with a few sickly lindens. The houses in this part of town are better built than elsewhere, and that of the Descoings's was one of the finest. It stands opposite to the house of Monsieur Hochon, and has three windows in front on the first storey, and a porte-cochere on the ground-floor which gives entrance to a courtyard, beyond which lies the garden. Under the archway of the porte-cochere is the door of a large hall lighted by two windows on the street. The kitchen is behind this hall, part of the space being used for a staircase which leads to the upper floor and to the attic above that. Beyond the kitchen is a wood-shed and wash-house, a stable for two horses and a coach-house, over which are some little lofts for the storage of oats, hay, and straw, where, at that time, the doctor's servant slept.

The hall which the little peasant and her uncle admired with such wonder is decorated with wooden carvings of the time of Louis XV., painted gray, and a handsome marble chimney-piece, over which Flore beheld herself in a large mirror without any upper division and with a carved and gilded frame. On the panelled walls of the room, from space to space, hung several pictures, the spoil of various religious houses, such as the abbeys of Deols, Issoudun, Saint-Gildas, La Pree, Chezal-Beniot, Saint-Sulpice, and the convents of Bourges and Issoudun, which the liberality of our kings had enriched with the precious gifts of the glorious works called forth by the Renaissance. Among the pictures obtained by the Descoings and inherited by Rouget, was a Holy Family by Albano, a Saint-Jerome of Demenichino, a Head of Christ by Gian Bellini, a Virgin of Leonardo, a Bearing of the Cross by Titian, which formerly belonged to the Marquis de Belabre (the one who sustained a siege and had his head cut off under Louis XIII.); a Lazarus of Paul Veronese, a Marriage of the Virgin by the priest Genois, two church paintings by Rubens, and a replica of a picture by Perugino, done either by Perugino himself or by Raphael; and finally, two Correggios and one Andrea del Sarto.

The Descoings had culled these treasures from three hundred church pictures, without knowing their value, and selecting them only for their good preservation. Many were not only in magnificent frames, but some were still under glass. Perhaps it was the beauty of the frames and the value of the glass that led the Descoings to retain the pictures. The furniture of the room was not wanting in the sort of luxury we prize in these days, though at that time it had no value in Issoudun. The clock, standing on the mantle-shelf between two superb silver candlesticks with six branches, had an ecclesiastical splendor which revealed the hand of Boulle. The armchairs of carved oak, covered with tapestry-work due to the devoted industry of women of high rank, would be treasured in these days, for each was surmounted with a crown and coat-of-arms. Between the windows stood a rich console, brought from some castle, on whose marble slab stood an immense China jar, in which the doctor kept his tobacco. But neither Rouget, nor his son, nor the cook, took the slightest care of all these treasures. They spat upon a hearth of exquisite delicacy, whose gilded mouldings were now green with verdigris. A handsome chandelier, partly of semi-transparent porcelain, was peppered, like the ceiling from which it hung, with black speckles, bearing witness to the immunity enjoyed by the flies. The Descoings had draped the windows with brocatelle curtains torn from the bed of some monastic prior. To the left of the entrance-door, stood a chest or coffer, worth many thousand francs, which the doctor now used for a sideboard.

"Here, Fanchette," cried Rouget to his cook, "bring two glasses; and give us some of the old wine."

Fanchette, a big Berrichon countrywoman, who was considered a better cook than even La Cognette, ran in to receive the order with a celerity which said much for the doctor's despotism, and something also for her own curiosity.

"What is an acre of vineyard worth in your parts?" asked the doctor, pouring out a glass of wine for Brazier.

"Three hundred francs in silver."

"Well, then! leave your niece here as my servant; she shall have three hundred francs in wages, and, as you are her guardian, you can take them."

"Every year?" exclaimed Brazier, with his eyes as wide as saucers.

"I leave that to your conscience," said the doctor. "She is an orphan; up to eighteen, she has no right to what she earns."

"Twelve to eighteen—that's six acres of vineyard!" said the uncle. "Ay, she's a pretty one, gentle as a lamb, well made and active, and obedient as a kitten. She were the light o' my poor brother's eyes—"

"I will pay a year in advance," observed the doctor.

"Bless me! say two years, and I'll leave her with you, for she'll be better off with you than with us; my wife beats her, she can't abide her. There's none but I to stand up for her, and the little saint of a creature is as innocent as a new-born babe."

When he heard the last part of this speech, the doctor, struck by the word "innocent," made a sign to the uncle and took him out into the courtyard and from thence to the garden; leaving the Rabouilleuse at the table with Fanchette and Jean-Jacques, who immediately questioned her, and to whom she naively related her meeting with the doctor.

"There now, my little darling, good-by," said Uncle Brazier, coming back and kissing Flore on the forehead; "you can well say I've made your happiness by leaving you with this kind and worthy father of the poor; you must obey him as you would me. Be a good girl, and behave nicely, and do everything he tells you."

"Get the room over mine ready," said the doctor to Fanchette. "Little Flore—I am sure she is worthy of the name—will sleep there in future. To-morrow, we'll send for a shoemaker and a dressmaker. Put another plate on the table; she shall keep us company."

That evening, all Issoudun could talk of nothing else than the sudden appearance of the little "rabouilleuse" in Doctor Rouget's house. In that region of satire the nickname stuck to Mademoiselle Brazier before, during, and after the period of her good fortune.

The doctor no doubt intended to do with Flore Brazier, in a small way, what Louis XV. did in a large one with Mademoiselle de Romans; but he was too late about it; Louis XV. was still young, whereas the doctor was in the flower of old age. From twelve to fourteen, the charming little Rabouilleuse lived a life of unmixed happiness. Always well-dressed, and often much better tricked out than the richest girls in Issoudun, she sported a gold watch and jewels, given by the doctor to encourage her studies, and she had a master who taught her to read, write, and cipher. But the almost animal life of the true peasant had instilled into Flore such deep repugnance to the bitter cup of knowledge, that the doctor stopped her education at that point. His intentions with regard to the child, whom he cleansed and clothed, and taught, and formed with a care which was all the more remarkable because he was thought to be utterly devoid of tenderness, were interpreted in a variety of ways by the cackling society of the town, whose gossip often gave rise to fatal blunders, like those relating to the birth of Agathe and that of Max. It is not easy for the community of a country town to disentangle the truth from the mass of conjecture and contradictory reports to which a single fact gives rise. The provinces insist—as in former days the politicians of the little Provence at the Tuileries insisted—on full explanations, and they usually end by knowing everything. But each person clings to the version of the event which he, or she, likes best; proclaims it, argues it, and considers it the only true one. In spite of the strong light cast upon people's lives by the constant spying of a little town, truth is thus often obscured; and to be recognized, it needs the impartiality which historians or superior minds acquire by looking at the subject from a higher point of view.

"What do you suppose that old gorilla wants at his age with a little girl only fifteen years old?" society was still saying two years after the arrival of the Rabouilleuse.

"Ah! that's true," they answered, "his days of merry-making are long past."

"My dear fellow, the doctor is disgusted at the stupidity of his son, and he persists in hating his daughter Agathe; it may be that he has been living a decent life for the last two years, intending to marry little Flore; suppose she were to give him a fine, active, strapping boy, full of life like Max?" said one of the wise heads of the town.

"Bah! don't talk nonsense! After such a life as Rouget and Lousteau led from 1770 to 1787, is it likely that either of them would have children at sixty-five years of age? The old villain has read the Scriptures, if only as a doctor, and he is doing as David did in his old age; that's all."

"They say that Brazier, when he is drunk, boasts in Vatan that he cheated him," cried one of those who always believed the worst of people.

"Good heavens! neighbor; what won't they say at Issoudun?"

From 1800 to 1805, that is, for five years, the doctor enjoyed all the pleasures of educating Flore without the annoyances which the ambitions and pretensions of Mademoiselle de Romans inflicted, it is said, on Louis le Bien-Aime. The little Rabouilleuse was so satisfied when she compared the life she led at the doctor's with that she would have led at her uncle Brazier's, that she yielded no doubt to the exactions of her master as if she had been an Eastern slave. With due deference to the makers of idylls and to philanthropists, the inhabitants of the provinces have very little idea of certain virtues; and their scruples are of a kind that is roused by self-interest, and not by any sentiment of the right or the becoming. Raised from infancy with no prospect before them but poverty and ceaseless labor, they are led to consider anything that saves them from the hell of hunger and eternal toil as permissible, particularly if it is not contrary to any law.

Exceptions to this rule are rare. Virtue, socially speaking, is the companion of a comfortable life, and comes only with education.

Thus the Rabouilleuse was an object of envy to all the young peasant-girls within a circuit of ten miles, although her conduct, from a religious point of view, was supremely reprehensible. Flore, born in 1787, grew up in the midst of the saturnalias of 1793 and 1798, whose lurid gleams penetrated these country regions, then deprived of priests and faith and altars and religious ceremonies; where marriage was nothing more than legal coupling, and revolutionary maxims left a deep impression. This was markedly the case at Issoudun, a land where, as we have seen, revolt of all kinds is traditional. In 1802, Catholic worship was scarcely re-established. The Emperor found it a difficult matter to obtain priests. In 1806, many parishes all over France were still widowed; so slowly were the clergy, decimated by the scaffold, gathered together again after their violent dispersion.

In 1802, therefore, nothing was likely to reproach Flore Brazier, unless it might be her conscience; and conscience was sure to be weaker than self-interest in the ward of Uncle Brazier. If, as everybody chose to suppose, the cynical doctor was compelled by his age to respect a child of fifteen, the Rabouilleuse was none the less considered very "wide awake," a term much used in that region. Still, some persons thought she could claim a certificate of innocence from the cessation of the doctor's cares and attentions in the last two years of his life, during which time he showed her something more than coldness.

Old Rouget had killed too many people not to know when his own end was nigh; and his notary, finding him on his death-bed, draped as it were, in the mantle of encyclopaedic philosophy, pressed him to make a provision in favor of the young girl, then seventeen years old.

"So I do," he said, cynically; "my death sets her at liberty."

This speech paints the nature of the old man. Covering his evil doings with witty sayings, he obtained indulgence for them, in a land where wit is always applauded,—especially when addressed to obvious self-interest. In those words the notary read the concentrated hatred of a man whose calculations had been balked by Nature herself, and who revenged himself upon the innocent object of an impotent love. This opinion was confirmed to some extent by the obstinate resolution of the doctor to leave nothing to the Rabouilleuse, saying with a bitter smile, when the notary again urged the subject upon him,—

"Her beauty will make her rich enough!"

CHAPTER IX

Jean-Jacques Rouget did not mourn his father, though Flore Brazier did. The old doctor had made his son extremely unhappy, especially since he came of age, which happened in 1791; but he had given the little peasant-girl the material pleasures which are the ideal of happiness to country-folk. When Fanchette asked Flore, after the funeral, "Well, what is to become of you, now that monsieur is dead?" Jean-Jacques's eyes lighted up, and for the first time in his life his dull face grew animated, showed feeling, and seemed to brighten under the rays of a thought.

"Leave the room," he said to Fanchette, who was clearing the table.

At seventeen, Flore retained that delicacy of feature and form, that distinction of beauty which attracted the doctor, and which women of the world know how to preserve, though it fades among the peasant-girls like the flowers of the field. Nevertheless, the tendency to embonpoint, which handsome countrywomen develop when they no longer live a life of toil and hardship in the fields and in the sunshine, was already noticeable about her. Her bust had developed. The plump white shoulders were modelled on rich lines that harmoniously blended with those of the throat, already showing a few folds of flesh. But the outline of the face was still faultless, and the chin delicate.

"Flore," said Jean-Jacques, in a trembling voice, "you feel at home in this house?"

"Yes, Monsieur Jean."

As the heir was about to make his declaration, he felt his tongue stiffen at the recollection of the dead man, just put away in his grave, and a doubt seized him as to what lengths his father's benevolence might have gone. Flore, who was quite unable even to suspect his simplicity of mind, looked at her future master and waited for a time, expecting Jean-Jacques to go on with what he was saying; but she finally left him without knowing what to think of such obstinate silence. Whatever teaching the Rabouilleuse may have received from the doctor, it was many a long day before she finally understood the character of Jean-Jacques, whose history we now present in a few words.

At the death of his father, Jacques, then thirty-seven, was as timid and submissive to paternal discipline as a child of twelve years old. That timidity ought to explain his childhood, youth, and after-life to those who are reluctant to admit the existence of such characters, or such facts as this history relates,—though proofs of them are, alas, common everywhere, even among princes; for Sophie Dawes was taken by the last of the Condes under worse circumstances than the Rabouilleuse. There are two species of timidity,—the timidity of the mind, and the timidity of the nerves; a physical timidity, and a moral timidity. The one is independent of the other. The body may fear and tremble, while the mind is calm and courageous, or vice versa. This is the key to many moral eccentricities. When the two are united in one man, that man will be a cipher all his life; such double-sided timidity makes him what we call "an imbecile." Often fine suppressed qualities are hidden within that imbecile. To this double infirmity we may, perhaps, owe the lives of certain monks who lived in ecstasy; for this unfortunate moral and physical disposition is produced quite as much by the perfection of the soul and of the organs, as by defects which are still unstudied.

The timidity of Jean-Jacques came from a certain torpor of his faculties, which a great teacher or a great surgeon, like Despleins, would have roused. In him, as in the cretins, the sense of love had inherited a strength and vigor which were lacking to his mental qualities, though he had mind enough to guide him in ordinary affairs. The violence of passion, stripped of the ideal in which most young men expend it, only increased his timidity. He had never brought himself to court, as the saying is, any woman in Issoudun. Certainly no young girl or matron would make advances to a young man of mean stature, awkward and shame-faced in attitude; whose vulgar face, with its flattened features and pallid skin, making him look old before his time, was rendered still more hideous by a pair of large and prominent light-green eyes. The presence of a woman stultified the poor fellow, who was driven by passion on the one hand as violently as the lack of ideas, resulting from his education, held him back on the other. Paralyzed between these opposing forces, he had not a word to say, and feared to be spoken to, so much did he dread the obligation of replying. Desire, which usually sets free the tongue, only petrified his powers of speech. Thus it happened that Jean-Jacques Rouget was solitary and sought solitude because there alone he was at his ease.

The doctor had seen, too late for remedy, the havoc wrought in his son's life by a temperament and a character of this kind. He would have been glad to get him married; but to do that, he must deliver him over to an influence that was certain to become tyrannical, and the doctor hesitated. Was it not practically giving the whole management of the property into the hands of a stranger, some unknown girl? The doctor knew how difficult it was to gain true indications of the moral character of a woman from any study of a young girl. So, while he continued to search for a daughter-in-law whose sentiments and education offered some guarantees for the future, he endeavored to push his son into the ways of avarice; meaning to give the poor fool a sort of instinct that might eventually take the place of intelligence.

He trained him, in the first place, to mechanical habits of life; and instilled into him fixed ideas as to the investment of his revenues: and he spared him the chief difficulties of the management of a fortune, by leaving his estates all in good order, and leased for long periods. Nevertheless, a fact which was destined to be of paramount importance in the life of the poor creature escaped the notice of the wily old doctor. Timidity is a good deal like dissimulation, and is equally secretive. Jean-Jacques was passionately in love with the Rabouilleuse. Nothing, of course, could be more natural. Flore was the only woman who lived in the bachelor's presence, the only one he could see at his ease; and at all hours he secretly contemplated her and watched her. To him, she was the light of his paternal home; she gave him, unknown to herself, the only pleasures that brightened his youth. Far from being jealous of his father, he rejoiced in the education the old man was giving to Flore: would it not make her all he wanted, a woman easy to win, and to whom, therefore, he need pay no court? The passion, observe, which is able to reflect, gives even to ninnies, fools, and imbeciles a species of intelligence, especially in youth. In the lowest human creature we find an animal instinct whose persistency resembles thought.

The next day, Flore, who had been reflecting on her master's silence, waited in expectation of some momentous communication; but although he kept near her, and looked at her on the sly with passionate glances, Jean-Jacques still found nothing to say. At last, when the dessert was on the table, he recommenced the scene of the night before.

"You like your life here?" he said to Flore.

"Yes, Monsieur Jean."

"Well, stay here then."

"Thank you, Monsieur Jean."

This strange situation lasted three weeks. One night, when no sound broke the stillness of the house, Flore, who chanced to wake up, heard the regular breathing of human lungs outside her door, and was frightened to discover Jean-Jacques, crouched like a dog on the landing.

"He loves me," she thought; "but he will get the rheumatism if he keeps up that sort of thing."

The next day Flore looked at her master with a certain expression. This mute almost instinctive love had touched her; she no longer thought the poor ninny so ugly, though his forehead was crowned with pimples resembling ulcers, the signs of a vitiated blood.

"You don't want to go back and live in the fields, do you?" said Jean-Jacques when they were alone.

"Why do you ask me that?" she said, looking at him.

"To know—" replied Rouget, turning the color of a boiled lobster.

"Do you wish to send me back?" she asked.

"No, mademoiselle."

"Well, what is it you want to know? You have some reason—"

"Yes, I want to know—"

"What?" said Flore.

"You won't tell me?" exclaimed Rouget.

"Yes I will, on my honor—"

"Ah! that's it," returned Rouget, with a frightened air. "Are you an honest girl?"

"I'll take my oath—"

"Are you, truly?"

"Don't you hear me tell you so?"

"Come; are you the same as you were when your uncle brought you here barefooted?"

"A fine question, faith!" cried Flore, blushing.

The heir lowered his head and did not raise it again. Flore, amazed at such an encouraging sign from a man who had been overcome by a fear of that nature, left the room.

Three days later, at the same hour (for both seemed to regard the dessert as a field of battle), Flore spoke first, and said to her master,—

"Have you anything against me?"

"No, mademoiselle," he answered, "No—" (a pause) "On the contrary."

"You seemed annoyed the other day to hear I was an honest girl."

"No, I only wished to know—" (a pause) "But you would not tell me—"

"On my word!" she said, "I will tell you the whole truth."

"The whole truth about—my father?" he asked in a strangled voice.

"Your father," she said, looking full into her master's eye, "was a worthy man—he liked a joke—What of that?—there was nothing in it. But, poor dear man, it wasn't the will that was wanting. The truth is, he had some spite against you, I don't know what, and he meant—oh! he meant you harm. Sometimes he made me laugh; but there! what of that?"

"Well, Flore," said the heir, taking her hand, "as my father was nothing to you—"

"What did you suppose he was to me?" she cried, as if offended by some unworthy suspicion.

"Well, but just listen—"

"He was my benefactor, that was all. Ah! he would have liked to make me his wife, but—"

"But," said Rouget, taking the hand which Flore had snatched away from him, "if he was nothing to you you can stay here with me, can't you?"

"If you wish it," she said, dropping her eyes.

"No, no! if you wish it, you!" exclaimed Rouget. "Yes, you shall be—mistress here. All that is here shall be yours; you shall take care of my property, it is almost yours now—for I love you; I have always loved you since the day you came and stood there—there!—with bare feet."

Flore made no answer. When the silence became embarrassing, Jean-Jacques had recourse to a terrible argument.

"Come," he said, with visible warmth, "wouldn't it be better than returning to the fields?"

"As you will, Monsieur Jean," she answered.

Nevertheless, in spite of her "as you will," Jean-Jacques got no further. Men of his nature want certainty. The effort that they make in avowing their love is so great, and costs them so much, that they feel unable to go on with it. This accounts for their attachment to the first woman who accepts them. We can only guess at circumstances by results. Ten months after the death of his father, Jean-Jacques changed completely; his leaden face cleared, and his whole countenance breathed happiness. Flore exacted that he should take minute care of his person, and her own vanity was gratified in seeing him well-dressed; she always stood on the sill of the door, and watched him starting for a walk, until she could see him no longer. The whole town noticed these changes, which had made a new man of the bachelor.

"Have you heard the news?" people said to each other in Issoudun.

"What is it?"

"Jean-Jacques inherits everything from his father, even the Rabouilleuse."

"Don't you suppose the old doctor was wicked enough to provide a ruler for his son?"

"Rouget has got a treasure, that's certain," said everybody.

"She's a sly one! She is very handsome, and she will make him marry her."

"What luck that girl has had, to be sure!"

"The luck that only comes to pretty girls."

"Ah, bah! do you believe that? look at my uncle Borniche-Herau. You have heard of Mademoiselle Ganivet? she was as ugly as seven capital sins, but for all that, she got three thousand francs a year out of him."

"Yes, but that was in 1778."

"Still, Rouget is making a mistake. His father left him a good forty thousand francs' income, and he ought to marry Mademoiselle Herau."

"The doctor tried to arrange it, but she would not consent; Jean-Jacques is so stupid—"

"Stupid! why women are very happy with that style of man."

"Is your wife happy?"

Such was the sort of tattle that ran through Issoudun. If people, following the use and wont of the provinces, began by laughing at this quasi-marriage, they ended by praising Flore for devoting herself to the poor fellow. We now see how it was that Flore Brazier obtained the management of the Rouget household,—from father to son, as young Goddet had said. It is desirable to sketch the history of that management for the edification of old bachelors.

Fanchette, the cook, was the only person in Issoudun who thought it wrong that Flore Brazier should be queen over Jean-Jacques Rouget and his home. She protested against the immorality of the connection, and took a tone of injured virtue; the fact being that she was humiliated by having, at her age, a crab-girl for a mistress,—a child who had been brought barefoot into the house. Fanchette owned three hundred francs a year in the Funds, for the doctor made her invest her savings in that way, and he had left her as much more in an annuity; she could therefore live at her ease without the necessity of working, and she quitted the house nine months after the funeral of her old master, April 15, 1806. That date may indicate, to a perspicacious observer, the epoch at which Flore Brazier ceased to be an honest girl.

The Rabouilleuse, clever enough to foresee Fanchette's probable defection,—there is nothing like the exercise of power for teaching policy,—was already resolved to do without a servant. For six months she had studied, without seeming to do so, the culinary operations that made Fanchette a cordon-bleu worthy of cooking for a doctor. In the matter of choice living, doctors are on a par with bishops. The doctor had brought Fanchette's talents to perfection. In the provinces the lack of occupation and the monotony of existence turn all activity of mind towards the kitchen. People do not dine as luxuriously in the country as they do in Paris, but they dine better; the dishes are meditated upon and studied. In rural regions we often find some Careme in petticoats, some unrecognized genius able to serve a simple dish of haricot-beans worthy of the nod with which Rossini welcomed a perfectly-rendered measure.

When studying for his degree in Paris, the doctor had followed a course of chemistry under Rouelle, and had gathered some ideas which he afterwards put to use in the chemistry of cooking. His memory is famous in Issoudun for certain improvements little known outside of Berry. It was he who discovered that an omelette is far more delicate when the whites and the yolks are not beaten together with the violence which cooks usually put into the operation. He considered that the whites should be beaten to a froth and the yolks gently added by degrees; moreover a frying-pan should never be used, but a "cagnard" of porcelain or earthenware. The "cagnard" is a species of thick dish standing on four feet, so that when it is placed on the stove the air circulates underneath and prevents the fire from cracking it. In Touraine the "cagnard" is called a "cauquemarre." Rabelais, I think, speaks of a "cauquemarre" for cooking cockatrice eggs, thus proving the antiquity of the utensil. The doctor had also found a way to prevent the tartness of browned butter; but his secret, which unluckily he kept to his own kitchen, has been lost.

Flore, a born fryer and roaster, two qualities that can never be acquired by observation nor yet by labor, soon surpassed Fanchette. In making herself a cordon-bleu she was thinking of Jean-Jacques's comfort; though he was, it must be owned, tolerably dainty. Incapable, like all persons without education, of doing anything with her brains, she spent her activity upon household matters. She rubbed up the furniture till it shone, and kept everything about the house in a state of cleanliness worthy of Holland. She managed the avalanches of soiled linen and the floods of water that go by the name of "the wash," which was done, according to provincial usage, three times a year. She kept a housewifely eye to the linen, and mended it carefully. Then, desirous of learning little by little the secret of the family property, she acquired the very limited business knowledge which Rouget possessed, and increased it by conversations with the notary of the late doctor, Monsieur Heron. Thus instructed, she gave excellent advice to her little Jean-

Jacques. Sure of being always mistress, she was as eager and solicitous about the old bachelor's interests as if they had been her own. She was not obliged to guard against the exactions of her uncle, for two months before the doctor's death Brazier died of a fall as he was leaving a wine-shop, where, since his rise in fortune, he spent most of his time. Flore had also lost her father; thus she served her master with all the affection which an orphan, thankful to make herself a home and a settlement in life, would naturally feel.

This period of his life was paradise to poor Jean-Jacques, who now acquired the gentle habits of an animal, trained into a sort of monastic regularity. He slept late. Flore, who was up at daybreak attending to her housekeeping, woke him so that he should find his breakfast ready as soon as he had finished dressing. After breakfast, about eleven o'clock, Jean-Jacques went to walk; talked with the people he met, and came home at three in the afternoon to read the papers,—those of the department, and a journal from Paris which he received three days after publication, well greased by the thirty hands through which it came, browned by the snuffy noses that had pored over it, and soiled by the various tables on which it had lain. The old bachelor thus got through the day until it was time for dinner; over that meal he spent as much time as it was possible to give to it. Flore told him the news of the town, repeating the cackle that was current, which she had carefully picked up. Towards eight o'clock the lights were put out. Going to bed early is a saving of fire and candles very commonly practised in the provinces, which contributes no doubt to the empty-mindedness of the inhabitants. Too much sleep dulls and weakens the brain.

Such was the life of these two persons during a period of nine years, the great events of which were a few journeys to Bourges, Vierzon, Chateauroux, or somewhat further, if the notaries of those towns and Monsieur Heron had no investments ready for acceptance. Rouget lent his money at five per cent on a first mortgage, with release of the wife's rights in case the owner was married. He never lent more than a third of the value of the property, and required notes payable to his order for an additional interest of two and a half per cent spread over the whole duration of the loan. Such were the rules his father had told him to follow. Usury, that clog upon the ambition of the peasantry, is the destroyer of country regions. This levy of seven and a half per cent seemed, therefore, so reasonable to the borrowers that Jean-Jacques Rouget had his choice of investments; and the notaries of the different towns, who got a fine commission for themselves from clients for whom they obtained money on such good terms, gave due notice to the old bachelor.

During these nine years Flore obtained in the long run, insensibly and without aiming for it, an absolute control over her master. From the first, she treated him very familiarly; then, without failing him in proper respect, she so far surpassed him in superiority of mind and force of character that he became in fact the servant of his servant. Elderly child that he was, he met this mastery half-way by letting Flore take such care of him that she treated him more as a mother would a son; and he himself ended by clinging to her with the feeling of a child dependent on a mother's protection. But there were other ties between them not less tightly knotted. In the first place, Flore kept the house and managed all its business. Jean-Jacques left everything to the crab-girl so completely that life without her would have seemed to him not only difficult, but impossible. In every way, this woman had become the one need of his existence; she indulged all his fancies, for she knew them well. He loved to see her bright face always smiling at him,—the only face that had ever smiled upon him, the only one to which he could look for a smile. This happiness, a purely material happiness, expressed in the homely words which come readiest to the tongue in a Berrichon household, and visible on the fine countenance of the young woman, was like a reflection of his own inward content. The state into which Jean-Jacques was thrown when Flore's brightness was clouded over by some passing annoyance revealed to the girl her power over him, and, to make sure of it, she sometimes liked to use it. Using such power means, with women of her class, abusing it. The Rabouilleuse, no doubt, made her master play some of those scenes buried in the mysteries of private life, of which Otway gives a specimen in the tragedy of "Venice Preserved," where the scene between the senator and Aquilina is the realization of the magnificently horrible. Flore felt so secure of her power that, unfortunately for her, and for the bachelor himself, it did not occur to her to make him marry her.

Towards the close of 1815, Flore, who was then twenty-seven, had reached the perfect development of her beauty. Plump and fresh, and white as a Norman countrywoman, she was the ideal of what our ancestors used to call "a buxom housewife." Her beauty, always that of a handsome barmaid, though higher in type and better kept, gave her a likeness to Mademoiselle George in her palmy days, setting aside the latter's imperial dignity. Flore had the dazzling white round arms, the ample modelling, the satiny textures of the skin, the alluring though less rigidly correct outlines of the great actress. Her expression was one of sweetness and tenderness; but her glance commanded less respect than that of the noblest Agrippina that ever trod the French stage since the days of Racine: on the contrary, it evoked a vulgar joy. In 1816 the Rabouilleuse saw Maxence Gilet, and fell in love with him at first sight. Her heart was cleft by the mythological arrow,—admirable description of an effect of nature which the Greeks, unable to conceive the chivalric, ideal, and melancholy love begotten of Christianity, could represent in no other way. Flore was too handsome to be disdained, and Max accepted his conquest.

Thus, at twenty-eight years of age, the Rabouilleuse felt for the first time a true love, an idolatrous love, the love which includes all ways of loving,—that of Gulnare and that of Medora. As soon as the penniless officer found out the respective situations of Flore and Jean-Jacques Rouget, he saw something more desirable than an "amourette" in an intimacy with the Rabouilleuse. He asked nothing better for his future prosperity than to take up his abode at the Rouget's, recognizing perfectly the feeble nature of the old bachelor. Flore's passion necessarily affected the life and household affairs of her master. For a month the old man, now grown excessively timid, saw the laughing and kindly face of his mistress change to something terrible and gloomy and sullen. He was made to endure flashes of angry temper purposely displayed, precisely like a married man whose wife is meditating an infidelity. When, after some cruel rebuff, he nerved himself to ask Flore the reason of the change, her eyes were so full of hatred, and her voice so aggressive and contemptuous, that the poor creature quailed under them.

"Good heavens!" she cried; "you have neither heart nor soul! Here's sixteen years that I have spent my youth in this house, and I have only just found out that you have got a stone there (striking her breast). For two months you have seen before your eyes that brave captain, a victim of the Bourbons, who was cut out for a general, and is down in the depths of poverty, hunted into a hole of a place where there's no way to make a penny of money! He's forced to sit on a stool all day in the mayor's office to earn—what? Six hundred miserable francs,—a fine thing, indeed! And here are you, with six hundred and fifty-nine thousand well invested, and sixty thousand francs' income,—thanks to me, who never spend more than three thousand a year, everything included, even my own clothes, yes, everything!—and you never think of offering him a home here, though there's the second floor empty! You'd rather the rats and mice ran riot in it than put a human being there,—and he a lad your father always allowed to be his own son! Do you want to know what you are? I'll tell you,—a fratricide! And I know why, too. You see I take an interest in him, and that provokes you. Stupid as you seem, you have got more spite in you than the spitefullest of men. Well, yes! I do take an interest in him, and a keen one—"

"But, Flore—"

"'*But, Flore*', indeed! What's that got to do with it? You may go and find another Flore (if you can!), for I hope this glass of wine may poison me if I don't get away from your dungeon of a house. I haven't, God be thanked! cost you one penny during the twelve years I've been with you, and you have had the pleasure of my company into the bargain. I could have earned my own living anywhere with the work that I've done here,—washing, ironing, looking after the linen, going to market, cooking, taking care of your interests before everything, slaving myself to death from morning till night,—and this is my reward!"

"But, Flore—"

"Oh, yes, '*Flore*'! find another Flore, if you can, at your time of life, fifty-one years old, and getting feeble,—for the way your health is failing is frightful, I know that! and besides, you are none too amusing—"

"But, Flore—"

"Let me alone!"

She went out, slamming the door with a violence that echoed through the house, and seemed to shake it to its foundations. Jean-Jacques softly opened the door and went, still more softly, into the kitchen where she was muttering to herself.

"But, Flore," said the poor sheep, "this is the first time I have heard of this wish of yours; how do you know whether I will agree to it or not?"

"In the first place," she said, "there ought to be a man in the house. Everybody knows you have ten, fifteen, twenty thousand francs here; if they came to rob you we should both be murdered. For my part, I don't care to wake up some fine morning chopped in quarters, as happened to that poor servant-girl who was silly enough to defend her master. Well! if the robbers knew there was a man in the house as brave as Caesar and who wasn't born yesterday,— for Max could swallow three burglars as quick as a flash,—well, then I should sleep easy. People may tell you a lot of stuff,—that I love him, that I adore him,—and some say this and some say that! Do you know what you ought to say? You ought to answer that you know it; that your father told you on his deathbed to take care of his poor Max. That will stop people's tongues; for every stone in Issoudun can tell you he paid Max's schooling—and so! Here's nine years that I have eaten your bread—"

"Flore,—Flore!"

"—and many a one in this town has paid court to me, I can tell you! Gold chains here, and watches there,—what don't they offer me? 'My little Flore,' they say, 'why won't you leave that old fool of a Rouget,'—for that's what they call you. 'I leave him!' I always answer, 'a poor innocent like that? I think I see myself! what would become of him? No, no, where the kid is tethered, let her browse—'"

"Yes, Flore; I've none but you in this world, and you make me happy. If it will give you pleasure, my dear, well, we will have Maxence Gilet here; he can eat with us—"

"Heavens! I should hope so!"

"There, there! don't get angry—"

"Enough for one is enough for two," she answered laughing. "I'll tell you what you can do, my lamb, if you really mean to be kind; you must go and walk up and down near the Mayor's office at four o'clock, and manage to meet Monsieur Gilet and invite him to dinner. If he makes excuses, tell him it will give me pleasure; he is too polite to refuse. And after dinner, at dessert, if he tells you about his misfortunes, and the hulks and so forth—for you can easily get him to talk about all that—then you can make him the offer to come and live here. If he makes any objection, never mind, I shall know how to settle it."

Walking slowly along the boulevard Baron, the old celibate reflected, as much as he had the mind to reflect, over this incident. If he were to part from Flore (the mere thought confused him) where could he find another woman? Should he marry? At his age he should be married for his money, and a legitimate wife would use him far more cruelly than Flore. Besides, the thought of being deprived of her tenderness, even if it were a mere pretence, caused him horrible anguish. He was therefore as polite to Captain Gilet as he knew how to be. The invitation was given, as Flore had requested, before witnesses, to guard the hero's honor from all suspicion.

A reconciliation took place between Flore and her master; but from that day forth Jean-Jacques noticed many a trifle that betokened a total change in his mistress's affections. For two or three weeks Flore Brazier complained to the tradespeople in the markets, and to the women with whom she gossiped, about Monsieur Rouget's tyranny,—how he had taken it into his head to invite his self-styled natural brother to live with him. No one, however, was taken in by this comedy; and Flore was looked upon as a wonderfully clever and artful creature. Old Rouget really found himself very comfortable after Max became the master of his house; for he thus gained a companion who paid him many attentions, without, however, showing any servility. Gilet talked, discussed politics, and sometimes went to walk with Rouget. After Max was fairly installed, Flore did not choose to do the cooking; she said it spoiled her hands. At the request of the grand master of the Order of the Knights of Idleness, Mere Cognette produced one of her relatives, an old maid whose master, a curate, had lately died without leaving her anything,—an excellent cook, withal,—who declared she would devote herself for life or death to Max and Flore. In the name of the two powers, Mere Cognette promised her an annuity of three hundred francs a year at the end of ten years, if she served them loyally, honestly, and discreetly. The Vedie, as she was called, was noticeable for a face deeply pitted by the small-pox, and correspondingly ugly.

After the new cook had entered upon her duties, the Rabouilleuse took the title of Madame Brazier. She wore corsets; she had silk, or handsome woollen and cotton dresses, according to the season, expensive neckerchiefs, embroidered caps and collars, lace ruffles at her throat, boots instead of shoes, and, altogether, adopted a richness and elegance of apparel which renewed the youthfulness of her appearance. She was like a rough diamond, that needed cutting and mounting by a jeweller to bring out its full value. Her desire was to do honor to Max. At the end of the first year, in 1817, she brought a horse, styled English, from Bourges, for the poor cavalry captain, who was weary of going afoot. Max had picked up in the purlieus of Issoudun an old lancer of the Imperial Guard, a Pole named Kouski, now very poor, who asked nothing better than to quarter himself in Monsieur Rouget's house as the captain's servant. Max was Kouski's idol, especially after the duel with the three royalists. So, from 1817, the household of the old bachelor was made up of five persons, three of whom were masters, and the expenses advanced to about eight thousand francs a year.

CHAPTER X

At the time when Madame Bridau returned to Issoudun to save—as Maitre Desroches expressed it—an inheritance that was seriously threatened, Jean-Jacques Rouget had reached by degrees a condition that was semi-vegetative. In the first place, after Max's instalment, Flore put the table on an episcopal footing. Rouget, thrown in the way of good living, ate more and still more, enticed by the Vedie's excellent dishes. He grew no fatter, however, in spite of this abundant and luxurious nourishment. From day to day he weakened like a worn-out man,—

fatigued, perhaps, with the effort of digestion,—and his eyes had dark circles around them. Still, when his friends and neighbors met him in his walks and questioned him about his health, he always answered that he was never better in his life. As he had always been thought extremely deficient in mind, people did not notice the constant lowering of his faculties. His love for Flore was the one thing that kept him alive; in fact, he existed only for her, and his weakness in her presence was unbounded; he obeyed the creature's mere look, and watched her movements as a dog watches every gesture of his master. In short, as Madame Hochon remarked, at fifty-seven years of age he seemed older than Monsieur Hochon, an octogenarian.

Every one will suppose, and with reason, that Max's *appartement* was worthy of so charming a fellow. In fact, in the course of six years our captain had by degrees perfected the comfort of his abode and adorned every detail of it, as much for his own pleasure as for Flore's. But it was, after all, only the comfort and luxury of Issoudun,—colored tiles, rather elegant wallpapers, mahogany furniture, mirrors in gilt frames, muslin curtains with red borders, a bed with a canopy, and draperies arranged as the provincial upholsterers arrange them for a rich bride; which in the eyes of Issoudun seemed the height of luxury, but are so common in vulgar fashion-plates that even the petty shopkeepers in Paris have discarded them at their weddings. One very unusual thing appeared, which caused much talk in Issoudun, namely, a rush-matting on the stairs, no doubt to muffle the sound of feet. In fact, though Max was in the habit of coming in at daybreak, he never woke any one, and Rouget was far from suspecting that his guest was an accomplice in the nocturnal performances of the Knights of Idleness.

About eight o'clock the next morning, Flore, wearing a dressing-gown of some pretty cotton stuff with narrow pink stripes, a lace cap on her head, and her feet in furred slippers, softly opened the door of Max's chamber; seeing that he slept, she remained standing beside the bed.

"He came in so late!" she said to herself. "It was half-past three. He must have a good constitution to stand such amusements. Isn't he strong, the dear love! I wonder what they did last night."

"Oh, there you are, my little Flore!" said Max, waking like a soldier trained by the necessities of war to have his wits and his self-possession about him the instant that he waked, however suddenly it might happen.

"You are sleepy; I'll go away."

"No, stay; there's something serious going on."

"Were you up to some mischief last night?"

"Ah, bah! It concerns you and me and that old fool. You never told me he had a family! Well, his family are coming,—coming here,—no doubt to turn us out, neck and crop."

"Ah! I'll shake him well," said Flore.

"Mademoiselle Brazier," said Max gravely, "things are too serious for giddiness. Send me my coffee; I'll take it in bed, where I'll think over what we had better do. Come back at nine o'clock, and we'll talk about it. Meanwhile, behave as if you had heard nothing."

Frightened at the news, Flore left Max and went to make his coffee; but a quarter of an hour later, Baruch burst into Max's bedroom, crying out to the grand master,—

"Fario is hunting for his barrow!"

In five minutes Max was dressed and in the street, and though he sauntered along with apparent indifference, he soon reached the foot of the tower embankment, where he found quite a collection of people.

"What is it?" asked Max, making his way through the crowd and reaching the Spaniard.

Fario was a withered little man, as ugly as though he were a blue-blooded grandee. His fiery eyes, placed very close to his nose and piercing as a gimlet, would have won him the name of a sorcerer in Naples. He seemed gentle because he was calm, quiet, and slow in his movements; and for this reason people commonly called him "goodman Fario." But his skin— the color of gingerbread—and his softness of manner only hid from stupid eyes, and disclosed to observing ones, the half-Moorish nature of a peasant of Granada, which nothing had as yet roused from its phlegmatic indolence.

"Are you sure," Max said to him, after listening to his grievance, "that you brought your cart to this place? for, thank God, there are no thieves in Issoudun."

"I left it just there—"

"If the horse was harnessed to it, hasn't he drawn it somewhere."

"Here's the horse," said Fario, pointing to the animal, which stood harnessed thirty feet away.

Max went gravely up to the place where the horse stood, because from there the bottom of the tower at the top of the embankment could be seen,—the crowd being at the foot of the mound. Everybody followed Max, and that was what the scoundrel wanted.

62

"Has anybody thoughtlessly put a cart in his pocket?" cried Francois.

"Turn out your pockets, all of you!" said Baruch.

Shouts of laughter resounded on all sides. Fario swore. Oaths, with a Spaniard, denote the highest pitch of anger.

"Was your cart light?" asked Max.

"Light!" cried Fario. "If those who laugh at me had it on their feet, their corns would never hurt them again."

"Well, it must be devilishly light," answered Max, "for look there!" pointing to the foot of the tower; "it has flown up the embankment."

At these words all eyes were lifted to the spot, and for a moment there was a perfect uproar in the market-place. Each man pointed at the barrow bewitched, and all their tongues wagged.

"The devil makes common cause with the inn-keepers," said Goddet to the astonished Spaniard. "He means to teach you not to leave your cart about in the streets, but to put it in the tavern stables."

At this speech the crowd hooted, for Fario was thought to be a miser.

"Come, my good fellow," said Max, "don't lose heart. We'll go up to the tower and see how your barrow got there. Thunder and cannon! we'll lend you a hand! Come along, Baruch."

"As for you," he whispered to Francois, "get the people to stand back, and make sure there is nobody at the foot of the embankment when you see us at the top."

Fario, Max, Baruch, and three other knights climbed to the foot of the tower. During the rather perilous ascent Max and Fario noticed that no damage to the embankment, nor even trace of the passage of the barrow, could be seen. Fario began to imagine witchcraft, and lost his head. When they reached the top and examined into the matter, it really seemed a thing impossible that the cart had got there.

"How shall I ever get it down?" said the Spaniard, whose little eyes began for the first time to show fear; while his swarthy yellow face, which seemed as it if could never change color, whitened.

"How?" said Max. "Why, that's not difficult."

And taking advantage of the Spaniard's stupefaction, he raised the barrow by the shafts with his robust arms and prepared to fling it down, calling in thundering tones as it left his grasp, "Look out there, below!"

No accident happened, for the crowd, persuaded by Francois and eaten up with curiosity, had retired to a distance from which they could see more clearly what went on at the top of the embankment. The cart was dashed to an infinite number of pieces in a very picturesque manner.

"There! you have got it down," said Baruch.

"Ah, brigands! ah, scoundrels!" cried Fario; "perhaps it was you who brought it up here!"

Max, Baruch, and their three comrades began to laugh at the Spaniard's rage.

"I wanted to do you a service," said Max coolly, "and in handling the damned thing I came very near flinging myself after it; and this is how you thank me, is it? What country do you come from?"

"I come from a country where they never forgive," replied Fario, trembling with rage. "My cart will be the cab in which you shall drive to the devil!—unless," he said, suddenly becoming as meek as a lamb, "you will give me a new one."

"We will talk about that," said Max, beginning to descend.

When they reached the bottom and met the first hilarious group, Max took Fario by the button of his jacket and said to him,—

"Yes, my good Fario, I'll give you a magnificent cart, if you will give me two hundred and fifty francs; but I won't warrant it to go, like this one, up a tower."

At this last jest Fario became as cool as though he were making a bargain.

"Damn it!" he said, "give me the wherewithal to replace my barrow, and it will be the best use you ever made of old Rouget's money."

Max turned livid; he raised his formidable fist to strike Fario; but Baruch, who knew that the blow would descend on others besides the Spaniard, plucked the latter away like a feather and whispered to Max,—

"Don't commit such a folly!"

The grand master, thus called to order, began to laugh and said to Fario,—

"If I, by accident, broke your barrow, and you in return try to slander me, we are quits."

"Not yet," muttered Fario. "But I am glad to know what my barrow was worth."

"Ah, Max, you've found your match!" said a spectator of the scene, who did not belong to the Order of Idleness.

"Adieu, Monsieur Gilet. I haven't thanked you yet for lending me a hand," cried the Spaniard, as he kicked the sides of his horse and disappeared amid loud hurrahs.

"We will keep the tires of the wheels for you," shouted a wheelwright, who had come to inspect the damage done to the cart.

One of the shafts was sticking upright in the ground, as straight as a tree. Max stood by, pale and thoughtful, and deeply annoyed by Fario's speech. For five days after this, nothing was talked of in Issoudun but the tale of the Spaniard's barrow; it was even fated to travel abroad, as Goddet remarked,—for it went the round of Berry, where the speeches of Fario and Max were repeated, and at the end of a week the affair, greatly to the Spaniard's satisfaction, was still the talk of the three departments and the subject of endless gossip. In consequence of the vindictive Spaniard's terrible speech, Max and the Rabouilleuse became the object of certain comments which were merely whispered in Issoudun, though they were spoken aloud in Bourges, Vatan, Vierzon, and Chateauroux. Maxence Gilet knew enough of that region of the country to guess how envenomed such comments would become.

"We can't stop their tongues," he said at last. "Ah! I did a foolish thing!"

"Max!" said Francois, taking his arm. "They are coming to-night."

"They! Who!"

"The Bridaus. My grandmother has just had a letter from her goddaughter."

"Listen, my boy," said Max in a low voice. "I have been thinking deeply of this matter. Neither Flore nor I ought to seem opposed to the Bridaus. If these heirs are to be got rid of, it is for you Hochons to drive them out of Issoudun. Find out what sort of people they are. To-morrow at Mere Cognette's, after I've taken their measure, we can decide what is to be done, and how we can set your grandfather against them."

"The Spaniard found the flaw in Max's armor," said Baruch to his cousin Francois, as they turned into Monsieur Hochon's house and watched their comrade entering his own door.

While Max was thus employed, Flore, in spite of her friend's advice, was unable to restrain her wrath; and without knowing whether she would help or hinder Max's plans, she burst forth upon the poor bachelor. When Jean-Jacques incurred the anger of his mistress, the little attentions and vulgar fondlings which were all his joy were suddenly suppressed. Flore sent her master, as the children say, into disgrace. No more tender glances, no more of the caressing little words in various tones with which she decked her conversation,—"my kitten," "my old darling," "my bibi," "my rat," etc. A "you," cold and sharp and ironically respectful, cut like the blade of a knife through the heart of the miserable old bachelor. The "you" was a declaration of war. Instead of helping the poor man with his toilet, handing him what he wanted, forestalling his wishes, looking at him with the sort of admiration which all women know how to express, and which, in some cases, the coarser it is the better it pleases,—saying, for instance, "You look as fresh as a rose!" or, "What health you have!" "How handsome you are, my old Jean!"—in short, instead of entertaining him with the lively chatter and broad jokes in which he delighted, Flore left him to dress alone. If he called her, she answered from the foot of the staircase, "I can't do everything at once; how can I look after your breakfast and wait upon you up there? Are not you big enough to dress your own self?"

"Oh, dear! what have I done to displease her?" the old man asked himself that morning, as he got one of these rebuffs after calling for his shaving-water.

"Vedie, take up the hot water," cried Flore.

"Vedie!" exclaimed the poor man, stupefied with fear of the anger that was crushing him. "Vedie, what is the matter with Madame this morning?"

Flore Brazier required her master and Vedie and Kouski and Max to call her Madame.

"She seems to have heard something about you which isn't to your credit," answered Vedie, assuming an air of deep concern. "You are doing wrong, monsieur. I'm only a poor servant-woman, and you may say I have no right to poke my nose into your affairs; but I do say you may search through all the women in the world, like that king in holy Scripture, and you won't find the equal of Madame. You ought to kiss the ground she steps on. Goodness! if you make her unhappy, you'll only spoil your own life. There she is, poor thing, with her eyes full of tears."

Vedie left the poor man utterly cast down; he dropped into an armchair and gazed into vacancy like the melancholy imbecile that he was, and forgot to shave. These alternations of tenderness and severity worked upon this feeble creature whose only life was through his amorous fibre, the same morbid effect which great changes from tropical heat to arctic cold produce upon the human body. It was a moral pleurisy, which wore him out like a physical disease. Flore alone could thus affect him; for to her, and to her alone, he was as good as he was foolish.

"Well, haven't you shaved yet?" she said, appearing at his door.

Her sudden presence made the old man start violently; and from being pale and cast down he grew red for an instant, without, however, daring to complain of her treatment.

"Your breakfast is waiting," she added. "You can come down as you are, in dressing-gown and slippers; for you'll breakfast alone, I can tell you."

Without waiting for an answer, she disappeared. To make him breakfast alone was the punishment he dreaded most; he loved to talk to her as he ate his meals. When he got to the foot of the staircase he was taken with a fit of coughing; for emotion excited his catarrh.

"Cough away!" said Flore in the kitchen, without caring whether he heard her or not. "Confound the old wretch! he is able enough to get over it without bothering others. If he coughs up his soul, it will only be after—"

Such were the amenities the Rabouilleuse addressed to Rouget when she was angry. The poor man sat down in deep distress at a corner of the table in the middle of the room, and looked at his old furniture and the old pictures with a disconsolate air.

"You might at least have put on a cravat," said Flore. "Do you think it is pleasant for people to see such a neck as yours, which is redder and more wrinkled than a turkey's?"

"But what have I done?" he asked, lifting his big light-green eyes, full of tears, to his tormentor, and trying to face her hard countenance.

"What have you done?" she exclaimed. "As if you didn't know? Oh, what a hypocrite! Your sister Agathe—who is as much your sister as I am sister of the tower of Issoudun, if one's to believe your father, and who has no claim at all upon you—is coming here from Paris with her son, a miserable two-penny painter, to see you."

"My sister and my nephews coming to Issoudun!" he said, bewildered.

"Oh, yes! play the surprised, do; try to make me believe you didn't send for them! sewing your lies with white bread, indeed! Don't fash yourself; we won't trouble your Parisians—before they set their feet in this house, we shall have shaken the dust of it off ours. Max and I will be gone, never to return. As for your will, I'll tear it in quarters under your nose, and to your very beard—do you hear? Leave your property to your family, if you don't think we are your family; and then see if you'll be loved for yourself by a lot of people who have not seen you for thirty years,—who in fact have never seen you! Is it that sort of sister who can take my place? A pinchbeck saint!"

"If that's all, my little Flore," said the old man, "I won't receive my sister, or my nephews. I swear to you this is the first word I have heard of their coming. It is all got up by that Madame Hochon—a sanctimonious old—"

Max, who had overheard old Rouget's words, entered suddenly, and said in a masterful tone,—

"What's all this?"

"My good Max," said the old man, glad to get the protection of the soldier who, by agreement with Flore, always took his side in a dispute, "I swear by all that is most sacred, that I now hear this news for the first time. I have never written to my sister; my father made me promise not to leave her any of my property; to leave it to the Church sooner than to her. Well, I won't receive my sister Agathe to this house, or her sons—"

"Your father was wrong, my dear Jean-Jacques, and Madame Brazier is still more wrong," answered Max. "Your father no doubt had his reasons, but he is dead, and his hatred should die with him. Your sister is your sister, and your nephews are your nephews. You owe it to yourself to welcome them, and you owe it to us as well. What would people say in Issoudun? Thunder! I've got enough upon my shoulders as it is, without hearing people say that we shut you up and don't allow you a will of your own, or that we influence you against your relations and are trying to get hold of your property. The devil take me if I don't pull up stakes and be off, if that sort of calumny is to be flung at me! the other is bad enough! Let's eat our breakfast."

Flore, who was now as mild as a weasel, helped Vedie to set the table. Old Rouget, full of admiration for Max, took him by both hands and led him into the recess of a window, saying in a low voice:—

"Ah! Max, if I had a son, I couldn't love him better than I love you. Flore is right: you two are my real family. You are a man of honor, Max, and what you have just said is true."

"You ought to receive and entertain your sister and her son, but not change the arrangements you have made about your property," said Max. "In that way you will do what is right in the eyes of the world, and yet keep your promise to your father."

"Well! my dear loves!" cried Flore, gayly, "the salmi is getting cold. Come, my old rat, here's a wing for you," she said, smiling on Jean-Jacques.

At the words, the long-drawn face of the poor creature lost its cadaverous tints, the smile of a Theriaki flickered on his pendent lips; but he was seized with another fit of coughing; for the joy of being taken back to favor excited as violent an emotion as the punishment itself. Flore

65

rose, pulled a little cashmere shawl from her own shoulders, and tied it round the old man's throat, exclaiming: "How silly to put yourself in such a way about nothing. There, you old goose, that will do you good; it has been next my heart—"

"What a good creature!" said Rouget to Max, while Flore went to fetch a black velvet cap to cover the nearly bald head of the old bachelor.

"As good as she is beautiful"; answered Max, "but she is quick-tempered, like all people who carry their hearts in their hands."

The baldness of this sketch may displease some, who will think the flashes of Flore's character belong to the sort of realism which a painter ought to leave in shadow. Well! this scene, played again and again with shocking variations, is, in its coarse way and its horrible veracity, the type of such scenes played by women on whatever rung of the social ladder they are perched, when any interest, no matter what, draws them from their own line of obedience and induces them to grasp at power. In their eyes, as in those of politicians, all means to an end are justifiable. Between Flore Brazier and a duchess, between a duchess and the richest bourgeoise, between a bourgeoise and the most luxuriously kept mistress, there are no differences except those of the education they have received, and the surroundings in which they live. The pouting of a fine lady is the same thing as the violence of a Rabouilleuse. At all levels, bitter sayings, ironical jests, cold contempt, hypocritical complaints, false quarrels, win as much success as the low outbursts of this Madame Everard of Issoudun.

Max began to relate, with much humor, the tale of Fario and his barrow, which made the old man laugh. Vedie and Kouski, who came to listen, exploded in the kitchen, and as to Flore, she laughed convulsively. After breakfast, while Jean-Jacques read the newspapers (for they subscribed to the "Constitutionel" and the "Pandore"), Max carried Flore to his own quarters.

"Are you quite sure he has not made any other will since the one in which he left the property to you?"

"He hasn't anything to write with," she answered.

"He might have dictated it to some notary," said Max; "we must look out for that. Therefore it is well to be cordial to the Bridaus, and at the same time endeavor to turn those mortgages into money. The notaries will be only too glad to make the transfers; it is grist to their mill. The Funds are going up; we shall conquer Spain, and deliver Ferdinand VII. and the Cortez, and then they will be above par. You and I could make a good thing out of it by putting the old fellow's seven hundred and fifty thousand francs into the Funds at eighty-nine. Only you must try to get it done in your name; it will be so much secured anyhow."

"A capital idea!" said Flore.

"And as there will be an income of fifty thousand francs from eight hundred and ninety thousand, we must make him borrow one hundred and forty thousand francs for two years, to be paid back in two instalments. In two years, we shall get one hundred thousand francs *in* Paris, and ninety thousand here, and risk nothing."

"If it were not for you, my handsome Max, what would become of me now?" she said.

"Oh! to-morrow night at Mere Cognette's, after I have seen the Parisians, I shall find a way to make the Hochons themselves get rid of them."

"Ah! what a head you've got, my angel! You are a love of a man."

The place Saint-Jean is at the centre of a long street called at the upper end the rue Grand Narette, and at the lower the rue Petite Narette. The word "Narette" is used in Berry to express the same lay of the land as the Genoese word "salita" indicates,—that is to say, a steep street. The Grand Narette rises rapidly from the place Saint-Jean to the port Vilatte. The house of old Monsieur Hochon is exactly opposite that of Jean-Jacques Rouget. From the windows of the room where Madame Hochon usually sat, it was easy to see what went on at the Rouget household, and vice versa, when the curtains were drawn back or the doors were left open. The Hochon house was like the Rouget house, and the two were doubtless built by the same architect. Monsieur Hochon, formerly tax-collector at Selles in Berry, born, however, at Issoudun, had returned to his native place and married the sister of the sub-delegate, the gay Lousteau, exchanging his office at Selles for another of the same kind at Issoudun. Having retired before 1787, he escaped the dangers of the Revolution, to whose principles, however, he firmly adhered, like all other "honest men" who howl with the winners. Monsieur Hochon came honestly by the reputation of miser, but it would be mere repetition to sketch him here. A single specimen of the avarice which made him famous will suffice to make you see Monsieur Hochon as he was.

At the wedding of his daughter, now dead, who married a Borniche, it was necessary to give a dinner to the Borniche family. The bridegroom, who was heir to a large fortune, had suffered great mortification from having mismanaged his property, and still more because his father and mother refused to help him out. The old people, who were living at the time of the marriage, were delighted to see Monsieur Hochon step in as guardian,—for the purpose, of course, of making his daughter's dowry secure. On the day of the dinner, which was given to celebrate the signing of the marriage contract, the chief relations of the two families were assembled in the salon, the Hochons on one side, the Borniches on the other,—all in their best clothes. While the contract was being solemnly read aloud by young Heron, the notary, the cook came into the room and asked Monsieur Hochon for some twine to truss up the turkey,—an essential feature of the repast. The old man dove into the pocket of his surtout, pulled out an end of string which had evidently already served to tie up a parcel, and gave it to her; but before she could leave the room he called out, "Gritte, mind you give it back to me!" (Gritte is the abbreviation used in Berry for Marguerite.)

From year to year old Hochon grew more petty in his meanness, and more penurious; and at this time he was eighty-five years old. He belonged to the class of men who stop short in the street, in the middle of a lively dialogue, and stoop to pick up a pin, remarking, as they stick it in the sleeve of their coat, "There's the wife's stipend." He complained bitterly of the poor quality of the cloth manufactured now-a-days, and called attention to the fact that his coat had lasted only ten years. Tall, gaunt, thin, and sallow; saying little, reading little, and doing nothing to fatigue himself; as observant of forms as an oriental,—he enforced in his own house a discipline of strict abstemiousness, weighing and measuring out the food and drink of the family, which, indeed, was rather numerous, and consisted of his wife, nee Lousteau, his grandson Borniche with a sister Adolphine, the heirs of old Borniche, and lastly, his other grandson, Francois Hochon.

Hochon's eldest son was taken by the draft of 1813, which drew in the sons of well-to-do families who had escaped the regular conscription, and were now formed into a corps styled the "guards of honor." This heir-presumptive, who was killed at Hanau, had married early in life a rich woman, intending thereby to escape all conscriptions; but after he was enrolled, he wasted his substance, under a presentiment of his end. His wife, who followed the army at a distance, died at Strasburg in 1814, leaving debts which her father-in-law Hochon refused to pay,—answering the creditors with an axiom of ancient law, "Women are minors."

The house, though large, was scantily furnished; on the second floor, however, there were two rooms suitable for Madame Bridau and Joseph. Old Hochon now repented that he had kept them furnished with two beds, each bed accompanied by an old armchair of natural wood covered with needlework, and a walnut table, on which figured a water-pitcher of the wide-mouthed kind called "gueulard," standing in a basin with a blue border. The old man kept his winter store of apples and pears, medlars and quinces on heaps of straw in these rooms, where the rats and mice ran riot, so that they exhaled a mingled odor of fruit and vermin. Madame Hochon now directed that everything should be cleaned; the wall-paper, which had peeled off in places, was fastened up again with wafers; and she decorated the windows with little curtains which she pieced together from old hoards of her own. Her husband having refused to let her buy a strip of drugget, she laid down her own bedside carpet for her little Agathe,—"Poor little thing!" as she called the mother, who was now over forty-seven years old. Madame Hochon borrowed two night-tables from a neighbor, and boldly hired two chests of drawers with brass handles from a dealer in second-hand furniture who lived next to Mere Cognette. She herself had preserved two pairs of candlesticks, carved in choice woods by her own father, who had the "turning" mania. From 1770 to 1780 it was the fashion among rich people to learn a trade, and Monsieur Lousteau, the father, was a turner, just as Louis XVI. was a locksmith. These candlesticks were ornamented with circlets made of the roots of rose, peach, and apricot trees. Madame Hochon actually risked the use of her precious relics! These preparations and this sacrifice increased old Hochon's anxiety; up to this time he had not believed in the arrival of the Bridaus.

The morning of the day that was celebrated by the trick on Fario, Madame Hochon said to her husband after breakfast:—

"I hope, Hochon, that you will receive my goddaughter, Madame Bridau, properly." Then, after making sure that her grandchildren were out of hearing, she added: "I am mistress of my own property; don't oblige me to make up to Agathe in my will for any incivility on your part."

"Do you think, madame," answered Hochon, in a mild voice, "that, at my age, I don't know the forms of decent civility?"

"You know very well what I mean, you crafty old thing! Be friendly to our guests, and remember that I love Agathe."

"And you love Maxence Gilet also, who is getting the property away from your dear Agathe! Ah! you've warmed a viper in your bosom there; but after all, the Rouget money is bound to go to a Lousteau."

After making this allusion to the supposed parentage and both Max and Agathe, Hochon turned to leave the room; but old Madame Hochon, a woman still erect and spare, wearing a round cap with ribbon knots and her hair powdered, a taffet petticoat of changeable colors like a pigeon's breast, tight sleeves, and her feet in high-heeled slippers, deposited her snuff-box on a little table, and said:—

"Really, Monsieur Hochon, how can a man of your sense repeat absurdities which, unhappily, cost my poor friend her peace of mind, and Agathe the property which she ought to have had from her father. Max Gilet is not the son of my brother, whom I often advised to save the money he paid for him. You know as well as I do that Madame Rouget was virtue itself—"

"And the daughter takes after her; for she strikes me as uncommonly stupid. After losing all her fortune, she brings her sons up so well that here is one in prison and likely to be brought up on a criminal indictment before the Court of Peers for a conspiracy worthy of Berton. As for the other, he is worse off; he's a painter. If your proteges are to stay here till they have extricated that fool of a Rouget from the claws of Gilet and the Rabouilleuse, we shall eat a good deal more than half a measure of salt with them."

"That's enough, Monsieur Hochon; you had better wish they may not have two strings to their bow."

Monsieur Hochon took his hat, and his cane with an ivory knob, and went away petrified by that terrible speech; for he had no idea that his wife could show such resolution. Madame Hochon took her prayer-book to read the service, for her advanced age prevented her from going daily to church; it was only with difficulty that she got there on Sundays and holidays. Since receiving her goddaughter's letter she had added a petition to her usual prayers, supplicating God to open the eyes of Jean-Jacques Rouget, and to bless Agathe and prosper the expedition into which she herself had drawn her. Concealing the fact from her grandchildren, whom she accused of being "parpaillots," she had asked the curate to say a mass for Agathe's success during a neuvaine which was being held by her granddaughter, Adolphine Borniche, who thus made her prayers in church by proxy.

Adolphine, then eighteen,—who for the last seven years had sewed at the side of her grandmother in that cold household of monotonous and methodical customs,—had undertaken her neuvaine all the more willingly because she hoped to inspire some feeling in Joseph Bridau, in whom she took the deepest interest because of the monstrosities which her grandfather attributed in her hearing to the young Parisian.

All the old people and sensible people of the town, and the fathers of families approved of Madame Hochon's conduct in receiving her goddaughter; and their good wishes for the latter's success were in proportion to the secret contempt with which the conduct of Maxence Gilet had long inspired them. Thus the news of the arrival of Rouget's sister and nephew raised two parties in Issoudun,—that of the higher and older bourgeoisie, who contented themselves with offering good wishes and in watching events without assisting them, and that of the Knights of Idleness and the partisans of Max, who, unfortunately, were capable of committing many high-handed outrages against the Parisians.

CHAPTER XI

Agathe and Joseph arrived at the coach-office of the Messageries-Royales in the place Misere at three o'clock. Though tired with the journey, Madame Bridau felt her youth revive at sight of her native land, where at every step she came upon memories and impressions of her girlish days. In the then condition of public opinion in Issoudun, the arrival of the Parisians was known all over the town in ten minutes. Madame Hochon came out upon her doorstep to welcome her godchild, and kissed her as though she were really a daughter. After seventy-two years of a barren and monotonous existence, exhibiting in their retrospect the graves of her three children, all unhappy in their lives, and all dead, she had come to feel a sort of fictitious motherhood for the young girl whom she had, as she expressed it, carried in her pouch for sixteen years. Through the gloom of provincial life the old woman had cherished this early friendship, this girlish memory, as closely as if Agathe had remained near her, and she had also taken the deepest interest in Bridau. Agathe was led in triumph to the salon where Monsieur Hochon was stationed, chilling as a tepid oven.

"Here is Monsieur Hochon; how does he seem to you?" asked his wife.

"Precisely the same as when I last saw him," said the Parisian woman.

"Ah! it is easy to see you come from Paris; you are so complimentary," remarked the old man.

The presentations took place: first, young Baruch Borniche, a tall youth of twenty-two; then Francois Hochon, twenty-four; and lastly little Adolphine, who blushed and did not know what to do with her arms; she was anxious not to seem to be looking at Joseph Bridau, who in his turn was narrowly observed, though from different points of view, by the two young men and by old Hochon. The miser was saying to himself, "He is just out of the hospital; he will be as hungry as a convalescent." The young men were saying, "What a head! what a brigand! we shall have our hands full!"

"This is my son, the painter; my good Joseph," said Agathe at last, presenting the artist.

There was an effort in the accent that she put upon the word "good," which revealed the mother's heart, whose thoughts were really in the prison of the Luxembourg.

"He looks ill," said Madame Hochon; "he is not at all like you."

"No, madame," said Joseph, with the brusque candor of an artist; "I am like my father, and very ugly at that."

Madame Hochon pressed Agathe's hand which she was holding, and glanced at her as much as to say, "Ah! my child; I understand now why you prefer your good-for-nothing Philippe."

"I never saw your father, my dear boy," she said aloud; "it is enough to make me love you that you are your mother's son. Besides, you have talent, so the late Madame Descoings used to write to me; she was the only one of late years who told me much about you."

"Talent!" exclaimed the artist, "not as yet; but with time and patience I may win fame and fortune."

"By painting?" said Monsieur Hochon ironically.

"Come, Adolphine," said Madame Hochon, "go and see about dinner."

"Mother," said Joseph, "I will attend to the trunks which they are bringing in."

"Hochon," said the grandmother to Francois, "show the rooms to Monsieur Bridau."

As the dinner was to be served at four o'clock and it was now only half past three, Baruch rushed into the town to tell the news of the Bridau arrival, describe Agathe's dress, and more particularly to picture Joseph, whose haggard, unhealthy, and determined face was not unlike the ideal of a brigand. That evening Joseph was the topic of conversation in all the households of Issoudun.

"That sister of Rouget must have seen a monkey before her son was born," said one; "he is the image of a baboon."

"He has the face of a brigand and the eyes of a basilisk."

"All artists are like that."

"They are as wicked as the red ass, and as spiteful as monkeys."

"It is part of their business."

"I have just seen Monsieur Beaussier, and he says he would not like to meet him in a dark wood; he saw him in the diligence."

"He has got hollows over the eyes like a horse, and he laughs like a maniac."

"The fellow looks as though he were capable of anything; perhaps it's his fault that his brother, a fine handsome man they tell me, has gone to the bad. Poor Madame Bridau doesn't seem as if she were very happy with him."

"Suppose we take advantage of his being here, and have our portraits painted?"

The result of all these observations, scattered through the town was, naturally, to excite curiosity. All those who had the right to visit the Hochons resolved to call that very night and examine the Parisians. The arrival of these two persons in the stagnant town was like the falling of a beam into a community of frogs.

After stowing his mother's things and his own into the two attic chambers, which he examined as he did so, Joseph took note of the silent house, where the walls, the stair-case, the wood-work, were devoid of decoration and humid with frost, and where there was literally nothing beyond the merest necessaries. He felt the brusque transition from his poetic Paris to the dumb and arid province; and when, coming downstairs, he chanced to see Monsieur Hochon cutting slices of bread for each person, he understood, for the first time in his life, Moliere's Harpagon.

"We should have done better to go to an inn," he said to himself.

The aspect of the dinner confirmed his apprehensions. After a soup whose watery clearness showed that quantity was more considered than quality, the bouilli was served, ceremoniously garnished with parsley; the vegetables, in a dish by themselves, being counted into the items of the repast. The bouilli held the place of honor in the middle of the table, accompanied with three other dishes: hard-boiled eggs on sorrel opposite to the vegetables; then a salad dressed with nut-oil to face little cups of custard, whose flavoring of burnt oats did service as vanilla, which it resembles much as coffee made of chiccory resembles mocha. Butter and radishes, in two plates, were at each end of the table; pickled gherkins and horse-radish completed the spread, which won Madam Hochon's approbation. The good old woman gave a contented little nod when she saw that her husband had done things properly, for the first day at least. The old man answered with a glance and a shrug of his shoulders, which it was easy to translate into—

"See the extravagances you force me to commit!"

As soon as Monsieur Hochon had, as it were, slivered the bouilli into slices, about as thick as the sole of a dancing-shoe, that dish was replaced by another, containing three pigeons. The wine was of the country, vintage 1811. On a hint from her grandmother, Adolphine had decorated each end of the table with a bunch of flowers.

"At Rome as the Romans do," thought the artist, looking at the table, and beginning to eat,—like a man who had breakfasted at Vierzon, at six o'clock in the morning, on an execrable cup of coffee. When Joseph had eaten up all his bread and asked for more, Monsieur Hochon rose, slowly searched in the pocket of his surtout for a key, unlocked a cupboard behind him, broke off a section of a twelve-pound loaf, carefully cut a round of it, then divided the round in two, laid the pieces on a plate, and passed the plate across the table to the young painter, with the silence and coolness of an old soldier who says to himself on the eve of battle, "Well, I can meet death." Joseph took the half-slice, and fully understood that he was not to ask for any more. No member of the family was the least surprised at this extraordinary performance. The conversation went on. Agathe learned that the house in which she was born, her father's house before he inherited that of the old Descoings, had been bought by the Borniches; she expressed a wish to see it once more.

"No doubt," said her godmother, "the Borniches will be here this evening; we shall have half the town—who want to examine you," she added, turning to Joseph, "and they will all invite you to their houses."

Gritte, who in spite of her sixty years, was the only servant of the house, brought in for dessert the famous ripe cheese of Touraine and Berry, made of goat's milk, whose mouldy discolorations so distinctly reproduce the pattern of the vine-leaves on which it is served, that Touraine ought to have invented the art of engraving. On either side of these little cheeses Gritte, with a company air, placed nuts and some time-honored biscuits.

"Well, Gritte, the fruit?" said Madame Hochon.

"But, madame, there is none rotten," answered Gritte.

Joseph went off into roars of laughter, as though he were among his comrades in the atelier; for he suddenly perceived that the parsimony of eating only the fruits which were beginning to rot had degenerated into a settled habit.

"Bah! we can eat them all the same," he exclaimed, with the heedless gayety of a man who will have his say.

"Monsieur Hochon, pray get some," said the old lady.

Monsieur Hochon, much incensed at the artist's speech, fetched some peaches, pears, and Saint Catherine plums.

"Adolphine, go and gather some grapes," said Madame Hochon to her granddaughter.

Joseph looked at the two young men as much as to say: "Is it to such high living as this that you owe your healthy faces?"

Baruch understood the keen glance and smiled; for he and his cousin Hochon were behaving with much discretion. The home-life was of less importance to youths who supped three times the week at Mere Cognette's. Moreover, just before dinner, Baruch had received notice that the grand master convoked the whole Order at midnight for a magnificent supper, in the course of which a great enterprise would be arranged. The feast of welcome given by old Hochon to his guests explains the more necessary were the nocturnal repasts at the Cognette's to two young fellows blessed with good appetites, who, we may add, never missed any of them.

"We will take the liqueur in the salon," said Madame Hochon, rising and motioning to Joseph to give her his arm. As they went out before the others, she whispered to the painter:—

"Eh! my poor boy; this dinner won't give you an indigestion; but I had hard work to get it for you. It is always Lent here; you will get enough just to keep life in you, and no more. So you must bear it patiently."

The kind-heartedness of the old woman, who thus drew her own predicament, pleased the artist.

"I have lived fifty years with that man, without ever hearing half-a-dozen gold pieces chink in my purse," she went on. "Oh! if I did not hope that you might save your property, I would never have brought you and your mother into my prison."

"But how can you survive it?" cried Joseph naively, with the gayety which a French artist never loses.

"Ah, you may well ask!" she said. "I pray."

Joseph quivered as he heard the words, which raised the old woman so much in his estimation that he stepped back a little way to look into her face; it was radiant with so tender a serenity that he said to her,—

"Let me paint your portrait."

"No, no," she answered, "I am too weary of life to wish to remain here on canvas."

Gayly uttering the sad words, she opened a closet, and brought out a flask containing ratafia, a domestic manufacture of her own, the receipt for which she obtained from the far-famed nuns to whom is also due the celebrated cake of Issoudun,—one of the great creations of French confectionery; which no chef, cook, pastry-cook, or confectioner has ever been able to reproduce. Monsieur de Riviere, ambassador at Constantinople, ordered enormous quantities every year for the Seraglio.

Adolphine held a lacquer tray on which were a number of little old glasses with engraved sides and gilt edges; and as her mother filled each of them, she carried it to the company.

"It seems as though my father's turn were coming round!" exclaimed Agathe, to whom this immutable provincial custom recalled the scenes of her youth.

"Hochon will go to his club presently to read the papers, and we shall have a little time to ourselves," said the old lady in a low voice.

In fact, ten minutes later, the three women and Joseph were alone in the salon, where the floor was never waxed, only swept, and the worsted-work designs in oaken frames with grooved mouldings, and all the other plain and rather dismal furniture seemed to Madame Bridau to be in exactly the same state as when she had left Issoudun. Monarchy, Revolution, Empire, and Restoration, which respected little, had certainly respected this room where their glories and their disasters had left not the slightest trace.

"Ah! my godmother, in comparison with your life, mine has been cruelly tried," exclaimed Madame Bridau, surprised to find even a canary which she had known when alive, stuffed, and standing on the mantleshelf between the old clock, the old brass brackets, and the silver candlesticks.

"My child," said the old lady, "trials are in the heart. The greater and more necessary the resignation, the harder the struggle with our own selves. But don't speak of me, let us talk of your affairs. You are directly in front of the enemy," she added, pointing to the windows of the Rouget house.

"They are sitting down to dinner," said Adolphine.

The young girl, destined for a cloister, was constantly looking out of the window, in hopes of getting some light upon the enormities imputed to Maxence Gilet, the Rabouilleuse, and Jean-Jacques, of which a few words reached her ears whenever she was sent out of the room that others might talk about them. The old lady now told her granddaughter to leave her alone with Madame Bridau and Joseph until the arrival of visitors.

"For," she said, turning to the Parisians, "I know my Issoudun by heart; we shall have ten or twelve batches of inquisitive folk here to-night."

In fact Madame Hochon had hardly related the events and the details concerning the astounding influence obtained by Maxence Gilet and the Rabouilleuse over Jean-Jacques Rouget (without, of course, following the synthetical method with which they have been presented here), adding the many comments, descriptions, and hypotheses with which the good and evil tongues of the town embroidered them, before Adolphine announced the approach of the Borniche, Beaussier, Lousteau-Prangin, Fichet, Goddet-Herau families; in all, fourteen persons looming in the distance.

"You now see, my dear child," said the old lady, concluding her tale, "that it will not be an easy matter to get this property out of the jaws of the wolf—"

"It seems to me so difficult—with a scoundrel such as you represent him, and a daring woman like that crab-girl—as to be actually impossible," remarked Joseph. "We should have to stay a year in Issoudun to counteract their influence and overthrow their dominion over my uncle. Money isn't worth such a struggle,—not to speak of the meannesses to which we should have to condescend. My mother has only two weeks' leave of absence; her place is a permanent one, and she must not risk it. As for me, in the month of October I have an important work, which Schinner has just obtained for me from a peer of France; so you see, madame, my future fortune is in my brushes."

This speech was received by Madame Hochon with much amazement. Though relatively superior to the town she lived in, the old lady did not believe in painting. She glanced at her goddaughter, and again pressed her hand.

"This Maxence is the second volume of Philippe," whispered Joseph in his mother's ear, "—only cleverer and better behaved. Well, madame," he said, aloud, "we won't trouble Monsieur Hochon by staying very long."

"Ah! you are young; you know nothing of the world," said the old lady. "A couple of weeks, if you are judicious, may produce great results; listen to my advice, and act accordingly."

"Oh! willingly," said Joseph, "I know I have a perfectly amazing incapacity for domestic statesmanship: for example, I am sure I don't know what Desroches himself would tell us to do if my uncle declines to see us."

Mesdames Borniche, Goddet-Herau, Beaussier, Lousteau-Prangin and Fichet, decorated with their husbands, here entered the room.

When the fourteen persons were seated, and the usual compliments were over, Madame Hochon presented her goddaughter Agathe and Joseph. Joseph sat in his armchair all the evening, engaged in slyly studying the sixty faces which, from five o'clock until half past nine, posed for him gratis, as he afterwards told his mother. Such behavior before the aristocracy of Issoudun did not tend to change the opinion of the little town concerning him: every one went home ruffled by his sarcastic glances, uneasy under his smiles, and even frightened at his face, which seemed sinister to a class of people unable to recognize the singularities of genius.

After ten o'clock, when the household was in bed, Madame Hochon kept her goddaughter in her chamber until midnight. Secure from interruption, the two women told each other the sorrows of their lives, and exchanged their sufferings. As Agathe listened to the last echoes of a soul that had missed its destiny, and felt the sufferings of a heart, essentially generous and charitable, whose charity and generosity could never be exercised, she realized the immensity of the desert in which the powers of this noble, unrecognized soul had been wasted, and knew that she herself, with the little joys and interests of her city life relieving the bitter trials sent from God, was not the most unhappy of the two.

"You who are so pious," she said, "explain to me my shortcomings; tell me what it is that God is punishing in me."

"He is preparing us, my child," answered the old woman, "for the striking of the last hour."

At midnight the Knights of Idleness were collecting, one by one like shadows, under the trees of the boulevard Baron, and speaking together in whispers.

"What are we going to do?" was the first question of each as he arrived.

"I think," said Francois, "that Max means merely to give us a supper."

"No; matters are very serious for him, and for the Rabouilleuse: no doubt, he has concocted some scheme against the Parisians."

"It would be a good joke to drive them away."

"My grandfather," said Baruch, "is terribly alarmed at having two extra mouths to feed, and he'd seize on any pretext—"

"Well, comrades!" cried Max softly, now appearing on the scene, "why are you star-gazing? the planets don't distil kirschwasser. Come, let us go to Mere Cognette's!"

"To Mere Cognette's! To Mere Cognette's!" they all cried.

The cry, uttered as with one voice, produced a clamor which rang through the town like the hurrah of troops rushing to an assault; total silence followed. The next day, more than one inhabitant must have said to his neighbor: "Did you hear those frightful cries last night, about one o'clock? I thought there was surely a fire somewhere."

A supper worthy of La Cognette brightened the faces of the twenty-two guests; for the whole Order was present. At two in the morning, as they were beginning to "siroter" (a word in the vocabulary of the Knights which admirably expresses the act of sipping and tasting the wine in small quantities), Max rose to speak:—

"My dear fellows! the honor of your grand master was grossly attacked this morning, after our memorable joke with Fario's cart,—attacked by a vile peddler, and what is more, a Spaniard (oh, Cabrera!); and I have resolved to make the scoundrel feel the weight of my vengeance; always, of course, within the limits we have laid down for our fun. After reflecting about it all day, I have found a trick which is worth putting into execution,—a famous trick, that will drive him crazy. While avenging the insult offered to the Order in my person, we shall be feeding the sacred animals of the Egyptians,—little beasts which are, after all, the creatures of God, and which man unjustly persecutes. Thus we see that good is the child of evil, and evil is the offspring of good; such is the paramount law of the universe! I now order you all, on pain of displeasing your very humble grand master, to procure clandestinely, each one of you, twenty rats, male or female as heaven pleases. Collect your contingent within three days. If you can get more, the surplus will be welcome. Keep the interesting rodents without food; for it is essential that the delightful little beasts be ravenous with hunger. Please observe that I will accept both house-mice and field-mice as rats. If we multiply twenty-two by twenty, we shall have four hundred; four hundred accomplices let loose in the old church of the Capuchins, where Fario has stored all his grain, will consume a not insignificant quantity! But be lively about it! There's no time to lose.

Fario is to deliver most of the grain to his customers in a week or so; and I am determined that that Spaniard shall find a terrible deficit. Gentlemen, I have not the merit of this invention," continued Max, observing the signs of general admiration. "Render to Caesar that which is Caesar's, and to God that which is God's. My scheme is only a reproduction of Samson's foxes, as related in the Bible. But Samson was an incendiary, and therefore no philanthropist; while we, like the Brahmins, are the protectors of a persecuted race. Mademoiselle Flore Brazier has already set all her mouse-traps, and Kouski, my right-arm, is hunting field-mice. I have spoken."

"I know," said Goddet, "where to find an animal that's worth forty rats, himself alone."

"What's that?"

"A squirrel."

"I offer a little monkey," said one of the younger members, "he'll make himself drunk on wheat."

"Bad, very bad!" exclaimed Max, "it would show who put the beasts there."

"But we might each catch a pigeon some night," said young Beaussier, "taking them from different farms; if we put them through a hole in the roof, they'll attract thousands of others."

"So, then, for the next week, Fario's storehouse is the order of the night," cried Max, smiling at Beaussier. "Recollect; people get up early in Saint-Paterne. Mind, too, that none of you go there without turning the soles of your list shoes backward. Knight Beaussier, the inventor of pigeons, is made director. As for me, I shall take care to leave my imprint on the sacks of wheat. Gentlemen, you are, all of you, appointed to the commissariat of the Army of Rats. If you find a watchman sleeping in the church, you must manage to make him drunk,—and do it cleverly,—so as to get him far away from the scene of the Rodents' Orgy."

"You don't say anything about the Parisians?" questioned Goddet.

"Oh!" exclaimed Max, "I want time to study them. Meantime, I offer my best shotgun— the one the Emperor gave me, a treasure from the manufactory at Versailles—to whoever finds a way to play the Bridaus a trick which shall get them into difficulties with Madame and Monsieur Hochon, so that those worthy old people shall send them off, or they shall be forced to go of their own accord,—without, understand me, injuring the venerable ancestors of my two friends here present, Baruch and Francois."

"All right! I'll think of it," said Goddet, who coveted the gun.

"If the inventor of the trick doesn't care for the gun, he shall have my horse," added Max.

After this night twenty brains were tortured to lay a plot against Agathe and her son, on the basis of Max's programme. But the devil alone, or chance, could really help them to success; for the conditions given made the thing well-nigh impossible.

The next morning Agathe and Joseph came downstairs just before the second breakfast, which took place at ten o'clock. In Monsieur Hochon's household the name of first breakfast was given to a cup of milk and slice of bread and butter which was taken in bed, or when rising. While waiting for Madame Hochon, who notwithstanding her age went minutely through the ceremonies with which the duchesses of Louis XV.'s time performed their toilette, Joseph noticed Jean-Jacques Rouget planted squarely on his feet at the door of his house across the street. He naturally pointed him out to his mother, who was unable to recognize her brother, so little did he look like what he was when she left him.

"That is your brother," said Adolphine, who entered, giving an arm to her grandmother.

"What an idiot he looks like!" exclaimed Joseph.

Agathe clasped her hands, and raised her eyes to heaven.

"What a state they have driven him to! Good God! can that be a man only fifty-seven years old?"

She looked attentively at her brother, and saw Flore Brazier standing directly behind him, with her hair dressed, a pair of snowy shoulders and a dazzling bosom showing through a gauze neckerchief, which was trimmed with lace; she was wearing a dress with a tight-fitting waist, made of grenadine (a silk material then much in fashion), with leg-of-mutton sleeves so-called, fastened at the wrists by handsome bracelets. A gold chain rippled over the crab-girl's bosom as she leaned forward to give Jean-Jacques his black silk cap lest he should take cold. The scene was evidently studied.

"Hey!" cried Joseph, "there's a fine woman, and a rare one! She is made, as they say, to paint. What flesh-tints! Oh, the lovely tones! what surface! what curves! Ah, those shoulders! She's a magnificent caryatide. What a model she would have been for one of Titians' Venuses!"

Adolphine and Madame Hochon thought he was talking Greek; but Agathe signed to them behind his back, as if to say that she was accustomed to such jargon.

"So you think a creature who is depriving you of your property handsome?" said Madame Hochon.

"That doesn't prevent her from being a splendid model!—just plump enough not to spoil the hips and the general contour—"

"My son, you are not in your studio," said Agathe. "Adolphine is here."

"Ah, true! I did wrong. But you must remember that ever since leaving Paris I have seen nothing but ugly women—"

"My dear godmother," said Agathe hastily, "how shall I be able to meet my brother, if that creature is always with him?"

"Bah!" said Joseph. "I'll go and see him myself. I don't think him such an idiot, now I find he has the sense to rejoice his eyes with a Titian's Venus."

"If he were not an idiot," said Monsieur Hochon, who had come in, "he would have married long ago and had children; and then you would have no chance at the property. It is an ill wind that blows no good."

"Your son's idea is very good," said Madame Hochon; "he ought to pay the first visit. He can make his uncle understand that if you call there he must be alone."

"That will affront Mademoiselle Brazier," said old Hochon. "No, no, madame; swallow the pill. If you can't get the whole property, secure a small legacy."

The Hochons were not clever enough to match Max. In the middle of breakfast Kouski brought over a letter from Monsieur Rouget, addressed to his sister, Madame Bridau. Madame Hochon made her husband read it aloud, as follows:—

My dear Sister,—I learn from strangers of your arrival in   Issoudun. I can guess the reason which made you prefer the house   of Monsieur and Madame Hochon to mine; but if you will come to see   me you shall be received as you ought to be. I should certainly   pay you the first visit if my health did not compel me just now to keep the house; for which I offer my affectionate regrets. I shall   be delighted to see my nephew, whom I invite to dine with me   to-morrow,—young men are less sensitive than women about the   company. It will give me pleasure if Messrs. Baruch Borniche and   Francois Hochon will accompany him.   Your affectionate brother,   J.-J. Rouget.

"Say that we are at breakfast, but that Madame Bridau will send an answer presently, and the invitations are all accepted," said Monsieur Hochon to the servant.

The old man laid a finger on his lips, to require silence from everybody. When the street-door was shut, Monsieur Hochon, little suspecting the intimacy between his grandsons and Max, threw one of his slyest looks at his wife and Agathe, remarking,—

"He is just as capable of writing that note as I am of giving away twenty-five louis; it is the soldier who is corresponding with us!"

"What does that portend?" asked Madame Hochon. "Well, never mind; we will answer him. As for you, monsieur," she added, turning to Joseph, "you must dine there; but if—"

The old lady was stopped short by a look from her husband. Knowing how warm a friendship she felt for Agathe, old Hochon was in dread lest she should leave some legacy to her goddaughter in case the latter lost the Rouget property. Though fifteen years older than his wife, the miser hoped to inherit her fortune, and to become eventually the sole master of their whole property. That hope was a fixed idea with him. Madame Hochon knew that the best means of obtaining a few concessions from her husband was to threaten him with her will. Monsieur Hochon now took sides with his guests. An enormous fortune was at stake; with a sense of social justice, he wished it to go to the natural heirs, instead of being pillaged by unworthy outsiders. Moreover, the sooner the matter was decided, the sooner he should get rid of his guests. Now that the struggle between the interlopers and the heirs, hitherto existing only in his wife's mind, had become an actual fact, Monsieur Hochon's keen intelligence, lulled to sleep by the monotony of provincial life, was fully roused. Madame Hochon had been agreeably surprised that morning to perceive, from a few affectionate words which the old man had said to her about Agathe, that so able and subtle an auxiliary was on the Bridau side.

Towards midday the brains of Monsieur and Madame Hochon, of Agathe, and Joseph (the latter much amazed at the scrupulous care of the old people in the choice of words), were delivered of the following answer, concocted solely for the benefit of Max and Flore:—

My dear Brother,—If I have stayed away from Issoudun, and kept up   no intercourse with any one, not even with you, the fault lies not   merely with the strange and false ideas my father conceived about   me, but with the joys and sorrows of my life in Paris; for if God   made me a happy wife, he has also deeply afflicted me as a mother.   You are aware that my son, your nephew Philippe, lies under   accusation of a capital offence in consequence of his devotion to   the Emperor. Therefore you can hardly be surprised if a widow,   compelled to take a humble situation in a lottery-office for a   living, should come to seek consolation from those among whom she was born.   The profession adopted by the son who accompanies me is one that   requires great talent, many sacrifices, and prolonged studies   before any results can be obtained. Glory for an artist precedes   fortune; is not that to say that Joseph, though he may bring honor   to the family, will still be poor? Your sister, my dear Jean-Jacques, would have borne in silence the penalties of paternal   injustice, but you will pardon a mother for reminding you that you have two nephews; one of whom carried the Emperor's orders at the battle of Montereau and served in the Guard at Waterloo, and is now in prison for his devotion to Napoleon; the other, from his thirteenth year, has been impelled by natural gifts to enter a difficult though glorious career. I thank you for your letter, my dear brother, with heart-felt warmth, for my own sake, and also for Joseph's, who will certainly accept your invitation. Illness excuses everything, my dear Jean-Jacques, and I shall therefore go to see you in your own house. A sister is always at home with a brother, no matter what may be the life he has adopted. I embrace you tenderly. Agathe Rouget

"There's the matter started. Now, when you see him," said Monsieur Hochon to Agathe, "you must speak plainly to him about his nephews."

The letter was carried over by Gritte, who returned ten minutes later to render an account to her masters of all that she had seen and heard, according to a settled provincial custom.

"Since yesterday Madame has had the whole house cleaned up, which she left—"

"Whom do you mean by Madame?" asked old Hochon.

"That's what they call the Rabouilleuse over there," answered Gritte. "She left the salon and all Monsieur Rouget's part of the house in a pitiable state; but since yesterday the rooms have been made to look like what they were before Monsieur Maxence went to live there. You can see your face on the floors. La Vedie told me that Kouski went off on horseback at five o'clock this morning, and came back at nine, bringing provisions. It is going to be a grand dinner!—a dinner fit for the archbishop of Bourges! There's a fine bustle in the kitchen, and they are as busy as bees. The old man says, 'I want to do honor to my nephew,' and he pokes his nose into everything. It appears *the Rougets* are highly flattered by the letter. Madame came and told me so. Oh! she had on such a dress! I never saw anything so handsome in my life. Two diamonds in her ears!—two diamonds that cost, Vedie told me, three thousand francs apiece; and such lace! rings on her fingers, and bracelets! you'd think she was a shrine; and a silk dress as fine as an altar-cloth. So then she said to me, 'Monsieur is delighted to find his sister so amiable, and I hope she will permit us to pay her all the attention she deserves. We shall count on her good opinion after the welcome we mean to give her son. Monsieur is very impatient to see his nephew.' Madame had little black satin slippers; and her stockings! my! they were marvels,—flowers in silk and openwork, just like lace, and you could see her rosy little feet through them. Oh! she's in high feather, and she had a lovely little apron in front of her which, Vedie says, cost more than two years of our wages put together."

"Well done! We shall have to dress up," said the artist laughing.

"What do you think of all this, Monsieur Hochon?" said the old lady when Gritte had departed.

Madame Hochon made Agathe observe her husband, who was sitting with his head in his hands, his elbows on the arms of his chair, plunged in thought.

"You have to do with a Maitre Bonin!" said the old man at last. "With your ideas, young man," he added, looking at Joseph, "you haven't force enough to struggle with a practised scoundrel like Maxence Gilet. No matter what I say to you, you will commit some folly. But, at any rate, tell me everything you see, and hear, and do to-night. Go, and God be with you! Try to get alone with your uncle. If, in spite of all your genius, you can't manage it, that in itself will throw some light upon their scheme. But if you do get a moment alone with him, out of ear-shot, damn it, you must pull the wool from his eyes as to the situation those two have put him in, and plead your mother's cause."

CHAPTER XII

At four o'clock, Joseph crossed the open space which separated the Rouget house from the Hochon house,—a sort of avenue of weakly lindens, two hundred feet long and of the same width as the rue Grande Narette. When the nephew arrived, Kouski, in polished boots, black cloth trousers, white waistcoat, and black coat, announced him. The table was set in the large hall, and Joseph, who easily distinguished his uncle, went up to him, kissed him, and bowed to Flore and Max.

"We have not seen each other since I came into the world, my dear uncle," said the painter gayly; "but better late than never."

"You are very welcome, my friend," said the old man, looking at his nephew in a dull way.

"Madame," Joseph said to Flore with an artist's vivacity, "this morning I was envying my uncle the pleasure he enjoys in being able to admire you every day."

"Isn't she beautiful?" said the old man, whose dim eyes began to shine.

"Beautiful enough to be the model of a great painter."

"Nephew," said Rouget, whose elbow Flore was nudging, "this is Monsieur Maxence Gilet; a man who served the Emperor, like your brother, in the Imperial Guard."

Joseph rose, and bowed.

"Your brother was in the dragoons, I believe," said Maxence. "I was only a dust-trotter."

"On foot or on horseback," said Flore, "you both of you risked your skins."

Joseph took note of Max quite as much as Max took note of Joseph. Max, who got his clothes from Paris, was dressed as the young dandies of that day dressed themselves. A pair of light-blue cloth trousers, made with very full plaits, covered his feet so that only the toes and the spurs of his boots were seen. His waist was pinched in by a white waistcoat with chased gold buttons, which was laced behind to serve as a belt. The waistcoat, buttoned to the throat, showed off his broad chest, and a black satin stock obliged him to hold his head high, in soldierly fashion. A handsome gold chain hung from a waistcoat pocket, in which the outline of a flat watch was barely seen. He was twisting a watch-key of the kind called a "criquet," which Breguet had lately invented.

"The fellow is fine-looking," thought Joseph, admiring with a painter's eye the eager face, the air of strength, and the intellectual gray eyes which Max had inherited from his father, the noble. "My uncle must be a fearful bore, and that handsome girl takes her compensations. It is a triangular household; I see that."

At this instant, Baruch and Francois entered.

"Have you been to see the tower of Issoudun?" Flore asked Joseph. "No? then if you would like to take a little walk before dinner, which will not be served for an hour, we will show you the great curiosity of the town."

"Gladly," said the artist, quite incapable of seeing the slightest impropriety in so doing.

While Flore went to put on her bonnet, gloves, and cashmere shawl, Joseph suddenly jumped up, as if an enchanter had touched him with his wand, to look at the pictures.

"Ah! you have pictures, indeed, uncle!" he said, examining the one that had caught his eye.

"Yes," answered the old man. "They came to us from the Descoings, who bought them during the Revolution, when the convents and churches in Berry were dismantled."

Joseph was not listening; he was lost in admiration of the pictures.

"Magnificent!" he cried. "Oh! what painting! that fellow didn't spoil his canvas. Dear, dear! better and better, as it is at Nicolet's—"

"There are seven or eight very large ones up in the garret, which were kept on account of the frames," said Gilet.

"Let me see them!" cried the artist; and Max took him upstairs.

Joseph came down wildly enthusiastic. Max whispered a word to the Rabouilleuse, who took the old man into the embrasure of a window, where Joseph heard her say in a low voice, but still so that he could hear the words:—

"Your nephew is a painter; you don't care for those pictures; be kind, and give them to him."

"It seems," said Jean-Jacques, leaning on Flore's arm to reach the place were Joseph was standing in ecstasy before an Albano, "—it seems that you are a painter—"

"Only a 'rapin,'" said Joseph.

"What may that be?" asked Flore.

"A beginner," replied Joseph.

"Well," continued Jean-Jacques, "if these pictures can be of any use to you in your business, I give them to you,—but without the frames. Oh! the frames are gilt, and besides, they are very funny; I will put—"

"Well done, uncle!" cried Joseph, enchanted; "I'll make you copies of the same dimensions, which you can put into the frames."

"But that will take your time, and you will want canvas and colors," said Flore. "You will have to spend money. Come, Pere Rouget, offer your nephew a hundred francs for each copy; here are twenty-seven pictures, and I think there are eleven very big ones in the garret which ought to cost double,—call the whole four thousand francs. Oh, yes," she went on, turning to Joseph, "your uncle can well afford to pay you four thousand francs for making the copies, since he keeps the frames—but bless me! you'll want frames; and they say frames cost more than pictures; there's more gold on them. Answer, monsieur," she continued, shaking the old man's arm. "Hein? it isn't dear; your nephew will take four thousand francs for new pictures in the place of the old ones. It is," she whispered in his ear, "a very good way to give him four thousand francs; he doesn't look to me very flush—"

"Well, nephew, I will pay you four thousand francs for the copies—"

"No, no!" said the honest Joseph; "four thousand francs and the pictures, that's too much; the pictures, don't you see, are valuable—"

"Accept, simpleton!" said Flore; "he is your uncle, you know."

"Very good, I accept," said Joseph, bewildered by the luck that had befallen him; for he had recognized a Perugino.

The result was that the artist beamed with satisfaction as he went out of the house with the Rabouilleuse on his arm, all of which helped Maxence's plans immensely. Neither Flore, nor Rouget, nor Max, nor indeed any one in Issoudun knew the value of the pictures, and the crafty Max thought he had bought Flore's triumph for a song, as she paraded triumphantly before the eyes of the astonished town, leaning on the arm of her master's nephew, and evidently on the best of terms with him. People flocked to their doors to see the crab-girl's triumph over the family. This astounding event made the sensation on which Max counted; so that when they all returned at five o'clock, nothing was talked of in every household but the cordial understanding between Max and Flore and the nephew of old Rouget. The incident of the pictures and the four thousand francs circulated already. The dinner, at which Lousteau, one of the court judges, and the Mayor of Issoudun were present, was splendid. It was one of those provincial dinners lasting five hours. The most exquisite wines enlivened the conversation. By nine o'clock, at dessert, the painter, seated opposite to his uncle, and between Flore and Max, had fraternized with the soldier, and thought him the best fellow on earth. Joseph returned home at eleven o'clock somewhat tipsy. As to old Rouget, Kouski had carried him to his bed dead-drunk; he had eaten as though he were an actor from foreign parts, and had soaked up the wine like the sands of the desert.

"Well," said Max when he was alone with Flore, "isn't this better than making faces at them? The Bridaus are well received, they get small presents, and are smothered with attentions, and the end of it is they will sing our praises; they will go away satisfied and leave us in peace. To-morrow morning you and I and Kouski will take down all those pictures and send them over to the painter, so that he shall see them when he wakes up. We will put the frames in the garret, and cover the walls with one of those varnished papers which represent scenes from Telemachus, such as I have seen at Monsieur Mouilleron's."

"Oh, that will be much prettier!" said Flore.

On the morrow, Joseph did not wake up till midday. From his bed he saw the pictures, which had been brought in while he was asleep, leaning one against another on the opposite wall. While he examined them anew, recognizing each masterpiece, studying the manner of each painter, and searching for the signature, his mother had gone to see and thank her brother, urged thereto by old Hochon, who, having heard of the follies the painter had committed the night before, almost despaired of the Bridau cause.

"Your adversaries have the cunning of foxes," he said to Agathe. "In all my days I never saw a man carry things with such a high hand as that soldier; they say war educates young men! Joseph has let himself be fooled. They have shut his mouth with wine, and those miserable pictures, and four thousand francs! Your artist hasn't cost Maxence much!"

The long-headed old man instructed Madame Bridau carefully as to the line of conduct she ought to pursue,—advising her to enter into Maxence's ideas and cajole Flore, so as to set up a sort of intimacy with her, and thus obtain a few moments' interview with Jean-Jacques alone. Madame Bridau was very warmly received by her brother, to whom Flore had taught his lesson. The old man was in bed, quite ill from the excesses of the night before. As Agathe, under the circumstances, could scarcely begin at once to speak of family matters, Max thought it proper and magnanimous to leave the brother and sister alone together. The calculation was a good one. Poor Agathe found her brother so ill that she would not deprive him of Madame Brazier's care.

"Besides," she said to the old bachelor, "I wish to know a person to whom I am grateful for the happiness of my brother."

These words gave evident pleasure to the old man, who rang for Madame Flore. Flore, as we may well believe, was not far off. The female antagonists bowed to each other. The Rabouilleuse showed the most servile attentions and the utmost tenderness to her master; fancied his head was too low, beat up the pillows, and took care of him like a bride of yesterday. The poor creature received it with a rush of feeling.

"We owe you much gratitude, mademoiselle," said Agathe, "for the proofs of attachment you have so long given to my brother, and for the way in which you watch over his happiness."

"That is true, my dear Agathe," said the old man; "she has taught me what happiness is; she is a woman of excellent qualities."

"And therefore, my dear brother, you ought to have recompensed Mademoiselle by making her your wife. Yes! I am too sincere in my religion not to wish to see you obey the precepts of the church. You would each be more tranquil in mind if you were not at variance with morality and the laws. I have come here, dear brother, to ask for help in my affliction; but do not suppose that we wish to make any remonstrance as to the manner in which you may dispose of your property—"

"Madame," said Flore, "we know how unjust your father was to you. Monsieur, here, can tell you," she went on, looking fixedly at her victim, "that the only quarrels we have ever had were about you. I have always told him that he owes you part of the fortune he received from his father, and your father, my benefactor,—for he was my benefactor," she added in a tearful voice; "I shall ever remember him! But your brother, madame, has listened to reason—"

"Yes," said the old man, "when I make my will you shall not be forgotten."

"Don't talk of these things, my dear brother; you do not yet know my nature."

After such a beginning, it is easy to imagine how the visit went on. Rouget invited his sister to dinner on the next day but one.

We may here mention that during these three days the Knights of Idleness captured an immense quantity of rats and mice, which were kept half-famished until they were let loose in the grain one fine night, to the number of four hundred and thirty-six, of which some were breeding mothers. Not content with providing Fario's store-house with these boarders, the Knights made holes in the roof of the old church and put in a dozen pigeons, taken from as many different farms. These four-footed and feathered creatures held high revels,—all the more securely because the watchman was enticed away by a fellow who kept him drunk from morning till night, so that he took no care of his master's property.

Madame Bridau believed, contrary to the opinion of old Hochon, that her brother has as yet made no will; she intended asking him what were his intentions respecting Mademoiselle Brazier, as soon as she could take a walk with him alone,—a hope which Flore and Maxence were always holding out to her, and, of course, always disappointing.

Meantime the Knights were searching for a way to put the Parisians to flight, and finding none that were not impracticable follies.

At the end of a week—half the time the Parisians were to stay in Issoudun—the Bridaus were no farther advanced in their object than when they came.

"Your lawyer does not understand the provinces," said old Hochon to Madame Bridau. "What you have come to do can't be done in two weeks, nor in two years; you ought never to leave your brother, but live here and try to give him some ideas of religion. You cannot countermine the fortifications of Flore and Maxence without getting a priest to sap them. That is my advice, and it is high time to set about it."

"You certainly have very singular ideas about the clergy," said Madame Hochon to her husband.

"Bah!" exclaimed the old man, "that's just like you pious women."

"God would never bless an enterprise undertaken in a sacrilegious spirit," said Madame Bridau. "Use religion for such a purpose! Why, we should be more criminal than Flore."

This conversation took place at breakfast,—Francois and Baruch listening with all their ears.

"Sacrilege!" exclaimed old Hochon. "If some good abbe, keen as I have known many of them to be, knew what a dilemma you are in, he would not think it sacrilege to bring your brother's lost soul back to God, and call him to repentance for his sins, by forcing him to send away the woman who causes the scandal (with a proper provision, of course), and showing him how to set his conscience at rest by giving a few thousand francs a year to the seminary of the archbishop and leaving his property to the rightful heirs."

The passive obedience which the old miser had always exacted from his children, and now from his grandchildren (who were under his guardianship and for whom he was amassing a small fortune, doing for them, he said, just as he would for himself), prevented Baruch and Francois from showing signs of surprise or disapproval; but they exchanged significant glances expressing how dangerous and fatal such a scheme would be to Max's interest.

"The fact is, madame," said Baruch, "that if you want to secure your brother's property, the only sure and true way will be to stay in Issoudun for the necessary length of time—"

"Mother," said Joseph hastily, "you had better write to Desroches about all this. As for me, I ask nothing more than what my uncle has already given me."

After fully recognizing the great value of his thirty-nine pictures, Joseph had carefully unnailed the canvases and fastened paper over them, gumming it at the edges with ordinary glue; he then laid them one above another in an enormous wooden box, which he sent to Desroches by the carrier's waggon, proposing to write him a letter about it by post. The precious freight had been sent off the night before.

"You are satisfied with a pretty poor bargain," said Monsieur Hochon.

"I can easily get a hundred and fifty thousand francs for those pictures," replied Joseph.

"Painter's nonsense!" exclaimed old Hochon, giving Joseph a peculiar look.

"Mother," said Joseph, "I am going to write to Desroches and explain to him the state of things here. If he advises you to remain, you had better do so. As for your situation, we can always find you another like it."

"My dear Joseph," said Madame Hochon, following him as he left the table, "I don't know anything about your uncle's pictures, but they ought to be good, judging by the places from which they came. If they are worth only forty thousand francs,—a thousand francs apiece,—tell no one. Though my grandsons are discreet and well-behaved, they might, without intending harm, speak of this windfall; it would be known all over Issoudun; and it is very important that our adversaries should not suspect it. You behave like a child!"

In fact, before evening many persons in Issoudun, including Max, were informed of this estimate, which had the immediate effect of causing a search for all the old paintings which no one had ever cared for, and the appearance of many execrable daubs. Max repented having driven the old man into giving away the pictures, and the rage he felt against the heirs after hearing from Baruch old Hochon's ecclesiastical scheme, was increased by what he termed his own stupidity. The influence of religion upon such a feeble creature as Rouget was the one thing to fear. The news brought by his two comrades decided Maxence Gilet to turn all Rouget's investments into money, and to borrow upon his landed property, so as to buy into the Funds as soon as possible; but he considered it even more important to get rid of the Parisians at once. The genius of the Mascarilles and Scapins out together would hardly have solved the latter problem easily.

Flore, acting by Max's advice, pretended that Monsieur was too feeble to take walks, and that he ought, at his age, to have a carriage. This pretext grew out of the necessity of not exciting inquiry when they went to Bourges, Vierzon, Chateauroux, Vatan, and all the other places where the project of withdrawing investments obliged Max and Flore to betake themselves with Rouget. At the close of the week, all Issoudun was amazed to learn that the old man had gone to Bourges to buy a carriage,—a step which the Knights of Idleness regarded as favorable to the Rabouilleuse. Flore and Max selected a hideous "berlingot," with cracked leather curtains and windows without glass, aged twenty-two years and nine campaigns, sold on the decease of a colonel, the friend of grand-marshal Bertrand, who, during the absence of that faithful companion of the Emperor, was left in charge of the affairs of Berry. This "berlingot," painted bright green, was somewhat like a caleche, though shafts had taken the place of a pole, so that it could be driven with one horse. It belonged to a class of carriages brought into vogue by diminished fortunes, which at that time bore the candid name of "demi-fortune"; at its first introduction it was called a "seringue." The cloth lining of this demi-fortune, sold under the name of caleche, was moth-eaten; its gimps looked like the chevrons of an old Invalide; its rusty joints squeaked,—but it only cost four hundred and fifty francs; and Max bought a good stout mare, trained to harness, from an officer of a regiment then stationed at Bourges. He had the carriage repainted a dark brown, and bought a tolerable harness at a bargain. The whole town of Issoudun was shaken to its centre in expectation of Pere Rouget's equipage; and on the occasion of its first appearance, every household was on its door-step and curious faces were at all the windows.

The second time the old bachelor went out he drove to Bourges, where, to escape the trouble of attending personally to the business, or, if you prefer it, being ordered to do so by Flore, he went before a notary and signed a power of attorney in favor of Maxence Gilet, enabling him to make all the transfers enumerated in the document. Flore reserved to herself the business of making Monsieur sell out the investments in Issoudun and its immediate neighborhood. The principal notary in Bourges was requested by Rouget to get him a loan of one hundred and forty thousand francs on his landed estate. Nothing was known at Issoudun of these proceedings, which were secretly and cleverly carried out. Maxence, who was a good rider, went with his own horse to Bourges and back between five in the morning and five in the afternoon. Flore never left the old bachelor. Rouget consented without objection to the action Flore dictated to him; but he insisted that the investment in the Funds, producing fifty thousand francs a year, should stand in Flore's name as holding a life-interest only, and in his as owner of the principal. The tenacity the old man displayed in the domestic disputes which this idea created caused Max a good deal of anxiety; he thought he could see the result of reflections inspired by the sight of the natural heirs.

Amid all these movements, which Max concealed from the knowledge of everyone, he forgot the Spaniard and his granary. Fario came back to Issoudun to deliver his corn, after various trips and business manoeuvres undertaken to raise the price of cereals. The morning after his arrival he noticed that the roof the church of the Capuchins was black with pigeons. He cursed himself for having neglected to examine its condition, and hurried over to look into his storehouse, where he found half his grain devoured. Thousands of mice-marks and rat-marks scattered about showed a second cause of ruin. The church was a Noah's-ark. But anger turned the Spaniard white as a bit of cambric when, trying to estimate the extent of the destruction and his consequence losses, he noticed that the grain at the bottom of the heap, near the floor, was sprouting from the effects of water, which Max had managed to introduce by means of tin tubes into the very centre of the pile of wheat. The pigeons and the rats could be explained by animal instinct; but the hand of man was plainly visible in this last sign of malignity.

Fario sat down on the steps of a chapel altar, holding his head between his hands. After half an hour of Spanish reflections, he spied the squirrel, which Goddet could not refrain from giving him as a guest, playing with its tail upon a cross-beam, on the middle of which rested one of the uprights that supported the roof. The Spaniard rose and turned to his watchman with a face that was as calm and cold as an Arab's. He made no complaint, but went home, hired laborers to gather into sacks what remained of the sound grain, and to spread in the sun all that was moist, so as to save as much as possible; then, after estimating that his losses amounted to about three fifths, he attended to filling his orders. But his previous manipulations of the market had raised the price of cereals, and he lost on the three fifths he was obliged to buy to fill his orders; so that his losses amounted really to more than half. The Spaniard, who had no enemies, at once attributed this revenge to Gilet. He was convinced that Maxence and some others were the authors of all the nocturnal mischief, and had in all probability carried his cart up the embankment of the tower, and now intended to amuse themselves by ruining him. It was a matter to him of over three thousand francs,—very nearly the whole capital he had scraped together since the peace. Driven by the desire for vengeance, the man now displayed the cunning and stealthy persistence of a detective to whom a large reward is offered. Hiding at night in different parts of Issoudun, he soon acquired proof of the proceedings of the Knights of Idleness; he saw them all, counted them, watched their rendezvous, and knew of their suppers at Mere Cognette's; after that he lay in wait to witness one of their deeds, and thus became well informed as to their nocturnal habits.

In spite of Max's journeys and pre-occupations, he had no intention of neglecting his nightly employments,—first, because he did not wish his comrades to suspect the secret of his operations with Pere Rouget's property; and secondly, to keep the Knights well in hand. They were therefore convened for the preparation of a prank which might deserve to be talked of for years to come. Poisoned meat was to be thrown on a given night to every watch-dog in the town and in the environs. Fario overheard them congratulating each other, as they came out from a supper at the Cognettes', on the probable success of the performance, and laughing over the general mourning that would follow this novel massacre of the innocents,—revelling, moreover, in the apprehensions it would excite as to the sinister object of depriving all the households of their guardian watch-dogs.

"It will make people forget Fario's cart," said Goddet.

Fario did not need that speech to confirm his suspicions; besides, his mind was already made up.

After three weeks' stay in Issoudun, Agathe was convinced, and so was Madame Hochon, of the truth of the old miser's observation, that it would take years to destroy the influence which Max and the Rabouilleuse had acquired over her brother. She had made no progress in Jean-Jacques's confidence, and she was never left alone with him. On the other hand, Mademoiselle Brazier triumphed openly over the heirs by taking Agathe to drive in the caleche, sitting beside her on the back seat, while Monsieur Rouget and his nephew occupied the front. Mother and son impatiently awaited an answer to the confidential letter they had written to Desroches. The day before the night on which the dogs were to be poisoned, Joseph, who was nearly bored to death in Issoudun, received two letters: the first from the great painter Schinner,—whose age allowed him a closer intimacy than Joseph could have with Gros, their master,—and the second from Desroches.

Here is the first, postmarked Beaumont-sur-Oise:—

My dear Joseph,—I have just finished the principal panel-paintings at the chateau de Presles for the Comte de Serizy. I have left all the mouldings and the decorative painting; and I have recommended you so strongly to the count, and also to Gridot the architect, that you have nothing to do but pick up your brushes and come at once. Prices are arranged to please you. I am off to Italy with my wife; so you can have Mistigris to help you along. The young scamp has talent, and I put him at your disposal. He is twittering like a sparrow at the very idea of amusing himself at the chateau de Presles. Adieu, my dear Joseph; if I am still absent, and should send nothing to next year's Salon, you must take my place. Yes, dear Jojo, I know your picture is a masterpiece, but a masterpiece which will rouse a hue and cry about romanticism; you are doomed to lead the life of a devil in holy water. Adieu. Thy friend, Schinner

Here follows the letter of Desroches:—

My dear Joseph,—Your Monsieur Hochon strikes me as an old man full of common-sense, and you give me a high idea of his methods; he is perfectly right. My advice, since you ask it, is that your mother should

80

remain at Issoudun with Madame Hochon, paying a small board,—say four hundred francs a year,—to reimburse her hosts for what she eats. Madame Bridau ought, in my opinion, to follow Monsieur Hochon's advice in everything; for your excellent mother will have many scruples in dealing with persons who have no scruple at all, and whose behavior to her is a master-stroke of policy. That Maxence, you are right enough, is dangerous. He is another Philippe, but of a different calibre. The scoundrel makes his vices serve his fortunes, and gets his amusement gratis; whereas your brother's follies are never useful to him. All that you say alarms me, but I could do no good by going to Issoudun. Monsieur Hochon, acting behind your mother, will be more useful to you than I. As for you, you had better come back here; you are good for nothing in a matter which requires continual attention, careful observation, servile civilities, discretion in speech, and a dissimulation of manner and gesture which is wholly against the grain of artists. If they have told you no will has been made, you may be quite sure they have possessed one for a long time. But wills can be revoked, and as long as your fool of an uncle lives he is no doubt susceptible of being worked upon by remorse and religion. Your inheritance will be the result of a combat between the Church and the Rabouilleuse. There will inevitably come a time when that woman will lose her grip on the old man, and religion will be all-powerful. So long as your uncle makes no gift of the property during his lifetime, and does not change the nature of his estate, all may come right whenever religion gets the upper hand. For this reason, you must beg Monsieur Hochon to keep an eye, as well as he can, on the condition of your uncle's property. It is necessary to know if the real estate is mortgaged, and if so, where and in whose name the proceeds are invested. It is so easy to terrify an old man with fears about his life, in case you find him despoiling his own property for the sake of these interlopers, that almost any heir with a little adroitness could stop the spoliation at its outset. But how should your mother, with her ignorance of the world, her disinterestedness, and her religious ideas, know how to manage such an affair? However, I am not able to throw any light on the matter. All that you have done so far has probably given the alarm, and your adversaries may already have secured themselves—

"That is what I call an opinion in good shape," exclaimed Monsieur Hochon, proud of being himself appreciated by a Parisian lawyer.

"Oh! Desroches is a famous fellow," answered Joseph.

"It would be well to read that letter to the two women," said the old man.

"There it is," said Joseph, giving it to him; "as to me, I want to be off to-morrow; and I am now going to say good-by to my uncle."

"Ah!" said Monsieur Hochon, "I see that Monsieur Desroches tells you in a postscript to burn the letter."

"You can burn it after showing it to my mother," said the painter.

Joseph dressed, crossed the little square, and called on his uncle, who was just finishing breakfast. Max and Flore were at table.

"Don't disturb yourself, my dear uncle; I have only come to say good-by."

"You are going?" said Max, exchanging glances with Flore.

"Yes; I have some work to do at the chateau of Monsieur de Serizy, and I am all the more glad of it because his arm is long enough to do a service to my poor brother in the Chamber of Peers."

"Well, well, go and work"; said old Rouget, with a silly air. Joseph thought him extraordinarily changed within a few days. "Men must work—I am sorry you are going."

"Oh! my mother will be here some time longer," remarked Joseph.

Max made a movement with his lips which the Rabouilleuse observed, and which signified: "They are going to try the plan Baruch warned me of."

"I am very glad I came," said Joseph, "for I have had the pleasure of making your acquaintance and you have enriched my studio—"

"Yes," said Flore, "instead of enlightening your uncle on the value of his pictures, which is now estimated at over one hundred thousand francs, you have packed them off in a hurry to Paris. Poor dear man! he is no better than a baby! We have just been told of a little treasure at Bourges,—what did they call it? a Poussin,—which was in the choir of the cathedral before the Revolution and is now worth, all by itself, thirty thousand francs."

"That was not right of you, my nephew," said Jean-Jacques, at a sign from Max, which Joseph could not see.

"Come now, frankly," said the soldier, laughing, "on your honor, what should you say those pictures were worth? You've made an easy haul out of your uncle! and right enough, too,—uncles are made to be pillaged. Nature deprived me of uncles, but damn it, if I'd had any I should have shown them no mercy."

"Did you know, monsieur," said Flore to Rouget, "what *your* pictures were worth? How much did you say, Monsieur Joseph?"

"Well," answered the painter, who had grown as red as a beetroot,—"the pictures are certainly worth something."

81

"They say you estimated them to Monsieur Hochon at one hundred and fifty thousand francs," said Flore; "is that true?"

"Yes," said the painter, with childlike honesty.

"And did you intend," said Flore to the old man, "to give a hundred and fifty thousand francs to your nephew?"

"Never, never!" cried Jean-Jacques, on whom Flore had fixed her eye.

"There is one way to settle all this," said the painter, "and that is to return them to you, uncle."

"No, no, keep them," said the old man.

"I shall send them back to you," said Joseph, wounded by the offensive silence of Max and Flore. "There is something in my brushes which will make my fortune, without owing anything to any one, even an uncle. My respects to you, mademoiselle; good-day, monsieur—"

And Joseph crossed the square in a state of irritation which artists can imagine. The entire Hochon family were in the salon. When they saw Joseph gesticulating and talking to himself, they asked him what was the matter. The painter, who was as open as the day, related before Baruch and Francois the scene that had just taken place; and which, two hours later, thanks to the two young men, was the talk of the whole town, embroidered with various circumstances that were more or less ridiculous. Some persons insisted that the painter was maltreated by Max; others that he had misbehaved to Flore, and that Max had turned him out of doors.

"What a child your son is!" said Hochon to Madame Bridau; "the booby is the dupe of a scene which they have been keeping back for the last day of his visit. Max and the Rabouilleuse have known the value of those pictures for the last two weeks,—ever since he had the folly to tell it before my grandsons, who never rested till they had blurted it out to all the world. Your artist had better have taken himself off without taking leave."

"My son has done right to return the pictures if they are really so valuable," said Agathe.

"If they are worth, as he says, two hundred thousand francs," said old Hochon, "it was folly to put himself in the way of being obliged to return them. You might have had that, at least, out of the property; whereas, as things are going now, you won't get anything. And this scene with Joseph is almost a reason why your brother should refuse to see you again."

CHAPTER XIII

Between midnight and one o'clock, the Knights of Idleness began their gratuitous distribution of comestibles to the dogs of the town. This memorable expedition was not over till three in the morning, the hour at which these reprobates went to sup at Cognette's. At half-past four, in the early dawn, they crept home. Just as Max turned the corner of the rue l'Avenier into the Grande rue, Fario, who stood ambushed in a recess, struck a knife at his heart, drew out the blade, and escaped by the moat towards Vilatte, wiping the blade of his knife on his handkerchief. The Spaniard washed the handkerchief in the Riviere forcee, and returned quietly to his lodgings at Saint-Paterne, where he got in by a window he had left open, and went to bed: later, he was awakened by his new watchman, who found him fast asleep.

As he fell, Max uttered a fearful cry which no one could mistake. Lousteau-Prangin, son of a judge, a distant relation to the family of the sub-delegate, and young Goddet, who lived at the lower end of the Grande rue, ran at full speed up the street, calling to each other,—

"They are killing Max! Help! help!"

But not a dog barked; and all the town, accustomed to the false alarms of these nightly prowlers, stayed quietly in their beds. When his two comrades reached him, Max had fainted. It was necessary to rouse Monsieur Goddet, the surgeon. Max had recognized Fario; but when he came to his senses, with several persons about him, and felt that his wound was not mortal, it suddenly occurred to him to make capital out of the attack, and he said, in a faint voice,—

"I think I recognized that cursed painter!"

Thereupon Lousteau-Prangin ran off to his father, the judge. Max was carried home by Cognette, young Goddet, and two other persons. Mere Cognette and Monsieur Goddet walked beside the stretcher. Those who carried the wounded man naturally looked across at Monsieur Hochon's door while waiting for Kouski to let them in, and saw Monsieur Hochon's servant sweeping the steps. At the old miser's, as everywhere else in the provinces, the household was early astir. The few words uttered by Max had roused the suspicions of Monsieur Goddet, and he called to the woman,—

"Gritte, is Monsieur Joseph Bridau in bed?"

"Bless me!" she said, "he went out at half-past four. I don't know what ailed him; he walked up and down his room all night."

This simple answer drew forth such exclamations of horror that the woman came over, curious to know what they were carrying to old Rouget's house.

"A precious fellow he is, that painter of yours!" they said to her. And the procession entered the house, leaving Gritte open-mouthed with amazement at the sight of Max in his bloody shirt, stretched half-fainting on a mattress.

Artists will readily guess what ailed Joseph, and kept him restless all night. He imagined the tale the bourgeoisie of Issoudun would tell of him. They would say he had fleeced his uncle; that he was everything but what he had tried to be,—a loyal fellow and an honest artist! Ah! he would have given his great picture to have flown like a swallow to Paris, and thrown his uncle's paintings at Max's nose. To be the one robbed, and to be thought the robber!—what irony! So at the earliest dawn, he had started for the poplar avenue which led to Tivoli, to give free course to his agitation.

While the innocent fellow was vowing, by way of consolation, never to return to Issoudun, Max was preparing a horrible outrage for his sensitive spirit. When Monsieur Goddet had probed the wound and discovered that the knife, turned aside by a little pocket-book, had happily spared Max's life (though making a serious wound), he did as all doctors, and particularly country surgeons, do; he paved the way for his own credit by "not answering for the patient's life"; and then, after dressing the soldier's wound, and stating the verdict of science to the Rabouilleuse, Jean-Jacques Rouget, Kouski, and the Vedie, he left the house. The Rabouilleuse came in tears to her dear Max, while Kouski and the Vedie told the assembled crowd that the captain was in a fair way to die. The news brought nearly two hundred persons in groups about the place Saint-Jean and the two Narettes.

"I sha'n't be a month in bed; and I know who struck the blow," whispered Max to Flore. "But we'll profit by it to get rid of the Parisians. I have said I thought I recognized the painter; so pretend that I am expected to die, and try to have Joseph Bridau arrested. Let him taste a prison for a couple of days, and I know well enough the mother will be off in a jiffy for Paris when she gets him out. And then we needn't fear the priests they talk of setting on the old fool."

When Flore Brazier came downstairs, she found the assembled crowd quite prepared to take the impression she meant to give them. She went out with tears in her eyes, and related, sobbing, how the painter, "who had just the face for that sort of thing," had been angry with Max the night before about some pictures he had "wormed out" of Pere Rouget.

"That brigand—for you've only got to look at him to see what he is—thinks that if Max were dead, his uncle would leave him his fortune; as if," she cried, "a brother were not more to him than a nephew! Max is Doctor Rouget's son. The old one told me so before he died!"

"Ah! he meant to do the deed just before he left Issoudun; he chose his time, for he was going away to-day," said one of the Knights of Idleness.

"Max hasn't an enemy in Issoudun," said another.

"Besides, Max recognized the painter," said the Rabouilleuse.

"Where's that cursed Parisian? Let us find him!" they all cried.

"Find him?" was the answer, "why, he left Monsieur Hochon's at daybreak."

A Knight of Idleness ran off at once to Monsieur Mouilleron. The crowd increased; and the tumult became threatening. Excited groups filled up the whole of the Grande-Narette. Others stationed themselves before the church of Saint-Jean. An assemblage gathered at the porte Vilatte, which is at the farther end of the Petite-Narette. Monsieur Lousteau-Prangin and Monsieur Mouilleron, the commissary of police, the lieutenant of gendarmes, and two of his men, had some difficulty in reaching the place Saint-Jean through two hedges of people, whose cries and exclamations could and did prejudice them against the Parisian; who was, it is needless to say, unjustly accused, although, it is true, circumstances told against him.

After a conference between Max and the magistrates, Monsieur Mouilleron sent the commissary of police and a sergeant with one gendarme to examine what, in the language of the ministry of the interior, is called "the theatre of the crime." Then Messieurs Mouilleron and Lousteau-Prangin, accompanied by the lieutenant of gendarmes crossed over to the Hochon house, which was now guarded by two gendarmes in the garden and two at the front door. The crowd was still increasing. The whole town was surging in the Grande rue.

Gritte had rushed terrified to her master, crying out: "Monsieur, we shall be pillaged! the town is in revolt; Monsieur Maxence Gilet has been assassinated; he is dying! and they say it is Monsieur Joseph who has done it!"

Monsieur Hochon dressed quickly, and came downstairs; but seeing the angry populace, he hastily retreated within the house, and bolted the door. On questioning Gritte, he learned that his guest had left the house at daybreak, after walking the floor all night in great agitation, and had not yet come in. Much alarmed, he went to find Madame Hochon, who was already awakened by the noise, and to whom he told the frightful news which, true or false, was causing almost a riot in Issoudun.

"He is innocent, of course," said Madame Hochon.

"Before his innocence can be proved, the crowd may get in here and pillage us," said Monsieur Hochon, livid with fear, for he had gold in his cellar.

"Where is Agathe?"

"Sound asleep."

"Ah! so much the better," said Madame Hochon. "I wish she may sleep on till the matter is cleared up. Such a shock might kill the poor child."

But Agathe woke up and came down half-dressed; for the evasive answers of Gritte, whom she questioned, had disturbed both her head and heart. She found Madame Hochon, looking very pale, with her eyes full of tears, at one of the windows of the salon beside her husband.

"Courage, my child. God sends us our afflictions," said the old lady. "Joseph is accused—"

"Of what?"

"Of a bad action which he could never have committed," answered Madame Hochon.

Hearing the words, and seeing the lieutenant of gendarmes, who at this moment entered the room accompanied by the two gentlemen, Agathe fainted away.

"There now!" said Monsieur Hochon to his wife and Gritte, "carry off Madame Bridau; women are only in the way at these times. Take her to her room and stay there, both of you. Sit down, gentlemen," continued the old man. "The mistake to which we owe your visit will soon, I hope, be cleared up."

"Even if it should be a mistake," said Monsieur Mouilleron, "the excitement of the crowd is so great, and their minds are so exasperated, that I fear for the safety of the accused. I should like to get him arrested, and that might satisfy these people."

"Who would ever have believed that Monsieur Maxence Gilet had inspired so much affection in this town?" asked Lousteau-Prangin.

"One of my men says there's a crowd of twelve hundred more just coming in from the faubourg de Rome," said the lieutenant of gendarmes, "and they are threatening death to the assassin."

"Where is your guest?" said Monsieur Mouilleron to Monsieur Hochon.

"He has gone to walk in the country, I believe."

"Call Gritte," said the judge gravely. "I was in hopes he had not left the house. You are aware that the crime was committed not far from here, at daybreak."

While Monsieur Hochon went to find Gritte, the three functionaries looked at each other significantly.

"I never liked that painter's face," said the lieutenant to Monsieur Mouilleron.

"My good woman," said the judge to Gritte, when she appeared, "they say you saw Monsieur Joseph Bridau leave the house this morning?"

"Yes, monsieur," she answered, trembling like a leaf.

"At what hour?"

"Just as I was getting up: he walked about his room all night, and was dressed when I came downstairs."

"Was it daylight?"

"Barely."

"Did he seem excited?"

"Yes, he was all of a twitter."

"Send one of your men for my clerk," said Lousteau-Prangin to the lieutenant, "and tell him to bring warrants with him—"

"Good God! don't be in such a hurry," cried Monsieur Hochon. "The young man's agitation may have been caused by something besides the premeditation of this crime. He meant to return to Paris to-day, to attend to a matter in which Gilet and Mademoiselle Brazier had doubted his honor."

"Yes, the affair of the pictures," said Monsieur Mouilleron. "Those pictures caused a very hot quarrel between them yesterday, and it is a word and a blow with artists, they tell me."

"Who is there in Issoudun who had any object in killing Gilet?" said Lousteau. "No one,—neither a jealous husband nor anybody else; for the fellow has never harmed a soul."

"But what was Monsieur Gilet doing in the streets at four in the morning?" remarked Monsieur Hochon.

"Now, Monsieur Hochon, you must allow us to manage this affair in our own way," answered Mouilleron; "you don't know all: Gilet recognized your painter."

At this instant a clamor was heard from the other end of the town, growing louder and louder, like the roll of thunder, as it followed the course of the Grande-Narette.

"Here he is! here he is!—he's arrested!"

These words rose distinctly on the ear above the hoarse roar of the populace. Poor Joseph, returning quietly past the mill at Landrole intending to get home in time for breakfast, was spied by the various groups of people, as soon as he reached the place Misere. Happily for him, a couple of gendarmes arrived on a run in time to snatch him from the inhabitants of the faubourg de Rome, who had already pinioned him by the arms and were threatening him with death.

"Give way! give way!" cried the gendarmes, calling to some of their comrades to help them, and putting themselves one before and the other behind Bridau.

"You see, monsieur," said the one who held the painter, "it concerns our skin as well as yours at this moment. Innocent or guilty, we must protect you against the tumult raised by the murder of Captain Gilet. And the crowd is not satisfied with suspecting you; they declare, hard as iron, that you are the murderer. Monsieur Gilet is adored by all the people, who—look at them!—want to take justice into their own hands. Ah! didn't we see them, in 1830, dusting the jackets of the tax-gatherers? whose life isn't a bed of roses, anyway!"

Joseph Bridau grew pale as death, and collected all his strength to walk onward.

"After all," he said, "I am innocent. Go on!"

Poor artist! he was forced to bear his cross. Amid the hooting and insults and threats from the mob, he made the dreadful transit from the place Misere to the place Saint-Jean. The gendarmes were obliged to draw their sabres on the furious mob, which pelted them with stones. One of the officers was wounded, and Joseph received several of the missiles on his legs, and shoulders, and hat.

"Here we are!" said one of the gendarmes, as they entered Monsieur Hochon's hall, "and not without difficulty, lieutenant."

"We must now manage to disperse the crowd; and I see but one way, gentlemen," said the lieutenant to the magistrates. "We must take Monsieur Bridau to the Palais accompanied by all of you; I and my gendarmes will make a circle round you. One can't answer for anything in presence of a furious crowd of six thousand—"

"You are right," said Monsieur Hochon, who was trembling all the while for his gold.

"If that's your only way to protect innocence in Issoudun," said Joseph, "I congratulate you. I came near being stoned—"

"Do you wish your friend's house to be taken by assault and pillaged?" asked the lieutenant. "Could we beat back with our sabres a crowd of people who are pushed from behind by an angry populace that knows nothing of the forms of justice?"

"That will do, gentlemen, let us go; we can come to explanations later," said Joseph, who had recovered his self-possession.

"Give way, friends!" said the lieutenant to the crowd; "*He* is arrested, and we are taking him to the Palais."

"Respect the law, friends!" said Monsieur Mouilleron.

"Wouldn't you prefer to see him guillotined?" said one of the gendarmes to an angry group.

"Yes, yes, they shall guillotine him!" shouted one madman.

"They are going to guillotine him!" cried the women.

By the time they reached the end of the Grande-Narette the crowd were shouting: "They are taking him to the guillotine!" "They found the knife upon him!" "That's what Parisians are!" "He carries crime on his face!"

Though all Joseph's blood had flown to his head, he walked the distance from the place Saint-Jean to the Palais with remarkable calmness and self-possession. Nevertheless, he was very glad to find himself in the private office of Monsieur Lousteau-Prangin.

"I need hardly tell you, gentlemen, that I am innocent," said Joseph, addressing Monsieur Mouilleron, Monsieur Lousteau-Prangin, and the clerk. "I can only beg you to assist me in proving my innocence. I know nothing of this affair."

When the judge had stated all the suspicious facts which were against him, ending with Max's declaration, Joseph was astounded.

"But," said he, "it was past five o'clock when I left the house. I went up the Grande rue, and at half-past five I was standing looking up at the facade of the parish church of Saint-Cyr. I talked there with the sexton, who came to ring the angelus, and asked him for information about the building, which seems to me fantastic and incomplete. Then I passed through the vegetable-market, where some women had already assembled. From there, crossing the place Misere, I went as far as the mill of Landrole by the Pont aux Anes, where I watched the ducks for five or six minutes, and the miller's men must have noticed me. I saw the women going to wash; they are probably still there. They made a little fun of me, and declared that I was not handsome; I told them it was not all gold that glittered. From there, I followed the long avenue to Tivoli, where I talked with the gardener. Pray have these facts verified; and do not even arrest me, for I give you my word of honor that I will stay quietly in this office till you are convinced of my innocence."

These sensible words, said without the least hesitation, and with the ease of a man who is perfectly sure of his facts, made some impression on the magistrates.

"Yes, we must find all these persons and summon them," said Monsieur Mouilleron; "but it is more than the affair of a day. Make up your mind, therefore, in your own interests, to be imprisoned in the Palais."

"Provided I can write to my mother, so as to reassure her, poor woman—oh! you can read the letter," he added.

This request was too just not to be granted, and Joseph wrote the following letter:—

"Do not be uneasy, dear mother; the mistake of which I am a victim can easily be rectified; I have already given them the means of doing so. To-morrow, or perhaps this evening, I shall be at liberty. I kiss you, and beg you to say to Monsieur and Madame Hochon how grieved I am at this affair; in which, however, I have had no hand,—it is the result of some chance which, as yet, I do not understand."

When the note reached Madame Bridau, she was suffering from a nervous attack, and the potions which Monsieur Goddet was trying to make her swallow were powerless to soothe her. The reading of the letter acted like balm; after a few quiverings, Agathe subsided into the depression which always follows such attacks. Later, when Monsieur Goddet returned to his patient he found her regretting that she had ever quitted Paris.

"Well," said Madame Hochon to Monsieur Goddet, "how is Monsieur Gilet?"

"His wound, though serious, is not mortal," replied the doctor. "With a month's nursing he will be all right. I left him writing to Monsieur Mouilleron to request him to set your son at liberty, madame," he added, turning to Agathe. "Oh! Max is a fine fellow. I told him what a state you were in, and he then remembered a circumstance which goes to prove that the assassin was not your son; the man wore list shoes, whereas it is certain that Monsieur Joseph left the house in his boots—"

"Ah! God forgive him the harm he has done me—"

The fact was, a man had left a note for Max, after dark, written in type-letters, which ran as follows:—

"Captain Gilet ought not to let an innocent man suffer. He who struck the blow promises not to strike again if Monsieur Gilet will have Monsieur Joseph Bridau set at liberty, without naming the man who did it."

After reading this letter and burning it, Max wrote to Monsieur Mouilleron stating the circumstance of the list shoes, as reported by Monsieur Goddet, begging him to set Joseph at liberty, and to come and see him that he might explain the matter more at length.

By the time this letter was received, Monsieur Lousteau-Prangin had verified, by the testimony of the bell-ringer, the market-women and washerwomen, and the miller's men, the truth of Joseph's explanation. Max's letter made his innocence only the more certain, and Monsieur Mouilleron himself escorted him back to the Hochons'. Joseph was greeted with such overflowing tenderness by his mother that the poor misunderstood son gave thanks to ill-luck— like the husband to the thief, in La Fontaine's fable—for a mishap which brought him such proofs of affection.

"Oh," said Monsieur Mouilleron, with a self-satisfied air, "I knew at once by the way you looked at the angry crowd that you were innocent; but whatever I may have thought, any one who knows Issoudun must also know that the only way to protect you was to make the arrest as we did. Ah! you carried your head high."

"I was thinking of something else," said the artist simply. "An officer in the army told me that he was once stopped in Dalmatia under similar circumstances by an excited populace, in the early morning as he was returning from a walk. This recollection came into my mind, and I looked at all those heads with the idea of painting a revolt of the year 1793. Besides, I kept saying to myself: Blackguard that I am! I have only got my deserts for coming here to look after an inheritance, instead of painting in my studio."

"If you will allow me to offer you a piece of advice," said the procureur du roi, "you will take a carriage to-night, which the postmaster will lend you, and return to Paris by the diligence from Bourges."

"That is my advice also," said Monsieur Hochon, who was burning with a desire for the departure of his guests.

"My most earnest wish is to get away from Issoudun, though I leave my only friend here," said Agathe, kissing Madame Hochon's hand. "When shall I see you again?"

"Ah! my dear, never until we meet above. We have suffered enough here below," she added in a low voice, "for God to take pity upon us."

Shortly after, while Monsieur Mouilleron had gone across the way to talk with Max, Gritte greatly astonished Monsieur and Madame Hochon, Agathe, Joseph, and Adolphine by announcing the visit of Monsieur Rouget. Jean-Jacques came to bid his sister good-by, and to offer her his caleche for the drive to Bourges.

"Ah! your pictures have been a great evil to us," said Agathe.

"Keep them, my sister," said the old man, who did not even now believe in their value.

"Neighbor," remarked Monsieur Hochon, "our best friends, our surest defenders, are our own relations; above all, when they are such as your sister Agathe, and your nephew Joseph."

"Perhaps so," said old Rouget in his dull way.

"We ought all to think of ending our days in a Christian manner," said Madame Hochon.

"Ah! Jean-Jacques," said Agathe, "what a day this has been!"

"Will you accept my carriage?" asked Rouget.

"No, brother," answered Madame Bridau, "I thank you, and wish you health and comfort."

Rouget let his sister and nephew kiss him, and then he went away without manifesting any feeling himself. Baruch, at a hint from his grandfather, had been to see the postmaster. At eleven o'clock that night, the two Parisians, ensconced in a wicker cabriolet drawn by one horse and ridden by a postilion, quitted Issoudun. Adolphine and Madame Hochon parted from them with tears in their eyes; they alone regretted Joseph and Agathe.

"They are gone!" said Francois Hochon, going, with the Rabouilleuse, into Max's bedroom.

"Well done! the trick succeeded," answered Max, who was now tired and feverish.

"But what did you say to old Mouilleron?" asked Francois.

"I told him that I had given my assassin some cause to waylay me; that he was a dangerous man and likely, if I followed up the affair, to kill me like a dog before he could be captured. Consequently, I begged Mouilleron and Prangin to make the most active search ostensibly, but really to let the assassin go in peace, unless they wished to see me a dead man."

"I do hope, Max," said Flore, "that you will be quiet at night for some time to come."

"At any rate, we are delivered from the Parisians!" cried Max. "The fellow who stabbed me had no idea what a service he was doing us."

The next day, the departure of the Parisians was celebrated as a victory of the provinces over Paris by every one in Issoudun, except the more sober and staid inhabitants, who shared the opinions of Monsieur and Madame Hochon. A few of Max's friends spoke very harshly of the Bridaus.

"Do those Parisians fancy we are all idiots," cried one, "and think they have only got to hold their hats and catch legacies?"

"They came to fleece, but they have got shorn themselves," said another; "the nephew is not to the uncle's taste."

"And, if you please, they actually consulted a lawyer in Paris—"

"Ah! had they really a plan?"

"Why, of course,—a plan to get possession of old Rouget. But the Parisians were not clever enough; that lawyer can't crow over us Berrichons!"

"How abominable!"

"That's Paris for you!"

"The Rabouilleuse knew they came to attack her, and she defended herself."

"She did gloriously right!"

To the townspeople at large the Bridaus were Parisians and foreigners; they preferred Max and Flore.

We can imagine the satisfaction with which, after this campaign, Joseph and Agathe re-entered their little lodging in the rue Mazarin. On the journey, the artist recovered his spirits, which had, not unnaturally, been put to flight by his arrest and twenty-four hours' confinement; but he could not cheer up his mother. The Court of Peers was about to begin the trial of the military conspirators, and that was sufficient to keep Agathe from recovering her peace of mind. Philippe's conduct, in spite of the clever defender whom Desroches recommended to him, roused suspicions that were unfavorable to his character. In view of this, Joseph, as soon as he had put Desroches in possession of all that was going on at Issoudun, started with Mistigris for the chateau of the Comte de Serizy, to escape hearing about the trial of the conspirators, which lasted for twenty days.

It is useless to record facts that may be found in contemporaneous histories. Whether it were that he played a part previously agreed upon, or that he was really an informer, Philippe was condemned to five years' surveillance by the police department, and ordered to leave Paris the same day for Autun, the town which the director-general of police selected as the place of his exile for five years. This punishment resembled the detention of prisoners on parole who have a town for a prison. Learning that the Comte de Serizy, one of the peers appointed by the Chamber on the court-martial, was employing Joseph to decorate his chateau at Presles, Desroches begged the minister to grant him an audience, and found Monsieur de Serizy most amiably disposed toward Joseph, with whom he had happened to make personal acquaintance. Desroches explained the financial condition of the two brothers, recalling the services of the father, and the neglect shown to them under the Restoration.

"Such injustice, monseigneur," said the lawyer, "is a lasting cause of irritation and discontent. You knew the father; give the sons a chance, at least, of making a fortune—"

And he drew a succinct picture of the situation of the family affairs at Issoudun, begging the all-powerful vice-president of the Council of State to take steps to induce the director-general of police to change Philippe's place of residence from Autun to Issoudun. He also spoke of Philippe's extreme poverty, and asked a dole of sixty francs a month, which the minister of war ought, he said, for mere shame's sake, to grant to a former lieutenant-colonel.

"I will obtain all you ask of me, for I think it just," replied the count.

Three days later, Desroches, furnished with the necessary authority, fetched Philippe from the prison of the Court of Peers, and took him to his own house, rue de Bethizy. Once there, the young barrister read the miserable vagabond one of those unanswerable lectures in which lawyers rate things at their actual value; using plain terms to qualify the conduct, and to analyze and reduce to their simplest meaning the sentiments and ideas of clients toward whom they feel enough interest to speak plainly. After humbling the Emperor's staff-officer by reproaching him with his reckless dissipations, his mother's misfortunes, and the death of Madame Descoings, he went on to tell him the state of things at Issoudun, explaining it according to his lights, and probing both the scheme and the character of Maxence Gilet and the Rabouilleuse to their depths. Philippe, who was gifted with a keen comprehension in such directions, listened with much more interest to this part of Desroches's lecture than to what had gone before.

"Under these circumstances," continued the lawyer, "you can repair the injury you have done to your estimable family,—so far at least as it is reparable; for you cannot restore life to the poor mother you have all but killed. But you alone can—"

"What can I do?" asked Philippe.

"I have obtained a change of residence for you from Autun to Issoudun.—"

Philippe's sunken face, which had grown almost sinister in expression and was furrowed with sufferings and privation, instantly lighted up with a flash of joy.

"And, as I was saying, you alone can recover the inheritance of old Rouget's property; half of which may by this time be in the jaws of the wolf named Gilet," replied Desroches. "You now know all the particulars, and it is for you to act accordingly. I suggest no plan; I have no ideas at all as to that; besides, everything will depend on local circumstances. You have to deal with a strong force; that fellow is very astute. The way he attempted to get back the pictures your uncle had given to Joseph, the audacity with which he laid a crime on your poor brother's shoulders, all go to prove that the adversary is capable of everything. Therefore, be prudent; and try to behave properly out of policy, if you can't do so out of decency. Without telling Joseph, whose artist's pride would be up in arms, I have sent the pictures to Monsieur Hochon, telling him to give them up to no one but you. By the way, Maxence Gilet is a brave man."

"So much the better," said Philippe; "I count on his courage for success; a coward would leave Issoudun."

"Well,—think of your mother who has been so devoted to you, and of your brother, whom you made your milch cow."

"Ah! did he tell you that nonsense?" cried Philippe.

"Am I not the friend of the family, and don't I know much more about you than they do?" asked Desroches.

"What do you know?" said Philippe.

"That you betrayed your comrades."

"I!" exclaimed Philippe. "I! a staff-officer of the Emperor! Absurd! Why, we fooled the Chamber of Peers, the lawyers, the government, and the whole of the damned concern. The king's people were completely hood-winked."

"That's all very well, if it was so," answered the lawyer. "But, don't you see, the Bourbons can't be overthrown; all Europe is backing them; and you ought to try to make your peace with the war department,—you could do that readily enough if you were rich. To get rich, you and your brother, you must lay hold of your uncle. If you will take the trouble to manage an affair which needs great cleverness, patience, and caution, you have enough work before you to occupy your five years."

"No, no," cried Philippe, "I must take the bull by the horns at once. This Maxence may alter the investment of the property and put it in that woman's name; and then all would be lost."

"Monsieur Hochon is a good adviser, and sees clearly; consult him. You have your orders from the police; I have taken your place in the Orleans diligence for half-past seven o'clock this evening. I suppose your trunk is ready; so, now come and dine."

"I own nothing but what I have got on my back," said Philippe, opening his horrible blue overcoat; "but I only need three things, which you must tell Giroudeau, the uncle of Finot, to send me,—my sabre, my sword, and my pistols."

"You need more than that," said the lawyer, shuddering as he looked at his client. "You will receive a quarterly stipend which will clothe you decently."

"Bless me! are you here, Godeschal?" cried Philippe, recognizing in Desroches's head-clerk, as they passed out, the brother of Mariette.

"Yes, I have been with Monsieur Desroches for the last two months."

"And he will stay with me, I hope, till he gets a business of his own," said Desroches.

"How is Mariette?" asked Philippe, moved at his recollections.

"She is getting ready for the opening of the new theatre."

"It would cost her little trouble to get my sentence remitted," said Philippe. "However, as she chooses!"

After a meagre dinner, given by Desroches who boarded his head-clerk, the two lawyers put the political convict in the diligence, and wished him good luck.

CHAPTER XIV

On the second of November, All-Souls' day, Philippe Bridau appeared before the commissary of police at Issoudun, to have the date of his arrival recorded on his papers; and by that functionary's advice he went to lodge in the rue l'Avenier. The news of the arrival of an officer, banished on account of the late military conspiracy, spread rapidly through the town, and caused all the more excitement when it was known that this officer was a brother of the painter who had been falsely accused. Maxence Gilet, by this time entirely recovered from his wound, had completed the difficult operation of turning all Pere Rouget's mortgages into money, and putting the proceeds in one sum, on the "grand-livre." The loan of one hundred and forty thousand francs obtained by the old man on his landed property had caused a great sensation,—for everything is known in the provinces. Monsieur Hochon, in the Bridau interest, was much put about by this disaster, and questioned old Monsieur Heron, the notary at Bourges, as to the object of it.

"The heirs of old Rouget, if old Rouget changes his mind, ought to make me a votive offering," cried Monsieur Heron. "If it had not been for me, the old fellow would have allowed the fifty thousand francs' income to stand in the name of Maxence Gilet. I told Mademoiselle Brazier that she ought to look to the will only, and not run the risk of a suit for spoliation, seeing what numerous proofs these transfers in every direction would give against them. To gain time, I advised Maxence and his mistress to keep quiet, and let this sudden change in the usual business habits of the old man be forgotten."

"Protect the Bridaus, for they have nothing," said Monsieur Hochon, who in addition to all other reasons, could not forgive Gilet the terrors he had endured when fearing the pillage of his house.

Maxence Gilet and Flore Brazier, now secure against all attack, were very merry over the arrival of another of old Rouget's nephews. They knew they were able, at the first signal of danger, to make the old man sign a power of attorney under which the money in the Funds could be transferred either to Max or Flore. If the will leaving Flore the principal, should be revoked, an income of fifty thousand francs was a very tolerable crumb of comfort,—more particularly after squeezing from the real estate that mortgage of a hundred and forty thousand.

The day after his arrival, Philippe called upon his uncle about ten o'clock in the morning, anxious to present himself in his dilapidated clothing. When the convalescent of the Hopital du Midi, the prisoner of the Luxembourg, entered the room, Flore Brazier felt a shiver pass over her at the repulsive sight. Gilet himself was conscious of that particular disturbance both of mind and body, by which Nature sometimes warns us of a latent enmity, or a coming danger. If there was something indescribably sinister in Philippe's countenance, due to his recent misfortunes, the effect was heightened by his clothes. His forlorn blue great-coat was buttoned in military fashion to the throat, for painful reasons; and yet it showed much that it pretended to conceal. The bottom edges of the trousers, ragged like those of an almshouse beggar, were the sign of abject poverty. The boots left wet splashes on the floor, as the mud oozed from fissures in the soles. The gray hat, which the colonel held in his hand, was horribly greasy round the rim. The malacca cane, from which the polish had long disappeared, must have stood in all the corners of all the cafes in Paris, and poked its worn-out end into many a corruption. Above the velvet collar, rubbed and worn till the frame showed through it, rose a head like that which Frederick Lemaitre makes up for the last act in "The Life of a Gambler,"—where the exhaustion of a man still in the prime of life is betrayed by the metallic, brassy skin, discolored as if with verdigris. Such tints are seen on the faces of debauched gamblers who spend their nights in play: the eyes are sunken in a dusky circle, the lids are reddened rather than red, the brow is menacing from the wreck and ruin it reveals. Philippe's cheeks, which were sunken and wrinkled, showed signs of the illness from which he had scarcely recovered. His head was bald, except for a fringe of hair at the back which ended at the ears. The pure blue of his brilliant eyes had acquired the cold tones of polished steel.

"Good-morning, uncle," he said, in a hoarse voice. "I am your nephew, Philippe Bridau,— a specimen of how the Bourbons treat a lieutenant-colonel, an old soldier of the old army, one who carried the Emperor's orders at the battle of Montereau. If my coat were to open, I should be put to shame in presence of Mademoiselle. Well, it is the rule of the game! We hoped to begin it again; we tried it, and we have failed! I am to reside in your city by the order of the police, with a full pay of sixty francs a month. So the inhabitants needn't fear that I shall raise the price of provisions! I see you are in good and lovely company."

"Ah! you are my nephew," said Jean-Jacques.

"Invite monsieur le colonel to breakfast with us," said Flore.

"No, I thank you, madame," answered Philippe, "I have breakfasted. Besides, I would cut off my hand sooner than ask a bit of bread or a farthing from my uncle, after the treatment my mother and brother received in this town. It did not seem proper, however, that I should settle here, in Issoudun, without paying my respects to him from time to time. You can do what you like," he added, offering the old man his hand, into which Rouget put his own, which Philippe shook, "—whatever you like. I shall have nothing to say against it; provided the honor of the Bridaus is untouched."

Gilet could look at the lieutenant-colonel as much as he pleased, for Philippe pointedly avoided casting his eyes in his direction. Max, though the blood boiled in his veins, was too well aware of the importance of behaving with political prudence—which occasionally resembles cowardice—to take fire like a young man; he remained, therefore, perfectly calm and cold.

"It wouldn't be right, monsieur," said Flore, "to live on sixty francs a month under the nose of an uncle who has forty thousand francs a year, and who has already behaved so kindly to Captain Gilet, his natural relation, here present—"

"Yes, Philippe," cried the old man, "you must see that!"

On Flore's presentation, Philippe made a half-timid bow to Max.

"Uncle, I have some pictures to return to you; they are now at Monsieur Hochon's. Will you be kind enough to come over some day and identify them."

Saying these last words in a curt tone, lieutenant-colonel Philippe Bridau departed. The tone of his visit made, if possible, a deeper impression on Flore's mind, and also on that of Max, than the shock they had felt at the first sight of that horrible campaigner. As soon as Philippe had slammed the door, with the violence of a disinherited heir, Max and Flore hid behind the window-curtains to watch him as he crossed the road, to the Hochons'.

"What a vagabond!" exclaimed Flore, questioning Max with a glance of her eye.

"Yes; unfortunately there were men like him in the armies of the Emperor; I sent seven to the shades at Cabrera," answered Gilet.

"I do hope, Max, that you won't pick a quarrel with that fellow," said Mademoiselle Brazier.

"He smelt so of tobacco," complained the old man.

"He was smelling after your money-bags," said Flore, in a peremptory tone. "My advice is that you don't let him into the house again."

"I'd prefer not to," replied Rouget.

"Monsieur," said Gritte, entering the room where the Hochon family were all assembled after breakfast, "here is the Monsieur Bridau you were talking about."

Philippe made his entrance politely, in the midst of a dead silence caused by general curiosity. Madame Hochon shuddered from head to foot as she beheld the author of all Agathe's woes and the murderer of good old Madame Descoings. Adolphine also felt a shock of fear. Baruch and Francois looked at each other in surprise. Old Hochon kept his self-possession, and offered a seat to the son of Madame Bridau.

"I have come, monsieur," said Philippe, "to introduce myself to you; I am forced to consider how I can manage to live here, for five years, on sixty francs a month."

"It can be done," said the octogenarian.

Philippe talked about things in general, with perfect propriety. He mentioned the journalist Lousteau, nephew of the old lady, as a "rara avis," and won her good graces from the moment she heard him say that the name of Lousteau would become celebrated. He did not hesitate to admit his faults of conduct. To a friendly admonition which Madame Hochon addressed to him in a low voice, he replied that he had reflected deeply while in prison, and could promise that in future he would live another life.

On a hint from Philippe, Monsieur Hochon went out with him when he took his leave. When the miser and the soldier reached the boulevard Baron, a place where no one could overhear them, the colonel turned to the old man,—

"Monsieur," he said, "if you will be guided by me, we will never speak together of matters and things, or people either, unless we are walking in the open country, or in places where we cannot be heard. Maitre Desroches has fully explained to me the influence of the gossip of a little town. Therefore I don't wish you to be suspected of advising me; though Desroches has told me to ask for your advice, and I beg you not to be chary of giving it. We have a powerful enemy in our front, and it won't do to neglect any precaution which may help to defeat him. In the first place, therefore, excuse me if I do not call upon you again. A little coldness between us will clear you of all suspicion of influencing my conduct. When I want to consult you, I will pass along the square at half-past nine, just as you are coming out after breakfast. If you see me carry my cane on my shoulder, that will mean that we must meet—accidentally—in some open space which you will point out to me."

"I see you are a prudent man, bent on success," said old Hochon.

"I shall succeed, monsieur. First of all, give me the names of the officers of the old army now living in Issoudun, who have not taken sides with Maxence Gilet; I wish to make their acquaintance."

"Well, there's a captain of the artillery of the Guard, Monsieur Mignonnet, a man about forty years of age, who was brought up at the Ecole Polytechnique, and lives in a quiet way. He is a very honorable man, and openly disapproves of Max, whose conduct he considers unworthy of a true soldier."

"Good!" remarked the lieutenant-colonel.

"There are not many soldiers here of that stripe," resumed Monsieur Hochon; "the only other that I know is an old cavalry captain."

"That is my arm," said Philippe. "Was he in the Guard?"

"Yes," replied Monsieur Hochon. "Carpentier was, in 1810, sergeant-major in the dragoons; then he rose to be sub-lieutenant in the line, and subsequently captain of cavalry."

"Giroudeau may know him," thought Philippe.

"This Monsieur Carpentier took the place in the mayor's office which Gilet threw up; he is a friend of Monsieur Mignonnet."

"How can I earn my living here?"

"They are going, I think, to establish a mutual insurance agency in Issoudun, for the department of the Cher; you might get a place in it, but the pay won't be more than fifty francs a month at the outside."

"That will be enough."

At the end of a week Philippe had a new suit of clothes,—coat, waistcoat, and trousers,— of good blue Elbeuf cloth, bought on credit, to be paid for at so much a month; also new boots, buckskin gloves, and a hat. Giroudeau sent him some linen, with his weapons and a letter for Carpentier, who had formerly served under Giroudeau. The letter secured him Carpentier's good-will, and the latter presented him to his friend Mignonnet as a man of great merit and the highest character. Philippe won the admiration of these worthy officers by confiding to them a few facts about the late conspiracy, which was, as everybody knows, the last attempt of the old army against the Bourbons; for the affair of the sergeants at La Rochelle belongs to another order of ideas.

Warned by the fate of the conspiracy of the 19th of August, 1820, and of those of Berton and Caron, the soldiers of the old army resigned themselves, after their failure in 1822, to await events. This last conspiracy, which grew out of that of the 19th of August, was really a continuation of the latter, carried on by a better element. Like its predecessor, it was absolutely unknown to the royal government. Betrayed once more, the conspirators had the wit to reduce their vast enterprise to the puny proportions of a barrack plot. This conspiracy, in which several regiments of cavalry, infantry, and artillery were concerned, had its centre in the north of France. The strong places along the frontier were to be captured at a blow. If success had followed, the treaties of 1815 would have been broken by a federation with Belgium, which, by a military compact made among the soldiers, was to withdraw from the Holy Alliance. Two thrones would have been plunged in a moment into the vortex of this sudden cyclone. Instead of this formidable scheme—concerted by strong minds and supported by personages of high rank— being carried out, one small part of it, and that only, was discovered and brought before the Court of Peers. Philippe Bridau consented to screen the leaders, who retired the moment the plot was discovered (either by treachery or accident), and from their seats in both Chambers lent their co-operation to the inquiry only to work for the ultimate success of their purpose at the heart of the government.

To recount this scheme, which, since 1830, the Liberals have openly confessed in all its ramifications, would trench upon the domain of history and involve too long a digression. This glimpse of it is enough to show the double part which Philippe Bridau undertook to play. The former staff-officer of the Emperor was to lead a movement in Paris solely for the purpose of masking the real conspiracy and occupying the mind of the government at its centre, while the great struggle should burst forth at the north. When the latter miscarried before discovery, Philippe was ordered to break all links connecting the two plots, and to allow the secrets of the secondary plot only to become known. For this purpose, his abject misery, to which his state of health and his clothing bore witness, was amply sufficient to undervalue the character of the conspiracy and reduce its proportions in the eyes of the authorities. The role was well suited to the precarious position of the unprincipled gambler. Feeling himself astride of both parties, the crafty Philippe played the saint to the royal government, all the while retaining the good opinion of the men in high places who were of the other party,—determined to cast in his lot at a later day with whichever side he might then find most to his advantage.

These revelations as to the vast bearings of the real conspiracy made Philippe a man of great distinction in the eyes of Carpentier and Mignonnet, to whom his self-devotion seemed a state-craft worthy of the palmy days of the Convention. In a short time the tricky Bonapartist was seen to be on friendly terms with the two officers, and the consideration they enjoyed in the town was, of course, shared by him. He soon obtained, through their recommendation, the situation in the insurance office that old Hochon had suggested, which required only three hours of his day. Mignonnet and Carpentier put him up at their club, where his good manners and bearing, in keeping with the high opinion which the two officers expressed about him, won him a respect often given to external appearances that are only deceitful.

Philippe, whose conduct was carefully considered and planned, had indeed made many reflections while in prison as to the inconveniences of leading a debauched life. He did not need Desroches's lecture to understand the necessity of conciliating the people at Issoudun by decent, sober, and respectable conduct. Delighted to attract Max's ridicule by behaving with the propriety of a Mignonnet, he went further, and endeavored to lull Gilet's suspicions by deceiving him as to his real character. He was bent on being taken for a fool by appearing generous and disinterested; all the while drawing a net around his adversary, and keeping his eye on his uncle's property. His mother and brother, on the contrary, who were really disinterested, generous, and lofty, had been accused of greed because they had acted with straightforward simplicity. Philippe's covetousness was fully roused by Monsieur Hochon, who gave him all the details of his uncle's property. In the first secret conversation which he held with the octogenarian, they agreed that Philippe must not awaken Max's suspicions; for the game would be lost if Flore and Max were to carry off their victim, though no further than Bourges.

Once a week the colonel dined with Mignonnet; another day with Carpentier; and every Thursday with Monsieur Hochon. At the end of three weeks he received other invitations for the remaining days, so that he had little more than his breakfast to provide. He never spoke of his uncle, nor of the Rabouilleuse, nor of Gilet, unless it were in connection with his mother and his brother's stay in Issoudun. The three officers—the only soldiers in the town who were decorated, and among whom Philippe had the advantage of the rosette, which in the eyes of all provincials gave him a marked superiority—took a habit of walking together every day before dinner, keeping, as the saying is, to themselves. This reserve and tranquillity of demeanor had an excellent effect on Issoudun. All Max's adherents thought Philippe a "sabreur,"—an expression applied by soldiers to the commonest sort of courage in their superior officers, while denying that they possess the requisite qualities of a commander.

"He is a very honorable man," said Goddet the surgeon, to Max.

"Bah!" replied Gilet, "his behavior before the Court of Peers proves him to have been either a dupe or a spy; he is, as you say, ninny enough to have been duped by the great players."

After obtaining his situation, Philippe, who was well informed as to the gossip of the town, wished to conceal certain circumstances of his present life as much as possible from the knowledge of the inhabitants; he therefore went to live in a house at the farther end of the faubourg Saint-Paterne, to which was attached a large garden. Here he was able in the utmost secrecy to fence with Carpentier, who had been a fencing-master in the infantry before entering the cavalry. Philippe soon recovered his early dexterity, and learned other and new secrets from Carpentier, which convinced him that he need not fear the prowess of any adversary. This done, he began openly to practise with pistols, with Mignonnet and Carpentier, declaring it was for amusement, but really intending to make Max believe that, in case of a duel, he should rely on that weapon. Whenever Philippe met Gilet he waited for him to bow first, and answered the salutation by touching the brim of his hat cavalierly, as an officer acknowledges the salute of a private. Maxence Gilet gave no sign of impatience or displeasure; he never uttered a single word about Bridau at the Cognettes' where he still gave suppers; although, since Fario's attack, the pranks of the Order of Idleness were temporarily suspended.

After a while, however, the contempt shown by Lieutenant-colonel Bridau for the former cavalry captain, Gilet, was a settled fact, which certain Knights of Idleness, who were less bound to Max than Francois, Baruch, and three or four others, discussed among themselves. They were much surprised to see the violent and fiery Max behave with such discretion. No one in Issoudun, not even Potel or Renard, dared broach so delicate a subject with him. Potel, somewhat disturbed by this open misunderstanding between two heroes of the Imperial Guard, suggested that Max might be laying a net for the colonel; he asserted that some new scheme might be looked for from the man who had got rid of the mother and one brother by making use of Fario's attack upon him, the particulars of which were now no longer a mystery. Monsieur Hochon had taken care to reveal the truth of Max's atrocious accusation to the best people of the town. Thus it happened that in talking over the situation of the lieutenant-colonel in relation to Max, and in trying to guess what might spring from their antagonism, the whole town regarded the two men, from the start, as adversaries.

Philippe, who had carefully investigated all the circumstances of his brother's arrest and the antecedents of Gilet and the Rabouilleuse, was finally brought into rather close relations with Fario, who lived near him. After studying the Spaniard, Philippe thought he might trust a man of that quality. The two found their hatred so firm a bond of union, that Fario put himself at Philippe's disposal, and related all that he knew about the Knights of Idleness. Philippe promised, in case he succeeded in obtaining over his uncle the power now exercised by Gilet, to indemnify Fario for his losses; this bait made the Spaniard his henchman. Maxence was now face to face with a dangerous foe; he had, as they say in those parts, some one to handle. Roused by much gossip and various rumors, the town of Issoudun expected a mortal combat between the two men, who, we must remark, mutually despised each other.

One morning, toward the end of November, Philippe met Monsieur Hochon about twelve o'clock, in the long avenue of Frapesle, and said to him:—

"I have discovered that your grandsons Baruch and Francois are the intimate friends of Maxence Gilet. The rascals are mixed up in all the pranks that are played about this town at night. It was through them that Maxence knew what was said in your house when my mother and brother were staying there."

"How did you get proof of such a monstrous thing?"

"I overheard their conversation one night as they were leaving a drinking-shop. Your grandsons both owe Max more than three thousand francs. The scoundrel told the lads to try and find out our intentions; he reminded them that you had once thought of getting round my uncle by priestcraft, and declared that nobody but you could guide me; for he thinks, fortunately, that I am nothing more than a 'sabreur.'"

"My grandsons! is it possible?"

"Watch them," said Philippe. "You will see them coming home along the place Saint-Jean, at two or three o'clock in the morning, as tipsy as champagne-corks, and in company with Gilet—"

"That's why the scamps keep so sober at home!" cried Monsieur Hochon.

"Fario has told me all about their nocturnal proceedings," resumed Philippe; "without him, I should never have suspected them. My uncle is held down under an absolute thraldom, if I may judge by certain things which the Spaniard has heard Max say to your boys. I suspect Max and the Rabouilleuse of a scheme to make sure of the fifty thousand francs' income from the Funds, and then, after pulling that feather from their pigeon's wing, to run away, I don't know where, and get married. It is high time to know what is going on under my uncle's roof, but I don't see how to set about it."

"I will think of it," said the old man.

They separated, for several persons were now approaching.

Never, at any time in his life, did Jean-Jacques suffer as he had done since the first visit of his nephew Philippe. Flore was terrified by the presentiment of some evil that threatened Max.

Weary of her master, and fearing that he might live to be very old, since he was able to bear up under their criminal practices, she formed the very simple plan of leaving Issoudun and being married to Maxence in Paris, after obtaining from Jean-Jacques the transfer of the income in the Funds. The old bachelor, guided, not by any justice to his family, nor by personal avarice, but solely by his passion, steadily refused to make the transfer, on the ground that Flore was to be his sole heir. The unhappy creature knew to what extent Flore loved Max, and he believed he would be abandoned the moment she was made rich enough to marry. When Flore, after employing the tenderest cajoleries, was unable to succeed, she tried rigor; she no longer spoke to her master; Vedie was sent to wait upon him, and found him in the morning with his eyes swollen and red with weeping. For a week or more, poor Rouget had breakfasted alone, and Heaven knows on what food!

The day after Philippe's conversation with Monsieur Hochon, he determined to pay a second visit to his uncle, whom he found much changed. Flore stayed beside the old man, speaking tenderly and looking at him with much affection; she played the comedy so well that Philippe guessed some immediate danger, merely from the solicitude thus displayed in his presence. Gilet, whose policy it was to avoid all collision with Philippe, did not appear. After watching his uncle and Flore for a time with a discerning eye, the colonel judged that the time had come to strike his grand blow.

"Adieu, my dear uncle," he said, rising as if to leave the house.

"Oh! don't go yet," cried the old man, who was comforted by Flore's false tenderness. "Dine with us, Philippe."

"Yes, if you will come and take a walk with me."

"Monsieur is very feeble," interposed Mademoiselle Brazier; "just now he was unwilling even to go out in the carriage," she added, turning upon the old man the fixed look with which keepers quell a maniac.

Philippe took Flore by the arm, compelling her to look at him, and looking at her in return as fixedly as she had just looked at her victim.

"Tell me, mademoiselle," he said, "is it a fact that my uncle is not free to take a walk with me?"

"Why, yes he is, monsieur," replied Flore, who was unable to make any other answer.

"Very well. Come, uncle. Mademoiselle, give him his hat and cane."

"But—he never goes out without me. Do you, monsieur?"

"Yes, Philippe, yes; I always want her—"

"It would be better to take the carriage," said Flore.

"Yes, let us take the carriage," cried the old man, in his anxiety to make his two tyrants agree.

"Uncle, you will come with me, alone, and on foot, or I shall never return here; I shall know that the town of Issoudun tells the truth, when it declares you are under the dominion of Mademoiselle Flore Brazier. That my uncle should love you, is all very well," he resumed, holding Flore with a fixed eye; "that you should not love my uncle is also on the cards; but when it comes to your making him unhappy—halt! If people want to get hold of an inheritance, they must earn it. Are you coming, uncle?"

Philippe saw the eyes of the poor imbecile roving from himself to Flore, in painful hesitation.

"Ha! that's how it is, is it?" resumed the lieutenant-colonel. "Well, adieu, uncle. Mademoiselle, I kiss your hands."

He turned quickly when he reached the door, and caught Flore in the act of making a menacing gesture at his uncle.

"Uncle," he said, "if you wish to go with me, I will meet you at your door in ten minutes: I am now going to see Monsieur Hochon. If you and I do not take that walk, I shall take upon myself to make some others walk."

So saying, he went away, and crossed the place Saint-Jean to the Hochons.

Every one can imagine the scenes which the revelations made by Philippe to Monsieur Hochon had brought about within that family. At nine o'clock, old Monsieur Heron, the notary, presented himself with a bundle of papers, and found a fire in the hall which the old miser, contrary to all his habits, had ordered to be lighted. Madame Hochon, already dressed at this unusual hour, was sitting in her armchair at the corner of the fireplace. The two grandsons, warned the night before by Adolphine that a storm was gathering about their heads, had been ordered to stay in the house. Summoned now by Gritte, they were alarmed at the formal preparations of their grandparents, whose coldness and anger they had been made to feel in the air for the last twenty-four hours.

"Don't rise for them," said their grandfather to Monsieur Heron; "you see before you two miscreants, unworthy of pardon."

"Oh, grandpapa!" said Francois.

"Be silent!" said the old man sternly. "I know of your nocturnal life and your intimacy with Monsieur Maxence Gilet. But you will meet him no more at Mere Cognette's at one in the morning; for you will not leave this house, either of you, until you go to your respective destinations. Ha! it was you who ruined Fario, was it? you, who have narrowly escaped the police-courts—Hold your tongue!" he said, seeing that Baruch was about to speak. "You both owe money to Monsieur Maxence Gilet; who, for six years, has paid for your debauchery. Listen, both of you, to my guardianship accounts; after that, I shall have more to say. You will see, after these papers are read, whether you can still trifle with me,—still trifle with family laws by betraying the secrets of this house, and reporting to a Monsieur Maxence Gilet what is said and what is done here. For three thousand francs, you became spies; for ten thousand, you would, no doubt, become assassins. You did almost kill Madame Bridau; for Monsieur Gilet knew very well it was Fario who stabbed him when he threw the crime upon my guest, Monsieur Joseph Bridau. If that jail-bird did so wicked an act, it was because you told him what Madame Bridau meant to do. You, my grandsons, the spies of such a man! You, house-breakers and marauders! Don't you know that your worthy leader killed a poor young woman, in 1806? I will not have assassins and thieves in my family. Pack your things; you shall go hang elsewhere!"

The two young men turned white and stiff as plaster casts.

"Read on, Monsieur Heron," said Hochon.

The old notary read the guardianship accounts; from which it appeared that the net fortune of the two Borniche children amounted to seventy thousand francs, a sum derived from the dowry of their mother: but Monsieur Hochon had lent his daughter various large sums, and was now, as creditor, the owner of a part of the property of his Borniche grandchildren. The portion coming to Baruch amounted to only twenty thousand francs.

"Now you are rich," said the old man, "take your money, and go. I remain master of my own property and that of Madame Hochon, who in this matter shares all my intentions, and I shall give it to whom I choose; namely, our dear Adolphine. Yes, we can marry her if we please to the son of a peer of France, for she will be an heiress."

"A noble fortune!" said Monsieur Heron.

"Monsieur Maxence Gilet will make up this loss to you," said Madame Hochon.

"Let my hard-saved money go to a scapegrace like you? no, indeed!" cried Monsieur Hochon.

"Forgive me!" stammered Baruch.

"'Forgive, and I won't do it again,'" sneered the old man, imitating a child's voice. "If I were to forgive you, and let you out of this house, you would go and tell Monsieur Maxence what has happened, and warn him to be on his guard. No, no, my little men. I shall keep my eye on you, and I have means of knowing what you do. As you behave, so shall I behave to you. It will be by a long course of good conduct, not that of a day or a month, but of years, that I shall judge you. I am strong on my legs, my eyes are good, my health is sound; I hope to live long enough to see what road you take. Your first move will be to Paris, where you will study banking under Messieurs Mongenod and Sons. Ill-luck to you if you don't walk straight; you will be watched. Your property is in the hand of Messieurs Mongenod; here is a cheque for the amount. Now then, release me as guardian, and sign the accounts, and also this receipt," he added, taking the papers from Monsieur Heron and handing them to Baruch.

"As for you, Francois Hochon, you owe me money instead of having any to receive," said the old man, looking at his other grandson. "Monsieur Heron, read his account; it is all clear—perfectly clear."

The reading was done in the midst of perfect stillness.

"You will have six hundred francs a year, and with that you will go to Poitiers and study law," said the grandfather, when the notary had finished. "I had a fine life in prospect for you; but now, you must earn your living as a lawyer. Ah! my young rascals, you have deceived me for six years; you now know it has taken me but one hour to get even with you: I have seven-leagued boots."

Just as old Monsieur Heron was preparing to leave with the signed papers, Gritte announced Colonel Bridau. Madame Hochon left the room, taking her grandsons with her, that she might, as old Hochon said, confess them privately and find out what effect this scene had produced upon them.

Philippe and the old man stood in the embrasure of a window and spoke in low tones.

"I have been reflecting on the state of your affairs over there," said Monsieur Hochon pointing to the Rouget house. "I have just had a talk with Monsieur Heron. The security for the fifty thousand francs a year from the property in the Funds cannot be sold unless by the owner himself or some one with a power of attorney from him. Now, since your arrival here, your uncle has not signed any such power before any notary; and, as he has not left Issoudun, he can't have signed one elsewhere. If he attempts to give a power of attorney here, we shall know it instantly; if he goes away to give one, we shall also know it, for it will have to be registered, and that excellent Heron has means of finding it out. Therefore, if Rouget leaves Issoudun, have him followed, learn where he goes, and we will find a way to discover what he does."

"The power of attorney has not been given," said Philippe; "they are trying to get it; but—they—will—not—suc—ceed—" added the vagabond, whose eye just then caught sight of his uncle on the steps of the opposite house: he pointed him out to Monsieur Hochon, and related succinctly the particulars, at once so petty and so important, of his visit.

"Maxence is afraid of me, but he can't evade me. Mignonnet says that all the officers of the old army who are in Issoudun give a yearly banquet on the anniversary of the Emperor's coronation; so Maxence Gilet and I are sure to meet in a few days."

"If he gets a power of attorney by the morning of the first of December," said Hochon, "he might take the mail-post for Paris, and give up the banquet."

"Very good. The first thing is, then, to get possession of my uncle; I've an eye that cows a fool," said Philippe, giving Monsieur Hochon an atrocious glance that made the old man tremble.

"If they let him walk with you, Maxence must believe he has found some means to win the game," remarked the old miser.

"Oh! Fario is on the watch," said Philippe, "and he is not alone. That Spaniard has discovered one of my old soldiers in the neighborhood of Vatan, a man I once did some service to. Without any one's suspecting it, Benjamin Bourdet is under Fario's orders, who has lent him a horse to get about with."

"If you kill that monster who has corrupted my grandsons, I shall say you have done a good deed."

"Thanks to me, the town of Issoudun now knows what Monsieur Maxence Gilet has been doing at night for the last six years," replied Philippe; "and the cackle, as you call it here, is now started on him. Morally his day is over."

The moment Philippe left his uncle's house Flore went to Max's room to tell him every particular of the nephew's bold visit.

"What's to be done?" she asked.

"Before trying the last means,—which will be to fight that big reprobate," replied Maxence, "—we must play double or quits, and try our grand stroke. Let the old idiot go with his nephew."

"But that big brute won't mince matters," remonstrated Flore; "he'll call things by their right names."

"Listen to me," said Maxence in a harsh voice. "Do you think I've not kept my ears open, and reflected about how we stand? Send to Pere Cognette for a horse and a char-a-banc, and say we want them instantly: they must be here in five minutes. Pack all your belongings, take Vedie, and go to Vatan. Settle yourself there as if you mean to stay; carry off the twenty thousand francs in gold which the old fellow has got in his drawer. If I bring him to you in Vatan, you are to refuse to come back here unless he signs the power of attorney. As soon as we get it I'll slip off to Paris, while you're returning to Issoudun. When Jean-Jacques gets back from his walk and finds you gone, he'll go beside himself, and want to follow you. Well! when he does, I'll give him a talking to."

CHAPTER XV

While the foregoing plot was progressing, Philippe was walking arm in arm with his uncle along the boulevard Baron.

"The two great tacticians are coming to close quarters at last," thought Monsieur Hochon as he watched the colonel marching off with his uncle; "I am curious to see the end of the game, and what becomes of the stake of ninety thousand francs a year."

"My dear uncle," said Philippe, whose phraseology had a flavor of his affinities in Paris, "you love this girl, and you are devilishly right. She is damnably handsome! Instead of billing and cooing she makes you trot like a valet; well, that's all simple enough; but she wants to see you six feet underground, so that she may marry Max, whom she adores."

"I know that, Philippe, but I love her all the same."

"Well, I have sworn by the soul of my mother, who is your own sister," continued Philippe, "to make your Rabouilleuse as supple as my glove, and the same as she was before that scoundrel, who is unworthy to have served in the Imperial Guard, ever came to quarter himself in your house."

"Ah! if you could do that!—" said the old man.

"It is very easy," answered Philippe, cutting his uncle short. "I'll kill Max as I would a dog; but—on one condition," added the old campaigner.

"What is that?" said Rouget, looking at his nephew in a stupid way.

"Don't sign that power of attorney which they want of you before the third of December; put them off till then. Your torturers only want it to enable them to sell the fifty thousand a year you have in the Funds, so that they may run off to Paris and pay for their wedding festivities out of your millions."

"I am afraid so," replied Rouget.

"Well, whatever they may say or do to you, put off giving that power of attorney until next week."

"Yes; but when Flore talks to me she stirs my very soul, till I don't know what I do. I give you my word, when she looks at me in a certain way, her blue eyes seem like paradise, and I am no longer master of myself,—especially when for some days she had been harsh to me."

"Well, whether she is sweet or sour, don't do more than promise to sign the paper, and let me know the night before you are going to do it. That will answer. Maxence shall not be your proxy unless he first kills me. If I kill him, you must agree to take me in his place, and I'll undertake to break in that handsome girl and keep her at your beck and call. Yes, Flore shall love you, and if she doesn't satisfy you—thunder! I'll thrash her."

"Oh! I never could allow that. A blow struck at Flore would break my heart."

"But it is the only way to govern women and horses. A man makes himself feared, or loved, or respected. Now that is what I wanted to whisper in your ear—Good-morning, gentlemen," he said to Mignonnet and Carpentier, who came up at the moment; "I am taking my uncle for a walk, as you see, and trying to improve him; for we are in an age when children are obliged to educate their grandparents."

They all bowed to each other.

"You behold in my dear uncle the effects of an unhappy passion. Those two want to strip him of his fortune and leave him in the lurch—you know to whom I refer? He sees the plot; but he hasn't the courage to give up his SUGAR-PLUM for a few days so as to baffle it."

Philippe briefly explained his uncle's position.

"Gentlemen," he remarked, in conclusion, "you see there are no two ways of saving him: either Colonel Bridau must kill Captain Gilet, or Captain Gilet must kill Colonel Bridau. We celebrate the Emperor's coronation on the day after to-morrow; I rely upon you to arrange the seats at the banquet so that I shall sit opposite to Gilet. You will do me the honor, I hope, of being my seconds."

"We will appoint you to preside, and sit ourselves on either side of you. Max, as vice-president, will of course sit opposite," said Mignonnet.

"Oh! the scoundrel will have Potel and Renard with him," said Carpentier. "In spite of all that Issoudun now knows and says of his midnight maraudings, those two worthy officers, who have already been his seconds, remain faithful to him."

"You see how it all maps out, uncle," said Philippe. "Therefore, sign no paper before the third of December; the next day you shall be free, happy, and beloved by Flore, without having to coax for it."

"You don't know him, Philippe," said the terrified old man. "Maxence has killed nine men in duels."

"Yes; but ninety thousand francs a year didn't depend on it," answered Philippe.

"A bad conscience shakes the hand," remarked Mignonnet sententiously.

"In a few days from now," resumed Philippe, "you and the Rabouilleuse will be living together as sweet as honey,—that is, after she gets through mourning. At first she'll twist like a worm, and yelp, and weep; but never mind, let the water run!"

The two soldiers approved of Philippe's arguments, and tried to hearten up old Rouget, with whom they walked about for nearly two hours. At last Philippe took his uncle home, saying as they parted:—

"Don't take any steps without me. I know women. I have paid for one, who cost me far more than Flore can ever cost you. But she taught me how to behave to the fair sex for the rest of my days. Women are bad children; they are inferior animals to men; we must make them fear us; the worst condition in the world is to be governed by such brutes."

It was about half-past two in the afternoon when the old man got home. Kouski opened the door in tears,—that is, by Max's orders, he gave signs of weeping.

"Oh! Monsieur, Madame has gone away, and taken Vedie with her!"

"Gone—a—way!" said the old man in a strangled voice.

The blow was so violent that Rouget sat down on the stairs, unable to stand. A moment after, he rose, looked about the hall, into the kitchen, went up to his own room, searched all the chambers, and returned to the salon, where he threw himself into a chair, and burst into tears.

"Where is she?" he sobbed. "Oh! where is she? where is Max?"

"I don't know," answered Kouski. "The captain went out without telling me."

Gilet thought it politic to be seen sauntering about the town. By leaving the old man alone with his despair, he knew he should make him feel his desertion the more keenly, and reduce him to docility. To keep Philippe from assisting his uncle at this crisis, he had given Kouski strict orders not to open the door to any one. Flore away, the miserable old man grew frantic, and the situation of things approached a crisis. During his walk through the town, Maxence Gilet was avoided by many persons who a day or two earlier would have hastened to shake hands with him. A general reaction had set in against him. The deeds of the Knights of Idleness were ringing on every tongue. The tale of Joseph Bridau's arrest, now cleared up, disgraced Max in the eyes of all; and his life and conduct received in one day their just award. Gilet met Captain Potel, who was looking for him, and seemed almost beside himself.

"What's the matter with you, Potel?"

"My dear fellow, the Imperial Guard is being black-guarded all over the town! These civilians are crying you down! and it goes to the bottom of my heart."

"What are they complaining of?" asked Max.

"Of what you do at night."

"As if we couldn't amuse ourselves a little!"

"But that isn't all," said Potel.

Potel belonged to the same class as the officer who replied to the burgomasters: "Eh! your town will be paid for, if we do burn it!" So he was very little troubled about the deeds of the Order of Idleness.

"What more?" inquired Gilet.

"The Guard is against the Guard. It is that that breaks my heart. Bridau has set all these bourgeois on you. The Guard against the Guard! no, it ought not to be! You can't back down, Max; you must meet Bridau. I had a great mind to pick a quarrel with the low scoundrel myself and send him to the shades; I wish I had, and then the bourgeois wouldn't have seen the spectacle of the Guard against the Guard. In war times, I don't say anything against it. Two heroes of the Guard may quarrel, and fight,—but at least there are no civilians to look on and sneer. No, I say that big villain never served in the Guard. A guardsman would never behave as he does to another guardsman, under the very eyes of the bourgeois; impossible! Ah! it's all wrong; the Guard is disgraced—and here, at Issoudun! where it was once so honored."

"Come, Potel, don't worry yourself," answered Max; "even if you do not see me at the banquet—"

"What! do you mean that you won't be there the day after to-morrow?" cried Potel, interrupting his friend. "Do you wish to be called a coward? and have it said you are running away from Bridau? No, no! The unmounted grenadiers of the Guard can not draw back before the dragoons of the Guard. Arrange your business in some other way and be there!"

"One more to send to the shades!" said Max. "Well, I think I can manage my business so as to get there—For," he thought to himself, "that power of attorney ought not to be in my name; as old Heron says, it would look too much like theft."

This lion, tangled in the meshes Philippe Bridau was weaving for him, muttered between his teeth as he went along; he avoided the looks of those he met and returned home by the boulevard Vilatte, still talking to himself.

"I will have that money before I fight," he said. "If I die, it shall not go to Philippe. I must put it in Flore's name. She will follow my instructions, and go straight to Paris. Once there, she can marry, if she chooses, the son of some marshal of France who has been sent to the right-about. I'll have that power of attorney made in Baruch's name, and he'll transfer the property by my order."

Max, to do him justice, was never more cool and calm in appearance than when his blood and his ideas were boiling. No man ever united in a higher degree the qualities which make a great general. If his career had not been cut short by his captivity at Cabrera, the Emperor would certainly have found him one of those men who are necessary to the success of vast enterprises. When he entered the room where the hapless victim of all these comic and tragic scenes was still weeping, Max asked the meaning of such distress; seemed surprised, pretended that he knew nothing, and heard, with well-acted amazement, of Flore's departure. He questioned Kouski, to obtain some light on the object of this inexplicable journey.

"Madame said like this," Kouski replied, "—that I was to tell monsieur she had taken twenty thousand francs in gold from his drawer, thinking that monsieur wouldn't refuse her that amount as wages for the last twenty-two years."

"Wages?" exclaimed Rouget.

"Yes," replied Kouski. "Ah! I shall never come back," she said to Vedie as she drove away. "Poor Vedie, who is so attached to monsieur, remonstrated with madame. 'No, no,' she answered, 'he has no affection for me; he lets his nephew treat me like the lowest of the low'; and she wept—oh! bitterly."

"Eh! what do I care for Philippe?" cried the old man, whom Max was watching. "Where is Flore? how can we find out where she is?"

"Philippe, whose advice you follow, will help you," said Max coldly.

"Philippe?" said the old man, "what has he to do with the poor child? There is no one but you, my good Max, who can find Flore. She will follow you—you could bring her back to me—"

"I don't wish to oppose Monsieur Bridau," observed Max.

"As for that," cried Rouget, "if that hinders you, he told me he meant to kill you."

"Ah!" exclaimed Gilet, laughing, "we will see about it!"

"My friend," said the old man, "find Flore, and I will do all she wants of me."

"Some one must have seen her as she passed through the town," said Maxence to Kouski. "Serve dinner; put everything on the table, and then go and make inquiries from place to place. Let us know, by dessert, which road Mademoiselle Brazier has taken."

This order quieted for a time the poor creature, who was moaning like a child that has lost its nurse. At this moment Rouget, who hated Max, thought his tormentor an angel. A passion like that of this miserable old man for Flore is astonishingly like the emotions of childhood. At six o'clock, the Pole, who had merely taken a walk, returned to announce that Flore had driven towards Vatan.

"Madame is going back to her own people, that's plain," said Kouski.

"Would you like to go to Vatan to-night?" said Max. "The road is bad, but Kouski knows how to drive, and you'll make your peace better to-night than to-morrow morning."

"Let us go!" cried Rouget.

"Put the horse in quietly," said Max to Kouski; "manage, if you can, that the town shall not know of this nonsense, for Monsieur Rouget's sake. Saddle my horse," he added in a whisper. "I will ride on ahead of you."

Monsieur Hochon had already notified Philippe of Flore's departure; and the colonel rose from Monsieur Mignonnet's dinner-table to rush to the place Saint-Jean; for he at once guessed the meaning of this clever strategy. When Philippe presented himself at his uncle's house, Kouski answered through a window that Monsieur Rouget was unable to see any one.

"Fario," said Philippe to the Spaniard, who was stationed in the Grande-Narette, "go and tell Benjamin to mount his horse; it is all-important that I shall know what Gilet does with my uncle."

"They are now putting the horse into the caleche," said Fario, who had been watching the Rouget stable.

"If they go towards Vatan," answered Philippe, "get me another horse, and come yourself with Benjamin to Monsieur Mignonnet's."

"What do you mean to do?" asked Monsieur Hochon, who had come out of his own house when he saw Philippe and Fario standing together.

"The genius of a general, my dear Monsieur Hochon," said Philippe, "consists not only in carefully observing the enemy's movements, but also in guessing his intentions from those movements, and in modifying his own plan whenever the enemy interferes with it by some unexpected action. Now, if my uncle and Max drive out together, they are going to Vatan; Maxence will have promised to reconcile him with Flore, who 'fugit ad salices,'—the manoeuvre is General Virgil's. If that's the line they take, I don't yet know what I shall do; I shall have some hours to think it over, for my uncle can't sign a power of attorney at ten o'clock at night; the notaries will all be in bed. If, as I rather fancy, Max goes on in advance of my uncle to teach Flore her lesson,—which seems necessary and probable,—the rogue is lost! you will see the sort of revenge we old soldiers take in a game of this kind. Now, as I need a helper for this last stroke, I must go back to Mignonnet's and make an arrangement with my friend Carpentier."

Shaking hands with Monsieur Hochon, Philippe went off down the Petite-Narette to Mignonnet's house. Ten minutes later, Monsieur Hochon saw Max ride off at a quick trot; and the old miser's curiosity was so powerfully excited that he remained standing at his window, eagerly expecting to hear the wheels of the old demi-fortune, which was not long in coming. Jean-Jacques's impatience made him follow Max within twenty minutes. Kouski, no doubt under orders from his master, walked the horse through the town.

"If they get to Paris, all is lost," thought Monsieur Hochon.

At this moment, a lad from the faubourg de Rome came to the Hochon house with a letter for Baruch. The two grandsons, much subdued by the events of the morning, had kept their rooms of their own accord during the day. Thinking over their prospects, they saw plainly that they had better be cautious with their grandparents. Baruch knew very well the influence which his grandfather Hochon exerted over his grandfather and grandmother Borniche: Monsieur Hochon would not hesitate to get their property for Adolphine if his conduct were such as to make them pin their hopes on the grand marriage with which his grandfather had threatened him that morning. Being richer than Francois, Baruch had the most to lose; he therefore counselled an absolute surrender, with no other condition than the payment of their debt to Max. As for Francois, his future was entirely in the hands of his grandfather; he had no expectations except from him, and by the guardianship account, he was now his debtor. The two young men accordingly gave solemn promises of amendment, prompted by their imperilled interests, and by the hope Madame Hochon held out, that the debt to Max should be paid.

"You have done very wrong," she said to them; "repair it by future good conduct, and Monsieur Hochon will forget it."

So, when Francois had read the letter which had been brought for Baruch, over the latter's shoulder, he whispered in his ear, "Ask grandpapa's advice."

"Read this," said Baruch, taking the letter to old Hochon.

"Read it to me yourself; I haven't my spectacles."

My dear Friend,—I hope you will not hesitate, under the serious circumstances in which I find myself, to do me the service of receiving a power of attorney from Monsieur Rouget. Be at Vatan to-morrow morning at nine o'clock. I shall probably send you to Paris, but don't be uneasy; I will furnish you with money for the journey, and join you there immediately. I am almost sure I shall be obliged to leave Issoudun, December third. Adieu. I count on your friendship; rely on that of your friend, Maxence

"God be praised!" exclaimed Monsieur Hochon; "the property of that old idiot is saved from the claws of the devil."

"It will be if you say so," said Madame Hochon; "and I thank God,—who has no doubt heard my prayers. The prosperity of the wicked is always fleeting."

"You must go to Vatan, and accept the power of attorney from Monsieur Rouget," said the old man to Baruch. "Their object is to get fifty thousand francs a year transferred to Mademoiselle Brazier. They will send you to Paris, and you must seem to go; but you are to stop at Orleans, and wait there till you hear from me. Let no one—not a soul—know where you lodge; go to the first inn you come to in the faubourg Bannier, no matter if it is only a post-house—"

"Look here!" cried Francois, who had rushed to the window at the sudden noise of wheels in the Grande-Narette. "Here's something new!—Pere Rouget and Colonel Bridau coming back together in the caleche, Benjamin and Captain Carpentier following on horseback!"

"I'll go over," cried Monsieur Hochon, whose curiosity carried the day over every other feeling.

Monsieur Hochon found old Rouget in his bedroom, writing the following letter at his nephew's dictation:

Mademoiselle,—If you do not start to return here the moment you receive this letter, your conduct will show such ingratitude for all my goodness that I shall revoke the will I have made in your favor, and give my property to my nephew Philippe. You will understand that Monsieur Gilet can no longer be my guest after staying with you at Vatan. I send this letter by Captain Carpentier, who will put it into your own hands. I hope you will listen to his advice; he will speak to you with authority from me. Your affectionate J.-J. Rouget.

"Captain Carpentier and I MET my uncle, who was so foolish as to follow Mademoiselle Brazier and Monsieur Gilet to Vatan," said Philippe, with sarcastic emphasis, to Monsieur Hochon. "I have made my uncle see that he was running his head into a noose; for that girl will abandon him the moment she gets him to sign a power of attorney, by which they mean to obtain the income of his money in the Funds. That letter will bring her back under his roof, the handsome runaway! this very night, or I'm mistaken. I promise to make her as pliable as a bit of whalebone for the rest of her days, if my uncle allows me to take Maxence Gilet's place; which, in my opinion, he ought never to have had in the first place. Am I not right?—and yet here's my uncle bemoaning himself!"

"Neighbor," said Monsieur Hochon, "you have taken the best means to get peace in your household. Destroy your will, and Flore will be once more what she used to be in the early days."

"No, she will never forgive me for what I have made her suffer," whimpered the old man; "she will no longer love me."

"She shall love you, and closely too; I'll take care of that," said Philippe.

"Come, open your eyes!" exclaimed Monsieur Hochon. "They mean to rob you and abandon you."

"Oh! I was sure of it!" cried the poor imbecile.

"See, here is a letter Maxence has written to my grandson Borniche," said old Hochon. "Read it."

"What infamy!" exclaimed Carpentier, as he listened to the letter, which Rouget read aloud, weeping.

"Is that plain enough, uncle?" demanded Philippe. "Hold that hussy by her interests and she'll adore you as you deserve."

"She loves Maxence too well; she will leave me," cried the frightened old man.

"But, uncle, Maxence or I,—one or the other of us—won't leave our footsteps in the dust of Issoudun three days hence."

"Well then go, Monsieur Carpentier," said Rouget; "if you promise me to bring her back, go! You are a good man; say to her in my name all you think you ought to say."

"Captain Carpentier will whisper in her ear that I have sent to Paris for a woman whose youth and beauty are captivating; that will bring the jade back in a hurry!"

The captain departed, driving himself in the old caleche; Benjamin accompanied him on horseback, for Kouski was nowhere to be found. Though threatened by the officers with arrest and the loss of his situation, the Pole had gone to Vatan on a hired horse, to warn Max and Flore of the adversary's move. After fulfilling his mission, Carpentier, who did not wish to drive back with Flore, was to change places with Benjamin, and take the latter's horse.

When Philippe was told of Kouski's flight he said to Benjamin, "You will take the Pole's place, from this time on. It is all mapping out, papa Hochon!" cried the lieutenant-colonel. "That banquet will be jovial!"

"You will come and live here, of course," said the old miser.

"I have told Fario to send me all my things," answered Philippe. "I shall sleep in the room adjoining Gilet's apartment,—if my uncle consents."

"What will come of all this?" cried the terrified old man.

"Mademoiselle Flore Brazier is coming, gentle as a paschal lamb," replied Monsieur Hochon.

"God grant it!" exclaimed Rouget, wiping his eyes.

"It is now seven o'clock," said Philippe; "the sovereign of your heart will be here at half-past eleven: you'll never see Gilet again, and you will be as happy ever after as a pope.—If you want me to succeed," he whispered to Monsieur Hochon, "stay here till the hussy comes; you can help me in keeping the old man up to his resolution; and, together, we'll make that crab-girl see on which side her bread is buttered."

Monsieur Hochon felt the reasonableness of the request and stayed: but they had their hands full, for old Rouget gave way to childish lamentations, which were only quieted by Philippe's repeating over and over a dozen times:—

"Uncle, you will see that I am right when Flore returns to you as tender as ever. You shall be petted; you will save your property: be guided by my advice, and you'll live in paradise for the rest of your days."

When, about half-past eleven, wheels were heard in the Grande-Narette, the question was, whether the carriage were returning full or empty. Rouget's face wore an expression of agony, which changed to the prostration of excessive joy when he saw the two women, as the carriage turned to enter the courtyard.

"Kouski," said Philippe, giving a hand to Flore to help her down. "You are no longer in Monsieur Rouget's service. You will not sleep here to-night; get your things together, and go. Benjamin takes your place."

"Are you the master here?" said Flore sarcastically.

"With your permission," replied Philippe, squeezing her hand as if in a vice. "Come! we must have an understanding, you and I"; and he led the bewildered woman out into the place Saint-Jean.

"My fine lady," began the old campaigner, stretching out his right hand, "three days hence, Maxence Gilet will be sent to the shades by that arm, or his will have taken me off guard. If I die, you will be the mistress of my poor imbecile uncle; 'bene sit.' If I remain on my pins, you'll have to walk straight, and keep him supplied with first-class happiness. If you don't, I know girls in Paris who are, with all due respect, much prettier than you; for they are only seventeen years old: they would make my uncle excessively happy, and they are in my interests. Begin your attentions this very evening; if the old man is not as gay as a lark to-morrow morning, I have only a word to say to you; it is this, pay attention to it,—there is but one way to kill a man without the interference of the law, and that is to fight a duel with him; but I know three ways to get rid of a woman: mind that, my beauty!"

During this address, Flore shook like a person with the ague.

"Kill Max—?" she said, gazing at Philippe in the moonlight.

"Come, here's my uncle."

Old Rouget, turning a deaf ear to Monsieur Hochon's remonstrances, now came out into the street, and took Flore by the hand, as a miser might have grasped his treasure; he drew her back to the house and into his own room and shut the door.

"This is Saint-Lambert's day, and he who deserts his place, loses it," remarked Benjamin to the Pole.

"My master will shut your mouth for you," answered Kouski, departing to join Max who established himself at the hotel de la Poste.

On the morrow, between nine and eleven o'clock, all the women talked to each other from door to door throughout the town. The story of the wonderful change in the Rouget household spread everywhere. The upshot of the conversations was the same on all sides,—

"What will happen at the banquet between Max and Colonel Bridau?"

Philippe said but few words to the Vedie,—"Six hundred francs' annuity, or dismissal." They were enough, however, to keep her neutral, for a time, between the two great powers, Philippe and Flore.

Knowing Max's life to be in danger, Flore became more affectionate to Rouget than in the first days of their alliance. Alas! in love, a self-interested devotion is sometimes more agreeable than a truthful one; and that is why many men pay so much for clever deceivers. The Rabouilleuse did not appear till the next morning, when she came down to breakfast with Rouget on her arm. Tears filled her eyes as she beheld, sitting in Max's place, the terrible adversary, with his sombre blue eyes, and the cold, sinister expression on his face.

"What is the matter, mademoiselle?" he said, after wishing his uncle good-morning.

"She can't endure the idea of your fighting Maxence," said old Rouget.

"I have not the slightest desire to kill Gilet," answered Philippe. "He need only take himself off from Issoudun and go to America on a venture. I should be the first to advise you to give him an outfit, and to wish him a safe voyage. He would soon make a fortune there, and that is far more honorable than turning Issoudun topsy-turvy at night, and playing the devil in your household."

"Well, that's fair enough," said Rouget, glancing at Flore.

"A-mer-i-ca!" she ejaculated, sobbing.

"It is better to kick his legs about in a free country than have them rot in a pine box in France. However, perhaps you think he is a good shot, and can kill me; it's on the cards," observed the colonel.

"Will you let me speak to him?" said Flore, imploring Philippe in a humble and submissive tone.

"Certainly; he can come here and pack up his things. I will stay with my uncle during that time; for I shall not leave the old man again," replied Philippe.

"Vedie," cried Flore, "run to the hotel, and tell Monsieur Gilet that I beg him—"

"—to come and get his belongings," said Philippe, interrupting Flore's message.

"Yes, yes, Vedie; that will be a good pretext to see me; I must speak to him."

Terror controlled her hatred; and the shock which her whole being experienced when she first encountered this strong and pitiless nature was now so overwhelming that she bowed before Philippe just as Rouget had been in the habit of bending before her. She anxiously awaited Vedie's return. The woman brought a formal refusal from Max, who requested Mademoiselle Brazier to send his things to the hotel de la Poste.

"Will you allow me to take them to him?" she said to Jean-Jacques Rouget.

"Yes, but will you come back?" said the old man.

"If Mademoiselle is not back by midday, you will give me a power of attorney to attend to your property," said Philippe, looking at Flore. "Take Vedie with you, to save appearances, mademoiselle. In future you are to think of my uncle's honor."

Flore could get nothing out of Max. Desperate at having allowed himself, before the eyes of the whole town, to be routed out of his shameless position, Gilet was too proud to run away from Philippe. The Rabouilleuse combated this objection, and proposed that they should fly together to America; but Max, who did not want Flore without her money, and yet did not wish the girl to see the bottom of his heart, insisted on his intention of killing Philippe.

"We have committed a monstrous folly," he said. "We ought all three to have gone to Paris and spent the winter there; but how could one guess, from the mere sight of that fellow's big carcass, that things would turn out as they have? The turn of events is enough to make one giddy! I took the colonel for one of those fire-eaters who haven't two ideas in their head; that was the blunder I made. As I didn't have the sense to double like a hare in the beginning, I'll not be such a coward as to back down before him. He has lowered me in the estimation of this town, and I cannot get back what I have lost unless I kill him."

"Go to America with forty thousand francs. I'll find a way to get rid of that scoundrel, and join you. It would be much wiser."

"What would people say of me?" he exclaimed. "No; I have buried nine already. The fellow doesn't seem as if he knew much; he went from school to the army, and there he was always fighting till 1815; then he went to America, and I doubt if the brute ever set foot in a fencing-alley; while I have no match with the sabre. The sabre is his arm; I shall seem very generous in offering it to him,—for I mean, if possible, to let him insult me,—and I can easily run him through. Unquestionably, it is my wisest course. Don't be uneasy; we shall be masters of the field in a couple of days."

That it was that a stupid point of honor had more influence over Max than sound policy. When Flore got home she shut herself up to cry at ease. During the whole of that day gossip ran wild in Issoudun, and the duel between Philippe and Maxence was considered inevitable.

"Ah! Monsieur Hochon," said Mignonnet, who, accompanied by Carpentier, met the old man on the boulevard Baron, "we are very uneasy; for Gilet is clever with all weapons."

"Never mind," said the old provincial diplomatist; "Philippe has managed this thing well from the beginning. I should never have thought that big, easy-going fellow would have succeeded as he has. The two have rolled together like a couple of thunder-clouds."

"Oh!" said Carpentier, "Philippe is a remarkable man. His conduct before the Court of Peers was a masterpiece of diplomacy."

"Well, Captain Renard," said one of the townsfolk to Max's friend. "They say wolves don't devour each other, but it seems that Max is going to set his teeth in Colonel Bridau. That's pretty serious among you gentlemen of the Old Guard."

"You make fun of it, do you? Because the poor fellow amused himself a little at night, you are all against him," said Potel. "But Gilet is a man who couldn't stay in a hole like Issoudun without finding something to do."

"Well, gentlemen," remarked another, "Max and the colonel must play out their game. Bridau had to avenge his brother. Don't you remember Max's treachery to the poor lad?"

"Bah! nothing but an artist," said Renard.

"But the real question is about the old man's property," said a third. "They say Monsieur Gilet was laying hands on fifty thousand francs a year, when the colonel turned him out of his uncle's house."

"Gilet rob a man! Come, don't say that to any one but me, Monsieur Canivet," cried Potel. "If you do, I'll make you swallow your tongue,—and without any sauce."

Every household in town offered prayers for the honorable Colonel Bridau.

CHAPTER XVI

Towards four o'clock the following day, the officers of the old army who were at Issoudun or its environs, were sauntering about the place du Marche, in front of an eating-house kept by a man named Lacroix, and waiting the arrival of Colonel Philippe Bridau. The banquet in honor of the coronation was to take place with military punctuality at five o'clock. Various groups of persons were talking of Max's discomfiture, and his dismissal from old Rouget's house; for not only were the officers to dine at Lacroix's, but the common soldiers had determined on a meeting at a neighboring wine-shop. Among the officers, Potel and Renard were the only ones who attempted to defend Max.

"Is it any of our business what takes place among the old man's heirs?" said Renard.

"Max is weak with women," remarked the cynical Potel.

"There'll be sabres unsheathed before long," said an old sub-lieutenant, who cultivated a kitchen-garden in the upper Baltan. "If Monsieur Maxence Gilet committed the folly of going to live under old Rouget's roof, he would be a coward if he allowed himself to be turned off like a valet without asking why."

"Of course," said Mignonnet dryly. "A folly that doesn't succeed becomes a crime."

At this moment Max joined the old soldiers of Napoleon, and was received in significant silence. Potel and Renard each took an arm of their friend, and walked about with him, conversing. Presently Philippe was seen approaching in full dress; he trailed his cane after him with an imperturbable air which contrasted with the forced attention Max was paying to the remarks of his two supporters. Bridau's hand was grasped by Mignonnet, Carpentier, and several others. This welcome, so different from that accorded to Max, dispelled the last feeling of cowardice, or, if you prefer it, wisdom, which Flore's entreaties, and above all, her tendernesses, had awakened in the latter's mind.

"We shall fight," he said to Renard, "and to the death. Therefore don't talk to me any more; let me play my part well."

After these words, spoken in a feverish tone, the three Bonapartists returned to the group of officers and mixed among them. Max bowed first to Bridau, who returned his bow, and the two exchanged a frigid glance.

"Come, gentlemen, let us take our seats," said Potel.

"And drink to the health of the Little Corporal, who is now in the paradise of heroes," cried Renard.

The company poured into the long, low dining-hall of the restaurant Lacroix, the windows of which opened on the market-place. Each guest took his seat at the table, where, in compliance with Philippe's request, the two adversaries were placed directly opposite to each other. Some young men of the town, among them several Knights of Idleness, anxious to know what might happen at the banquet, were walking about the street and discussing the critical position into which Philippe had contrived to force Max. They all deplored the crisis, though each considered the duel to be inevitable.

Everything went off well until the dessert, though the two antagonists displayed, in spite of the apparent joviality of the dinner, a certain vigilance that resembled disquietude. While waiting for the quarrel that both were planning, Philippe showed admirable coolness, and Max a distracting gayety; but to an observer, each was playing a part.

When the desert was served Philippe rose and said: "Fill your glasses, my friends! I ask permission to propose the first toast."

"He said *my friends*, don't fill your glass," whispered Renard to Max.

Max poured out some wine.

"To the Grand Army!" cried Philippe, with genuine enthusiasm.

"To the Grand Army!" was repeated with acclamation by every voice.

At this moment eleven private soldiers, among whom were Benjamin and Kouski, appeared at the door of the room and repeated the toast,—

"To the Grand Army!"

"Come in, my sons; we are going to drink His health."

The old soldiers came in and stood behind the officers.

"You see He is not dead!" said Kouski to an old sergeant, who had perhaps been grieving that the Emperor's agony was over.

"I claim the second toast," said Mignonnet, as he rose. "Let us drink to those who attempted to restore his son!"

Every one present, except Maxence Gilet, bowed to Philippe Bridau, and stretched their glasses towards him.

"One word," said Max, rising.

"It is Max! it is Max!" cried voices outside; and then a deep silence reigned in the room and in the street, for Gilet's known character made every one expect a taunt.

"May we *all* meet again at this time next year," said Max, bowing ironically to Philippe.

"It's coming!" whispered Kouski to his neighbor.

"The Paris police would never allow a banquet of this kind," said Potel to Philippe.

"Why do the devil to you mention the police to Colonel Bridau?" said Maxence insolently.

"Captain Potel—*he*—meant no insult," said Philippe, smiling coldly. The stillness was so profound that the buzzing of a fly could have been heard if there had been one.

"The police were sufficiently afraid of me," resumed Philippe, "to send me to Issoudun,— a place where I have had the pleasure of meeting old comrades, but where, it must be owned, there is a dearth of amusement. For a man who doesn't despise folly, I'm rather restricted. However, it is certainly economical, for I am not one of those to whom feather-beds give incomes; Mariette of the Grand Opera cost me fabulous sums."

"Is that remark meant for me, my dear colonel?" asked Max, sending a glance at Philippe which was like a current of electricity.

"Take it as you please," answered Bridau.

"Colonel, my two friends here, Renard and Potel, will call to-morrow on—"

"—on Mignonnet and Carpentier," answered Philippe, cutting short Max's sentence, and motioning towards his two neighbors.

"Now," said Max, "let us go on with the toasts."

The two adversaries had not raised their voices above the tone of ordinary conversation; there was nothing solemn in the affair except the dead silence in which it took place.

"Look here, you others!" cried Philippe, addressing the soldiers who stood behind the officers; "remember that our affairs don't concern the bourgeoisie—not a word, therefore, on what goes on here. It is for the Old Guard only."

"They'll obey orders, colonel," said Renard. "I'll answer for them."

"Long live His little one! May he reign over France!" cried Potel.

"Death to Englishmen!" cried Carpentier.

That toast was received with prodigious applause.

"Shame on Hudson Lowe," said Captain Renard.

The dessert passed off well; the libations were plentiful. The antagonists and their four seconds made it a point of honor that a duel, involving so large a fortune, and the reputation of two men noted for their courage, should not appear the result of an ordinary squabble. No two gentlemen could have behaved better than Philippe and Max; in this respect the anxious waiting of the young men and townspeople grouped about the market-place was balked. All the guests, like true soldiers, kept silence as to the episode which took place at dessert. At ten o'clock that night the two adversaries were informed that the sabre was the weapon agreed upon by the seconds; the place chosen for the rendezvous was behind the chancel of the church of the Capuchins at eight o'clock the next morning. Goddet, who was at the banquet in his quality of former army surgeon, was requested to be present at the meeting. The seconds agreed that, no matter what might happen, the combat should last only ten minutes.

At eleven o'clock that night, to Colonel Bridau's amazement, Monsieur Hochon appeared at his rooms just as he was going to bed, escorting Madame Hochon.

"We know what has happened," said the old lady, with her eyes full of tears, "and I have come to entreat you not to leave the house to-morrow morning without saying your prayers. Lift your soul to God!"

"Yes, madame," said Philippe, to whom old Hochon made a sign from behind his wife's back.

"That is not all," said Agathe's godmother. "I stand in the place of your poor mother, and I divest myself, for you, of a thing which I hold most precious,—here," she went on, holding towards Philippe a tooth, fastened upon a piece of black velvet embroidered in gold, to which she had sewn a pair of green strings. Having shown it to him, she replaced it in a little bag. "It is a relic of Sainte Solange, the patron saint of Berry," she said, "I saved it during the Revolution; wear it on your breast to-morrow."

"Will it protect me from a sabre-thrust?" asked Philippe.

"Yes," replied the old lady.

"Then I have no right to wear that accoutrement any more than if it were a cuirass," cried Agathe's son.

"What does he mean?" said Madame Hochon.

"He says it is not playing fair," answered Hochon.

"Then we will say no more about it," said the old lady, "I shall pray for you."

"Well, madame, prayer—and a good point—can do no harm," said Philippe, making a thrust as if to pierce Monsieur Hochon's heart.

The old lady kissed the colonel on his forehead. As she left the house, she gave thirty francs—all the money she possessed—to Benjamin, requesting him to sew the relic into the pocket of his master's trousers. Benjamin did so,—not that he believed in the virtue of the tooth, for he said his master had a much better talisman than that against Gilet, but because his conscience constrained him to fulfil a commission for which he had been so liberally paid. Madame Hochon went home full of confidence in Saint Solange.

At eight o'clock the next morning, December third, the weather being cloudy, Max, accompanied by his seconds and the Pole, arrived on the little meadow which then surrounded the apse of the church of the Capuchins. There he found Philippe and his seconds, with Benjamin, waiting for him. Potel and Mignonnet paced off twenty-four feet; at each extremity, the two attendants drew a line on the earth with a spade: the combatants were not allowed to retreat beyond that line, on pain of being thought cowardly. Each was to stand at his own line, and advance as he pleased when the seconds gave the word.

"Do we take off our coats?" said Philippe to his adversary coldly.

"Of course," answered Maxence, with the assumption of a bully.

They did so; the rosy tints of their skin appearing through the cambric of their shirts. Each, armed with a cavalry sabre selected of equal weight, about three pounds, and equal length, three feet, placed himself at his own line, the point of his weapon on the ground, awaiting the signal. Both were so calm that, in spite of the cold, their muscles quivered no more than if they had been made of iron. Goddet, the four seconds, and the two soldiers felt an involuntary admiration.

"They are a proud pair!"

The exclamation came from Potel.

Just as the signal was given, Max caught sight of Fario's sinister face looking at them through the hole which the Knights of Idleness had made for the pigeons in the roof of the church. Those eyes, which sent forth streams of fire, hatred, and revenge, dazzled Max for a moment. The colonel went straight to his adversary, and put himself on guard in a way that gained him an advantage. Experts in the art of killing, know that, of two antagonists, the ablest takes the "inside of the pavement,"—to use an expression which gives the reader a tangible idea of the effect of a good guard. That pose, which is in some degree observant, marks so plainly a duellist of the first rank that a feeling of inferiority came into Max's soul, and produced the same disarray of powers which demoralizes a gambler when, in presence of a master or a lucky hand, he loses his self-possession and plays less well than usual.

"Ah! the lascar!" thought Max, "he's an expert; I'm lost!"

He attempted a "moulinet," and twirled his sabre with the dexterity of a single-stick. He wanted to bewilder Philippe, and strike his weapon so as to disarm him; but at the first encounter he felt that the colonel's wrist was iron, with the flexibility of a steel string. Maxence was then forced, unfortunate fellow, to think of another move, while Philippe, whose eyes were darting gleams that were sharper than the flash of their blades, parried every attack with the coolness of a fencing-master wearing his plastron in an armory.

Between two men of the calibre of these combatants, there occurs a phenomenon very like that which takes place among the lower classes, during the terrible tussle called "the savante," which is fought with the feet, as the name implies. Victory depends on a false movement, on some error of the calculation, rapid as lightning, which must be made and followed almost instinctively. During a period of time as short to the spectators as it seems long to the combatants, the contest lies in observation, so keen as to absorb the powers of mind and body, and yet concealed by preparatory feints whose slowness and apparent prudence seem to show that the antagonists are not intending to fight. This moment, which is followed by a rapid and decisive struggle, is terrible to a connoisseur. At a bad parry from Max the colonel sent the sabre spinning from his hand.

"Pick it up," he said, pausing; "I am not the man to kill a disarmed enemy."

There was something atrocious in the grandeur of these words; they seemed to show such consciousness of superiority that the onlookers took them for a shrewd calculation. In fact, when Max replaced himself in position, he had lost his coolness, and was once more confronted with his adversary's raised guard which defended the colonel's whole person while it menaced his. He resolved to redeem his shameful defeat by a bold stroke. He no longer guarded himself, but took his sabre in both hands and rushed furiously on his antagonist, resolved to kill him, if he had to lose his own life. Philippe received a sabre-cut which slashed open his forehead and a part of his face, but he cleft Max's head obliquely by the terrible sweep of a "moulinet," made to break the force of the annihilating stroke Max aimed at him. These two savage blows ended the combat, at the ninth minute. Fario came down to gloat over the sight of his enemy in the convulsions of death; for the muscles of a man of Maxence Gilet's vigor quiver horribly. Philippe was carried back to his uncle's house.

Thus perished a man destined to do great deeds had he lived his life amid environments which were suited to him; a man treated by Nature as a favorite child, for she gave him courage, self-possession, and the political sagacity of a Cesar Borgia. But education had not bestowed upon him that nobility of conduct and ideas without which nothing great is possible in any walk of life. He was not regretted, because of the perfidy with which his adversary, who was a worse man than he, had contrived to bring him into disrepute. His death put an end to the exploits of the Order of Idleness, to the great satisfaction of the town of Issoudun. Philippe therefore had nothing to fear in consequence of the duel, which seemed almost the result of divine vengeance: its circumstances were related throughout that whole region of country, with unanimous praise for the bravery of the two combatants.

"But they had better have been both been killed," remarked Monsieur Mouilleron; "it would have been a good riddance for the Government."

The situation of Flore Brazier would have been very embarrassing were it not for the condition into which she was thrown by Max's death. A brain-fever set in, combined with a dangerous inflammation resulting from her escapade to Vatan. If she had had her usual health, she might have fled the house where, in the room above her, Max's room, and in Max's bed, lay and suffered Max's murderer. She hovered between life and death for three months, attended by Monsieur Goddet, who was also attending Philippe.

As soon as Philippe was able to hold a pen, he wrote the following letters:—

To Monsieur Desroches: I have already killed the most venomous of the two reptiles; not however without getting my own head split open by a sabre; but the rascal struck with a dying hand. The other viper is here, and I must come to an understanding with her, for my uncle clings to her like the apple of his eye. I have been half afraid the girl, who is devilishly handsome, might run away, and then my uncle would have followed her; but an illness which seized her suddenly has kept her in bed. If God desired to protect me, he would call her soul to himself, now, while she is repenting of her sins. Meantime, on my side I have, thanks to that old trump, Hochon, the doctor of Issoudun, one named Goddet, a worthy soul who conceives that the property of uncles ought to go to nephews rather than to sluts. Monsieur Hochon has some influence on a certain papa Fichet, who is rich, and whose daughter Goddet wants as a wife for his son: so the thousand francs they have promised him if he mends up my pate is not the chief cause of his devotion. Moreover, this Goddet, who was formerly head-surgeon to the 3rd regiment of the line, has been privately advised by my staunch friends, Mignonnet and Carpentier; so he is now playing the hypocrite with his other patient. He says to Mademoiselle Brazier, as he feels her pulse, "You see, my child, that there's a God after all. You have been the cause of a great misfortune, and you must now repair it. The finger of God is in all this (it is inconceivable what they don't say the finger of God is in!). Religion is religion: submit, resign yourself, and that will quiet you better than my drugs. Above all, resolve to stay here and take care of your master: forget and forgive,—that's Christianity." Goddet has promised to keep the Rabouilleuse three months in her bed. By degrees the girl will get accustomed to living under the same roof with me. I have bought over the cook. That abominable old woman tells her mistress Max would have led her a hard life; and declares she overheard him say that if, after the old man's death, he was obliged to marry Flore, he didn't mean to have his prospects ruined by it, and he should find a way to get rid of her. Thus, all goes well, so far. My uncle, by old Hochon's advice, has destroyed his will.

To Monsieur Giroudeau, care of Mademoiselle Florentine. Rue de Vendome, Marais:

My dear old Fellow,—Find out if the little rat Cesarine has any engagement, and if not, try to arrange that she can come to Issoudun in case I send for her; if I do, she must come at once. It is a matter this time of decent behavior; no theatre morals. She must present herself as the daughter of a brave soldier, killed on the battle-field. Therefore, mind,—sober manners, schoolgirl's clothes, virtue of the best quality; that's the watchword. If I need Cesarine, and if she answers my purpose, I will give her fifty thousand francs on my uncle's death. If Cesarine has other engagements, explain what I want to Florentine; and between you, find me some ballet-girl capable of playing the part. I have had my skull cracked in a duel with the fellow who was filching my inheritance, and is now feeding the worms. I'll tell you all about it some day. Ah! old fellow, the good times are coming back for you and me; we'll amuse ourselves once more, or we are not the pair we really are. If you can send me five hundred more cartridges I'll bite them. Adieu, my old fire-eater. Light your pipe with this letter. Mind, the daughter of the officer is to come from Chateauroux, and must seem to be in need of assistance. I hope however that I shall not be driven to such dangerous expedients. Remember me to Mariette and all our friends.

Agathe, informed by Madame Hochon of what had happened, rushed to Issoudun, and was received by her brother, who gave her Philippe's former room. The poor mother's tenderness for the worthless son revived in all its maternal strength; a few happy days were hers at last, as she listened to the praises which the whole town bestowed upon her hero.

"After all, my child," said Madame Hochon on the day of her arrival, "youth must have its fling. The dissipations of a soldier under the Empire must, of course, be greater than those of young men who are looked after by their fathers. Oh! if you only knew what went on here at night under that wretched Max! Thanks to your son, Issoudun now breathes and sleeps in peace. Philippe has come to his senses rather late; he told us frankly that those three months in the Luxembourg sobered him. Monsieur Hochon is delighted with his conduct here; every one thinks highly of it. If he can be kept away from the temptations of Paris, he will end by being a comfort to you."

Hearing these consolatory words Agathe's eyes filled with tears.

Philippe played the saint to his mother, for he had need of her. That wily politician did not wish to have recourse to Cesarine unless he continued to be an object of horror to Mademoiselle Brazier. He saw that Flore had been thoroughly broken to harness by Max; he knew she was an essential part of his uncle's life, and he greatly preferred to use her rather than send for the ballet-girl, who might take it into her head to marry the old man. Fouche advised Louis XVIII. to sleep in Napoleon's sheets instead of granting the charter; and Philippe would have liked to remain in Gilet's sheets; but he was reluctant to risk the good reputation he had made for himself in Berry. To take Max's place with the Rabouilleuse would be as odious on his part as on hers. He could, without discredit and by the laws of nepotism, live in his uncle's house and at his uncle's expense; but he could not have Flore unless her character were whitewashed. Hampered by this difficulty, and stimulated by the hope of finally getting hold of the property, the idea came into his head of making his uncle marry the Rabouilleuse. With this in view he requested his mother to go and see the girl and treat her in a sisterly manner.

"I must confess, my dear mother," he said, in a canting tone, looking at Monsieur and Madame Hochon who accompanied her, "that my uncle's way of life is not becoming; he could, however, make Mademoiselle Brazier respected by the community if he chose. Wouldn't it be far better for her to be Madame Rouget than the servant-mistress of an old bachelor? She had better obtain a definite right to his property by a marriage contract then threaten a whole family with disinheritance. If you, or Monsieur Hochon, or some good priest would speak of the matter to both parties, you might put a stop to the scandal which offends decent people. Mademoiselle Brazier would be only too happy if you were to welcome her as a sister, and I as an aunt."

On the morrow Agathe and Madame Hochon appeared at Flore's bedside, and repeated to the sick girl and to Rouget, the excellent sentiments expressed by Philippe. Throughout Issoudun the colonel was talked of as a man of noble character, especially because of his conduct towards Flore. For a month, the Rabouilleuse heard Goddet, her doctor, the individual who has paramount influence over a sick person, the respectable Madame Hochon, moved by religious principle, and Agathe, so gentle and pious, all representing to her the advantages of a marriage with Rouget. And when, attracted by the idea of becoming Madame Rouget, a dignified and virtuous bourgeoisie, she grew eager to recover, so that the marriage might speedily be celebrated, it was not difficult to make her understand that she would not be allowed to enter the family of the Rougets if she intended to turn Philippe from its doors.

"Besides," remarked the doctor, "you really owe him this good fortune. Max would never have allowed you to marry old Rouget. And," he added in her ear, "if you have children, you can revenge Max, for that will disinherit the Bridaus."

Two months after the fatal duel in February, 1823, the sick woman, urged by those about her, and implored by Rouget, consented to receive Philippe, the sight of whose scars made her weep, but whose softened and affectionate manner calmed her. By Philippe's wish they were left alone together.

"My dear child," said the soldier. "It is I, who, from the start, have advised your marriage with my uncle; if you consent, it will take place as soon as you are quite recovered."

"So they tell me," she replied.

"Circumstances have compelled me to give you pain, it is natural therefore that I should wish to do you all the good I can. Wealth, respect, and a family position are worth more than what you have lost. You wouldn't have been that fellow's wife long after my uncle's death, for I happen to know, through friends of his, that he intended to get rid of you. Come, my dear, let us understand each other, and live happily. You shall be my aunt, and nothing more than my aunt. You will take care that my uncle does not forget me in his will; on my side, you shall see how well I will have you treated in the marriage contract. Keep calm, think it over, and we will talk of it later. All sensible people, indeed the whole town, urge you to put an end to your illegal position; no one will blame you for receiving me. It is well understood in the world that interests go before feelings. By the day of your marriage you will be handsomer than ever. The pallor of illness has given you an air of distinction, and on my honor, if my uncle did not love you so madly, you should be the wife of Colonel Bridau."

Philippe left the room, having dropped this hint into Flore's mind to waken a vague idea of vengeance which might please the girl, who did, in fact, feel a sort of happiness as she saw this dreadful being at her feet. In this scene Philippe repeated, in miniature, that of Richard III. with the queen he had widowed. The meaning of it is that personal calculation, hidden under sentiment, has a powerful influence on the heart, and is able to dissipate even genuine grief. This is how, in individual life, Nature does that which in works of genius is thought to be consummate art: she works by self-interest,—the genius of money.

At the beginning of April, 1823, the hall of Jean-Jacques Rouget's house was the scene of a splendid dinner, given to celebrate the signing of the marriage contract between Mademoiselle Flore Brazier and the old bachelor. The guests were Monsieur Heron, the four witnesses, Messieurs Mignonnet, Carpentier, Hochon, and Goddet, the mayor and the curate, Agathe Bridau, Madame Hochon, and her friend Madame Borniche, the two old ladies who laid down the law to the society of Issoudun. The bride was much impressed by this concession, obtained by Philippe, and intended by the two ladies as a mark of protection to a repentant woman. Flore was in dazzling beauty. The curate, who for the last fortnight had been instructing the ignorant crab-girl, was to allow her, on the following day, to make her first communion. The marriage was the text of the following pious article in the "Journal du Cher," published at Bourges, and in the "Journal de l'Indre," published at Chateauroux:

Issoudun.—The revival of religion is progressing in Berry. Friends of the Church and all respectable persons in this town were yesterday witnesses of a marriage ceremony by which a leading man of property put an end to a scandalous connection, which began at the time when the authority of religion was overthrown in this region. This event, due to the enlightened zeal of the clergy of Issoudun will, we trust, have imitators, and put a stop to marriages, so-called, which have never been solemnized, and were only contracted during the disastrous epoch of revolutionary rule. One remarkable feature of the event to which we allude, is the fact that it was brought about at the entreaty of a colonel belonging to the old army, sent to our town by a sentence of the Court of Peers, who may, in consequence, lose the inheritance of his uncle's property. Such disinterestedness is so rare in these days that it deserves public mention.

By the marriage contract Rouget secured to Flore a dower of one hundred thousand francs, and a life annuity of thirty thousand more.

After the wedding, which was sumptuous, Agathe returned to Paris the happiest of mothers, and told Joseph and Desroches what she called the good news.

"Your son Philippe is too wily a man not to keep his paw on that inheritance," said the lawyer, when he had heard Madame Bridau to the end. "You and your poor Joseph will never get one penny of your brother's property."

"You, and Joseph too, will always be unjust to that poor boy," said the mother. "His conduct before the Court of Peers was worthy of a statesman; he succeeded in saving many heads. Philippe's errors came from his great faculties being unemployed. He now sees how faults of conduct injure the prospects of a man who has his way to make. He is ambitious; that I am sure of; and I am not the only one to predict his future. Monsieur Hochon firmly believes that Philippe has a noble destiny before him."

"Oh! if he chooses to apply his perverted powers to making his fortune, I have no doubt he will succeed: he is capable of everything; and such fellows go fast and far," said Desroches.

"Why do you suppose that he will not succeed by honest means?" demanded Madame Bridau.

"You will see!" exclaimed Desroches. "Fortunate or unfortunate, Philippe will remain the man of the rue Mazarin, the murderer of Madame Descoings, the domestic thief. But don't worry yourself; he will manage to appear honest to the world."

After breakfast, on the morning succeeding the marriage, Philippe took Madame Rouget by the arm when his uncle rose from table and went upstairs to dress,—for the pair had come down, the one in her morning-robe, and the other in his dressing-gown.

"My dear aunt," said the colonel, leading her into the recess of a window, "you now belong to the family. Thanks to me, the law has tied the knot. Now, no nonsense. I intend that you and I should play above board. I know the tricks you will try against me; and I shall watch you like a duenna. You will never go out of this house except on my arm; and you will never leave me. As to what passes within the house, damn it, you'll find me like a spider in the middle of his web. Here is something," he continued, showing the bewildered woman a letter, "which will prove to you that I could, while you were lying ill upstairs, unable to move hand or foot, have turned you out of doors without a penny. Read it."

He gave her the letter.

My dear Fellow,—Florentine, who has just made her debut at the new Opera House in a "pas de trois" with Mariette and Tullia, is thinking steadily about your affair, and so is Florine,—who has finally given up Lousteau and taken Nathan. That shrewd pair have found you a most delicious little creature,—only seventeen, beautiful as an English woman, demure as a "lady," up to all mischief, sly as Desroches, faithful as Godeschal. Mariette is forming her, so as to give you a fair chance. No woman could hold her own against this little angel, who is a devil under her skin; she can play any part you please; get complete possession of your uncle, or drive him crazy with love. She has that celestial look poor Coralie used to have; she can weep,—the tones of her voice will draw a thousand-franc note from a granite heart; and the young mischief soaks up champagne better than any of us. It is a precious discovery; she is under obligations to Mariette, and wants to pay them off. After squandering the fortunes of two Englishmen, a Russian, and an Italian prince, Mademoiselle Esther is now in poverty; give her ten thousand francs, that will satisfy her. She has just remarked, laughing, that she has never yet fricasseed a bourgeois, and it will get her hand in. Esther is well known to Finot, Bixiou, and des Lupeaulx, in fact to all our set. Ah! if there were any real fortunes left in France, she would be the greatest courtesan of modern times. All the editorial staff, Nathan, Finot, Bixiou, etc., are now joking the aforesaid Esther in a magnificent appartement just arranged for Florine by old Lord Dudley (the real father of de Marsay); the lively actress captured him by the dress of her new role. Tullia is with the Duc de Rhetore, Mariette is still with the Duc de Maufrigneuse; between them, they will get your sentence remitted in time for the King's fete. Bury your uncle under the roses before the Saint-Louis, bring away the property, and spend a little of it with Esther and your old friends, who sign this epistle in a body, to remind you of them. Nathan, Florine, Bixiou, Finot, Mariette, Florentine, Giroudeau, Tullia

The letter shook in the trembling hands of Madame Rouget, and betrayed the terror of her mind and body. The aunt dared not look at the nephew, who fixed his eyes upon her with terrible meaning.

"I trust you," he said, "as you see; but I expect some return. I have made you my aunt intending to marry you some day. You are worth more to me than Esther in managing my uncle.

In a year from now, we must be in Paris; the only place where beauty really lives. You will amuse yourself much better there than here; it is a perpetual carnival. I shall return to the army, and become a general, and you will be a great lady. There's our future; now work for it. But I must have a pledge to bind this agreement. You are to give me, within a month from now, a power of attorney from my uncle, which you must obtain under pretence of relieving him of the fatigues of business. Also, a month later, I must have a special power of attorney to transfer the income in the Funds. When that stands in my name, you and I have an equal interest in marrying each other. There it all is, my beautiful aunt, as plain as day. Between you and me there must be no ambiguity. I can marry my aunt at the end of a year's widowhood; but I could not marry a disgraced girl."

He left the room without waiting for an answer. When Vedie came in, fifteen minutes later, to clear the table, she found her mistress pale and moist with perspiration, in spite of the season. Flore felt like a woman who had fallen to the bottom of a precipice; the future loomed black before her; and on its blackness, in the far distance, were shapes of monstrous things, indistinctly perceptible, and terrifying. She felt the damp chill of vaults, instinctive fear of the man crushed her; and yet a voice cried in her ear that she deserved to have him for her master. She was helpless against her fate. Flore Brazier had had a room of her own in Rouget's house; but Madame Rouget belonged to her husband, and was now deprived of the free-will of a servant-mistress. In the horrible situation in which she now found herself, the hope of having a child came into her mind; but she soon recognized its impossibility. The marriage was to Jean-Jacques what the second marriage of Louis XII. was to that king. The incessant watchfulness of a man like Philippe, who had nothing to do and never quitted his post of observation, made any form of vengeance impossible. Benjamin was his innocent and devoted spy. The Vedie trembled before him. Flore felt herself deserted and utterly helpless. She began to fear death. Without knowing how Philippe might manage to kill her, she felt certain that whenever he suspected her of pregnancy her doom would be sealed. The sound of that voice, the veiled glitter of that gambler's eye, the slightest movement of the soldier, who treated her with a brutality that was still polite, made her shudder. As to the power of attorney demanded by the ferocious colonel, who in the eyes of all Issoudun was a hero, he had it as soon as he wanted it; for Flore fell under the man's dominion as France had fallen under that of Napoleon.

Like a butterfly whose feet are caught in the incandescent wax of a taper, Rouget rapidly dissipated his remaining strength. In presence of that decay, the nephew remained as cold and impassible as the diplomatists of 1814 during the convulsions of imperial France.

Philippe, who did not believe in Napoleon II., now wrote the following letter to the minister of war, which Mariette made the Duc de Maufrigneuse convey to that functionary:—

Monseigneur,—Napoleon is no more. I desired to remain faithful to him according to my oath; now I am free to offer my services to His Majesty. If your Excellency deigns to explain my conduct to His Majesty, the King will see that it is in keeping with the laws of honor, if not with those of his government. The King, who thought it proper that his aide-de-camp, General Rapp, should mourn his former master, will no doubt feel indulgently for me. Napoleon was my benefactor. I therefore entreat your Excellency to take into consideration the request I make for employment in my proper rank; and I beg to assure you of my entire submission. The King will find in me a faithful subject. Deign to accept the assurance of respect with which I have the honor to be, Your Excellency's very submissive and Very humble servant, Philippe Bridau Formerly chief of squadron in the dragoons of the Guard; officer of the Legion of honor; now under police surveillance at Issoudun.

To this letter was joined a request for permission to go to Paris on urgent family business; and Monsieur Mouilleron annexed letters from the mayor, the sub-prefect, and the commissary of police at Issoudun, all bestowing many praises on Philippe's conduct, and dwelling upon the newspaper article relating to his uncle's marriage.

Two weeks later, Philippe received the desired permission, and a letter, in which the minister of war informed him that, by order of the King, he was, as a preliminary favor, reinstated lieutenant-colonel in the royal army.

CHAPTER XVII

Lieutenant-Colonel Bridau returned to Paris, taking with him his aunt and the helpless Rouget, whom he escorted, three days after their arrival, to the Treasury, where Jean-Jacques signed the transfer of the income, which henceforth became Philippe's. The exhausted old man and the Rabouilleuse were now plunged by their nephew into the excessive dissipations of the dangerous and restless society of actresses, journalists, artists, and the equivocal women among whom Philippe had already wasted his youth; where old Rouget found excitements that soon after killed him. Instigated by Giroudeau, Lolotte, one of the handsomest of the Opera ballet-girls, was the amiable assassin of the old man. Rouget died after a splendid supper at Florentine's, and Lolotte threw the blame of his death upon a slice of pate de foie gras; as the Strasburg masterpiece could make no defence, it was considered settled that the old man died of indigestion.

Madame Rouget was in her element in the midst of this excessively decollete society; but Philippe gave her in charge of Mariette, and that monitress did not allow the widow—whose mourning was diversified with a few amusements—to commit any actual follies.

In October, 1823, Philippe returned to Issoudun, furnished with a power of attorney from his aunt, to liquidate the estate of his uncle; a business that was soon over, for he returned to Paris in March, 1824, with sixteen hundred thousand francs,—the net proceeds of old Rouget's property, not counting the precious pictures, which had never left Monsieur Hochon's hands. Philippe put the whole property into the hands of Mongenod and Sons, where young Baruch Borniche was employed, and on whose solvency and business probity old Hochon had given him satisfactory assurances. This house took his sixteen hundred thousand francs at six per cent per annum, on condition of three months' notice in case of the withdrawal of the money.

One fine day, Philippe went to see his mother, and invited her to be present at his marriage, which was witnessed by Giroudeau, Finot, Nathan, and Bixiou. By the terms of the marriage contract, the widow Rouget, whose portion of her late husband's property amounted to a million of francs, secured to her future husband her whole fortune in case she died without children. No invitations to the wedding were sent out, nor any "billets de faire part"; Philippe had his designs. He lodged his wife in an *appartement* in the rue Saint-Georges, which he bought ready-furnished from Lolotte. Madame Bridau the younger thought it delightful, and her husband rarely set foot in it. Without her knowledge, Philippe purchased in the rue de Clichy, at a time when no one suspected the value which property in that quarter would one day acquire, a magnificent hotel for two hundred and fifty thousand francs; of which he paid one hundred and fifty thousand down, taking two years to pay the remainder. He spent large sums in altering the interior and furnishing it; in fact, he put his income for two years into this outlay. The pictures, now restored, and estimated at three hundred thousand francs, appeared in such surroundings in all their beauty.

The accession of Charles X. had brought into still greater court favor the family of the Duc de Chaulieu, whose eldest son, the Duc de Rhetore, was in the habit of seeing Philippe at Tullia's. Under Charles X., the elder branch of the Bourbons, believing itself permanently seated on the throne, followed the advice previously given by Marshal Gouvion-Saint-Cyr to encourage the adherence of the soldiers of the Empire. Philippe, who had no doubt made invaluable revelations as to the conspiracies of 1820 and 1822, was appointed lieutenant-colonel in the regiment of the Duc de Maufrigneuse. That fascinating nobleman thought himself bound to protect the man from whom he had taken Mariette. The corps-de-ballet went for something, therefore, in the appointment. Moreover, it was decided in the private councils of Charles X., to give a faint tinge of liberalism to the surroundings of Monseigneur the Dauphin. Philippe, now a sort of equerry to the Duc de Maufrigneuse, was presented not only to the Dauphin, but also to the Dauphine, who was not averse to brusque and soldierly characters who had become noted for a past fidelity. Philippe thoroughly understood the part the Dauphin had to play; and he turned the first exhibition of that spurious liberalism to his own profit, by getting himself appointed aide-de-camp to a marshal who stood well at court.

In January, 1827, Philippe, who was now promoted to the Royal Guard as lieutenant-colonel in a regiment then commanded by the Duc de Maufrigneuse, solicited the honor of being ennobled. Under the Restoration, nobility became a sort of perquisite to the "roturiers" who served in the Guard. Colonel Bridau had lately bought the estate of Brambourg, and he now asked to be allowed to entail it under the title of count. This favor was accorded through the influence of his many intimacies in the highest rank of society, where he now appeared in all the luxury of horses, carriages, and liveries; in short, with the surroundings of a great lord. As soon as he saw himself gazetted in the Almanack under the title of Comte de Brambourg, he began to frequent the house of a lieutenant-general of artillery, the Comte de Soulanges.

Insatiable in his wants, and backed by the mistresses of influential men, Philippe now solicited the honor of being one of the Dauphin's aides-de-camp. He had the audacity to say to the Dauphin that "an old soldier, wounded on many a battle-field and who knew real warfare, might, on occasion, be serviceable to Monseigneur." Philippe, who could take the tone of all varieties of sycophancy, became in the regions of the highest social life exactly what the position required him to be; just as at Issoudun, he had copied the respectability of Mignonnet. He had, moreover, a fine establishment and gave fetes and dinners; admitting none of his old friends to his house if he thought their position in life likely to compromise his future. He was pitiless to the companions of his former debauches, and curtly refused Bixiou when that lively satirist asked him to say a word in favor of Giroudeau, who wanted to re-enter the army after the desertion of Florentine.

"The man has neither manners nor morals," said Philippe.

"Ha! did he say that of me?" cried Giroudeau, "of me, who helped him to get rid of his uncle!"

"We'll pay him off yet," said Bixiou.

Philippe intended to marry Mademoiselle Amelie de Soulanges, and become a general, in command of a regiment of the Royal Guard. He asked so many favors that, to keep him quiet, they made him a Commander of the Legion of honor, and also Commander of the order of Saint Louis. One rainy evening, as Agathe and Joseph were returning home along the muddy streets, they met Philippe in full uniform, bedizened with orders, leaning back in a corner of a handsome coupe lined with yellow silk, whose armorial bearings were surmounted with a count's coronet. He was on his way to a fete at the Elysee-Bourbon; the wheels splashed his mother and brother as he waved them a patronizing greeting.

"He's going it, that fellow!" said Joseph to his mother. "Nevertheless, he might send us something better than mud in our faces."

"He has such a fine position, in such high society, that we ought not to blame him for forgetting us," said Madame Bridau. "When a man rises to so great a height, he has many obligations to repay, many sacrifices to make; it is natural he should not come to see us, though he may think of us all the same."

"My dear fellow," said the Duc de Maufrigneuse one evening, to the new Comte de Brambourg, "I am sure that your addresses will be favorably received; but in order to marry Amelie de Soulanges, you must be free to do so. What have you done with your wife?"

"My wife?" said Philippe, with a gesture, look, and accent which Frederick Lemaitre was inspired to use in one of his most terrible parts. "Alas! I have the melancholy certainty of losing her. She has not a week to live. My dear duke, you don't know what it is to marry beneath you. A woman who was a cook, and has the tastes of a cook! who dishonors me—ah! I am much to be pitied. I have had the honor to explain my position to Madame la Dauphine. At the time of the marriage, it was a question of saving to the family a million of francs which my uncle had left by will to that person. Happily, my wife took to drinking; at her death, I come into possession of that million, which is now in the hands of Mongenod and Sons. I have thirty thousand francs a year in the five per cents, and my landed property, which is entailed, brings me in forty thousand more. If, as I am led to suppose, Monsieur de Soulanges gets a marshal's baton, I am on the high-road with my title of Comte de Brambourg, to becoming general and peer of France. That will be the proper end of an aide-de-camp of the Dauphin."

After the Salon of 1823, one of the leading painters of the day, a most excellent man, obtained the management of a lottery-office near the Markets, for the mother of Joseph Bridau. Agathe was fortunately able, soon after, to exchange it on equal terms with the incumbent of another office, situated in the rue de Seine, in a house where Joseph was able to have his atelier. The widow now hired an agent herself, and was no longer an expense to her son. And yet, as late as 1828, though she was the directress of an excellent office which she owed entirely to Joseph's fame, Madame Bridau still had no belief in that fame, which was hotly contested, as all true glory ever will be. The great painter, struggling with his genius, had enormous wants; he did not earn enough to pay for the luxuries which his relations to society, and his distinguished position in the young School of Art demanded. Though powerfully sustained by his friends of the Cenacle and by Mademoiselle des Touches, he did not please the Bourgeois. That being, from whom comes the money of these days, never unties its purse-strings for genius that is called in question; unfortunately, Joseph had the classics and the Institute, and the critics who cry up those two powers, against him. The brave artist, though backed by Gros and Gerard, by whose influence he was decorated after the Salon of 1827, obtained few orders. If the ministry of the interior and the King's household were with difficulty induced to buy some of his greatest pictures, the shopkeepers and the rich foreigners noticed them still less. Moreover, Joseph gave way rather too much, as we must all acknowledge, to imaginative fancies, and that produced a certain inequality in his work which his enemies made use of to deny his talent.

"High art is at a low ebb," said his friend Pierre Grassou, who made daubs to suit the taste of the bourgeoisie, in whose *appartements* fine paintings were at a discount.

"You ought to have a whole cathedral to decorate; that's what you want," declared Schinner; "then you would silence criticism with a master-stroke."

Such speeches, which alarmed the good Agathe, only corroborated the judgment she had long since formed upon Philippe and Joseph. Facts sustained that judgment in the mind of a woman who had never ceased to be a provincial. Philippe, her favorite child, was he not the great man of the family at last? in his early errors she saw only the ebullitions of youth. Joseph, to the merit of whose productions she was insensible, for she saw them too long in process of gestation to admire them when finished, seemed to her no more advanced in 1828 than he was in 1816. Poor Joseph owed money, and was bowed down by the burden of debt; he had chosen, she felt, a worthless career that made him no return. She could not conceive why they had given him the cross of the Legion of honor. Philippe, on the other hand, rich enough to cease gambling, a guest at the fetes of *Madame*, the brilliant colonel who at all reviews and in all processions appeared before her eyes in splendid uniforms, with his two crosses on his breast, realized all her maternal dreams. One such day of public ceremony effaced from Agathe's mind the horrible sight of Philippe's misery on the Quai de l'Ecole; on that day he passed his mother at the self-same spot, in attendance on the Dauphin, with plumes in his shako, and his pelisse gorgeous with gold and fur. Agathe, who to her artist son was now a sort of devoted gray sister, felt herself the mother of none but the dashing aide-de-camp to his Royal Highness, the Dauphin of France. Proud of Philippe, she felt he made the ease and happiness of her life,—forgetting that the lottery-office, by which she was enabled to live at all, came through Joseph.

One day Agathe noticed that her poor artist was more worried than usual by the bill of his color-man, and she determined, though cursing his profession in her heart, to free him from his debts. The poor woman kept the house with the proceeds of her office, and took care never to ask Joseph for a farthing. Consequently she had no money of her own; but she relied on Philippe's good heart and well-filled purse. For three years she had waited in expectation of his coming to see her; she now imagined that if she made an appeal to him he would bring some enormous sum; and her thoughts dwelt on the happiness she should feel in giving it to Joseph, whose judgment of his brother, like that of Madame Descoings, was so unfair.

Saying nothing to Joseph, she wrote the following letter to Philippe:—

To Monsieur le comte de Brambourg: My dear Philippe,—You have not given the least little word of remembrance to your mother for five years. That is not right. You   should remember the past, if only for the sake of your excellent   brother. Joseph is now in need of money, and you are floating in   wealth; he works, while you are flying from fete to fete. You now   possess, all to yourself, the property of my brother. Little   Borniche tells me you cannot have less than two hundred thousand   francs a year. Well, then, come and see Joseph. During your visit,   slip into the skull a few thousand-franc notes. Philippe, you owe   them to us; nevertheless, your brother will feel grateful to you,   not to speak of the happiness you will give   Your mother,   Agathe Bridau, nee Rouget

Two days later the concierge brought to the atelier, where poor Agathe was breakfasting with Joseph, the following terrible letter:—

My dear Mother,—A man does not marry a Mademoiselle Amelie de   Soulanges without the purse of Fortunatus, if under the name of   Comte de Brambourg he hides that of   Your son,   Philippe Bridau

As Agathe fell half-fainting on the sofa, the letter dropped to the floor. The slight noise made by the paper, and the smothered but dreadful exclamation which escaped Agathe startled Joseph, who had forgotten his mother for a moment and was vehemently rubbing in a sketch; he leaned his head round the edge of his canvas to see what had happened. The sight of his mother stretched out on the floor made him drop palette and brushes, and rush to lift what seemed a lifeless body. He took Agathe in his arms and carried her to her own bed, and sent the servant for his friend Horace Bianchon. As soon as he could question his mother she told him of her letter to Philippe, and of the answer she had received from him. The artist went to his atelier and picked up the letter, whose concise brutality had broken the tender heart of the poor mother, and shattered the edifice of trust her maternal preference had erected. When Joseph returned to her bedside he had the good feeling to be silent. He did not speak of his brother in the three weeks during which—we will not say the illness, but—the death agony of the poor woman lasted. Bianchon, who came every day and watched his patient with the devotion of a true friend, told Joseph the truth on the first day of her seizure.

"At her age," he said, "and under the circumstances which have happened to her, all we can hope to do is to make her death as little painful as possible."

She herself felt so surely called of God that she asked the next day for the religious help of old Abbe Loraux, who had been her confessor for more than twenty-two years. As soon as she was alone with him, and had poured into his heart her griefs, she said—as she had said to Madame Hochon, and had repeated to herself again and again throughout her life:—

"What have I done to displease God? Have I not loved Him with all my soul? Have I wandered from the path of grace? What is my sin? Can I be guilty of wrong when I know not what it is? Have I the time to repair it?"

"No," said the old man, in a gentle voice. "Alas! your life seems to have been pure and your soul spotless; but the eye of God, poor afflicted creature, is keener than that of his ministers. I see the truth too late; for you have misled even me."

Hearing these words from lips that had never spoken other than peaceful and pleasant words to her, Agathe rose suddenly in her bed and opened her eyes wide, with terror and distress.

"Tell me! tell me!" she cried.

"Be comforted," said the priest. "Your punishment is a proof that you will receive pardon. God chastens his elect. Woe to those whose misdeeds meet with fortunate success; they will be kneaded again in humanity until they in their turn are sorely punished for simple errors, and are brought to the maturity of celestial fruits. Your life, my daughter, has been one long error. You have fallen into the pit which you dug for yourself; we fail ever on the side we have ourselves weakened. You gave your heart to an unnatural son, in whom you made your glory, and you have misunderstood the child who is your true glory. You have been so deeply unjust that you never even saw the striking contrast between the brothers. You owe the comfort of your life to Joseph, while your other son has pillaged you repeatedly. The poor son, who loves you with no return of equal tenderness, gives you all the comfort that your life has had; the rich son, who never thinks of you, despises you and desires your death—"

"Oh! no," she cried.

"Yes," resumed the priest, "your humble position stands in the way of his proud hopes. Mother, these are your sins! Woman, your sorrows and your anguish foretell that you shall know the peace of God. Your son Joseph is so noble that his tenderness has never been lessened by the injustice your maternal preferences have done him. Love him now; give him all your heart during your remaining days; pray for him, as I shall pray for you."

The eyes of the mother, opened by so firm a hand, took in with one retrospective glance the whole course of her life. Illumined by this flash of light, she saw her involuntary wrong-doing and burst into tears. The old priest was so deeply moved at the repentance of a being who had sinned solely through ignorance, that he left the room hastily lest she should see his pity.

Joseph returned to his mother's room about two hours after her confessor had left her. He had been to a friend to borrow the necessary money to pay his most pressing debts, and he came in on tiptoe, thinking that his mother was asleep. He sat down in an armchair without her seeing him; but he sprang up with a cold chill running through him as he heard her say, in a voice broken with sobs,—

"Will he forgive me?"

"What is it, mother?" he exclaimed, shocked at the stricken face of the poor woman, and thinking the words must mean the delirium that precedes death.

"Ah, Joseph! can you pardon me, my child?" she cried.

"For what?" he said.

"I have never loved you as you deserved to be loved."

"Oh, what an accusation!" he cried. "Not loved me? For seven years have we not lived alone together? All these seven years have you not taken care of me and done everything for me? Do I not see you every day,—hear your voice? Are you not the gentle and indulgent companion of my miserable life? You don't understand painting?—Ah! but that's a gift not always given. I was saying to Grassou only yesterday: 'What comforts me in the midst of my trials is that I have such a good mother. She is all that an artist's wife should be; she sees to everything; she takes care of my material wants without ever troubling or worrying me.'"

"No, Joseph, no; you have loved me, but I have not returned you love for love. Ah! would that I could live a little longer—Give me your hand."

Agathe took her son's hand, kissed it, held it on her heart, and looked in his face a long time,—letting him see the azure of her eyes resplendent with a tenderness she had hitherto bestowed on Philippe only. The painter, well fitted to judge of expression, was so struck by the change, and saw so plainly how the heart of his mother had opened to him, that he took her in his arms, and held her for some moments to his heart, crying out like one beside himself,—"My mother! oh, my mother!"

"Ah! I feel that I am forgiven!" she said. "God will confirm the child's pardon of its mother."

"You must be calm: don't torment yourself; hear me. I feel myself loved enough in this one moment for all the past," he said, as he laid her back upon the pillows.

During the two weeks' struggle between life and death, there glowed such love in every look and gesture and impulse of the soul of the pious creature, that each effusion of her feelings seemed like the expression of a lifetime. The mother thought only of her son; she herself counted for nothing; sustained by love, she was unaware of her sufferings. D'Arthez, Michel Chrestien, Fulgence Ridal, Pierre Grassou, and Bianchon often kept Joseph company, and she heard them talking art in a low voice in a corner of her room.

"Oh, how I wish I knew what color is!" she exclaimed one evening as she heard them discussing one of Joseph's pictures.

Joseph, on his side, was sublimely devoted to his mother. He never left her chamber; answered tenderness by tenderness, cherishing her upon his heart. The spectacle was never afterwards forgotten by his friends; and they themselves, a band of brothers in talent and nobility of nature, were to Joseph and his mother all that they should have been,—friends who prayed, and truly wept; not saying prayers and shedding tears, but one with their friend in thought and action. Joseph, inspired as much by feeling as by genius, divined in the occasional expression of his mother's face a desire that was deep hidden in her heart, and he said one day to d'Arthez,—

"She has loved that brigand Philippe too well not to want to see him before she dies."

Joseph begged Bixiou, who frequented the Bohemian regions where Philippe was still occasionally to be found, to persuade that shameless son to play, if only out of pity, a little comedy of tenderness which might wrap the mother's heart in a winding-sheet of illusive happiness. Bixiou, in his capacity as an observing and misanthropical scoffer, desired nothing better than to undertake such a mission. When he had made known Madame Bridau's condition to the Comte de Brambourg, who received him in a bedroom hung with yellow damask, the colonel laughed.

"What the devil do you want me to do there?" he cried. "The only service the poor woman can render me is to die as soon as she can; she would be rather a sorry figure at my marriage with Mademoiselle de Soulanges. The less my family is seen, the better my position. You can easily understand that I should like to bury the name of Bridau under all the monuments in Pere-Lachaise. My brother irritates me by bringing the name into publicity. You are too knowing not to see the situation as I do. Look at it as if it were your own: if you were a deputy, with a tongue like yours, you would be as much feared as Chauvelin; you would be made Comte Bixiou, and director of the Beaux-Arts. Once there, how should you like it if your grandmother Descoings were to turn up? Would you want that worthy woman, who looked like a Madame Saint-Leon, to be hanging on to you? Would you give her an arm in the Tuileries, and present her to the noble family you were trying to enter? Damn it, you'd wish her six feet under ground, in a leaden night-gown. Come, breakfast with me, and let us talk of something else. I am a parvenu, my dear fellow, and I know it. I don't choose that my swaddling-clothes shall be seen. My son will be more fortunate than I; he will be a great lord. The scamp will wish me dead; I expect it,—or he won't be my son."

He rang the bell, and ordered the servant to serve breakfast.

"The fashionable world wouldn't see you in your mother's bedroom," said Bixiou. "What would it cost you to seem to love that poor woman for a few hours?"

"Whew!" cried Philippe, winking. "So you come from them, do you? I'm an old camel, who knows all about genuflections. My mother makes the excuse of her last illness to get something out of me for Joseph. No, thank you!"

When Bixiou related this scene to Joseph, the poor painter was chilled to the very soul.

"Does Philippe know I am ill?" asked Agathe in a piteous tone, the day after Bixiou had rendered an account of his fruitless errand.

Joseph left the room, suffocating with emotion. The Abbe Loraux, who was sitting by the bedside of his penitent, took her hand and pressed it, and then he answered, "Alas! my child, you have never had but one son."

The words, which Agathe understood but too well, conveyed a shock which was the beginning of the end. She died twenty hours later.

In the delirium which preceded death, the words, "Whom does Philippe take after?" escaped her.

Joseph followed his mother to the grave alone. Philippe had gone, on business it was said, to Orleans; in reality, he was driven from Paris by the following letter, which Joseph wrote to him a moment after their mother had breathed her last sigh:—

Monster! my poor mother has died of the shock your letter caused her. Wear mourning, but pretend illness; I will not suffer her assassin to stand at my side before her coffin. Joseph B.

The painter, who no longer had the heart to paint, though his bitter grief sorely needed the mechanical distraction which labor is wont to give, was surrounded by friends who agreed with one another never to leave him entirely alone. Thus it happened that Bixiou, who loved Joseph as much as a satirist can love any one, was sitting in the atelier with a group of other friends about two weeks after Agathe's funeral. The servant entered with a letter, brought by an old woman, she said, who was waiting below for the answer.

Monsieur,—To you, whom I scarcely dare to call my brother, I am forced to address myself, if only on account of the name I bear.—

Joseph turned the page and read the signature. The name "Comtesse Flore de Brambourg" made him shudder. He foresaw some new atrocity on the part of his brother.

"That brigand," he cried, "is the devil's own. And he calls himself a man of honor! And he wears a lot of crosses on his breast! And he struts about at court instead of being bastinadoed! And the scoundrel is called Monsieur le Comte!"

115

"There are many like him," said Bixiou.

"After all," said Joseph, "the Rabouilleuse deserves her fate, whatever it is. She is not worth pitying; she'd have had my neck wrung like a chicken's without so much as saying, 'He's innocent.'"

Joseph flung away the letter, but Bixiou caught it in the air, and read it aloud, as follows:—

Is it decent that the Comtesse Bridau de Brambourg should die in a hospital, no matter what may have been her faults? If such is to be my fate, if such is your determination and that of monsieur le comte, so be it; but if so, will you, who are the friend of Doctor Bianchon, ask him for a permit to let me enter a hospital? The person who carries this letter has been eleven consecutive days to the hotel de Brambourg, rue de Clichy, without getting any help from my husband. The poverty in which I now am prevents my employing a lawyer to make a legal demand for what is due to me, that I may die with decency. Nothing can save me, I know that. In case you are unwilling to see your unhappy sister-in-law, send me, at least, the money to end my days. Your brother desires my death; he has always desired it. He warned me that he knew three ways of killing a woman, but I had not the sense to foresee the one he has employed. In case you will consent to relieve me, and judge for yourself the misery in which I now am, I live in the rue du Houssay, at the corner of the rue Chantereine, on the fifth floor. If I cannot pay my rent to-morrow I shall be put out—and then, where can I go? May I call myself, Your sister-in-law, Comtesse Flore de Brambourg.

"What a pit of infamy!" cried Joseph; "there is something under it all."

"Let us send for the woman who brought the letter; we may get the preface of the story," said Bixiou.

The woman presently appeared, looking, as Bixiou observed, like perambulating rags. She was, in fact, a mass of old gowns, one on top of another, fringed with mud on account of the weather, the whole mounted on two thick legs with heavy feet which were ill-covered by ragged stockings and shoes from whose cracks the water oozed upon the floor. Above the mound of rags rose a head like those that Charlet has given to his scavenger-women, caparisoned with a filthy bandanna handkerchief slit in the folds.

"What is your name?" said Joseph, while Bixiou sketched her, leaning on an umbrella belonging to the year II. of the Republic.

"Madame Gruget, at your service. I've seen better days, my young gentleman," she said to Bixiou, whose laugh affronted her. "If my poor girl hadn't had the ill-luck to love some one too much, you wouldn't see me what I am. She drowned herself in the river, my poor Ida,—saving your presence! I've had the folly to nurse up a quaterne, and that's why, at seventy-seven years of age, I'm obliged to take care of sick folks for ten sous a day, and go—"

"—without clothes?" said Bixiou. "My grandmother nursed up a trey, but she dressed herself properly."

"Out of my ten sous I have to pay for a lodging—"

"What's the matter with the lady you are nursing?"

"In the first place, she hasn't got any money; and then she has a disease that scares the doctors. She owes me for sixty days' nursing; that's why I keep on nursing her. The husband, who is a count,—she is really a countess,—will no doubt pay me when she is dead; and so I've lent her all I had. And now I haven't anything; all I did have has gone to the pawn-brokers. She owes me forty-seven francs and twelve sous, beside thirty francs for the nursing. She wants to kill herself with charcoal. I tell her it ain't right; and, indeed, I've had to get the concierge to look after her while I'm gone, or she's likely to jump out of the window."

"But what's the matter with her?" said Joseph.

"Ah! monsieur, the doctor from the Sisters' hospital came; but as to the disease," said Madame Gruget, assuming a modest air, "he told me she must go to the hospital. The case is hopeless."

"Let us go and see her," said Bixiou.

"Here," said Joseph to the woman, "take these ten francs."

Plunging his hand into the skull and taking out all his remaining money, the painter called a coach from the rue Mazarin and went to find Bianchon, who was fortunately at home. Meantime Bixiou went off at full speed to the rue de Bussy, after Desroches. The four friends reached Flore's retreat in the rue du Houssay an hour later.

"That Mephistopheles on horseback, named Philippe Bridau," said Bixiou, as they mounted the staircase, "has sailed his boat cleverly to get rid of his wife. You know our old friend Lousteau? well, Philippe paid him a thousand francs a month to keep Madame Bridau in the society of Florine, Mariette, Tullia, and the Val-Noble. When Philippe saw his crab-girl so used to pleasure and dress that she couldn't do without them, he stopped paying the money, and left her to get it as she could—it is easy to know how. By the end of eighteen months, the brute had forced his wife, stage by stage, lower and lower; till at last, by the help of a young officer, he gave her a taste for drinking. As he went up in the world, his wife went down; and the countess is now

116

in the mud. The girl, bred in the country, has a strong constitution. I don't know what means Philippe has lately taken to get rid of her. I am anxious to study this precious little drama, for I am determined to avenge Joseph here. Alas, friends," he added, in a tone which left his three companions in doubt whether he was jesting or speaking seriously, "give a man over to a vice and you'll get rid of him. Didn't Hugo say: 'She loved a ball, and died of it'? So it is. My grandmother loved the lottery. Old Rouget loved a loose life, and Lolotte killed him. Madame Bridau, poor woman, loved Philippe, and perished of it. Vice! vice! my dear friends, do you want to know what vice is? It is the Bonneau of death."

"Then you'll die of a joke," said Desroches, laughing.

Above the fourth floor, the young men were forced to climb one of the steep, straight stairways that are almost ladders, by which the attics of Parisian houses are often reached. Though Joseph, who remembered Flore in all her beauty, expected to see some frightful change, he was not prepared for the hideous spectacle which now smote his artist's eye. In a room with bare, unpapered walls, under the sharp pitch of an attic roof, on a cot whose scanty mattress was filled, perhaps, with refuse cotton, a woman lay, green as a body that has been drowned two days, thin as a consumptive an hour before death. This putrid skeleton had a miserable checked handkerchief bound about her head, which had lost its hair. The circle round the hollow eyes was red, and the eyelids were like the pellicle of an egg. Nothing remained of the body, once so captivating, but an ignoble, bony structure. As Flore caught sight of the visitors, she drew across her breast a bit of muslin which might have been a fragment of a window-curtain, for it was edged with rust as from a rod. The young men saw two chairs, a broken bureau on which was a tallow-candle stuck into a potato, a few dishes on the floor, and an earthen fire-pot in a corner of the chimney, in which there was no fire; this was all the furniture of the room. Bixiou noticed the remaining sheets of writing-paper, brought from some neighboring grocery for the letter which the two women had doubtless concocted together. The word "disgusting" is a positive to which no superlative exists, and we must therefore use it to convey the impression caused by this sight. When the dying woman saw Joseph approaching her, two great tears rolled down her cheeks.

"She can still weep!" whispered Bixiou. "A strange sight,—tears from dominos! It is like the miracle of Moses."

"How burnt up!" cried Joseph.

"In the fires of repentance," said Flore. "I cannot get a priest; I have nothing, not even a crucifix, to help me see God. Ah, monsieur!" she cried, raising her arms, that were like two pieces of carved wood, "I am a guilty woman; but God never punished any one as he has punished me! Philippe killed Max, who advised me to do dreadful things, and now he has killed me. God uses him as a scourge!"

"Leave me alone with her," said Bianchon, "and let me find out if the disease is curable."

"If you cure her, Philippe Bridau will die of rage," said Desroches. "I am going to draw up a statement of the condition in which we have found his wife. He has not brought her before the courts as an adulteress, and therefore her rights as a wife are intact: he shall have the shame of a suit. But first, we must remove the Comtesse de Brambourg to the private hospital of Doctor Dubois, in the rue du Faubourg-Saint-Denis. She will be well cared for there. Then I will summon the count for the restoration of the conjugal home."

"Bravo, Desroches!" cried Bixiou. "What a pleasure to do so much good that will make some people feel so badly!"

Ten minutes later, Bianchon came down and joined them.

"I am going straight to Despleins," he said. "He can save the woman by an operation. Ah! he will take good care of the case, for her abuse of liquor has developed a magnificent disease which was thought to be lost."

"Wag of a mangler! Isn't there but one disease in life?" cried Bixiou.

But Bianchon was already out of sight, so great was his haste to tell Despleins the wonderful news. Two hours later, Joseph's miserable sister-in-law was removed to the decent hospital established by Doctor Dubois, which was afterward bought of him by the city of Paris. Three weeks later, the "Hospital Gazette" published an account of one of the boldest operations of modern surgery, on a case designated by the initials "F. B." The patient died,—more from the exhaustion produced by misery and starvation than from the effects of the treatment.

No sooner did this occur, than the Comte de Brambourg went, in deep mourning, to call on the Comte de Soulanges, and inform him of the sad loss he had just sustained. Soon after, it was whispered about in the fashionable world that the Comte de Soulanges would shortly marry his daughter to a parvenu of great merit, who was about to be appointed brigadier-general and receive command of a regiment of the Royal Guard. De Marsay told this news to Eugene de Rastignac, as they were supping together at the Rocher de Cancale, where Bixiou happened to be.

"It shall not take place!" said the witty artist to himself.

117

Among the many old friends whom Philippe now refused to recognize, there were some, like Giroudeau, who were unable to revenge themselves; but it happened that he had wounded Bixiou, who, thanks to his brilliant qualities, was everywhere received, and who never forgave an insult. One day at the Rocher de Cancale, before a number of well-bred persons who were supping there, Philippe had replied to Bixiou, who spoke of visiting him at the hotel de Brambourg: "You can come and see me when you are made a minister."

"Am I to turn Protestant before I can visit you?" said Bixiou, pretending to misunderstand the speech; but he said to himself, "You may be Goliath, but I have got my sling, and plenty of stones."

The next day he went to an actor, who was one of his friends, and metamorphosed himself, by the all-powerful aid of dress, into a secularized priest with green spectacles; then he took a carriage and drove to the hotel de Soulanges. Received by the count, on sending in a message that he wanted to speak with him on a matter of serious importance, he related in a feigned voice the whole story of the dead countess, the secret particulars of whose horrible death had been confided to him by Bianchon; the history of Agathe's death; the history of old Rouget's death, of which the Comte de Brambourg had openly boasted; the history of Madame Descoings's death; the history of the theft from the newspaper; and the history of Philippe's private morals during his early days.

"Monsieur le comte, don't give him your daughter until you have made every inquiry; interrogate his former comrades,—Bixiou, Giroudeau, and others."

Three months later, the Comte de Brambourg gave a supper to du Tillet, Nucingen, Eugene de Rastignac, Maxime de Trailles, and Henri de Marsay. The amphitryon accepted with much nonchalance the half-consolatory condolences they made to him as to his rupture with the house of Soulanges.

"You can do better," said Maxime de Trailles.

"How much money must a man have to marry a demoiselle de Grandlieu?" asked Philippe of de Marsay.

"You? They wouldn't give you the ugliest of the six for less than ten millions," answered de Marsay insolently.

"Bah!" said Rastignac. "With an income of two hundred thousand francs you can have Mademoiselle de Langeais, the daughter of the marquis; she is thirty years old, and ugly, and she hasn't a sou; that ought to suit you."

"I shall have ten millions two years from now," said Philippe Bridau.

"It is now the 16th of January, 1829," cried du Tillet, laughing. "I have been hard at work for ten years and I have not made as much as that yet."

"We'll take counsel of each other," said Bridau; "you shall see how well I understand finance."

"How much do you really own?" asked Nucingen.

"Three millions, excluding my house and my estate, which I shall not sell; in fact, I cannot, for the property is now entailed and goes with the title."

Nucingen and du Tillet looked at each other; after that sly glance du Tillet said to Philippe, "My dear count, I shall be delighted to do business with you."

De Marsay intercepted the look du Tillet had exchanged with Nucingen, and which meant, "We will have those millions." The two bank magnates were at the centre of political affairs, and could, at a given time, manipulate matters at the Bourse, so as to play a sure game against Philippe, when the probabilities might all seem for him and yet be secretly against him.

The occasion came. In July, 1830, du Tillet and Nucingen had helped the Comte de Brambourg to make fifteen hundred thousand francs; he could therefore feel no distrust of those who had given him such good advice. Philippe, who owed his rise to the Restoration, was misled by his profound contempt for "civilians"; he believed in the triumph of the Ordonnances, and was bent on playing for a rise; du Tillet and Nucingen, who were sure of a revolution, played against him for a fall. The crafty pair confirmed the judgment of the Comte de Brambourg and seemed to share his convictions; they encouraged his hopes of doubling his millions, and apparently took steps to help him. Philippe fought like a man who had four millions depending on the issue of the struggle. His devotion was so noticeable, that he received orders to go to Saint-Cloud with the Duc de Maufrigneuse and attend a council. This mark of favor probably saved Philippe's life; for when the order came, on the 25th of July, he was intending to make a charge and sweep the boulevards, when he would undoubtedly have been shot down by his friend Giroudeau, who commanded a division of the assailants.

A month later, nothing was left of Colonel Bridau's immense fortune but his house and furniture, his estates, and the pictures which had come from Issoudun. He committed the still further folly, as he said himself, of believing in the restoration of the elder branch, to which he remained faithful until 1834. The not imcomprehensible jealousy Philippe felt on seeing Giroudeau a colonel drove him to re-enter the service. Unluckily for himself, he obtained, in 1835, the command of a regiment in Algiers, where he remained three years in a post of danger, always hoping for the epaulets of a general. But some malignant influence—that, in fact, of General Giroudeau,—continually balked him. Grown hard and brutal, Philippe exceeded the ordinary severity of the service, and was hated, in spite of his bravery a la Murat.

At the beginning of the fatal year 1839, while making a sudden dash upon the Arabs during a retreat before superior forces, he flung himself against the enemy, followed by only a single company, and fell in, unfortunately, with the main body of the enemy. The battle was bloody and terrible, man to man, and only a few horsemen escaped alive. Seeing that their colonel was surrounded, these men, who were at some distance, were unwilling to perish uselessly in attempting to rescue him. They heard his cry: "Your colonel! to me! a colonel of the Empire!" but they rejoined the regiment. Philippe met with a horrible death, for the Arabs, after hacking him to pieces with their scimitars, cut off his head.

Joseph, who was married about this time, through the good offices of the Comte de Serizy, to the daughter of a millionaire farmer, inherited his brother's house in Paris and the estate of Brambourg, in consequence of the entail, which Philippe, had he foreseen this result, would certainly have broken. The chief pleasure the painter derived from his inheritance was in the fine collection of paintings from Issoudun. He now possesses an income of sixty thousand francs, and his father-in-law, the farmer, continues to pile up the five-franc pieces. Though Joseph Bridau paints magnificent pictures, and renders important services to artists, he is not yet a member of the Institute. As the result of a clause in the deed of entail, he is now Comte de Brambourg, a fact which often makes him roar with laughter among his friends in the atelier.

www.ingramcontent.com/pod-product-compliance
Lightning Source LLC
Chambersburg PA
CBHW061020080425

24772CB00014B/246